7

The Song In His Heart

by
John Monek

1663 LIBERTY DRIVE, SUITE 200
BLOOMINGTON, INDIANA 47403
(800) 839-8640
WWW.AUTHORHOUSE.COM

This book is a work of fiction. People, places, events, and situations are the product of the author's imagination. Any resemblance to actual persons, living or dead, or historical events, is purely coincidental.

© 2005 John Monek. All Rights Reserved.

No part of this book may be reproduced, stored in a retrieval system, or transmitted by any means without the written permission of the author.

First published by AuthorHouse 07/19/05

ISBN: 1-4208-6862-4 (sc)
ISBN: 1-4208-6863-2 (dj)

Registration Number: TXu-1-052-341
Created: 2002

Printed in the United States of America
Bloomington, Indiana

This book is printed on acid-free paper.

Dedication

I WOULD LIKE TO DEDICATE THIS BOOK TO
THE TWO MOST IMPORTANT WOMEN IN MY LIFE

MY MOTHER, CAROL B. MONEK

FOR ENCOURAGING ME TO READ IN MY
YOUNGER YEARS WHEN I FOUND IT DIFFICULT

MY WIFE, BECKY

WHO'S PATIENCE, SUPPORT, AND MOST OF
ALL LOVE MADE THE WRITING OF THIS BOOK
POSSIBLE

Special Thanks

Georgette Comuntzis Page, Sue O'Neil, and
Patty Papageorgiou who helped edit and critique the book

Rick Dorazil and Jim Kennett for their inspiration

Chapter One

The morning was so very cold. It was unusual for the temperature to be below freezing this early in the season. Of course, it was still an hour before daylight, and one would assume it would naturally warm up as the sun rose, but this year was hard to figure. Poppy had said the strange weather patterns lately were probably due to El Niño. Something about the warm water in the Pacific Ocean causing more moisture and extreme weather conditions. Well, there certainly had been more moisture. In fact, Colorado was having the wettest year in recent memory, and if the weather bulletins could be believed, there was more on the way. The only question was whether it would now come as snow or rain. Lonnie was hoping it would be snow. Elk hunting in the rain was the pits. True, according to Poppy, it did make for a quieter stalk, and it did help to cut down on scent, but little Lonnie hated to have to wear his rain gear. They were old hand-me-downs which were too big and torn in several places. The plastic or vinyl material did not breathe properly, and it would make him sweat too much when he was forced to climb. It wouldn't be so bad if they could just sit and wait, but Poppy didn't believe in hunting elk that way. "It's a big animal," he would say, "and it covers a lot of ground. If we are going to get one, we just have to cover a lot of ground ourselves." Unfortunately, that always meant for a cold, damp hunt. If the rain didn't get him wet, the sweat usually would. Oh, what he wouldn't do for a set of that fancy Gore-Tex raingear he had read about in the hunting catalog. In addition to breathing properly, it was also quiet in the woods. Even if they could afford it, which they couldn't, it was too fancy for a fourteen-year-old boy to wear.

Poppy and Lonnie had left home early the previous morning and hiked well up into the mountains by noon. It took almost six hours to travel the eight mile distance to camp. Going in was always tough because it was mostly up. There were no roads or horse trails so if one was going to the top, it had to be by foot. At times the terrain was almost impossible for a boy of such tender years, but when he needed help the most, Poppy was always there to lend a hand or more often, to offer words of encouragement. He tried to let Lonnie do it mostly by himself though. His son was fiercely independent and preferred it that way, even though sometimes he tended to push himself a little too far.

Camp was at 11,000 feet, right about at tree line. Even though it was a hard place to get to, Poppy was convinced he had found the best elk hunting area around. There were never any other hunters to be seen up here. He would say to Lonnie that nobody else had the strength or endurance or woodsmanship to hike in this far with their camps on their back. This made the boy feel especially good as he took pride in the fact that he was actually able to make the arduous trek up the mountain. Lonnie loved this time he was able to spend with his father. It was just the two of them with no outside distractions.

Even though this was only his third hunt, Lonnie looked forward all year long to the seven or eight days they would spend together up at their special camp. The two of them would have long conversations at night sitting around the campfire on their custom-made chairs that each had carved out of logs. Lonnie wanted to know so many things about the world that at times Poppy found himself hard pressed to give accurate answers. There was one subject, however, which came up often that he never had any trouble with. This had to do with the woods and hunting. In Lonnie's eyes and indeed in the eyes of just about everybody else in the county, Poppy was the expert. He was the first and finest. Although he was only thirty-seven years old, Poppy had a deep understanding of the woods and the creatures that lived in them. His wisdom was attained by spending his entire life surrounded by these things he loved so much.

It was unfortunate so much time had to be spent away from home working in the mine, up to sixty hours some weeks. It was for this reason that Poppy was ever mindful of the fact that he was not raising his son to his late wife's expectations. This was particularly evident when it came to his schooling. Lonnie was now a freshman in high school. There had been an obvious decline in his grades after the premature death of his mother three winters before.

Her name was Anjuli, and she had been the most beautiful woman in the world. This was not just the opinion of a young boy or a love-struck husband, but a general consensus of everyone who knew or came into contact with her. Anjuli had long raven black hair with beautiful brown eyes and high cheek bones. Her perfectly shaped teeth were as white as snow. At 5' 7" she was somewhat tall amongst her friends. Most people in Silvertown knew Anjuli. Her quick wit and outgoing personality coupled with extreme beauty and devotion to her family made Poppy the envy of every man in town. How he missed his lovely wife and how his heart would ache when he would think of her.

There had been no dating for Poppy after Anjuli, although many women had tried to attract his attention. He was by all rights a very good looking man, standing 6'2" with stylishly long thick black hair and striking blue eyes. Years of hard work in the mine shoveling coal had turned him into quite a specimen. His broad frame and narrow hips concealed his 230 pound bulk well. Poppy was of English descent. He was born Tyler James Burch. The name Poppy came about when his young son could not properly pronounce the name Papa. The new name just kind of stuck over the years and now most people thought it to be his given name. He never knew his parents. They were both killed in an auto crash when he was three. Poor visibility due to blowing snow and a mule deer buck caused his father to veer off the road into the side of a mountain. Death was instantaneous for him and his wife. If young Tyler hadn't been spending the night with his mother's sister, he also would have perished in the fiery crash. Auntie Rose took him in and raised the young boy as her own on a small ranch outside of town. They lived together until Poppy was seventeen. Auntie Rose passed away quietly in her sleep one night leaving the forty-acre ranch to him.

After the good Lord took his wife, Poppy soon began to realize what a difficult task it was to raise a young boy without a mother. She would spend each evening with Lonnie going over his lessons for the next day. Anjuli devoted the time to child rearing that Poppy just didn't have. More than once she had stayed by his bedside all night long when young Lonnie was sick and feverish. Anjuli made a special point of teaching her only child how to bake cookies. With a laugh she would say that when she was gone someone would have to cook for her poor husband. Little did they know she was foreshadowing things to come. There are so many things only a mother can give to a child that at times Poppy felt completely incompetent. After all, he was only a miner. He was not an educated man, nor was he a wealthy man. Life had been hard for him once he married. Rather than going on to college, which is what his Auntie Rose had always spoken of, the two newlyweds decided that it would be best if he went to work right away. At the time, the coal mine was the only place offering work to a man with his talents. That was seventeen years ago, and as the old miners would say, "It is easy to get into the mine, but damn difficult to get out of it."

As cruel as the fates had been in taking Anjuli, they did serve to bring the boy and his father closer together. In fact, over the past three years the two of them had formed a bond with each other that seemed to go well beyond a normal father son relationship. While Poppy would spend his time each day in the mine, Lonnie would rise early each morning in order to do the chores around the house. After attending school he would come home and prepare an evening meal for his father, as simple as it was. Both were completely independent of each other during the day, but came to rely on one another heavily the rest of the time. Their evenings were spent around home enjoying quiet time, sometimes fishing, sometimes just discussing the events of the day, but always reinforcing their family bond by sharing secrets and providing an outlet for each others frustrations.

As they moved silently through the forest, Lonnie could see the sky starting to lighten up in the East. This was always the coldest time of the day, just before dawn. He was grateful to be moving as it would soon warm him. Although the initial light of dawn was evident, the sky was still very dark. There were no stars this morning and the sky was overcast with a heavy cloud cover. The air was damp and Lonnie shivered a bit unconsciously. He was thankful he had remembered to bring along his polypropylene long underwear. It would help to keep him dry and warm once he started to sweat. As long as they didn't have to put on the rain clothes, it should be all right. The combination of polypropylene long johns and wool outer clothes would serve him well, according to Poppy. The wool absorbed the moisture the polypropylene would whisk away from his skin, thus, keeping him dry close to his body. The force of gravity would then allow for the moisture to flow down through the wool fibers in his outer clothes and collect around the pant cuffs where it would freeze if the weather was cold enough. This helped to prevent snow from getting into his boots by making a solid cuff. Somebody sure had it all figured out, Lonnie thought. Poppy said that if the mountain men had polypropylene long underwear, it would have made their lives a lot easier, at least in the wintertime-- certainly more comfortable.

The going was pretty easy now. They were skirting around the top of the mountain just inside the cover of a heavy band of spruce trees. An old elk trail served as the pathway. It led over to the next ridge where they could look down into the basin below the rock formation known as Baldy. The basin had a minimal tree cover and was always a good place to spot elk if they were in the area. Poppy liked to start each hunt looking down into this area with his binoculars. Over the years he had taken three elk from this spot. One of them was a very large 6' x 6' bull with a 44" spread. Quite a trophy for your regular hunter; however, Poppy just called it meat for the table. He would never consider sending the head to a taxidermist to be mounted, always preferring to save just the antlers for above the fireplace in their family room.

Poppy liked to hunt trophy elk, but not for the same reasons most hunters liked to. He explained to Lonnie that the big herd bulls are usually the first to die in a severe winter. They spend most of the fall season gathering up their harem of cows so they can breed them when they come into heat. In attempting to keep the herd together, the herd bull must constantly fend off other interlopers. These are usually lesser bulls that would like to get into the action of the rut. Between the almost constant battling with other bulls for control of the herd and the actual breeding of the cows, the herd bull is steadily worn down and his winter preserves of fat accumulated over the spring and summer are dangerously reduced. Once a severe winter comes, he will more than likely succumb to the elements. This is why Poppy hunted the trophy elk. He felt that by taking the reigning monarch once it had fulfilled its duty and passed on its genes to the next generation, he was not interfering with the natural flow of events in nature. The animal would surely die anyway, and this way he could tap into it with minimal impact and at the same time feed himself and his family. Now, this isn't to say he would not take a lesser bull on the last day of the season if no other opportunity presented itself, but it rarely ever came to that.

The trail beneath their feet was worn down by countless generations of elk moving along the top of the mountain from one ridge to the next. It showed no fresh signs of any recent passing; however, Lonnie had been taught to examine every detail. When the ground was frosted over and a twig, rock, or moss was disturbed and there was no frost in its old resting spot, then this was a fresh sign. Elk droppings were everywhere in the forest, but only by closely examining it could one tell whether or not it was fresh. Lonnie picked up what he thought might be fresh droppings and squeezed them. The hard marble like texture told him that in fact it was probably many days or even weeks old. In looking up he could see that Poppy had stopped and was watching him. The pride in his eyes was evident as he watched his boy. Lonnie was a quick learner and rarely had to be taught things more than once. He would make a good woodsman someday Poppy thought, perhaps even better than himself. With this comforting thought he turned and continued his trek towards Baldy.

Once they reached their destination, it was a short climb to the ridge top which overlooked the basin below. From this point on they both dropped to the ground and army crawled up over the crest so their silhouette could not be seen from the other side. Poppy had timed it perfectly. It was just light enough to make out the shapes in the valley. They dropped down a bit into the basin to an old rock formation which they used for cover. There was no movement below.

After a careful examination with his binoculars that took almost ten minutes, Poppy relaxed a bit. He removed a small plastic bottle with a pump spray from his pocket and with his free hand sprayed the contents onto his pants. This was part of the ritual Lonnie was not crazy about. The contents of the bottle was elk urine. In fact, it was cow elk in- heat urine. The scent is supposed to help cover up the human odor and perhaps maybe even attract an amorous bull elk that might be in the area. To Lonnie, it

7

just smelled awful. He could not imagine how anybody could make themselves smell so bad. There was no doubt in his mind that it certainly covered up his scent. When his father handed him the bottle and nodded with a grin, Lonnie reluctantly sprayed it onto himself. The good thing was that after a little while, his nose would become accustomed to the awful odor and he would not notice it so much. Then just about that time his dad would pull out the bottle once more and start spraying again. Poppy insisted on using scents when he hunted. The wind direction changes frequently during the winter in the mountains. Unless a hunter is able to mask his own scent, he can be discovered by his prey long before he even realizes it is in the area.

Today there was a gentle breeze blowing out of the northwest. The fact that it was in their faces made for ideal conditions to hunt the valley below. No human scent would drift down into the basin and give away their position. If, for some reason, the wind should shift slightly, the masking odor of the elk scent would help to conceal their presence.

As the two of them crouched behind the rocks, Poppy kept a wary eye on the edge of the trees beneath them. Only occasionally did they ever speak during these times, always preferring to use sign language instead. After all, there was no reason to alert the creatures of the forest with idle chatter. When something important had to be conveyed, they would speak to each other in very low whispers.

While Lonnie was fussing with his back pack in search of a hard piece of candy to suck on, he felt a sudden pressure on his shoulder. Looking immediately to his father he followed his nod down to the valley below. Just inside the tree line there was movement. Within moments, a large cow elk walked into the clearing. She was soon followed by three more cows, two calves, and a spike bull. They milled about in the open grazing on the exposed grass for almost ten minutes. Poppy was resting his old Belgium Browning 300 Winchester Mag on top of the rock he was using for cover. The rifle sat on top of his wool hunting hat so as not to scratch it in case he should fire a shot. Lonnie was lying in the prone position alongside their cover rock. He had a 270 Weatherby equipped with a Leopold 3x 9 variable scope. Poppy felt the Leopold was the best money could buy, so he was willing to pay for it. It was also a necessity when hunting big game in the Rocky Mountains.

The small herd of elk was about 250 yards away. Although no mature bull was in sight, each hunter knew there would undoubtedly be one in the immediate vicinity. It was early October and the rut seemed to be in full swing. As sudden as they appeared, the elk vanished. Within minutes a high shrill whistle could be heard coming from the thick stand of black timber adjacent to the meadow. It was followed by a deep guttural growl that sounded like some hungry beast from hell. The penetrating sound lasted for almost twenty seconds, then, once again, all became silent. This was the call of the bull elk, one of the most magnificent sounds in nature. It is called by the Indians, "wapiti" or "ghost of the forest." In this particular case, the bull sounded like a large one. As soon as Poppy heard the deep resonance of the bugle, he knew there was a giant lurking somewhere down below in the timber. He looked down at Lonnie, who returned his gaze and they both smiled. Each knew they were getting ready to embark on the most exciting aspect of the hunt, the stalk.

Chapter Two

The plan was to backtrack over the ridge keeping very low until they were out of sight from the lower valley. Then they could move quickly down the backside of the adjacent ridge to the approximate level where the bull was. Once in this position, the going would become very cautious as they moved in. With a bit of luck, they might be on his trail within an hour or so.

The sky never did clear as the dawn came and went. The gentle breeze was turning into more of a steady blow. It was still coming out of the northwest, so they didn't have to worry about being scented. A light flurry of snow had developed in the upper ranges. Poppy was confident as they moved down into position things were going well. With only two hours into the first day of the hunt, they were already putting the sneak on what he was guessing to be a very large bull elk. The impending snowfall did not concern him much. If things got too bad they could always abandon their stalk and make tracks back to camp where they could wait it out. On more than one occasion, Poppy had weathered out severe winter conditions while hunting elk at higher elevations. As long as you stayed dry and didn't do anything foolish, things usually turned out alright.

"Stay close behind me," Poppy said, "and make sure you keep the safety on your rifle. If we come on the herd first, the bull is sure to be close by. Follow my lead."

"Ok, Poppy. Do you think it could be Old Ivory Tips?" Lonnie was referring to a legendary bull elk that hunters and locals had spoken of for years. Its huge body was said to be upwards of 1,200 pounds. He had great massive beams with seven giant tines on each side. Each was topped off with ivory white tips where it had rubbed them clean. Old Maynard Kennicot reported the previous year that he had taken a shot at this monster bull while it was with a herd of twenty cows. After some gentle prodding from his buddies, Maynard admitted he had missed it completely several times and that he was convinced his rifle must be shooting wide. He trailed it through the aspens for almost a mile before giving up due to darkness. Poor Maynard has been talking about Old Ivory Tips ever since and will probably talk about it until his dying day. As far as Poppy knew no one had spotted the giant bull yet this year; and there was some speculation as to whether it had made it through the previous winter even though it had been a relatively mild one.

"I'm not certain if it is Old Ivory Tips," answered Poppy, "but I'll tell you one thing for sure. Based upon the baritone in that bugle we heard, it could be at least his first cousin. One way or another we should find out soon."

Silently, they moved forward into the black timber. It consisted of mostly spruce, but there was also an abundance of ponderosa pine. At this elevation, the aspen tree was relatively scarce, naturally growing between 8,000 and 10,000 feet. The forest floor was littered with countless trees of all sizes that were in various stages of decomposition. They accumulate over the years only to rot away and to be reincorporated back into the soil from which they came and from which new life will once again spring forth. Many of the dead falls were so advanced in rot that they were covered with spongy green moss. Whenever possible, Lonnie would try to step here because it was softer and more quiet. The barely recognizable trail they were following meandered through the tangle, and only a skilled and experienced eye kept them on track.

Poppy knelt down to examine some fresh elk droppings. He looked at Lonnie and gave a thumbs up. They were getting closer, and at least some of the group they had seen earlier were using the same trail they were now on. Their movement became very controlled. Every couple of steps they would stop for a few moments and look long and hard through the trees. Somewhere ahead, perhaps fifty yards, a pine squirrel started chattering. It sounded as if it were scolding somebody---or something. Many times when a squirrel chatters in the forest, it is for no particular reason, maybe just exercising its vocal chords. But once in a while, according to Poppy, squirrels chatter because they are disturbed. In this instance, Lonnie had every reason to believe it was a group of elk disturbing the squirrel. He grabbed Poppy's arm as if to tell him this, but his old man understood well enough what caused the chatter. Once again he gave his son a positive nod as if to say, "You are exactly right."

At that moment, the forest stillness was once again interrupted. This time by a high- pitched whistle that gradually changed tone into a long bellowing roar and then finally ended in a spasmodic ejaculation of grunts. Both hunters froze in their tracks. The hair on Lonnie's head literally stood on end. Poppy focused his eyes through the heavy cover of trees searching for any movement whatsoever--perhaps a shape or a color that was out of place. He estimated that the bull was within forty yards. Ever so slowly they crouched down to the ground. Off to the right, just beneath a low overhang of brush, Poppy was able to make out some legs. As he watched, more legs came into view. With his rifle horizontal in his arms, he began to army crawl very carefully towards the position.

Time began to pass very slowly. Lonnie could feel his heart pounding in his chest. There were moments when he thought the sound of it would actually give him away. His hands were shaking, and even though the wind was still blowing in his face, he felt warm all over. Poppy had explained to him that this was called 'buck fever'. Some less experienced hunters mistakenly felt buck fever happened when a novice froze out of fear and thereby became unable to actually pull the trigger. "Not so," explained Poppy. "Buck fever is simply when a hunter feels the anxiety and the excitement of the hunt. When the stalk gets to the critical stage where it can go either way, a certain amount of nervousness is only natural. In fact, I get it every time I hunt. It is nothing to be ashamed of. One must simply understand what these feelings are and be able to control them. These are marvelous creatures that we hunt, and we should thank God for giving us the ability to harvest them. Remember son, we take no pleasure in the kill, only in the stalk. When the final moment comes, concentrate on keeping your emotions under control. Hold your rifle steady. Rest it when you can. Take a deep breath and let half of it out, then hold. Put the crosshairs low on his front shoulder and gently squeeze the trigger. Under no circumstances do we want to wound an innocent animal. The kill must be quick and clean. If you have doubt about the outcome turning out any other way, do not take the shot. There is no shame in passing once in awhile if the conditions are not perfect."

Snow had begun to fall all around them now. Although it had not yet begun to accumulate, it would only be a matter of time for the ground was very cold. The two of them crawled single file along the forest floor. Whenever it seemed as though they might be getting closer, the small group of elk would slowly move forward, thus putting more distance between them once again. As of yet, there was still no sign of the bull. At least no visual sign. But it was evident that he was just ahead. Lonnie could hear him raking the tree limbs with his antlers and making whistling sounds. Occasionally a cow elk would come into clear view, but only for a moment. They were moving deeper into the forest where the foliage would offer more cover while they bedded down for the day. As long as the wind direction did not shift and the two stalkers didn't make any noise or sudden movements, they might remain undiscovered long enough to catch the bull in an opening and get their shot. It was important not to get over anxious. Just the slightest sound out of place would surely spook them into the next county.

After crawling for what seemed like an hour, but what could very well have been only twenty minutes, Poppy came upon two large trees that had fallen over years before and were blocking his path. There was no possible way for him to go under them for they were quite large in the trunk and rested solidly on the ground. The only way to deal with the situation was to stand up and step over them individually. He delayed this action for some time in the hope that the elk would continue to move on and therefore be less likely to notice the movement.

Several minutes later, Poppy could neither see nor hear the elk any longer, and he assumed they had moved safely out of view. Slowly, he motioned for Lonnie to stand with him, and they very carefully started to step over the old trees. It was at this exact moment that the obnoxious little pine squirrel decided to start scolding the two of them. It was standing on a tree limb just overhead, not ten feet away. There they were, in the midst of straddling the old tree, with this arrogant little creature making all the noise in the world directed right at them.

As they both turned their heads upward with murder in their eyes, there was a sudden crashing of timber directly in front of them. The startled hunters immediately looked forward just in time to see the most magnificent bull elk either had ever seen. He was standing there in all his glory less than fifty feet away. The majesty of this creature was overwhelming. It towered over the cows standing beside it. The almost prehistoric antler rack appeared quite dark and gnarled at the base and spread out easily 50 inches. Each tine had unusually solid mass and length and was topped off with great ivory white tips. He snorted and glared at the intruders as if to say, "Who dares to approach me?" There was mucus dripping from his open mouth and nose. The steam created by his warm breath hitting the frigid air made him look all the more incredible. Although it took only a moment, it was a sight neither of them would forget for the remainder of his life.

In a heartbeat, Old Ivory Tips turned and vanished into the forest he knew so well. Lonnie and Poppy could hear the crashing of timber for a full five minutes as the herd bull and his harem made their escape down into the deepest part of the forest. They could only stand and stare at each other with their jaws agape. Even the squirrel was stunned into silence. Finally, Poppy shook his head and laughed while saying, "Lonnie, my boy, we have just been introduced to Old Ivory Tips."

Chapter Three

The sighting and close encounter with Old Ivory Tips provided a major dose of adrenaline for both Poppy and Lonnie. Their next course of action naturally would be to pursue this giant elk, but it must be done very carefully and with the utmost stealth. Just to charge out after him with all due haste would serve no purpose other than to scare the animals. Spooked elk have been known to cover large distances especially if they feel they are being followed or their security is threatened.

"Let's sit here for a while and give those critters a chance to settle down," Poppy suggested. "If they discover we're on their trail, I'm quite confident we will have seen the last of them, perhaps for the rest of the hunt. I figure the smart thing to do now is to eat something. After about an hour we can start moving down the mountain again and try to cut their trail. That old bull will more than likely head into the saddle area down below with all that fallen timber in it. Just when he starts feeling safe again, we'll put the sneak on him once more, and this time we'll take him!"

After a suitable delay, father and son once again found themselves in the familiar routine of moving silently through the forest. The snow was falling steadily now, having already accumulated several inches. Each knew this fresh snow blanket would be a real asset in their tracking. In addition to helping them pick up fresh trails easier, it would also serve to cut down on visibility and scent. Whenever an elk's defenses can be minimized, the odds of encountering one in its natural habitat are greatly increased. Sight and smell are two of the elk's most important senses. The third, of course, is hearing. This snow would also greatly reduce sound travel. All things considered, Poppy figured their chances of re-encountering the giant bull were fairly good, but it would still take a lot of luck.

It was almost 1:30 in the afternoon when Poppy finally came across the trail of the small group of elk. There were a total of seven sets of tracks. The hoof prints of Old Ivory Tips were enormous compared to the others. His dew claws were easily visible. Lonnie knew large male ungulates had a tendency to stand very flat footed, thereby leaving the imprint of the small, toe-like claw behind their hoof in the ground. Female elk and deer more often walk on the ends of their hooves, or on their toes so to speak. They were keeping in a tight group and seemed to be heading to the heavily congested saddle area Poppy was quite familiar with. After trailing them for a short while, Poppy noticed another large bull was shadowing the herd. More than likely, he was on the scent of one of the cows which would be in heat. This could be the bit of luck they needed. If Old Ivory Tips had his mind occupied with keeping another male suitor away from his cows, then perhaps he might let his guard down with respect to possibly being followed by the two of them.

At first the cracking noise sounded like tree branches breaking under the heavy weight of snow and ice. When it continued over the next several moments, it immediately became apparent the sound was not anything as mundane as tree branches giving way, but, was rather the battle noise of two bull elk engaged in the most vicious combat imaginable. Indeed, two herd bulls had come together in order to establish which one would earn the right to breed. All creatures, large and small, focused their undivided attention on the two gladiators as they tore up the earth with their charging hoofs and crashed their heads together with locking antlers. Heads twisted and neck muscles bulged as each attempted to gore the flank of the other and thereby bring an early end to this dangerous display of aggression. Rarely are these battles ever fought to the death, but when two exceptionally powerful animals come together in order to determine which is dominant, the outcome can never be guaranteed.

Poppy recognized this commotion for what it was. He knew all eyes would be trained on the combatants. If he and Lonnie were going to be able to get close, they must move now while the two bulls were engaged with each other. Although the animals were not in sight, the loud raucous told the story. They would be just over the next ridge perhaps fifty or sixty yards. Immediately, Poppy explained his plan to Lonnie. It was simple considering the situation. The wind was blowing crosswise, not ideal, but it should be sufficient. "We'll move straight up over the ridge," he whispered, "keeping any tree cover between us and the elk. As soon as we spot the bull, look for a place to rest your rifle so you can get a clean shot. This one is yours, Lonnie. I'll be your backup if you need me."

Once over the ridge the battle scene came into full view. They were in a small meadow protected on each side by small rolling hills and heavy tree cover. Lonnie spotted Old Ivory Tips right off. He was locked head to head in a vicious pushing match with another bull elk. The small group of cows stood off to one side. They seemed to be showing very little interest in the spectacle, preferring to continue grazing. Although this new bull was not nearly the specimen Old Ivory Tips was, he was still quite an animal. It had a large heavy rack with six very dark tines on each side. His body was a very light tan almost yellowish color. There was a deep gash in his shoulder which oozed thick red blood. It had flowed most of the way down his leg and could be seen dripping onto the ground. The wound was probably not mortal in itself, but the blood would leave a very dangerous trail. Within hours a pack of coyotes or even a hungry mountain lion could very well be on him. His ultimate survival would depend on how soon he broke off his engagement with Old Ivory Tips and how lucky he would be in fending off potential predators.

It was at this time Lonnie noticed Old Ivory Tips had seven points on one side and what he thought must be eight points on the other side. If this proved to be in fact true, then this magnificent creature must indeed be a new world record bull elk. Once again he was amazed by the beauty and aura of this powerful animal. He watched the battle as if in a trance.

Very softly, Poppy squeezed Lonnie's shoulder and motioned for him to get ready to fire. The boy immediately knelt down behind a fallen tree and rested his rifle over it. Ever so slowly he pulled the bolt back and chambered a round. As he looked through his scope at his target, he saw something that made him pause. He had never really ever seen anything like this animal before, either alive or in picture books. It was remarkable. The phrase 'Forest Ghost' came into his mind. This creature was revered and respected by Indians and white men as well. Old Ivory Tips was without a doubt the king and reigning monarch of the entire species. No, he must not die! At least not by the hands of mankind. With that thought in his mind, Lonnie turned his rifle onto the wounded lesser bull and pulled the trigger.

His aim was true. The 180 grain bullet struck the wounded elk low behind his front shoulder. It was a heart shot. In the blink of an eye, the once proud animal lay motionless on the ground. Old Ivory Tips immediately associated the loud rifle shot with human danger. The fact that this once aggressive and belligerent elk which had been challenging him moments before now lay dead at his feet confirmed this. There was no hesitation in his reaction. A quick turn to his right followed by two large leaps and he was gone. The herd of cows took a little bit longer to digest what had just happened. At first they seemed inquisitive. The largest cow even approached the fallen bull. Then all of a sudden, as if she were slapped in the face, she bolted into the woods. The rest of the group followed closely behind. Perhaps it was the smell of death, or maybe it was the hunters' scent that finally alarmed them. One way or another, it would be a learning experience for the entire herd. The presence of man can only bring them harm. This is a lesson Old Ivory Tips had undoubtedly learned earlier in his life.

Poppy put his hand on young Lonnie's shoulder. He had not yet moved from his shooting position. Although it seemed to be a good deal longer, the entire episode had taken less than a minute. "I was wondering what you were going to do," he quietly stated.

"I'm sorry Poppy. When I looked at Old Ivory Tips, he was just so wonderful. Never in my life have I ever seen anything so magnificent! I wanted to get him so badly all morning, but when we got close to him, and I saw how important he was, there was just something telling me he must go on living. Then, when I saw the other was injured, it was like God telling me I should take that one instead. Did I do the right thing, Poppy?"

The boy's father looked at his son with deep understanding and sympathy. He saw before him no longer a little boy, but the beginnings of a fine young man. Poppy felt emotional and struggled to speak without revealing the lump which had formed in his throat. "Yes, Lonnie, you did the right thing. I'm so proud to call you my son. There are very few grown men who would have done what you did here today. Most would have tried to take the trophy, even though it was obvious the smaller bull would probably have died. Now, whenever you and I are up here in the mountains together, we will know that Old Ivory Tips is still here with us."

Chapter Four

The job of skinning and quartering a full grown elk normally takes a couple of hours under the best of conditions. Unfortunately, the weather was not cooperating as it continued to deteriorate. It was snowing quite heavily now and the wind had picked up dangerously. Nevertheless, Poppy felt it would be best if the quarters of the animal were hung from a tree branch. This would serve to protect the meat from scavengers, and it would also allow them more time to get back to the site after the blizzard in order to pack it out. Once this was accomplished, he marked it with a red handkerchief so it would be easier to find when they returned. It was well after dark by the time they finished with their task.

Lonnie had hesitated when his father suggested he put on his raingear prior to the skinning of the elk. He was wearing wool pants and a heavy wool sweater. The combination of four layers of shirts and sweater would surely keep him warm, but when Poppy reminded him about the importance of keeping dry from the falling snow, he capitulated. Now, as they prepared to head back up the mountain towards their camp and warm sleeping bags, he was happy he did.

The going was slow because the conditions were miserable. One would suspect they might want to hurry along back to camp, but Poppy was too experienced as a woodsman to let this happen. By moving quickly back up the mountainside, there was a very real chance they could get lost in the blowing snow. In addition to this, the long, hard climb would make them sweat unnecessarily, thus creating the potential danger of hypothermia. This is always a hazard when camping up in the high country during the colder months.

Poppy figured they were about a mile from camp as the crow flies. If they were to attempt this direct route, they must traverse an avalanche field strewn with large unstable rocks piled high on top of each other. The alternative route would add almost another mile to their trip. He wrestled with this in his mind as they moved along. He was not concerned about himself so much as the danger it could pose for the boy. When they finally reached the point in the forest where a decision would have to be made, Poppy decided it would be best to take the shorter route.

"Rather than climbing up and around this old rock slide area, I feel it would be best if we cut across here. It could be dangerous, but we can save almost an hour by taking the shortcut." Poppy called out.

"That sounds good to me," replied Lonnie. "I can't wait to eat some hot soup and get into my warm bag. This has been a long day and I'm beat."

"How do you feel? Should we stop for awhile and take a rest?" asked Poppy.

"No, let's keep moving. Other than my fingers being cold, I'm ok. The sooner we get back the better."

With that said, the two of them moved cautiously out of the protected woods and into the open avalanche field. The wind was blowing much harder here. It cut right through their clothes, rain gear and all, and chilled them to the very core. The rock field had been formed by countless years of spring thaws breaking apart the upper mountain, piece by piece, and sending it tumbling down the slope. Although Poppy had crossed over the steep avalanche field numerous times before, this did not lessen his trepidation. The deep snow cover was a cause for concern. It would conceal the treacherous rocks and make their footing very unstable. The blinding snow exacerbated the situation. Poppy rationalized that as long as he led the way, Lonnie should do all right following in his tracks. The distance across was less than one hundred and fifty yards. As he moved forward, Poppy placed each foot carefully onto the rock ahead and slowly put pressure on it before trusting his entire weight. In this manner, the two of them slowly moved along.

Lonnie was a half dozen steps behind when all of a sudden he lost his balance. With his rifle slung loosely over his shoulder, he quickly dropped to his knees and tried to grab hold of a large boulder. The icy snow did not afford him a good grip and he began to slide down the slope. In desperation he gave a cry of help as the rocks beneath his feet started to give way. Poppy turned just in time to see Lonnie clawing desperately at the ground in an effort to climb above the rapidly developing slide. In one quick motion, Poppy spun around while dropping his rifle onto the rocks and took two giant leaps down toward his son with the intent of catching hold of him and arresting his fall.

Poppy was barely able to accomplish this. As the boy slid by, his father grabbed him by the arm and pulled him to safety onto the more stable rocks alongside. While they continued to move downward with their momentum, Poppy stepped onto what he thought was solid footing, but what in reality turned out to be a hole in the rocks which was covered by snow. His left foot sunk in almost all the way to the knee. The ensuing crack was heard by both of them as Poppy's leg fractured midway up his shin.

The pain was immediate and excruciating. He dropped down onto his side and held his leg in disbelief. It took all of the will-power he could muster in order to extract his mangled leg from the unyielding hole. Upon feeling the afflicted area with his hands, Poppy realized his lower leg was most definitely broken. He cursed aloud at his carelessness and misfortune. At least it was not a compound fracture. This was a small bit of good news in a world that was rapidly going into the shitter, he thought.

Lonny looked truly worried. "Poppy, are you all right? Do you think you can walk? I couldn't help it. The ground just gave way underneath me."

"Don't worry Lonnie. It's not your fault, but damn, I'm pretty sure my leg is broken." Poppy had to speak very loudly to be heard over the howling wind. "We have to get off this slide area and into the shelter of the trees. Once we get there I'll have a better idea of how bad it is and whether I can go on. If I can't, we'll have to build a lean-to for shelter and spend the night down here. Don't worry about that though, we'll be all right."

With that said the boy and his father very slowly made their way across the remainder of the slide area. Lonnie carried both rifles over his shoulder so Poppy could use his hands freely as he crab crawled over the rocks with great difficulty.

Once they reached the shelter and safety of the forest on the opposite side of the slide area, Poppy was in a cold sweat. He knew immediately it would not be possible to continue the climb up the mountain. The only thing they could do now would be to build some type of shelter in order to protect them from the wind and snow and to prepare to spend the night out. They were forced to move deeper into the woods until finding an area suitable for building a lean-to. Lonnie reconnoitered the area and found a spot where it would be pretty good. It was situated right below a large outcropping of rock. If they built the shelter close to the face, the ground there was relatively flat. More importantly, the rock wall would serve as a wind breaker. There were also a lot of broken down trees nearby with plenty of smaller branches they could utilize to build the shelter. It would be a long, cold night and any advantage they could find to lessen their discomfort could go a long way toward possibly ensuring their very survival.

The Song In His Heart

Lonnie had been taught how to build a lean-to when he was a small boy. It had been fun constructing this monstrosity with his buddies in his back yard one warm evening in July. The circumstances on this cold snowy night were now quite different. He must gather all the wood himself under the harshest of conditions and under his father's guidance put together a structure that would prove to be sturdy and also act to block out the falling snow. The important task of locating two end pieces with a "Y" shape on one end took a bit of searching, but with Poppy's help, they were able to fabricate suitable pieces from a nearby fallen tree. The ground under the stone outcropping consisted of rock and frozen earth which made it virtually impossible to drive the wooden branches into it without breaking them. The alternative was to pile rocks and packed snow around the base of each so they would stand freely and be sturdy supports for the seven foot cross-pole and all the wooden branches and debris that would be leaned up against it. Lonnie made trip after trip to a fallen tree gathering pieces of wood that were roughly five feet long. When these were tilted up against the cross-pole, which was roughly four feet above the ground, it would allow enough room beneath for a grown man to sit up, yet it would be close enough to the ground to conserve heat that would be generated from a fire. After this, he stripped an old dead tree of its bark and carefully intertwined it between the sticks to act like a sort of waterproofing. When this was completed, Lonnie used his hunting knife to cut fresh pine branches to pile on top of the entire structure. With the addition of the tree bark and the fresh pine, the lean-to would be a good shelter to protect them against the elements. As the finishing touches were being tended to, Poppy scraped the snow out of the interior and piled it at the ends of the shelter for extra cover. More pine branches were laid on the ground to serve as a mattress and to protect them from the cold, hard earth.

Lonnie helped his father get settled inside before he put his fire-building skills to work. Only four or five feet separated the rock wall from the opening of the lean-to. He used this space for the fire. After collecting a sizable amount of wood and piling it off to the side, Lonnie broke off some small, dead under-branches from a large fir tree. Whenever building a fire in wet or snowy conditions, dry tinder could always be found here, Poppy had told him. He quickly set up a small teepee-style fire. It had a cone shape, with various size sticks coming together at the top. He placed smaller pieces of wood inside the cone that would ignite the outer layer of larger sticks. Before lighting it with the butane lighter he always carried in his pocket, Lonnie removed a tube of fire-starting paste from his backpack. Poppy would never allow a camping trip into the mountains without this necessity. A tablespoon size dollop of this squeezed onto a piece of wood, wet or dry, would burn for almost twenty minutes. It would easily ignite the dry tinder placed around it, which would then ignite the larger pieces of wood. The paste eliminated the need to use paper or dry leaves when building a fire. When everything is wet and tinder is hard to find, a person can run out of matches real quick, especially if his hands are numb from the cold. More than once, it had saved a camper's life by facilitating the fire building process.

The small fire was a welcome event. It provided both heat and light, but more importantly, it provided security and peace of mind. As long as the fire burned, there was little chance of freezing. It also gave them the luxury of heating up some hot tea. Poppy removed the tea bags and a tin cup from his back pack before placing it under his rapidly swelling leg. Lonnie removed quite a few things from his own pack. In addition to his cup, some beef jerky, and a Snickers, he unpacked an extra pair of dry socks and a hat that covered his entire head and was long enough to tuck into his sweater. The hat and socks were part of his survival gear that were always carried with him. He gave his dad the candy bar to eat while he melted some snow for hot tea, and then he devoured the jerky. It was the first thing they had eaten since dawn. Although Poppy was ravenous, he did not eat more than the chocolate. He knew they were not going to make it back to camp anytime soon, so it would be best to conserve what little food they had. One bit of good luck, however, was that he had made a point of bringing along the elk's tenderloins. He had planned on bringing them to camp and cooking them for breakfast the next day with eggs and potatoes. Unfortunately, the eggs and potatoes would have to wait.

Lonnie had spoken very little since they had returned to the forest. Although he had been quite fatigued, he went about setting up camp with minimal direction or help from Poppy. Now that the work for the evening was completed and the only thing left to do was to get through the night, the idleness began to prey on his mind. Lonnie found he could no longer hold back his emotions. With tears in his eyes, he looked at his father who was resting uncomfortably next to him and said; "Poppy, this is all my fault. If it weren't for me, you wouldn't have broken your leg and we wouldn't be in this mess right now. I know you're hurt bad, otherwise we would have kept going up the mountain. I don't know what we can do, but whatever happens, I'm to blame." The young boy sobbed uncontrollably. He reached out and touched his father's good leg, but would not look him in the eyes.

It was evident to Poppy the boy was deeply troubled. He took a moment to figure out how he might best deal with Lonnie's fragile state of mind. "Oh hogwash," he finally said. "For the first thing, it's not your fault. Accidents happen. Number two, if it's anybody's fault, it would be mine. I never should have tried to cross over that slide area in a blizzard. And number three, you're just a young boy. Sometimes I expect too much from you. Now stop the crying. This is just going to turn out to be another one of our great outdoor adventures together. Everything will work out fine, you'll see. You have my word on it." With that said, Poppy reached over and pulled Lonnie to him and gave the boy a reassuring hug. "Why don't you wrap yourself up now in your space blanket and catch some shut eye. I'll feed the fire from here while you sleep, but after awhile I might have to wake you to bring in some more wood."

"I'm sorry about crying Poppy. It won't happen again. Sure, we'll get out of here, and then we can tell everybody about our great adventure. I wish that someday I could be strong like you." Lonnie closed his eyes and stopped talking. He knew that Poppy did not like it when he cried. Only babies cry. While drifting off to sleep, he made a promise to himself that he would never cry again.

On this bitter cold and dangerous night, young Lonnie huddled close to his father. Although the weather outside their makeshift shelter was threatening, they were warm inside. As he tried to sleep, Lonnie thought about something that he hadn't thought about consciously for a long while---his mother, Anjuli. At this very moment he missed her something awful. She offered a different kind of comfort and warmth to him. When Poppy would get upset about his crying or pouting, his mother would be there to comfort him. She listened to his youthful problems with a sympathetic ear no matter how trivial they seemed. When Lonnie was afraid or distraught, Anjuli would sing a little song to him and hold him very close to her.

> "Don't be afraid my little boy, though danger's near
> I'll be watching over you, so there is nothing to fear.
> When you wake up tomorrow, the sun will shine
> So, now dry those tears, things will be fine."

Lonnie wondered if his mother still looked out over him. He bit his lower lip hard to keep from crying again. Poppy wouldn't like that.

It was more than just keeping the fire lit that kept Poppy awake for most of the night. He was truly troubled about the dilemma they were in. Tomorrow they would have to make some serious decisions. No matter how he figured it, Lonnie was going to have to play a major role in getting them off the mountain. As he lay there with an arm around the boy, his thoughts also turned to his late wife. How she had been cheated in life. The tumor that had started in her breast and spread throughout her body had robbed her of so much. Indeed, it had robbed them all. Poppy was saddened when he thought about how much Lonnie needed his mother, and how this void in his life was depriving him of an upbringing that his father was no substitute for. The change in his son after her death had been subtle. Although they didn't speak about it much, Poppy knew that Lonnie thought of her often. He knew his son missed her gentleness, and try as he would, Poppy found it difficult to relate to his son in "gentle" terms. Perhaps he had been selfish in not pursuing another woman. It was easier to just block those feelings out. But what about the boy's feelings? He would have to give that some serious thought in the future.

Chapter Five

Dawn brought more overcast skies and blowing snow. The storm seemed to have let up for the time being, but not until it had dumped nearly thirty inches of soft powdery snow on the mountain. It was the light, drier variety, that which is prone to blow more easily. The temperature had continued to drop during the night. Poppy checked the small thermometer he wore attached to his zipper. It read 12 degrees F. Although the fire still burned, it had decreased in size over the past few hours. Poppy knew it would be dangerous to let it go completely out. The heat generated from the burning coals was enough to take the edge off the frigid air in their little shelter.

As he lay there in the cramped conditions, Poppy's leg throbbed. This was the first time in his life he had ever broken a bone, and he felt foolish finding himself caught up in this predicament. It was apparent to him that attempting to make it back to camp was completely out of the question. It would be a long painful journey, and to what purpose in the end, only to come down once again? No, they had to move off the mountain. The question in his mind was whether or not he should make the attempt himself or possibly just send Lonnie for help. It had to be a good seven miles back to the ranch. Could the boy find his way out safely? Could he find his way back in with help? The terrain alternated between steep downgrades and rolling ridges. For the most part, however, it was all downhill.

The most dangerous aspect would be the potential of getting lost. If this were to happen, he could always follow his compass due northeast and eventually come out on a crossroad down below. The deep snow would be a hindrance as well, but Poppy figured the lower he got on the mountain, the less accumulation there was likely to be. The ranch elevation was 9,200 feet. It could be entirely possible there might not be any snow down there at all. Once Lonnie got home, he could contact their neighbor and good friend, Maynard Kennicot. There wasn't anybody on the mesa, other than Poppy himself, who knew these woods any better than Maynard. He could saddle a couple of horses and get back up here in a few hours if everything went well. If---that's a mighty big word sometimes. Unfortunately, there were a lot of 'ifs' to this plan, but what else could they do? Poppy continued to mull it over in his mind as Lonnie slept on and the wind howled outside the lean-to.

Lonnie slept until almost eight o'clock. He had a big day the day before and most certainly would have a bigger one today. Any extra bit of rest wouldn't hurt the boy. When he was fully awake, Poppy asked him to gather more wood and build the fire up a bit. They melted snow and had a cup of hot tea together. After a while Poppy insisted on making a little breakfast, so he unpacked one of the elk tenderloins and cut it into small pieces. These, he put into his cup with more snow and put it on the hot coals of the fire. Boiled elk would be better for them and easier to prepare as opposed to cooking it over the fire on a stick. The broth added a little variety as well. All things considered, it tasted pretty good, though a pinch of salt would have been nice.

"I have to tell you Poppy, this is the best elk I have ever tasted," Lonnie cheerfully said. "How are you feeling today? Are you ready to run up the mountain with me?"

"No, Son. I think perhaps the best thing for me to do today is just sit here for awhile. How do you feel about hiking down the mountain by yourself and rousting old Maynard out of bed? Maybe we could get him to ride Junie and Sugar back up here and pack us out. What do you think? Do you feel you could find your way home, and if so, how about being able to find your way back?"

Lonnie's heart leaped in his chest. Here was his opportunity to make up for all the trouble he perceived that he had caused. Over the past few years he had been up here many times with both his dad and Maynard. He certainly didn't know every inch of the mountainside, but he figured he knew it well enough to get home and back again.

"You bet I could. That's a great idea, Poppy. I bet it wouldn't take me more than a few hours to get home and then lead Maynard back up here again. We could be back by dark, but how about you? Will you be all right here alone?"

Poppy chuckled, "Yeah, I suppose I can manage for a few hours by myself." He was encouraged by Lonnie's enthusiasm, certainly a welcome change from his previous night's despondency. "Now Son, the important thing is not how fast you can make it, but rather making it safely, and not getting lost. I can manage up here for as long as it takes. Just leave me a pile of wood to burn."

"I'll do better than that," Lonnie said. "I'll hike back up to camp before leaving and bring back some supplies--food, sleeping bags, warm clothes, anything I can carry."

"Well, I can't say that wouldn't be a good idea. Check my pack for the medical kit. A few pain killers would be much appreciated."

The hike back up to camp proved to be uneventful. It took a bit less than an hour. Lonnie was surprised at how much snow had fallen. Although he was considered tall for his age, standing almost 5'7", the snow rose well above his knees. The tree branches bowed down low under their heavy burden of white. It truly looked like a winter wonderland. The change from the previous day was remarkable, he thought. When he entered their upper camp he noticed the pup-tent had practically collapsed from the weight of the snow. After brushing it off, Lonnie crawled inside and filled his small day pack with all the supplies it would hold. He eagerly took off his rain clothes and put on his heavier winter coat. After filling up the pockets with candy bars, beef jerky, and a flash light, he put together a bundle of warm clothes and then started back on his trail towards the lean-to and his father.

Inside of thirty minutes Lonnie was trudging back into their new camp where he found Poppy sitting on a log outside of the lean-to. The movement obviously had not done him much good. Once again, he looked to be sweating profusely and in considerable pain. The sight of this reminded the boy one more time about the predicament they were in, and how important his mission to get help actually was. For the first time in his young life, Lonnie realized his father really needed him. In fact, his very life might depend upon how well he performed. This new responsibility seemed to light a flame deep inside of him. It created a desire in the boy to want more than anything to succeed, to make his father proud of him.

"When you come on the mountain stream, follow it all the way down until it splits. Keep to the left fork for about a half mile. At the little waterfall veer off and head due north across the rolling ridges. You should be able to see Baldy over your left shoulder. In about two miles you'll come on another stream. That will be Porcupine Creek. Remember not to drink from that stream or you'll get sick. Follow Porcupine Creek all the way through the aspens until you come out on Maynard's back range. Now, do you think you can remember all of that? If you get lost, follow your compass due northeast, and eventually you will come out on a county road. There, it should be no problem flagging somebody down. Our ranch from here is five points off due north. The trip back is about seven miles. Normally, it should take four hours if you're hoofing it, but now, with all this snow, there is no telling."

When Lonnie finally left it was already close to noon. The sky continued to look dark and ominous, but the two of them, in discussing their predicament, decided that it was best to get going as soon as possible and to get the show on the road. Poppy insisted that Lonnie climb up a good distance before attempting to cross over the avalanche field. There was a spot that he had in mind for the traverse, but it would be a pretty good hike, maybe as much as a half mile. Rather safe than sorry, he rationalized. The last thing they needed now was for Lonnie to get hurt on the way down.

Lonnie moved along quickly. He was anxious to prove himself to his father. More than once he had to remind himself not to hurry too much going uphill. It would only cause him to sweat and that would not be good, especially if he were to get into some kind of trouble that might delay his getting down the mountain. It would be a long day no matter how fast he moved so better to pace himself. He carried only his day pack which contained the barest of necessities for survival--fire paste, matches, lighter, metal cup, dry socks and turtleneck, a pull over face mask, space blanket, candle, jerky, and a quart bottle of water. Altogether, it weighed less than three pounds. He carried his compass in his pocket so that it would be easy to get at whenever he wanted to check directions.

There was no need to tote along his rifle as it would only add extra weight and it would be of no real value to him. Farther north in Montana and into Canada it's a good idea to carry a firearm when in the back country to protect oneself against potential predators such as grizzly bears or the occasional mountain lion. Most of the time these animals will stay well clear of a human, but, on rare occasions they have been known to attack people. Lonnie had no fear of being attacked around here. There were no grizzlies in the state and any black bear in the area had probably already gone down for the winter. Mountain lions were always a potential problem, but they were rarely ever encountered in this region. Only once had he seen evidence of a cougar. Two years earlier he and

Maynard were out riding his horses, Junie and Sugar, through the aspens when they came upon a partially eaten mule deer carcass. Maynard was surprised to find a lion kill so close to home, but the abundant paw prints and cracked bones around the carcass were proof enough. Anyway, all things considered, Lonnie moved along relatively confident. He certainly wasn't afraid of any predator today. What goofy mountain lion would be moving around in weather like this?

Upon reaching the cross-over spot his father had told him about, Lonnie very carefully commenced to traverse the rock field. He had moved considerably higher up the mountain from where they had made their initial crossing the night before, and it was not as steep here, therefore the boulders were not quite as unstable. Within twenty minutes he had crossed safely to the other side. If only they had moved higher up the mountain last night before attempting to cross the avalanche field, they might have avoided this entire situation. Well, unfortunately, they didn't, and now they must deal with the consequences.

Lonnie checked his compass more out of habit than necessity. He had been bulling his way along the upper slope for almost an hour. The temperature was bitter cold but it helped to keep the snow dry and light. The going was agonizingly slow. He had been moving in a northerly direction and figured that the mountain stream should be coming up soon. Once again the gray blanket of clouds smothering the afternoon sky had let loose their burden. It was snowing steadily now and the wind continued to howl viscously. As long as he could keep to the cover of the forest the effects of the wind were minimized, but it certainly did make the trees sway. Sometimes the forest can be so silent he thought, but then other times it can make so much noise that it is almost deafening. The roar of the wind through the trees covered up the sound of the mountain stream until he was almost on top of it.

Lonnie was excited when he came upon the stream as it marked the first milestone in his journey off the mountain. From this point on, it should be easier to make good time. He moved along steadily keeping the stream to his right after crossing it. The whooshing noise that it made was hypnotic. He contemplated how minutes earlier the only sound he could hear was the roar of the wind, and now the only sound was the noise of the stream. It drowned out every other sound in the forest, yet it was amazing that he didn't hear the stream until he came to its edge.

At the fork, Lonnie kept to the left as he remembered. The small waterfall soon followed and at that point he checked his compass before heading off in a northerly direction once again. The deep snow and blowing wind made his progress much slower than he had hoped for. Visibility became increasingly limited. Once he got away from the stream and started to cut over the ridges the terrain became very broken and difficult. Many times he slipped and fell while trying to side step his way down the steeper embankments. Each time he would pick himself back up and continue his torturous journey to get help for his father. It was very frustrating for the young boy, and the cold biting wind only helped to wear down his stamina and mental fortitude. Lonnie climbed over so many fallen trees as he moved up and down over the ridges that after awhile he started to fear it might be impossible to get horses back in here. The timber in this section of the forest was very thick. The canopy that it made overhead, coupled with the continuous downfall of snow and dark cloud cover, made it seem as if it were almost dark. Checking his watch, he was shocked to realize that it was almost four o'clock in the afternoon. All of a sudden Lonnie started to feel cold and clammy. The realization that he might not make it out before darkness set in had never really occurred to him. Now that it could be a potentiality, it stirred something deep inside of him that he had never felt before. Lonnie became anxious and picked up his pace considerably. He did not notice that he was falling down more often, nor did he realize that he was no longer heading due north, but was rather tending to head more downhill, which ultimately would get him off the mountain, but only after an additional three or four miles of hard rugged hiking. In order to come across Porcupine Creek, it was important that he head due north for two miles. By heading down the mountain too soon, he would be moving northeast, and very possibly could miss Porcupine Creek entirely.

Fear is an interesting phenomenon. It can affect any human, male or female. Even if one is big and strong, it does not protect them from the slow insidious creeping of uncertainty that takes over their mind. As one is subjected to physical hardship and depredation, the process quickens. The mind becomes immune to rational thought. Irrational behavior is a common reaction. People do things that they don't mean to do. They do them without thinking of the consequences. When the desired outcome is not reached as a result of this irrational behavior, the fear quickens and the whole process continues to build until it reaches the point of climax- this is called panic!

Lonnie was close to panic as he stumbled and fell down the steep incline. Inside his head there was a voice telling him that he had to hurry and get off the mountain before dark. He set this timeline that he could not possibly meet and the closer the darkness came the more afraid he became, and the faster he would try to go. Finally, as he lay face down in the deep snow near exhaustion, he remembered what Poppy had told him before he left. "It doesn't matter how quickly you make it off the mountain, only that you make it safely. I'll be ok for as long as it takes you."

Lonnie lay there breathing hard for a long while. Over and over in his mind he heard the words, "Make it out safely." Slowly he sat up and opened his pack and took a long slow swallow from his water bottle. After a moment, realizing that this was the first water he had consumed since he left his father, he took another long drink. The snow had continued to fall all day. In fact, it was snowing harder now than at any time since it had begun the previous day. The wind was blowing, it seemed, from every direction. Lonnie was cold, very cold. To make matters worse, he had become dehydrated and wet with sweat. He knew he had approached the precipice of panic and that now he was at a very serious crossroad. Should he try to continue on and use his flashlight for light to guide him in the dark, or should he stay where he was at and try to survive the night the way he had been taught? Slowly, as he sat there and collected himself, his rational mind started to work once again. It became apparent to him that going on at this point would be tantamount to suicide. He must bivouac here or someplace very close by where the conditions were more favorable.

Once Lonnie set his mind to the notion of spending the night out, he became much more controlled and intelligent in his decision making. The idea of a lean-to did not seem to excite him. The snow was so deep that it would be difficult to find materials to build it with. Keeping a fire going all night in this wind would also pose a problem. He could very well freeze or die from hypothermia by morning. No, a lean-to was not the answer. The obvious solution was to build a snow cave. Even though he had never built one before or for that matter, ever even been in one, he was confident that he could do it.

It didn't take long for Lonnie to find a suitable place to start digging in. After a short search, he found a spot in the open where the snow had collected into a huge drift. It was relatively flat here and due to fading light, severe weather conditions, and a young boy's reserve running on near empty, he decided that the spot would be perfect. First, he stomped down the snow as much as he could in front of the drift in order to make an exposed wall. Next, he started to burrow into the drift using his metal cup that he carried in his pack. The snow was quite firm as a result of being packed by the strong winds over the past thirty-two hours. In less than thirty minutes, Lonnie had managed to dig his way completely into the drift and secured himself a cozy little den on the inside that was long enough for him to stretch out in completely. He kept the height of the chamber at about thirty-six inches, probably due more to his exhaustion than for his desire to have a more heat-efficient snow cave.

Very few gophers could have made as nice a den in as little time as Lonnie had. The final touch was to cut off numerous pine branches to lay on the bottom of his den in order to insulate him from the cold snow as he hunkered down for the night. With that being completed he quickly stripped off his coat, sweater, and shirt so that he might remove his wet turtleneck. In its place he put on the extra dry one that he was carrying in his pack. Once again he realized the advantage of wearing the first layer of polypropylene. All his body sweat had passed right through it and gone into the cotton turtleneck which he had now replaced with a dry one. After putting his outer clothing back on he crawled back into his den. The candle that he carried provided some heat as well as light. Poppy had told him that one day this candle just might save his life. Lonnie made a mental note to thank him when next they spoke. When everything was in order inside Lonnie pushed some loose snow into the entrance hole until it was almost completely covered. As soon as this final task was complete he put on dry socks and his pullover hat, wrapped himself in his space blanket, ate a Snickers, had a drink of water, and then finally laid down in the fetal position using his backpack for a pillow. For the first time in two full days he heard absolute silence as the storm raged on outside

Later, while Lonnie was dozing off, he could hear a beautiful female voice from his past singing an old familiar tune to him.

> "Don't be afraid my little boy, though danger's near
> I'll be watching over you, so nothing to fear.
> When you wake up tomorrow, the sun will shine;
> So now dry those tears, things will be fine."

As his conscious mind surrendered itself to fatigue, the soothing magic of her voice carried him to a place where he had known great happiness. He could see himself and his parents sitting together on their couch in front of a warm fire at home. His mother was singing softly to him as he curled up next to her. Although the boy was not aware of it, this recurring dream offered him comfort and provided a warmth and strength that allowed him to cast off his lingering fears. He soon drifted off into a peaceful sleep and didn't stir once until the early hours of the morning.

Chapter Six

For a good three hours Poppy lay in the lean-to and contemplated his situation. On the one hand he regretted sending his son down the mountain in this rapidly deteriorating weather but then, on the other hand, what could they do? Someone had to go for help. Lonnie was a good strong boy with a level head. There was no doubt in Poppy's mind that he might not make it. If there were, he wouldn't have let the boy go. The blizzard was his main cause for concern. By his reckoning, there had to be a good five hours of daylight remaining when Lonnie left. Even if he didn't make it all the way down by dark, if he could only find Porcupine Creek, that would lead him right to Maynard's ranch. In good weather a person could make it down from here in three hours, and that would be only covering about two miles an hour. This damn storm! Who would have thought that it could start up again after dumping all this snow. "My God, what a blizzard," he said aloud.

The earliest that he might expect help would certainly not be until late tomorrow afternoon. A man would have to be a fool to try and get back up here in the dark in weather like this, and

Maynard was no fool. He would take his time and carefully plan his course of action. If he had to wait an extra day on the storm, that would be understandable, after all, he would do the very same thing if the shoe were on the other foot. Until Lonnie made it down safely, he would continue to worry. Although he was quite strong for his age and had a drive to succeed like no other, Poppy couldn't stand the idea of his young son being out there in this storm all by himself with no one to help or guide him. Well, it was up to the boy now, he thought. All I can do is wait and pray.

Soon Poppy's mind started to dwell on other matters closer at hand. What do I do about this broken leg he pondered. Experience told him that it would have to be set, and the sooner the better. Many times while working in the mine he had taken part in helping to set broken bones when no doctors were available, but setting your own broken leg was a different matter, especially when there wasn't anyone around to help out. While feeling his shin, the break was evident. However, the best he could tell, it looked to be a clean break. All that needed to be done was a little bit of "realignment." He mused at the thought of this, having once used the very same words to a petrified co-worker when they were about to set his arm after a slight mining mishap. In that situation, the patient passed out and didn't come to for almost an hour. Poppy wondered if he would be as brave as he used to chide others to be.

After careful consideration, Poppy determined the best way to set the broken leg would be to wedge it in between two stationary rocks. Using his good leg, he could push on the one rock while pulling the other leg with both his hands around his thigh. There was no doubt in his mind whatsoever that this would be a desperate maneuver, and it would take all the courage and fortitude he could muster in order to carry it through. Even if help were to arrive immediately, the break would still have to be set. Riding down the mountain on horseback in all this snow would be no treat, especially with broken fragments of bone grating around the inside of his leg. His decision must stand. It had to be done now, no matter how ugly it was sure to be.

Poppy used a long staff to help him get around. First, he visited the dead tree where they had been getting their firewood from. He broke off two short lengths of wood that were each about two feet long. They were straight and solid. These he intended to use as a brace for either side of his leg after he attempted to set it. Rope that he always carried in his pack would be used to tie the supports in place. Next, he searched out a suitable outcropping of rock where he could sit and wedge his boot amongst them. This was no easy task, even with two good legs. Deep snow covered the entire area. Once Poppy had everything at hand that was needed, he methodically cleared a spot in the snow and carefully positioned himself on the ground, making sure his leg was secure and the rock would not give way. There was no need to go through the motions and ensuing pain only to have the rock move and then have to start all over again. This must be done correctly the first time as he was sure he would not have the stamina to attempt it a second time.

Poppy pushed with his good leg and pulled simultaneously with all his considerable might while leaning back towards the ground. The pain was excruciating. Though he was prepared for the sharp burning sensation, the effort left him feeling nauseated and light headed. He had experienced great pain before while working in the mine, but nothing could compare to this. Perhaps it was due to the fact that he expected it, or indeed, brought it on to himself. As he tried to focus through his bloodshot and bugged out eyes, he let out a growl from deep within his chest that would have turned the blood cold of anyone or anything that was within hearing distance. With a roar of fury, anger, and frustration, he continued to pull until he could feel the bone separating deep inside his leg. With his right hand, Poppy reached down to the break area and clamped his bear-like fist over the afflicted spot and squeezed it hard until he felt it go back into place. As he leaned forward and took the pressure off his leg, it did little to alleviate his suffering.

Through sheer power of will, he was able to remain conscious long enough to tie the wood supports onto each side of his now throbbing leg. Finally, in desperation, and with tears in his eyes, he crawled back to his shelter through the deep snow. It was all he could do to drop some wood on the fire and fall back into his lean-to on top of the sleeping bag that Lonnie had retrieved for him. Within minutes, Poppy lost consciousness as waves of pain battered him, one after another, until eventually his broken body could take it no longer and he drifted off into oblivion.

 Several hours later Poppy awoke to the sound of the howling wind. It had become very dark out as he slept. The extreme cold had penetrated his outer clothing while he lay there motionless for several hours, and now his limbs were numb. To make matters worse, the fire had died down to nothing but smoldering embers. Poppy cursed his carelessness in not attending to the fire. The last thing he needed at this time was a lot of unnecessary movement. The intense pain in his leg had subsided to a dull ache, but it was bearable as long as he kept it still. While restarting the fire he noticed that it was still snowing, and that it actually seemed to have picked up in intensity. Checking his watch he realized it was almost eleven o'clock. For the past six hours he had been dead to the world. If it weren't for the wind and intense cold waking him, he could very well have frozen to death as he lay there. All of a sudden a deep concern came over him as he thought about Lonnie. What about the boy? Could he have made it out in all this weather? As much as Poppy wanted to believe he did, there was a nagging feeling inside of him that created doubt. "Oh my God, Lord, please let him be all right. He is such a good boy and doesn't deserve this mess I have gotten him into." The distraught father looked out into the raging blizzard and called out aloud, "Lonnie, Lonnie my boy. Hold on, son. Hold on till morning. Help will come, you'll see, help will come." A great welling was rising up inside of him for he knew that indeed, no help would be coming on this miserable night. There was no way for anyone to know they were in trouble and that at this very moment, his beautiful boy might be freezing to death. His emotion finally became so intense he broke down and cried in great sobs, pounding the ground in frustration, for he knew there was nothing he could do. Finally, he covered himself with his sleeping bag and spent a very long night trying to stay warm, struggling with the thought of the possibility that his son was somewhere out there in desperate need.

Chapter Seven

Lonnie awoke the following morning feeling very secure and rested. The candle had burned itself out some hours earlier, but not before warming his little den to a comfortable degree. Thoughts from the previous day returned slowly to him as he lay there and gradually came back to life in the complete darkness. The call of nature ultimately roused him out of his protective womb-like chamber. He located the entrance hole and realized that it had completely filled in while he slept. With a gloved hand Lonnie pushed his way through the exit and was immediately rewarded with a blinding burst of sunlight that poured into his sanctuary and assaulted his senses. It took a full minute before his eyes were accustomed to the glare enough to peek his head out into the outside world. The sky had cleared up completely some time during the night and it once again revealed itself to be a deep blue.

With a burst of energy, a revitalized Lonnie dragged himself out of his snow cave into the crisp mountain air. It was a beautiful day. The sun was shining brightly in the early morning sky and the wind had almost completely died down. What a difference from the previous day. Lonnie felt like a million bucks! Yesterday the mountain had thrown its worst at him and he had been able to survive it, and quite comfortably at that. A quick reference to his compass along with a careful study of the upper peaks immediately enlightened him to the fact that he had strayed off course. With a new air of confidence and a renewed bounce in his step, he set out blazing a trail through the virgin snow heading due north.

Shortly before nine o'clock, Lonnie reached Porcupine Creek. His water bottle was empty and he was thirsty, but he remembered the warning that Poppy had given him about drinking the water from this creek. A beaver dam a ways up made the water not fit for human consumption unless it was first boiled. Giardia, a parasite that lives in the small intestine of many mammals, especially beaver, was a common occurrence in many mountain streams out here. The awful diarrhea that it causes in humans is enough to make even the most thirsty of campers sorry that they ever indulged in the not so pure Rocky Mountain spring water. Typically, streams above ten thousand feet are not much at risk for this ornery little bug. This is due to the absence of the aspen tree which is a staple of the beaver diet. Lonnie was content to pass on the cold drink. A mouthful of snow would do him just fine; after all, he realized that the difficult part of his journey had now been completed and that within a couple of hours Maynard's ranch would be within sight.

The wisp of smoke rising out of the stone chimney at Maynard's self built log cabin was a welcome sight indeed. It indicated that he more than likely would be at home. Lonnie had known Maynard for as long as he could remember. The old man was like a second father to him. In addition to being neighbors, he and Poppy were best of friends. After the death of his parents, when Poppy moved in with his Auntie Rose, Maynard was a frequent visitor. He had felt sorry for the orphan boy and took it upon himself to become the male influence in his life. Maynard had bought the two hundred acre ranch next door with the money he had earned from working as a mason. At twenty three years of age he had built his own log cabin, cutting the trees, notching them and all. Poppy at age six would often spend time helping his friend work on his home which never seemed to get finished. In fact, it took almost until he was a grown man that they could actually say that it was complete. Maynard watched as young Tyler, which is what he was called then, grew to be a giant of a man. He himself had chiseled features with rugged good looks, and a physique that resembled Michelangelo's David. Years of backbreaking labor working with stone and trying to build his own home at the same time had left him lean and sculpted. Even still, he was no match for Poppy. They had a brotherly type relationship, complete with minor spats and arguments. But the love and loyalty that these two felt for each other, even though they were separated in age by almost twenty years, was unparalleled. The coming of Lonnie and the subsequent tragedy in their life only strengthened the relationship. As a confirmed bachelor, Maynard reveled in the camaraderie that he shared with his friends.

Lonnie pounded on the door mercilessly for almost a full minute before Maynard answered. He was wearing nothing but a towel, having just gotten out of the shower.

"Hello there Lon, what are you trying to do, break my door down?" As soon as the words had left his mouth he recognized the urgency in the boy and immediately knew that something must be terribly wrong. "What's happened, son? Come inside and tell me."

For the next twenty minutes Lonnie relayed the entire story to his friend, from the point of killing the large elk, to Poppy breaking his leg in the slide area, to getting caught in the blizzard and having to spend the night out in a snow cave. Maynard insisted that he eat some warm chili as he continued with his story. While listening to the boy Maynard was already getting dressed into his backcountry clothes.

"You actually built and spent the night in a snow cave? Gadzooks Lon, even I have never done that. What ever gave you the idea?"

"Well, it just seemed like a good thing to do at the time. It was so cold and windy, I really didn't know what I should do. I got kind of panicky, you know. Maybe I should have tried to keep pushing on so I could have gotten back sooner so that we could get a quicker start.

"Lon, you did absolutely the right thing. I fear that if you had tried to continue on, the storm would have gotten you for sure, and then we never would have found out about what had happened until it was too late. This is the worst storm that has hit this area in as long as I can remember. I'll bet there is a good four and a half feet of snow up there. We got close to three down here. Why Son, I don't know how you made it. What an incredible amount of heart you must have. You're a real hero. Somebody important must be watching over you." With that said, Maynard gave the boy a great big bear hug and said, "Now, let's get Junie and Sugar saddled up. I feel that we are going to have another long day. At least for the next few hours we should be able to ride most of the time. By the way, I'm familiar with where this slide area is. If you don't feel up to it you can stay here at my place and rest until we get back."

"Are you nuts? Of course I'm going back up! Poppy needs me. Anyway, you're going to need all kinds of help. Remember, we have an elk to pack out, too. Poppy would have a fit if we somehow lost that."

"Lonnie, my boy, somehow I thought that would be your answer," Maynard said with a grin.

Chapter Eight

The sun glared down brightly as the two riders made their way up the meandering Porcupine Creek. Although the biting wind had died down to almost nothing, the temperature still hovered in the low teens. Maynard was following Lonnie's trail he had made earlier in the day on his way down the mountain. They had left the ranch with all due haste and were making every attempt to get back up to Poppy as quickly as they possibly could. The cawing of a lone raven as it flew overhead was the only sound they heard other than the heavy breathing and snorting of the horses as they moved laboriously through the snow. Lonnie noticed, with some satisfaction, how still it had become compared to the day before. He was amazed at how quickly things changed up here. Sometimes for the better and sometimes for the worse.

"I see where your trail crosses the stream here. If you had stayed higher up on the mountain while coming across, it wouldn't have been so thick and congested with deadfall. We'll continue on up for awhile before crossing so it will make our traverse much easier. The horses will like that, I'm sure."

"How long do you think it will take us?" asked Lonnie.

"I reckon a good three hours or so. This deep snow is tough on the horses. I'm afraid if I push them too hard, they'll get tired and start to stumble" replied Maynard. "We have to be careful, otherwise we won't be doing anybody any good. Don't worry yourself though, I'll get us there by nightfall."

After crossing over the stream, they continued to move due south. Baldy looked about as beautiful as it ever gets off to their right. There was a heavy covering of snow up top and the threat of avalanche was very real, Maynard thought. He knew well enough where Poppy would be laid up, and it couldn't be in a worse spot. His injury must be more severe than he led the boy to believe; otherwise, he would have tried to move off the steep face he was on. It was going to be one hell of a job getting Poppy across that slide area. There was no way the horses would ever be able to cross over. It was much too unstable. Even if they attempted to climb higher up the face of the mountain before crossing, it still wouldn't work. With the snow being so deep, the horses would have no sure footing as they tried to cross over. A rock giving way or a small stumble would panic them and before anything could be done, they would both be rolling down the shoot creating an avalanche of snow and rock as they went. If by some strange quirk of luck they should be able to cross with a horse, it would be nearly impossible for a person to ride it back again, let alone a large man with a broken leg. As they moved along, Maynard continued to think about this. He was pleased they were at least making decent time, considering the conditions.

Once they forded the mountain stream, the going got tougher. In addition to the terrain becoming steeper, there was now the added inconvenience of fallen down trees through which they had to maneuver. After awhile it became necessary to dismount and lead the horses on foot. When a tree would be too large for the animals to step over, they would have to walk all the way around it. They continued like this for almost two hours.

Shortly before four o'clock they came to the edge of the forest. Directly in front of them lay the large open expanse of the avalanche area. Maynard took this opportunity to tether the horses to a nearby sapling. They were tired and sweaty from the long climb, but that was okay for they were real mountain horses and were used to the hard work and altitude. Junie and Sugar were mother and daughter and had been raised in these very mountains by Maynard himself. They were his pride and joy, being the only family he had other than the friends he was now committed to helping. These horses had been packing elk out of the high country in every kind of weather for years. They were good sturdy animals.

"I see smoke," called out Lonnie. "There, down by that group of trees. He's just behind that large rock. That's where we built our lean-to. Why don't you go ahead and fire a shot to let him know we're here."

"No, that wouldn't be a good idea," replied Maynard. "There's no reason to risk the possibility of starting any of this snow moving."

Lonnie looked around as if it were for the first time, and suddenly, seemed to realize there were still some things that could go wrong. "Do you think?" he asked.

"I can't really say for sure, but there's no reason to take any unnecessary chances. We would best serve your father by keeping the rifle in its scabbard. Let's move up along the edge and look for a suitable place to cross. We can leave the horses here."

After hiking up the ridge for almost a half mile, Maynard decided that this was as good a place as any to cross over. Once again Lonnie found himself inching his way across the slide area, only this time there was almost four feet of snow on it; and rather than being in a howling blizzard, it was incredibly quiet and still. The traverse took almost thirty minutes, but they made it without any mishap. Once on the opposite side, they worked their way back into the woods where the snow wasn't so deep. Here they were able to make pretty good time moving down the slope. Lonnie took the lead, having a difficult time restraining his eagerness.

"I know the way Maynard, follow me. This is the way I came when I climbed up before crossing by myself." Lonnie continued to move rapidly down the slope. He was relieved to see smoke from the camp fire. It meant that Poppy was all right. Lonnie knew his father would be proud of him, and this made him beam with pride. He had made it all the way down the mountain in a blizzard, spent the night in a snow cave, and brought help all the way back up by himself. When he stopped for a moment to catch his breath, he realized that Maynard was some distance behind. He could see the old mountain man had stopped and was studying the avalanche chute intensely. When he turned back, Lonnie thought he recognized a look of concern on his weathered face; but in his eagerness, he put it out of his mind. Once again, he turned and hurried along to complete the rescue of his father.

"Hello, in the camp! It's me! I've come back, and I've brought Maynard and the horses to help! Poppy, are you awake?"

Poppy was sitting with his back up against the rock wall resting his leg on his pack. He was using a hot cup of tea to warm his hands, when in the distance, the sound of Lonnie's voice carried to him. At first, he wasn't sure he had heard anything at all. When the voice persisted, he finally realized his son had made it. All the fatalistic thoughts from the previous night vanished once he heard the call of his boy. With great exhilaration, he tried to stand and welcome his rescuers. Lonnie came bounding through the snow into camp with a large grin on his face. When father and son confronted each other, Poppy embraced him in a great hug like never before. He struggled to maintain his composure because he did not want his son to realize how worried he had been. Maynard soon found his way into camp as well.

"A mighty nice little retreat you have here, Tyler. So this is where you bust all those big elk." He also gave Poppy a big bear hug and a hearty slap on the back. "Now, what's this I hear about a broken leg? That's not supposed to happen when you're up here taking it easy. Why don't you sit back down and let old Maynard take a look at it. I brought along some pain killers and clean bandages just in case you might need them. Lon, how about rustling up some fresh firewood and building us a blaze? It's going to be dark soon and we can use the light."

As Lonnie hustled off to collect wood, Maynard became very sober while addressing Poppy. "I don't think I have to convince you we are in a dangerous position here. The threat of avalanche in this chute area is very real. The quicker we can vacate camp, the better. Like I mean right now! Why don't you tell me your situation as far as pain and movement is concerned."

Poppy agreed with his assessment relative to the potential for avalanche. He wasted no time in explaining how he had attempted to set his broken leg in the rocks, and how his mobility had been severely restricted over the past couple of days. Maynard listened to the story without revealing his awe and admiration for the man whom he had come to love as a son over the years. There was very little anyone could say about the incredible exploits of Tyler Burch that would amaze him. Here sat the most extraordinary man he had ever encountered, and if he said that he set his own broken leg in between two rocks by himself, without any help or painkillers, then by golly, that is exactly what he had done. Just like he, himself, would have done under the same circumstances. Yes, Tyler had a good teacher, Maynard thought with very little humility.

"Here, eat a couple of these Vicodin. They'll take the edge off. In an hour, you'll be in la la land, then I won't have to listen to your bellyaching," Maynard said half in jest. "We won't be able to cross here, and going down further is out of the question. Our best bet is to move up a ways, and cross over where we just came from. If we follow the trail already made through the snow, it will be easier. I don't imagine you will be able to walk, so plan on riding piggyback." When Poppy heard that, he started to protest, but Maynard would have none of it. "There is no other way, Tyler. Believe me. Even if you could stand the pain of walking through the snow on that leg, you would do more damage to yourself than a slew of doctors could fix in a lifetime. As of now, I'm in charge! You just sit back and enjoy the ride, and try not to get overly excited when riding on my back."

When Lonnie returned with an armful of wood for the fire, Maynard informed him they were breaking camp immediately. "But, I thought we could spend the night here," he said. "Do you think Poppy is ready to travel?"

"I'm afraid we have no choice, Lon. The snow is dangerously deep up top, and I'm worried that every extra minute we spend here is a risk we shouldn't be taking. Once we get back across the slide area and into the trees again, we can look for a good place to pitch camp. As for now, grab those rifles, stuff the sleeping bag in the pack, and let's move out. I'll be carrying your pa on my back. The plan is to backtrack all the way to Junie and Sugar, and I'm going to need you to lead the way. Try to bulldoze the snow as you walk by keeping your legs together. That should help to clear a better trail and make my life a little easier for the next couple of hours."

Lonnie immediately jumped to it. While working next to his father stuffing the pack, Poppy patted him on the shoulder and said, "It sure is good to see ya, Son. I reckon you have quite a story to tell. This adventure of ours just keeps getting better and better. I wonder what will happen next."

Darkness settled in around them as they slowly made their way up the slope adjacent to the open slide area. Maynard was sweating profusely under the weight of his friend. Before setting out, he wisely removed his heavy winter coat and tied it onto Lonnie's pack. With the amount of heat he was generating, there would be no need to trap it inside his clothing. Why make things more difficult than they already were? The clear sky and almost full moon offered good visibility to see by; however, Lonnie was still using his flashlight. He had opened up a gap of almost fifty yards when Maynard hollered for him to hold up while he took a short break. Lonnie sat down on a rock in an opening at the edge of the chute.

Poppy had been keeping his chatter to a minimum as he knew Maynard did not need the distraction. His job was difficult enough without having to concentrate on conversation. Maynard took a long pull on his water bottle that he carried in his fanny pack while they sat in the snow and rested. "You know Tyler, Lonnie spent last night out in a snow cave. He got turned around after dark and ended up in the lower basin with all that deadfall. Well, I guess it was pretty hairy, snowing and blowing pretty hard and all. He just decided to hunker down for the night; and it's a damn good thing. To do what he did is pretty amazing for a fourteen-year-old boy if you ask me, even Poppy Burch's son."

Poppy gave a long stare to his friend before he finally spoke. "Lonnie is an incredible athlete for any age. His stamina and drive never cease to amaze me. I'm concerned about him though. Ever since the death of Anj—well, you know, his mother, he has been very fragile emotionally. He has lost his motivation for school. Yes, he is advanced for his age physically, but all he wants to do is run around the mountains with you and me. He needs to pay more attention to his studies, but I don't have the time or know-how to make him do it. I feel he has the brains, if he would only apply himself more. I guess what I'm trying to say is, there's a void in his life I can't fill. He needs a mother. Someone who can give him the kind of attention and direction we can't. I fear if I don't do something, he will end up in the mine with his old man. That would kill me!"

Maynard nodded as he listened to his friend open up. Poppy took a short pause and the two of them sat and stared off into the darkness in silence. At first, it was barely noticeable, maybe just the sound of the wind through the trees. Then, as the seconds ticked by, the noise continued to build and it sounded like distant thunder. Suddenly, it was no longer a faint sound in the distance but a rapidly building roar. The two men locked eyes in recognizable horror. In a fraction of a second, Maynard jumped to his feet and started screaming for Lonnie to get into the woods. "RUN, LONNIE---RUN. AVALANCHE!" Poppy could only scream for the boy to run.

Lonnie sat and waited patiently for his companions to rest up. He was eager to continue his trek up the mountain, and then to cross over what he called 'No man's land.' Tonight, he would set up camp by himself and show them both what a good job he could do. As he sat there looking at the stars, he marveled at how beautiful it was up here. "This is where I want to spend the rest of my life," he thought. When the first sound of the impending disaster reached him, he thought it must be a high flying air force jet. He paid it no mind, preferring to enjoy the starry night and reveling in his recent accomplishments.

As the distant thunder grew in intensity, Lonnie realized that things weren't right. He stood and flashed his light up the mountain in a vain attempt to find the source of the building commotion. At that very moment, the shouts of Maynard and Poppy reached him, and he immediately realized what was happening. Without hesitation, he started to run through the snow. Rather than following his own trail back down the slope in the open, he veered off right and tried to make it into the trees; but the snow was deep and his movement was agonizingly slow. Within seconds the noise was deafening. Strong winds began to blow against him, and he could already feel the advanced spray of ice crystals stinging his face. In sheer panic, he dropped both rifles and made one last desperate attempt to reach a lone Ponderosa pine tree that had been standing out in the open for perhaps the last one hundred years. A tidal wave of snow came cascading down upon him. He was just able to lock his arms around the tree in a near hopeless attempt to thwart his inevitable plunge down the mountain to certain death.

When Maynard saw Lonnie heading for the forest, he quickly grabbed Poppy and with a super human burst of strength, hoisted him on to his shoulder and made for cover. They were lucky enough to make it behind a large outcropping of rock before the avalanche came down upon them. For what seemed like an eternity, thousands of tons of snow and ice rushed past them in a boiling melee of utter chaos. A hundred freight trains could not possibly have made more noise. As quickly as it was upon them it passed, continuing down the mountain taking along everything within its path. The terrifying roar subsided into a distant rumble as the avalanche ravaged the valley below.

They were fortunate in that the main flow of snow was more to their right. There was no doubt, however, the solid rock wall had saved their lives. What didn't go around the rock actually lofted over them, and the downward momentum carried it away so that only a few feet of spray landed upon them. Poppy was frantic. "We've got to get to Lonnie." Maynard saw the despondent look in his face and reacted immediately. He charged up the mountain like a man possessed. Poppy yelled from behind, "Check the tree, I think he made it to the tree!" and then more softly in anguish, "Oh God, please!"

The snow was much more solid after the avalanche had passed over. Maynard moved quickly over the ground that a moment before was flowing like water. He saw the large pine tree and made straight for it. Where the avalanche had only grazed them, the pine seemed to have taken the full force of the hit. Snow lay piled high around the solitary tree. When Maynard reached it, he frantically started to dig around the trunk. Discovering the snow was much too solid to dig with his bare hands, he quickly removed his hunting knife from his belt and used it to carve down into the drift. Poppy showed up moments later and savagely attacked the base of the tree where he had last seen his son. Together, the two of them dug into the snow without speaking a word. The minutes ticked by slowly, and still there was no sign of the boy.

Maynard got up and made a quick search of the area below the tree, but to no avail. Just as he turned back, Poppy yelled, "Here! Here is your coat!" With renewed vigor, the two of them scoured out an opening around the coat. Eventually, they realized that it was over Lonnie's head. The next few moments were an eternity for both men. When they were able to finally get the coat off his head, Poppy put his face to the boys and called his name. Lonnie's eyes were closed, and he was unresponsive.

Chapter Nine

    The moment Lonnie reached the large tree, he pulled Maynard's winter coat up over his head to protect his face and give himself some clear breathing space in case he was buried alive. From the deafening noise and the vibrating ground, Lonnie knew he must be in the direct path of the approaching avalanche. He also knew, in order to have any chance of survival, he must hold on to the tree at all costs. The last few seconds before it hit were terrorizing. The large diameter tree he had between him and the oncoming rush of snow offered little comfort to him. When the snow came, it was quick and totally encompassing. One moment he held on for his very life, and in the next instant, he was completely buried. It felt as if he were completely encased in concrete. Lonnie tried to move, but found it to be completely impossible. All he could manage to do was push away slightly from the tree and create a small air space. Disoriented and confused, he went completely limp. There was no reason to struggle. If he were to ever get out of this snowy tomb, it would be through no efforts of his own. Poppy had once told him that when a person is buried in an avalanche, many times they can survive for a long time if they don't panic. The important thing was to stay relaxed and try to breath shallow. Leave your rescue up to the people on top. If there is no one up top, well then, make peace with your maker, because you will soon be meeting him. Lonnie had no way of telling whether Poppy and Maynard had survived.

Lonnie's mind started to wonder. Initially he felt panic, but soon it gave way to more pleasant things. Many different thoughts and memories came to him from his life. Some were good and cheerful, but others definitely more fatalistic. He remembered how excited he was when Poppy first told him he could go on his next elk hunt, the joy he felt when Maynard had recently given him a new fly rod, and how he probably would never be able to try it out now. Lonnie could feel his heart pounding as he ran the six-hundred yard dash at school and how excited and proud he was when it later appeared in the town paper that he had set a new state middle school record for the event. He could see his best friend, Tony Bleuson, and all his other friends crying at his funeral. Most of all, he felt bad because Poppy would be so sad and alone without him. Somehow, he felt he was letting his father down by dying here. Slowly, Lonnie's thinking became more abstract. He could look down and see his body buried in the snow. There was no longer any fear as he resigned himself to the inevitable fact that he was dying. Things were very peaceful. He heard a voice calling him from afar. It was his mother. She was singing her little song; telling him not to be afraid. Lonnie let her know how happy he was to be with her. She told him how much she loved him and missed him. But he couldn't stay. His father needed him desperately; and there were still great things he must accomplish with his life. "I will be watching you my darling, there is nothing to fear; when you wake up tomorrow, the sun will shine; I will always be near...."

The vision of his mother slowly faded. Once again, Lonnie could hear voices calling from afar. This time they were male voices. "Lonnie! Lonnie! Come back to me!" "Please son, don't leave me!" Slowly, the boy regained consciousness. He could hear Poppy calling his name, but he still couldn't see him. As he opened his eyes, his mind started to clear. Eventually the boy became aware of events taking place around him. He could feel movement in the ground, the great thunder of the avalanche, the cold and dark pressure of being buried under the snow, the eerie silence. All these things came back to him in a rush. It was like awakening from a deep sleep. Poppy's face came into focus. He could see the frantic look in his eyes and realized that his mother was right. Poppy did need him. "Lonnie, can you hear me? Wake up son."

"Hey, Poppy. Am I glad to see you're okay! Don't worry, I'll take care of you."

"He must be delirious," said Maynard, "but thank God he's all right."

"Hey, Maynard. What are you guys doing up there? I think maybe I got buried or something. Am I okay?"

"Lonnie, you look just fine to me. Can you remember grabbing hold of this tree? I do believe we will now have to call it, 'Lonnie's Tree' because it sure as heck saved your life. Give us another few minutes and we'll have you out of there in a jiffy. You gave us quite a scare son."

"Dad, I was dreaming. Lots of dreams. In one of them, I was talking to mom. She told me I had to stay here and take care of you. It was like real."

"Well, your mother always knew what was right," replied Poppy. He locked eyes with Maynard, who had paused in his digging, and they both nodded.

Digging Lonnie out was like digging up a prehistoric fossil. They removed snow from all around him until eventually they were able to pull him out completely. Although his legs were a bit wobbly, he seemed to be no worse for wear. "Poppy, I dropped the rifles," said the boy sadly. "Do you think we can ever find them again?"

"Not this winter, but we'll sure enough get them in the springtime," replied his elated father who was happy to see his boy getting back his memory. "I think the most important thing we can do right now is to get out of here."

"I'll second that idea," added a haggard looking Maynard. "Are you ready for another piggyback ride, Tyler?"

"Sure as shootin' boss. Giddy-up!"

The passing of the avalanche had sufficiently packed down the snow so that it filled in the gaps between the rocks and made for a solid footing all the way across the exposed slope. Maynard was happy for small miracles. From this point on, Lonnie stayed closer to his travel companions as they completed the traverse and made their way down the opposite ridge to where Junie and Sugar were tied. Going down hill certainly seemed to be easier. Within an hour they were helping Poppy up onto Sugar's back. He had requested another Vicodin to stem off the pain in his leg, which had grown considerably worse since the recent excitement. Maynard led Sugar with her rider back along their earlier trail while Lonnie followed behind on foot with Junie. It was still a bit too steep and dangerous to ride the horses if it wasn't absolutely necessary. When the pain killers started to kick in, Poppy felt sufficiently invigorated enough to sing a few versus from one of his old mining songs.

> "Fifteen tons and whad'ya get, another day older
> and deeper in debt;
> Saint Peter don't you call me cause I can't go;
> I owe my soul to the company store."

His heavy mining accent and deep tenor voice made the song funny, and it picked up the spirits of the others, who joined in the refrain. For the next hour, the three weary travelers moved along under the almost full moon and starry night until Maynard decided they had done enough for one day.

Lonnie had never been more tired in his entire life. He made a half-hearted attempt with Maynard to help set up camp, but the old man would have none of it. He insisted the two of them stay put and out of his way while he went about building a fire. When that was completed, he found an old log that he moved closer to the fire so they could use it as a bench. Next, he cleared a spot in a suitably level area in order to pitch the small pup tent he had brought along. Among the three of them, they would have to make do with one sleeping bag and two blankets. Maynard figured it would be okay. They would be sleeping in close proximity to each other in an enclosed tent so they shouldn't get too cold. Dinner was a real gourmet affair. Being a confirmed life-long bachelor, Maynard considered himself to be a four star chef. On this night he proved it too; even if the two Burches were so hungry they would have gladly eaten old saddle leather with ketchup.

"This is as good as it gets Maynard. I can't remember the last time I had dogs and beans that tasted so good. On short notice, you can be our cook for any hunt," laughed Poppy.

"If I had a little more time to prepare for this, you wouldn't be joking about my meal. Unfortunately, I had to rush all the way up here to drag your sorry butt off the mountain. Next time, you can eat jerky and gorp. By the way, what's this I hear about a big bull elk hanging in a tree?"

"Little Lonnie has been booking all kinds of firsts up here over the past couple of days. On opening day we put the sneak on Old Ivory Tips. He led us down into the saddle area below the basin under Baldy. It turns out another bull had his eye on one of his cows. Well, Ivory Tips put a stop to that real quick. We sneaked up on them both while they were sparring, and it was all blood and guts. They were really going at it. I believe Ivory Tips would have killed that other bull if we hadn't come along. As it was, the smaller bull had been gored pretty badly. Lonnie used real good judgment and chose the wounded animal over Ivory Tips even though he could have taken either. It was a very mature decision. I wonder how many other hunters would have done that."

Maynard gave the boy an appraising stare. "Yes sir, son, you never cease to amaze me. I have been trying to get that critter in my crosshairs for as long as I can remember, and here you are passing on him to take another. I suppose we could all learn something from you, Lon."

Lonnie looked Maynard in the eyes and replied, "Old Ivory Tips is really something special. There is no other like him in all the world, I'm sure. He must never be hurt by any of us. It's very special to Poppy and me that he goes on living. Would you promise us never to shoot him, even if you get the opportunity?"

"After what you have gone through up here over the past couple of days Lon, it's the least I can do. As of this night, you have my solemn oath that I will never hunt or entice others to hunt Old Ivory Tips. We will let this beast live in peace up here on top of the mountain, and the legend can continue." Maynard crossed his heart with a reaffirming nod to both Lonnie and his Pa.

"What do you say we get some shut eye now," voiced in Poppy. "We still have to pick up that elk meat on the way out tomorrow."

Maynard gave his old buddy an incredulous stare and said, "You're actually up for that tomorrow morning Tyler, even with your banged up leg and all?"

"Sure, why not? It's on the way out. I'd hate to lose it to a flock of hungry ravens and jays. That's meat for our table, compliments of Lonnie here. If you're real nice to him maybe he'll let you have a front quarter."

"Would you do that for your old uncle Maynard, Lon?"

"You bet I would Maynard. After all, you're family now."

The following morning the elk quarters were still hanging in the tree where they had left them three days before. Even in this short period of time the scavenger birds had already discovered the free meal. They had started to pick around the edges of the quarters where they could get at the meat without having to go through the thick hide. There was no real damage done, as this portion typically is trimmed off anyway. It took Maynard the better part of an hour to load up Sugar's panyard with the meat and to secure it for the remainder of the journey down the mountain. He took pride in the fact that Sugar could pack out an entire elk by herself. Today it would be a must unless he wanted to tote some out on his own back. Junie had all she could deal with carrying Poppy and the miscellaneous supplies. Before setting out on the final leg of their trip back home, Poppy took a few minutes to remove the two teeth from the elk's upper jaw with his hunting knife. These are called whistlers. Many times, they are referred to as "ivories." He worked a hole into the base of each and ran a string through so that it could be worn as a necklace. This he presented to Lonnie as a remembrance of their elk hunt together while keeping the other for himself. "Now we both have a keepsake we can cherish," he said. "When we get home, we can polish them up real nice."

Lonnie put it on immediately and beamed with pride. He had seen these elk teeth necklaces before and had hoped to one day get his own. The fact that Poppy wore the other half of it made him feel especially good. He would always think of this trip with his father as one of those lifelong experiences, and the necklace would keep him from forgetting the great adventure they shared together.

The remainder of the trip down the mountain went by smoothly. Immediately upon their arrival back at the ranch, Maynard loaded Poppy into his four-wheel drive Chevy pickup truck and rushed him to the hospital. Although he wasn't complaining, Maynard knew Poppy's leg was giving him a good deal of pain. The sooner it was properly set and put into a cast the better it would be. Lonnie stayed behind, under protest, to unload the horses and put them out in the small corral. When he completed this, he walked the short distance to his own home and took a long bath after which he ate more than he had ever consumed at one time in his entire life. From there, it was a short hop to his bed and sixteen hours of uninterrupted sleep.

Chapter Ten

Over the next three weeks, Lonnie resumed his regular school time schedule, with one small alteration. Rather than being awakened at 6:00 a.m. by his father as he went out the door to work, Lonnie now woke himself at 6:00 a.m. and let Poppy sleep. The broken leg was technically called a fracture of the tibia. It required a hard cast all the way up to his groin for twelve weeks. Although Poppy was miffed that he would be out of work for such a long period of time, he was also somewhat relieved in that there were no serious complications. The doctor had made a point of trying to scare him with all the complications that could have arisen by trying to set his own leg such as shock, infection, or gangrene. There were more potential problems than he cared to even think about, not the least of which was losing his paycheck for the next three months. The new roof he planned on starting in the spring would now have to wait another year. He was hopeful that in a few more weeks when he became more mobile, he could fill in with a desk job at the mine. His supervisor had expressed a willingness to accommodate him in that regard. Poppy enjoyed enormous respect at the mine. Over the past seventeen years he had only missed a few days of work and that was because of his wife's illness and ultimate death. He was a team leader. Everybody involved with the mine, from management down, knew and liked him. Poppy missed the camaraderie he shared with his co-workers who were hard driven men that knew the value of a good days work. Shortly after Anjuli's death, Poppy was offered a supervisory position that would have given him relief from the back breaking labor he had become accustomed to over the years. At the time, he had turned it down preferring to continue digging with his buddies, somehow finding solace in hard exhaustive work. Now, once again, the offer had been put forward and Poppy knew it was time to reconsider it more seriously. As the days passed, he wallowed in his self pity sitting at home with nothing to do.

Lonnie, on the other hand, reveled in his newly found fame. Maynard had told the story to one of the attending nurses in the E.R. whose husband just happened to be a reporter for the local newspaper. Upon hearing from his wife about this young boy who saved his father's life at great risk to his own, he stopped by their ranch and interviewed both him and Poppy. The story opened on the front page of the Sunday edition. "Young Boy Hero Saves Father in Raging Blizzard!" Overnight Lonnie became a local celebrity. His school chums stopped him in the hallways and asked if it was true. In English, the teacher had him stand before the entire class and give his own version of the story. Kids who had never even spoken to him were now wanting to be his friend.

Yes, school at Silvertown High for the young freshman was definitely picking up, at least the social aspect of it. Lonnie still struggled in his daily academics, especially in Algebra. No matter how hard he seemed to try, the concept just wouldn't sink in. His teacher, Miss Evans, was certainly nice enough. She liked Lonnie. Perhaps because she was the girls cross country coach and Lonnie happened to be a stand out freshman varsity runner himself. Whatever the reason, she wanted him to do well in her class. One day, after the results came out on a particular devastating quiz, she approached Lonnie after class and asked if she could speak with him.

"Did you study your lessons, Lonnie? Were you prepared for the quiz?"

"Miss Evans, I study more math than any other subject, but I just don't seem to get it. Most of the time I don't understand the lesson. It's pointless."

"Nothing is pointless, Lon. Maybe we could set up a schedule where I could give you some extra help, you know, kind of like tutoring. Would you be open to that?"

"Well, I have basketball practice after school. I don't know when."

"And I have volleyball practice with the girls. Perhaps a little later in the evening, say around 7:30. We could meet once or twice a week. I might even be able to stop by your house. From what I hear, your father isn't getting around very well these days."

"I guess it would be okay if you think it would help. Can you call my dad and check it out with him though? I'm not sure about whether we can afford it."

"I'll call him today during lunch hour, and don't worry about the cost. We'll work something out."

Poppy was keeping his eye on a lone coyote as it moved through his back acres when the phone rang. Years earlier, a family of coyotes had moved into the area and pretty much destroyed his flock of chickens. He had been actively shooting them back then to keep the predation down, but now, since he didn't have any chickens left, he saw no point in killing the animals even though they put him out of the chicken business. After all, they were just trying to survive like everything else.

"Hello, Mr. Burch. This is Miss Evans, Lonnie's Algebra teacher."

"Yes, Miss Evans. What can I do for you? Is everything all right at school?"

"Well, we seem to have a bit of a problem with Lonnie and Algebra class. He is having a hard time grasping the fundamentals.

I've discussed it with him, and he assures me he is making every effort to keep up, but somehow I don't think that is enough."

"I can vouch for the boy. He works on it every night. Unfortunately, his old man isn't any good with all this new fangled math business, so I guess I'm not much help for him."

"It is difficult to understand if one hasn't been taught the rudimentary. In your son's case, I believe it's simply a situation where he needs a little extra explanation and reinforcement when he's working on his lessons, which brings me to the purpose of my call. If it is all right with you, I would like to offer my services to tutor Lonnie a couple nights a week. I'm sure it would do him a world of good. We could even conduct our lessons at your home if it meets with your approval. What do you think Mr. Burch?"

"I knew Lonnie was struggling with his schooling and I guess that I've been lax in doing anything about it. Perhaps this is a wake up call for the both of us. What would the fee be for your services, Miss Evans?"

"How does $10.00 an hour sound? We could meet from 7:30 to 8:30 on Tuesday and Thursday evenings. If he needs help in other subjects, maybe we could touch on them as well, time permitting."

"That sounds like a fair price to me and a good idea as far as the rest of the subjects are concerned. Miss Evans, I don't know how to thank you."

"The pleasure is all mine, sir. Your son is a fine boy, and I don't mind saying, he is one of my favorites. He is also a fine runner. As the girl's varsity cross country coach, I can tell you that your son could have a fine future if he continues to improve like he has over the past two years. There could even be a college scholarship somewhere in his future."

"You're telling me Lonnie could actually get a scholarship into college for running? Like maybe a financial scholarship?"

"It's still very early in his career, but from what I've seen, he certainly has potential. His times for a freshman are outstanding."

Poppy looked again at the coyote in his backyard without really seeing it. He was thinking about how nice it would be if Lonnie could just go to college and get a degree. It's what he and the boy's mother had always dreamed of. If it could be made easier by a scholarship; why, that would be just the greatest thing. "Lonnie has the heart of lion. If that is what he decides he wants to do, then there's no stopping him. I just hope he is willing to go on to college. So far, there doesn't seem to be much interest. He really doesn't like school except for maybe his sports teams. His mother always dreamed of Lonnie going to college."

"I don't understand. You speak in the past tense about Mrs. Burch," inquired Miss Evans.

"Lonnie's mother passed away three years ago from cancer. It has been difficult for us since then. She was a very stabilizing influence on the boy. I'm usually gone most of the time working in the mine. Unfortunately, that leaves him home alone more than I would like. When he started doing his running after school, I was thankful because it kept him out of mischief and offered a release for his pent up emotions. I never dreamed there could be a silver lining to it."

"I'm so sorry Mr. Burch. I didn't know. This is only my third year teaching here in Silvertown. Lonnie never speaks about his home life at school. I just assumed…."

"Don't worry about it. Things seem to work out in the end. I'm very grateful for your kind offer and will take you up on it. I'll let Lonnie know he now has his own private tutor, and maybe even a little extra coaching help on the side."

"You can count on that, Mr. Burch."

That evening Poppy had a long conversation with Lonnie about school and his grades, and about how he must do well if he ever expected to get into a good college. Lonnie stared at his father and didn't say much. Recently, he thought he might want to become a rancher. Maynard had shown him how easy it was to raise cattle over the past couple of summers. Surely, he wouldn't have to go to college for that. He could start making money right away rather than wasting his time going to four more years of school. They don't teach a person how to raise cattle there. They just teach things like Algebra. How will that ever help him to make money? Lonnie had no desire to extend his schooling any longer than absolutely necessary. He could even work in the mine, if he had to, in order to make money, just like his dad. Lonnie loved living on the ranch and spending time in the mountains. To be away at school didn't sound exciting. Anyway, what would Poppy do without him? Lonnie kept these thoughts inside so as not to upset his father. He knew how much his dad wanted him to get an education. There was no reason for arguing about it now. College was more than three years away and plenty could happen between now and then, he thought.

"So, how do you feel about Miss Evans coming over and tutoring you in Algebra?" questioned Poppy.

"I guess it's ok as long as we can afford it. Math is pretty tough and she seems to want to help me."

"Lon, we can certainly afford it. Anything we can do to help improve your grades is well worth the investment. Remember what I say when I tell you that only through education can a person better himself. It may not seem so important today, son, but one day you'll realize. The last thing you want in life is having to break your back doing physical labor when you can use your brains instead. It's so much easier."

"Yeah Poppy. You're right. I'll do good and get my grades up. You'll see."

"I know you will son, and I'm sorry to constantly harp on you about it. It's just that I don't want you to end up in the mine. My last promise to your mother was that you would go to college and get a good job away from the dangers of what your old man does." Having said this, Poppy leaned over on the couch where they had been sitting and gave Lonnie a hug. "Oh, and by the way, this Miss Evans tells me you're a regular Jim Thorpe at school. She seems to think one day you might actually be able to get an athletic scholarship into college with your running. That's when they pay all the bills just so you'll run for their team."

For the first time all evening, his dad had said something that actually caused him to stop and think. An athletic scholarship. He knew what that was. Some of the older boys on the basketball and football teams talked about getting one. To them, it seemed like the greatest thing in the world. Lonnie realized he was good in track. He could run faster and farther, jump higher and longer, and pretty much out throw any freshman or sophomore in the school. As an eighth grader, he had the fastest time in the state in the 600 yard dash. This was the main reason why the varsity cross country coach insisted on him running for the team even though he had wanted to play football instead. In the end, he decided to run. That's where he always excelled, and to get a varsity letter as a freshman was really something special. When he compared himself to the upper classmen on the team, however, Lonnie didn't really think he was very good, but the coach praised him in a big way saying, "Any freshman who can make the starting five on this team has a bright future." At the time, Lonnie just figured the coach didn't want him to give up and go out for football next season. Now, hearing this from Miss Evans, well, maybe he should keep on running.

Chapter Eleven

Miss Evans turned out to be just what Lonnie needed. After a few sessions with her, the boy's understanding of Algebra improved noticeably, even though he did still hate the subject. Over the weeks, she found him to be a hard-working young student who just had to study a little extra sometimes in order to get by like many other kids his age. Eventually, Lonnie was accepting help in the rest of his subjects as well. He didn't struggle with these as much as Algebra, but he grew to like Miss Evans and was happy to have her around. She bolstered his self-confidence in schoolwork to the point where Lonnie soon felt comfortable in classes that he had dreaded attending only weeks before.

Poppy also enjoyed having Miss Evans around. She was a breath of fresh air in the home shared by the two. Her outgoing personality and sense of humor made her a delight to be around. Soon, Poppy found himself looking forward to her scheduled visits almost as much as his son, but for different reasons. He enjoyed her feminine touch, which was something he had shut himself off from years earlier. At twenty-nine years of age, she was an attractive enough woman; so much so, Poppy secretly wondered how it could be she was still unattached this late in her life. He was careful, however, to keep these thoughts to himself.

Miss Evans, or Sara, as she insisted on being called by the two of them when tutoring, had medium length brown hair and striking blue eyes that seemed to twinkle when she smiled. At 5'7" she had an athletic physique, being thin and rather small breasted. Sara had an inner strength and confidence in her bearing that usually came from years of competitive sport. In fact, Sara had been quite an athlete herself earlier in her life. She was an accomplished distance runner in high school, and to this day, still found time to run twenty miles a week. Her real love had been girls' volleyball. She captained her junior and senior high school teams that placed third and first respectively in the state championships. One night, due to Lonnie's prodding, she brought over her scrapbook and let him look through it. He was amazed at all the newspaper articles and stories about her. There were individual pictures and interviews conducted by reporters that spanned her entire high school career. Lonnie studied page after page, all the while forming a new respect and friendship with his Algebra teacher. She started to build in him a desire to excel in his sports.

"You are so lucky Lonnie, to have all this natural ability. If you were to identify the sport today that you wanted to participate in, and then really trained in it, there would be no stopping you. The sky would be the limit! There is a tremendous amount of self-satisfaction that can be attained through sport. The competitive instincts and drive that great athletes are born with must be sharpened and honed like a knife by good coaches in order to bring out the best possible potential for that athlete. Sport builds a desire not only to succeed on the playing field, but to succeed in life as well, and it gives you the necessary tools in which to make it happen. Life is very competitive. In order to succeed and get ahead, one must take advantage of every asset they possess. In your case, it's the natural athletic ability coupled with your intense motivation to impress your father."

With that comment, Lonnie looked up at her and they locked eyes. "Yes, I've seen how you interact with him. It is very natural and good for a young boy to try to make his father proud of him. What helps to make the next generation succeed, Lonnie, is our desire to do well in front of our parents, coaches, and teachers. You are no exception here, but, you are exceptional in what you can actually accomplish with your life if you set your mind to it. Are you following me?"

Lonnie looked up again and answered, "You bet I am. I do like running and track, maybe even more than basketball. It's easier for me, and I get to play more. Plus, sitting on the bench in basketball is no fun. What do you think, Sara? Should I quit and concentrate on running all winter?"

"Why don't you finish the basketball season this year and see how you do with track in the spring. If you do well and still like it, then maybe it'll be easier to make your decision next year."

"I wish you were my track coach," Lonnie suddenly stated.

Sara blushed and responded, " Mr. Trapp is a very good track and cross country coach, Lonnie. In fact, our school is fortunate to have him. If you were to put yourself in his hands and follow his direction, he could help to develop your skills wonderfully."

Poppy had been in his bedroom with the door left ajar, just enough so that he could follow the conversation as teacher and student sat in the den discussing these things. He was pleased to overhear the solid advice and good counsel Sara provided for his son in addition to tutoring. She seemed to be a remarkable young woman who showed a real interest in helping the boy to find his way. It certainly was obvious that Lonnie had opened up to her over the past few weeks. Poppy could see the change in him and was pleased with it. Realizing the session had been over for some time, Poppy took the opportunity to join them.

"Hello. Is it okay if I hobble in here and join you two?"

"Absolutely, Mr. Burch. We were just finishing up. How is your leg doing? Does it still hurt?"

"Nah, it doesn't hurt much anymore. It itches more than anything. In another week I should be able to start work again. Management has offered me a temporary position where I will be working in mine safety. I get to move about the mines in the area looking for safety and health infractions. Typically, the brass that runs the mine likes to have an experienced mine worker perform this job. If it goes well and I like it, the position could become permanent. Sort of a promotion, I guess."

"That's wonderful Mr. Burch. I guess you were right when you said things usually work out."

"It's a tough decision to leave the men after seventeen years, but the increase in pay and lighter work load should agree with my tired old bones. Anyway, it's not like I would really be leaving their charming company. It's just that I wouldn't be operating the heavy machinery anymore. It might be nice to move more freely about the place. I definitely have some suggestions already."

"This is great, Poppy. Now you can stop using your brawn and start using your brains. That's what you always tell me!" laughed Lonnie.

"I guess it's time to start practicing what I preach," chuckled Poppy. If it gets me out of this house six weeks early, it will be worth it. How about hitting the shower, Son, and giving Sara and me a chance to talk a bit."

Lonnie said goodnight to Sara and thanked her for bringing the scrapbook over. He left the room whistling after giving Poppy a kiss goodnight.

"I've noticed quite a change in Lonnie over the past few weeks, Sara, and I must say, it's for the better. He actually seems to enjoy going to school. How are the lessons coming along?"

"Lonnie is an intelligent boy. It's amazing how quickly he can pick up on things with a little one-on-one attention. As far as his schooling is concerned, he is doing better. I believe he was just drifting prior to this, not really sure of what he wanted. In another couple weeks, you probably won't need me anymore. We'll see how it goes."

Poppy changed the subject, not really wanting to pursue that line of conversation. "Lonnie tells me you were quite the volleyball player."

"Well, I don't know about that, but I did play in high school a bit. It's a wonderful sport and I'm happy to be coaching it today. How about yourself, Mr. Burch? Are you the one and only Tyler Burch who holds all the high school football records to this day?"

"Gosh, are those old records still standing? I never would have thought--- Say, please don't call me 'Mr. Burch' any more. It's too formal. I'd prefer it if you called me 'Poppy' like everyone else does. After all, if I'm to call you Sara, then it's only fitting to call me by my name."

"Isn't your name, Tyler?"

"Only my late Auntie Rose and a few very old acquaintances call me that anymore. Lonnie renamed me Poppy when he was just a toddler. I've grown to like it more than my given name. Sentimental reasons, I guess."

"Ok, 'Poppy' it is then," laughed Sara. "But, what about all those old football records? Surely, you must have gone on to play in college? I'll bet the schools fought over you."

"No, I never went to college. Shortly after high school, I married Lonnie's mother, and went right to work in the mine. Been there ever since. This is why it is so important to me that Lonnie go on to college, but enough about me. How is it that an attractive, bright young woman like yourself is still unattached at this stage of your life? I would have figured some lucky guy would have snatched you up years ago."

Sara blushed. "I did date a boy throughout college and some years afterwards, but it never amounted to much. He turned out to be not the serious type. If I hadn't moved on, we would probably still be dating. He wasn't the marrying kind, I guess. Three years ago I told him I had accepted a teaching and coaching job here in Silvertown. It didn't seem to phase him the way I had hoped it would, so I just moved on, figuring it was better that way." Poppy gazed steadily into her blue eyes, but didn't say a word, preferring to

The Song In His Heart

let her continue. "At first, it was more than I had bargained for. My family lived in Denver, which is a bit larger than Silvertown, to say the least. I just up and left my parents and brother behind, along with most of my friends. It took a little getting used to, I guess. Now, I love it here and wouldn't go back for the world. There is something about being in the mountains that I love. Maybe it's the air or the water. I can't really say, but I love it just the same."

"Did he ever try to get you back?" Poppy questioned.

"Jack is his name, and yes, within a couple weeks he called, after tracking me down through my parents. He said he had made a big mistake and wanted me to come back. I lied and told him I had met someone else. He called one more time after that, and then never again. I'm a better person for it though, more independent. Plus, I love my job! Teaching is very satisfying and I especially like the coaching. It brings the best out of me."

Poppy and Sara continued to make small talk for almost another hour. He realized she had many desirable qualities, and he especially liked her free spirit. Without really meaning to, Poppy found himself drawing comparisons between her and Anjuli. They were very different in outward appearances but rather similar in personality traits. Sara made him feel relaxed and comfortable. Poppy enjoyed conversing with the younger woman. It had been a long time since he talked with an attractive woman for any length of time. Shortly after 10:00 pm, Sara indicated it was time for her to leave.

"Mr....I mean, Poppy, it was so very nice to chat with you. I'm sorry for going on and on about things. I'm sure you didn't need to hear about my life story and all."

"On the contrary Sara, I enjoyed it immensely and look forward to the next time when we might be able to pick up where we left off. It's not very often I get the chance to speak with a member of the opposite sex—uhh, you know, a woman," Poppy blushed.

"Somehow I find that hard to believe, Poppy. I would think you could have your pick of just about any female in the county."

"Ha, ha, Sara, I think I'll take that as a compliment, but it's not true. Here, let me walk you out to the car."

"You don't need to put yourself out on my account, Poppy."

"I'm not putting myself out, Sara. The pleasure is all mine. Anyway, I can use some of that mountain air you were talking about!"

As Sara drove home along the snowy roads she found herself to be in an exceptionally good mood. "Could he have possibly been flirting with me?" she asked herself. "An attractive, bright young woman!!! Yes, he did say those exact words. Oh, he was probably just being nice. But, then again, when he called me a woman, he turned red. That great big gorgeous man was blushing on account of me. Oh, but I acted dreadfully. I can't believe I told him all those things about myself. What will he ever think of me?"

Sara had never known anything about Poppy prior to the newspaper article, and Lonnie had been one of her favorites long before that. Her offer to tutor the boy was innocent enough as she was legitimately concerned with his ability to pass Algebra. But, on that first night when Poppy answered the door, she noticed a queasy feeling in the pit of her stomach that told her there might be something about this man, something special. She was self-conscious and nervous initially when he would address her, which was rather strange in itself, but as time passed, so did the nervousness. Now, she found Poppy quite pleasant to be around, and felt rather glib in his presence. Her sessions with Lonnie were going well. Indeed, they were going much better than she could have hoped for. He really was a good kid, and Sara had the distinct feeling the boy had developed a crush on her. Sara hummed a song to herself as she let the good feelings take control. Things definitely were picking up. The emotional stress she felt for the first year after moving to Silvertown was now a distant memory.

Jack had been the first true romance of her life. They had met her sophomore year at the University of Colorado where she majored in education. Jack was majoring in liberal arts and shared a history class with Sara. He was one of the original party animals back then and tried to lead Sara astray almost from the first day they met. The contrast between the two was considerable. Sara took her studies very seriously and worked to excel in everything she did. Jack, on the other hand, was more concerned with where he would get his next beer money. If it weren't for his wealthy parents and generous allowance, he certainly would have had a difficult time.

Sara eventually warmed up to the persistent young fellow, although they were quite the opposite in many ways. He showed her another side of the social scene, one of hard drinking frat parties and all night dorm keggers. On weekends Sara, Jack, and many of their friends would pile into his conversion van and head up into the mountains for camping trips in the fall and skiing trips in the winter. If not for her dedication and desire to succeed in college and to graduate in good standing, she would have found it nearly impossible with Jack as a boyfriend. Still, she found his wildness exciting. Sara led a somewhat sheltered life prior to college, and he provided an outlet for her to experience some of the more daring things she had always been afraid to try.

Her marijuana experiment had been the first of these. One evening a group of friends were going to a horror film marathon at the local theater, and they all got high on pot before going in. Sara had to be persuaded, but in the end, she let go and got stoned with the rest of them. It was not a good experience for her. Perhaps it was due to the subject matter of the movie, "The Night of the Living Dead." After the movie ended, she made Jack take her back to the dorm early because she was afraid. All in all, it was not a good evening, becoming the first and last time she ever tried smoking pot. Soon after that, Sara went so far as to forbid Jack to ever smoke it again, saying it would most likely cause him to go crazy. Certainly she could see that it was already making him both stupid and lazy. He refrained from doing it in her presence, but she could still smell it on his clothes at times. In the end, this was one of the major reasons she considered moving on.

Sara still maintained her virginity when she started dating Jack. Even though she was anxious to lose it, she wanted to make sure he was the right one. It took almost six months before feeling comfortable enough with him to accept his advances. The entire experience wasn't as romantic or as satisfying as she had hoped it would be. At least Jack was a considerate lover, if nothing else. Over time, their sex life improved, but in the end, it was the only cement that held them together. When Sara left, she realized that this was not the formula for a lasting relationship. To this day, Jack was the only man Sara had ever known romantically. As she drove up to her driveway, she found herself thinking about what it might be like to make love to a man like Poppy. When she realized where her thoughts had turned, modesty quickly prevailed, and she turned her mind to thoughts about the coming day.

Chapter Twelve

The following week Poppy returned to work after having his six-week follow up with the doctor. As promised, they reduced the size of his cast to just below his knee. This certainly improved his ability to walk, but, more importantly, it gave him the ability to drive which was essential if he was going to report to work each day.

The Lost Creek Mine got its name from its close proximity to the Lost Creek Canyon, which was located on the western slope of the Great Divide, just ten miles outside of Silvertown. The actual land area where the mine was located was owned by the BLM-Bureau of Land Management. This was state controlled property that was, in this instance, leased to the mining company. It was one of the smaller mines operating in western Colorado, employing just under 400 people. As coal mines went, the Lost Creek Mine was one of the more desirable ones, at least as far as the environmentalists were concerned. It was a room and pillar style mine with portal entries. This meant that all mining operations were conducted underground as opposed to the strip or pit mines which were carried out on the surface. In these mines, huge holes were scoured out of the earth in order to reach the minerals being mined. The locals were opposed to this method of mining because it scarred the landscape, at least until the mine was played out and the land could be reclaimed. Sometimes mining operations would continue for years.

In the case of the Lost Creek Mine, the coal was located at a depth of almost 2,000 feet below the surface. Each morning the miners would enter the mine riding in diesel powered trucks that would carry them almost four miles into the earth. Here they would spend their entire day hidden from the sun above, working heavy machinery in cramped conditions with minimal lighting. Although the old pick and shovel days of coal mining were largely a thing of the past, the dangers were still very real in this hazardous occupation. Coal miners throughout the United States continue to be killed and injured by cave-ins, falling rock, and explosions caused by an accumulation of methane gas and coal dust ignited by random sparks. Perhaps the greatest cause of injury and death in an underground mine is due to accidents involving machinery. Since 1900, over 100,000 American men have lost their lives in coal mine accidents and countless more have been injured and maimed for life. It is for this reason that the federal and state governments got involved. They set minimum health and safety standards that each coal company and every miner must follow. To ensure compliance with these standards, every mine now has a safety officer who works with management to establish safety procedures and then enforces them. His duties include making sure that the mines and miners follow these rules which are set up for their own protection. This was the new position that Poppy had been promoted to.

The physical demands of his first few weeks were rather insignificant as most of his time was spent in classroom sessions learning about the fundamentals of the new position. A federal Health and Safety inspector was responsible for his training. The fact that Poppy had been an actual working miner for so many years provided him with valuable insight and understanding in his new job. He was well aware of the many dangers inherent in this occupation. In addition to this, he had worked over the years on almost every piece of machinery in the mine. Early in his mining experience, he worked on the continuous miner machine. This was a huge improvement over previous mining techniques. The continuous miner allowed one man to operate a large piece of equipment which would gouge out the coal face using a rotating drum with drill bits mounted to it. The coal would then drop onto a conveyor belt which dumped it into shuttle trucks for transport to the surface. It was now possible for one man to dig out eleven metric tons of coal in a single minute. Because of its huge output potential, this piece of machinery had to be constantly stopped so that the loose coal could be hauled to the surface and so that the ceiling could have bolts drilled into it for support, thus helping to prevent roof cave-ins. Almost ten years ago, Poppy switched to a new piece of machinery introduced into the mine called a long-wall. This monstrosity used a round cutting tool mounted on an arm which moved back and forth across the coal face. It differed from the continuous miner in that as the area became more dug out, the long-wall actually provided steel props behind it that served as roof supports. As the long-wall moved forward, the supports would follow and allow the ceiling to collapse behind it. This proved to be more productive than the continuous miner which had to leave wall supports or 'pillars of coal' in its wake to shore up the ceiling or overburden. A developed mine actually looked like a honeycomb of many small rooms with the pillars being off-limits until the coal seam was played out. Then they were removed from the back area of the mine forward as the operation retreated. Most of the time the ceilings are allowed to collapse as the pillars are removed.

Poppy was taught how this collapsed portion of the mine known as the 'gob' area can provide an environment that is ripe for one of the deadliest of all mine mishaps. Spontaneous combustion or 'spon-com' can occur when excessive heat builds up in these areas. When it is combined with coal dust and air, an explosion can take place. This explosion can be greatly exacerbated when methane gas is present. As little as one percent detected in the mine brings all mining operations to a stop until giant fans have had a chance to clear it out. Spon-com can be detected early by recognizing an elevated reading of CO_2 and carbon monoxide in the mine. These gases are an indication of combustion. When this occurs, the room or shaft must be sealed off with metal panels known as a 'Kennedy Stopping.' Grout is used around the edges to keep out air. Eventually, when the inner fire is deprived of oxygen, it will go out naturally. It is imperative, however, that the air in the mine is constantly monitored for these elevated levels of gases. Dosimeters are used today to measure the concentrations of methane and carbon monoxide. Certainly an improvement over the 'canary in a cage' days.

In addition to this most deadly of mishaps, Poppy was also trained in equipment monitoring. Each piece of machinery used in the mine had to be first tested above ground to contain sparks. He was schooled in 'ground control', or the falling of rock or coal from ceilings and sidewalls, and how to prevent cave-ins by shoring up the ceilings. Whereby Poppy had always been one of the good old boys working in the mine, he would now have to become an enforcer. When men did not wear their hardhats, steel-toed shoes, or safety glasses, he would be required to write them up with a warning. Too many of these and a man could lose his bonus. For the most part though, these were good conscientious men who Poppy worked with and everybody inside and outside of the mine took the position of safety officer seriously. After all, it was their well being that he was working for. Poppy was not concerned whether he might ruffle anybody's feathers by enforcing these safety procedures, either inside the mine or inside the front office. He had a job to do and, as usual, he would do everything within his power to ensure that it was done properly to the best of his ability.

Once he had completed his classroom training, which took several weeks, Poppy began to make his regular rounds throughout the mine. Many of the miners knew him by name and he was well liked and respected by most everyone. The few individuals that had a beef with him had learned to keep it to themselves over the years for Poppy was a no nonsense sort of fellow. He had the reputation among the men of being a fierce fighter when provoked and had established himself at the top of the pecking order years before. He was also known as a considerate friend, one that could be relied upon in times of need. Poppy had always been a hard worker. He set a fine example of excellence in what can be accomplished with a solid work ethic. Overall, his co-workers were pleased with his promotion, and they welcomed his future efforts on their behalf relative to mine safety. If anyone could make a difference in this position, it was Poppy Burch, and that would benefit everyone.

"Yo Poppy! I heard a rumor that you finally broke down and accepted the safety officer spot!" called out Ralph Gromitz as Poppy made his way over to a large diesel truck that was getting ready to transport a group of miners through the entry shaft of the mine down to sub-level #4. Ralph was one of the old timers in the mine. At age sixty-one he had forty-two years of underground stories to tell. In that time he had seen quite a few changes come along. The mine operators weren't as concerned with safety issues in the old days. Most of the time they had a 'take it or leave it' attitude. Unfortunately, in some mining towns, which were owned and controlled by the mine operators themselves, it was very difficult to leave. Housing and food costs were priced so high that the common laborer could barely eek out a living. Many times they would actually get deeper into debt as time went on. Ralph talked about how it was a lot more violent back then. Mine owners thought nothing of bringing out a bunch of paid thugs with guns to intimidate the miners into accepting sub-standard wages and working conditions. His Uncle had actually been killed in the Ludlow Massacre.

By all accounts, this was one of the most ruthless and heinous episodes in coal mining history. It started in the fall of 1913 when a young labor organizer named Gerry Lippiatt was gunned down by two detectives who were working for the John D. Rockefeller's

Colorado Fuel and Iron Corporation. This so incensed the miners, who were mostly immigrants living in shanty towns controlled by Rockefeller, that they voted to strike the mine. In September, they were evicted from their shacks and were forced to march through a mountain blizzard to a tent colony many miles away which was set up by the United Mine Workers. Throughout the winter, they were terrorized repeatedly by roving bands of goons that fired randomly into their tents, killing many innocent men. Then, in the spring of 1914, the National Guard was called out to establish order. They immediately sided with the mine operators and commenced to wage a reign of terror against the miners which culminated on the morning of April 20, 1914. Before dawn, the guard surrounded the tent city. Unprovoked and with malicious intent, they fired machine guns into each tent before finally putting the entire city to the torch. In one tent alone, the bodies of two women and eleven children were recovered. In all, the death toll was staggering. It was ultimately the cause for President Woodrow Wilson's sending in federal troops to quell the unrest and future retaliations on the part of the mine workers.

"Those days of intimidation and terror now serve as a reminder of just how far we've come," stated Ralph when last he told his story to a group of young new recruits that were bellyaching about the hard work and less than adequate rest room facilities they had to deal with. As it turned out, one of the stalls was out of toilet paper!

Poppy replied to Ralph, "How ya doin, Ralphy? Yup, ya heard right. I accepted the position of mine safety officer. Hopefully, I'll be able to make a difference."

"I don't doubt it a minute, Pop. You're the man for the job. Say, I heard in the scuttle-butt about your most recent elk hunt. That's some boy you got there. How come you never bring him by to meet everyone no more?"

"You know I don't want him to get caught up in this business. He's gonna go to college and get a real education. I've got my hopes set on it, I do."

"Well, that sure would be nice, having a college educated young-un in the family. How's your leg? Aren't you up and about a little early?"

"Maybe so, but I got a job to do and after spending most of the past couple months sitting on my duff, it's high time I got at it again. Maynard gave me this nice old walking stick to use that his Father brought over from England. The wood is called malacca. It's nice and light, sturdy too. I can use it to clobber you guys when I catch ya loafin on the job. Watch out for me now, I'm one of the bad guys!"

"Yeah, right. Good luck Pop. We're all pullin for ya."

"Thanks Ralphy. Well, I guess I'll see ya in the hole later."

Poppy caught the next shuttle truck down to sub-level #5. He was on his way to one of the older areas in the mine which was now inactive. Two years previous, elevated levels of carbon monoxide were discovered indicating a spon-com in one of the old gob areas. It was immediately sealed off with a Kennedy wall, and now it was routine to check the area every week or so to make sure the seals were still intact. Air samples were also required to guarantee there were no additional hot spots.

After accomplishing this task, he moved about the subterranean labyrinth of tunnels checking on lights and electric power cables. Although all cords and lighting fixtures are first surface tested to ensure that there were no electrical shorts, they must also be continuously checked and rechecked for signs or wear or degradation. As Poppy moved along throughout the mine, he came into areas where there was considerable activity. This was in stark contrast to the more remote sections where mining operations had ceased years before. Many of these areas were familiar to Poppy having worked them in the past himself. Now they stood empty and abandoned for the most part, with only a single strand of dim lighting left to illuminate the empty shafts. These were the spots that must be constantly monitored for dangerous levels of gas. Although the position of safety officer much of the time was boring and unexciting work, it was nevertheless, perhaps the most critical position in the entire operation. One small oversight or miscalculation on his part could endanger the lives of every man below the surface. In a sense, the efficiency and performance of the entire mine hinged on how well he performed his duties.

Later in the day, Poppy moved back into an active area of the mine. He stood off to a side with his back up against the wall while he watched Andy Nelson on the long-wall machine. He didn't miss this old job of his. Andy filled in for him when he broke his leg, and now since he had accepted this new position, Andy's fill-in job had become permanent. He was a nice enough kid, about twenty-three years old, who kept pretty much to himself most of the time. Perhaps it was the money that lured him in. Poppy didn't know nor did he care. He knew that the enticement of quick decent earnings for an uneducated man was what the mine operators relied upon to keep their shifts running at full manpower. It was now his job to make sure these newer recruits followed the rules and didn't endanger their lives or anyone else's by reckless or lackadaisical behavior.

While Poppy watched, he once again realized how difficult it was to keep his mind from wandering under these conditions. The ear plugs that every machine operator are issued to deaden the thunderous noise of the long-wall worked well when it came to protecting the ears; however, when a man is working around loud machinery with ear muffs or plugs, he tends to go into his own little world. The mind wanders and leaves the operator less than focused on his task, thus increasing the potential for mishap. Perhaps this is what happened to Andy Nelson later that day. According to witnesses, everything seemed to be going along as well as could be expected. When the noise from the long-wall changed ever so slightly at first, it went unnoticed. Within a few brief moments, the deep roar of the huge cutting wheel scouring its way through the relatively soft bituminous coal changed to a screaming, high pitched, nearly ear shattering clamor as the heavy cutting wheel came into contact with a spar. The considerably harder material of the spar, igneous in makeup, stopped the momentum of the cutter instantly. By the time Andy reacted and cut the power, a large jagged rock weighing well over a ton was broken loose from the wall face and catapulted directly at the helpless young man. He took the hit in the chest and left shoulder area extending all the way down to his hip. By the time help could get to him, he had already perished from his massive injuries, literally being crushed. It happened late in the day, and by the time they could get the body out of the mine, it was already past dark.

When the news reached Poppy, he was devastated. Mining accidents involving casualties are always a reality when working under these conditions. The fact that it was Andy hit Poppy especially hard. This young man had come into the mine the previous year and done a good job. The lad had taken over the very same piece of equipment that he himself had worked on. If it weren't for his own broken leg experience, he could very well have been on that machine today. And if he had, and he hit the spar, what then? Would it have been his broken body they removed from the mine on this day? After so many years, and trying to be so careful for all that time, it was sobering to realize that sometimes, no matter how careful one is, a freak accident can occur and take you out in an instant. The shaken man shuddered as he contemplated the pressures and responsibility of his new job. He was also painfully aware of the young age of Andy and how one day this could be his boy Lonnie being reduced to a statistic. "No, I will not let that happen," he promised himself, "not under any circumstances."

Chapter Thirteen

Spring came slowly to the Silvertown area. The higher elevations usually permitted the snow to stick around for an additional month or so, until the inevitable rising temperatures caused by the lengthening days eventually melted it off completely. Lonnie looked forward to the beginning of the track season. He remembered his conversations with Sara over the winter about how important it was to get an early start with his training. The junior varsity basketball team had a mediocre season at best and he was glad it was over. Their record stood at fourteen wins, eleven losses. The final tournament at season's end, which determined whether their team could continue on to the state championships, was a disappointment. Due to a foot injury with Danny O'Neill, their star center, the team never made it past the first round. Normally, Lonnie would have been devastated to be eliminated in the preliminary round of anything; however, over the long season he had decided to dedicate all his energy to track and cross country from now on. In reality, the decision had not been that difficult to make. Lonnie was not a starter on the team, and he had too much competitive spirit to sit still on the bench. If his basketball coach couldn't recognize his talents perhaps the track coach would.

Track didn't officially start until April 7th, but the very next day after the end of basketball season, Lonnie was out running on the country roads. After their tutoring sessions, Sara and he would talk at length about shoes, nutrition, how to properly train, and anything else they could think of that had to do with running. She put together an early season training schedule for him to follow in the two weeks before the season began.

"It is important to ease into your training," Sara would say. "Under no circumstances do you want to push yourself too hard at the beginning until you've had some conditioning. A boy with your natural ability normally wants to start out too quickly. Before you know it, you're nursing an injury. Track season is ten to twelve weeks long. Training is not a sprint but rather a marathon. It is not important how well you do at the beginning of the season. In this sport, the only thing that counts is how well you finish the season. Then you can take all your conditioning at the end of the season and apply it toward cross country which starts the following September."

"Which events should I try out for?" questioned Lonnie.

"The more, the better!" responded Sara. "If I were you, I'd stick to the middle distance though. That way, you can add a few field events and maybe the hurdles or something. If you go right to the longer distance, you may not be able to compete as well in so many events. When cross country season begins in September, you'll be able to do your distance event then. That race is anywhere from 2.5 to 3 miles long. It's a one race sport. Everybody lines up together at the starting line, and the best runner finishes first. Not always the fastest but the best. A three mile race takes more than speed and endurance. It also takes skill and knowing your competitors. A person has to know when to run hard and when to hold back. If he runs too hard at the beginning, there may be nothing left for the finish. On the other hand, if he starts out too slow, he may not be able to catch the leaders before the race is finished. It takes four good years to train a fine runner like you to compete with the elite runners."

"Do you think I could ever become an elite runner, Sara?"

"Lonnie, you're an elite runner right now but only among freshman. It will take your whole high school career with continuing improvement to make you a state qualifier. Do I think you can do that? Yes, absolutely, but in the end it will be totally up to you. But only if you have the drive and motivation to train. Not just race mind you, but train. Some great athletes never reach their potential because they can't self motivate. If it takes an outside influence to force them to train and work out, they will never achieve greatness. It must come from within. The greatest runners have an inner force that propels them towards their goal."

The schedule Sara laid out for Lonnie included a six-mile run for each of the first five days. These were to be nice and easy miles. She called them L.S.D., which meant 'Long, Slow, Distance'. The sixth and seventh days were for stretching and light exercise. Week number two called for more of the same. The miles were meant to be easy and relaxing. It would be a precursor to the more rigorous training which would follow in the coming weeks and months. Sara stressed the importance of proper nutrition and plenty of sleep time. "If one doesn't recharge his body with good food and plenty of rest, it will run down like an old battery," she would say.

After the completion of these first two weeks of preseason training, Sara excused herself from any further coaching of Lonnie, preferring to let him get his instruction from the regular boys track coach. She didn't mind offering advice, but the actual coaching and training should come from the head coach. Herbie Trapp was more than happy to hear of the pre-season training schedule Lonnie had been following. He picked up right where Sara had left off with the boy. Each day after school the girls and boys track team reported to the athletic field for a two-hour workout. Silvertown High was not a large school, enrolling just under six hundred students, but it was noted for its great track teams year after year. Perhaps the greatest singular reason for this distinction was due to the fine coaching job of head coach Trapp.

Coach Herbie, as he was fondly called by returning alumni, was a good natured but intense man in his early sixties. Although not tall, just under 5'8", he had the muscle, structure and poise of a once great athlete. Among other things, Coach Herbie had been a nationally ranked track star in his college days. His specialty had been distance. In fact, for a time he had been considered one of the elite marathoners in the U.S.A. At the age of thirty, he ran the Boston Marathon in two hours and fourteen minutes. Coach Herbie completed a four-year scholarship in track at the University of Oregon in Portland. He had many distinctions and honors to his credit, but perhaps the greatest to him was when he ran the mile against a young man from England named Roger Bannister. There was a lot of press coverage for this particular race. Over the previous few months, excitement had been building over who would be the first man to break the four-minute mile. Although Herbie took dead last in the race, he still managed to run a time of 4 min. 7 sec. This run against the great Roger Bannister was his greatest accomplishment in track, he would later say. Roger ran a 3:59.9 second mile.

Shortly after college, Herbie moved back to his home state of Colorado where he took a job teaching Earth Science at Silvertown High School. When a position became available as assistant track coach, he quickly snatched it up as it was his one true love. Within another year, he would become the head coach of both cross country and track. Coach Herbie was able to take the young talent that tried out for his teams and turn them into state contenders. Four separate times his cross country team won the state championship; and his track team, not to be left behind, finished first three times, second three times, and third so many times that he lost count. The boys loved Coach Herbie. He was tough on them and would accept nothing but their best, but if a boy worked hard, he would do most anything for him. Slackers were not tolerated in any way, shape, or form. It broke his heart to do so, but each year he would feel compelled to kick a few of the less dedicated boys off the team. It was important in his eyes to set an early example each season and not allow the unmotivated kids to influence his teams. This never hurt his turnout, however. Track continuously enjoyed the highest rate of participation in any sport at the school.

The first meet of the season was always a big event. A number of the more powerful teams in the area had organized what became known as The Central Mountain Track and Field Comps. This early season event usually determined which schools would be the standouts in the mountain district. Of the twelve teams participating each year, only two or three had never gone on to distinguish themselves in the state championships held in early June. Coach Trapp was especially excited with the strong team he had been able to assemble this year. Most seasons, the distance runners formed the nucleus of his teams; but this year there were a number of very talented younger boys who excelled in the shorter distances as well as the field events. Although Coach Trapp typically refrained from running his freshman boys in varsity meets, this season he had made a decision early on that there were two underclassmen who certainly proved themselves worthy to make the squad. Lonnie was his number one pick for the 800-meters and the 110-meter high hurdles. He was also a strong candidate for the longer distances and the high jump, but due to the depth of this year's squad, he would only be competing there in a backup role.

The other standout freshman on this year's team was Tony Bleuson, known by his friends as Blue. He had been the only freshman at Silvertown High to make the varsity football team. Blue not only made the team, but was also voted second string on the all-state squad as defensive tackle. He weighed in at 245 pounds and stood 6'1". Early on in grade school, Blue and Lonnie were not good friends. Blue had been the school yard bully and made the mistake of picking on a much younger, but no less determined, Lonnie Burch. After a brief shoving match, Lonnie hit Blue with a one-two combination he had been taught by Maynard and broke his nose. Before Blue could retaliate, the fight was broken up, and the two of them were sent to the principal's office. Lonnie must have realized that even on his best day, he was probably no match for the much larger Bleuson boy, but due to his unwillingness to back down and his aggressive offense, he earned his respect. The following day, an embarrassed Tony Bleuson showed up for school with two black eyes, which were a direct result of the broken nose. Hence the name Blue, as in black and blue, not necessarily Bleuson. From that day forward, the two of them were fast friends and Blue was no longer the terror of the playground for it seems that the more timid nature of Lonnie rubbed off on his new friend. Due to the boy's incredible size, Coach Trapp figured he would be a natural for the shot-put and discus. When track season began, he was not to be disappointed, for Blue broke the school record by almost two feet on his very first throw of the shot.

As Lonnie approached the starting line, he felt a nervous excitement in the pit of his stomach. The event was the 800-meter run. Based on previous times in practice, Coach figured he could potentially place in the top six. This was the first time Lonnie had ever run the 800-meter on the varsity level. While checking out the other runners on the line, he couldn't help sizing them up. There were two boys he had heard about who were the favorites--Sam Costa from Ridgeway and Brian Pellitier from Golden. They were both returning lettermen in their senior years. Sam Costa had placed sixth in state the previous year and was looking to better that mark this season. The Pellitier boy hadn't done quite as well but supposedly his times had improved remarkably this year.

Coach Trapp had indicated it would be a very fast start. "Don't kill yourself trying to keep up with these guys in the lead pack," he said. "Get yourself established in the second group, preferably on the inside lane, and maintain your position for as long as you can. The winning time in this race will probably be around 1:56. If you can break your best time of 2:06, that will be just fine. We couldn't ask for anymore than that, especially from a freshman." Although he didn't show it, Lonnie resented that final comment. In his eyes there was no reason to expect any less from him because of his age.

Experience yes, but age, no way. Moments before the race started, Lonnie reached down to the good luck piece hanging from his neck on a leather string. It was the elk tooth his father had given him after their hunt the previous fall. He put it between his front teeth and held it there until the gun sounded. In this manner, he started the first track race of his high school career.

The pack of boys exploded off the starting line in a tight group and held it all the way through the first turn before they began to spread out. As expected, Sam Costa and Brian Pellitier moved out into an early lead. A few yards behind them were four more boys from various schools struggling to establish their positions before they entered the second turn. Lonnie found himself back in eleventh place going into the first straight-a-way. He did not have a good start. In addition to being elbowed several times by the other runners as they jockeyed for position, he also had his foot stepped on by a runner wearing racing cleats. The elbows were to be expected and were soon forgotten, but the top of his foot ached from the trauma of the spike bruising it. Due to the fact that Lonnie was a freshman and a relatively unknown runner, he had been required to begin the race in the second line. There were a total of twenty-six running the event spread out over two heats, the fast one and the slower one. Lonnie was now running eleventh out of thirteen runners in the fast heat. As he lengthened his stride and tried to relax going down the back stretch, his confidence and early season training kicked in as he slowly began to pass the runners in front of him. By the time he finished the first lap, which marked the half way point, Lonnie was running a strong fifth. The spectators and other athletes cheered them on as the gun once again went off marking the final lap of the race.

Lonnie ran as if he were in a dream. His total concentration was on the runner immediately in front of him. While running through the next turn, his attention was diverted to the sideline where he spotted both Blue and Sara. As head coach of the girls track team, she naturally was present at the meet even if her girls were not competing in it. "Run hard Lonnie! Pick them off one at a time! No one can stop you!" she cried.

"Atta boy, Lon. Kick ass!" he heard Blue yell.

With the extra bit of encouragement, Lonnie ran harder than ever. He soon passed the number four runner and set his sights on number three who was making a valiant attempt at passing the Pellitier boy currently running in second place. While running down the backstretch, Lonnie gave it all he had and sprinted past them both going into the final turn. He knew it was a gamble to make his final move so early, but the excitement of the moment and the possibility of placing well in this race clouded his judgment. With just 100 meters to go, Lonnie realized why they call the 800-meter run the hardest race in track. His legs had suddenly turned to lead and no matter how hard he tried there just was not enough air getting into his lungs. Everything seemed to be in slow motion. Up ahead Sam Costa seemed to be in control of the race. His movements were so fluid and relaxed. What he wouldn't do to be able to finish like that after a hard race. The closer Lonnie got to the finish line the more labored his efforts became. Somewhere behind him he could hear the heavy breathing and footsteps of another racer. Moments later Brian Pellitier sprinted past him followed closely by the number three runner Lonnie had just passed. They ran by him as if he were standing still he thought. Lonnie's heart sank as he realized his flirt with victory was little more than a weak attempt by a novice runner trying to upstage the more experienced athletes. It was all he could do to hold off the next competitor until he himself crossed the finish line in fourth place. Exhaustion quickly overcame him as he had to be helped off the track. When Coach Trapp finally confronted him, the disappointment in the boy's face was evident.

"Lonnie my boy, you just ran the race of your life. I have your unofficial time at 1:59.8. That's more than six seconds faster than you have ever run it before. Costa ran a 1:53.6 and Pellitier ran a 1:56.7. Son, you performed brilliantly. With a few strategy sessions and some more hard practices under your belt, you'll become a top competitor in no time at all."

All of a sudden, Lonnie didn't feel so tired any more. He shook off the helping hand of the race official and simply beamed at his coach. "I guess I made my move a little too early," he said. "Ran out of gas at the end. Next time I'll do better," he promised.

"I believe you will," said his coach. "Yes sir, I believe you will." Coach Trapp was already moving away towards the next event. In his mind he marveled at how well Lonnie had just done. Not very often in a coach's life is he able to work with and train a youngster with so much potential. Coach Trapp felt very good. His team was performing better than he had hoped for. Indeed, they would probably win the Comps, but more importantly he realized that young Lonnie Burch had the potential to become a world class track star, and he would be a guiding influence in the boy's life to make sure it happened. It had been a long time since he had seen young talent like this, and of course Blue in the discus and shot-put. Sure they had won lots of meets and championships in the past, but no real successes beyond that. There was something about the boy he couldn't quite put his finger on. He was driven, no doubt, but by what? Something was motivating him deep inside, but for the life of him, Coach Trapp couldn't figure out what it was. He shrugged his shoulders as he stowed this thought away in his mind for another day. There would be plenty of time to get into his head later for the boy was only a freshman and he still had another three years to go after this one.

"How are you feeling Lonnie?" asked Sara. "You were real impressive out there. Your father will be so proud of you. Pretty soon people are going to start recognizing you at these big meets."

"My legs got so heavy at the end. I have never experienced anything like that before."

"It's a sign that you went all out. If you don't feel that way at the end of a race, you're not trying hard enough no matter how good of shape you're in. Try to walk it off now. In a few minutes you'll be as good as new."

The Song In His Heart

"I better be. The 110-meter hurdles are coming up next." With that said, Lonnie jogged off to check on the progress of Blue, who was in the process of warming up for the discus throw. On his way over, Sam Costa trotted up alongside him.

"Nice race," he said. "I hear you almost beat Brian. Geez kid, you're good. Someone told me you are only a freshman. Is that true?"

"Yup, only a freshman," Lonnie proudly answered back. "I don't think I'll ever catch you though. As we were coming around the final turn, I saw you up ahead just kind of gliding in. You made it look easy. I don't know if I'll ever look that good."

"Don't sell yourself short kid, my best time as a sophomore was 2:01 and you just beat that time by more than two seconds as a freshman, in your first race no less! You stick with it and one day we'll all be watching you on TV. Well, nice race. See ya around. I'll be keeping track of your progress in the papers. Maybe we'll race again later in the season."

It was amazing how good that brief encounter with Sam Costa made him feel. To be recognized and acknowledged by one of the elite half-milers in the state was like icing on the cake. "Come on Blue. Send that thing into orbit," he called out as he approached the discus area. Blue looked over at him and gave a confident thumbs up before going into his spin. After a complete 360 degree twirl, Blue let out a deep grunt as he flung the four pound discus with all his might. It sailed through the air with an upward trajectory like a flying saucer and covered nearly 210 feet before landing with a plop, well ahead of any other throw up to that point. His effort put him firmly in first place. Blue made a pumping motion with his fist and let out a loud holler of approval before vacating the area. He puffed his chest out and strutted over to where Lonnie was standing.

"Hey, Lon, nice run. I think we're both going to have a good day. What did you think of my toss? I can do better if I have to, but with some luck, it won't be needed. Come on, walk with me over to the shot-put pit. I think I'm on a roll and you're bringing me luck." Blue's toss of the shot went much the same way as the discus throw.

After round one he was in first place for each event. This helped to swell his head more than ever. Modesty had never been one of his more admirable traits. Throughout his life, Blue had always relied upon his extraordinary size and sheer power to get what he wanted. Thus far, high school seemed to be just more of the same for the boy. He was basically a young kid in a grown man's body. As the two boys socialized with other members of their team the first call went up for the 110-meter high hurdles.

"Well, I guess that's me. I'll see you guys at the finish line," said Lonnie. He trotted over to where the hurdlers were stretching and began his pre-race warm-ups. Once again, Lonnie became conscious of the queasy feeling in his stomach as race time drew near. He tried to remember all the pointers Coach Trapp and some of the older, more experienced kids had given him about running the hurdles. There were a total of eight obstacles.

"Don't worry about knocking over a hurdle or two," Sara had told him. "There's no penalty for that. Just keep going and make sure you stay in your lane."

When the gun sounded, Lonnie charged out of the starting blocks. His long legs made him ideally suited for this event. For the first time in his life he actually felt like he was flying. Because the hurdles were evenly spaced, it was a simple matter of counting his steps in between each jump. Every eighth time his left foot would strike the ground, his right leg would then go up and clear the hurdle just like clockwork. With just one hurdle to clear and then a short sprint to the finish line, Lonnie realized that the race was his.

"Not bad," said Coach Gruenwald, "but I don't know if your time will be fast enough to place you in the top five. Even though Lonnie had won his heat, there were still three more heats to go. Over the next fifteen minutes he watched as his first place finish in his heat dwindled down to a fifth place overall finish. Coach Gruenwald seemed to be more pleased with the result than Lonnie. "Don't fret over it," he said. "The more experience you get in this event the better you'll become. Once we've refined your technique, you'll be unstoppable." The encouraging words helped to lessen his disappointment.

"Well, nobody ever said it would be easy," he thought to himself. "Now I know where I stand and how much I have to improve in order to become the best, and I will become the best." With that thought in mind, he walked slowly over to the stands and sat by himself to watch the rest of the meet.

The sixty-five mile bus ride back home was a festive affair. Once again, Coach Trapp's varsity track team had come out on top narrowly winning the prestigious meet by a margin of only two points. The enthusiasm the other boys showed was infectious for Lonnie, and after awhile he was laughing and joking with the rest of them. Not so for Tony Bleuson though. He was as depressed as could be. In the third round, an unknown had come out of nowhere and captured first place in both the discus and shot-put, forcing him to settle with two second place finishes. To make matters worse, the boy had completely ignored Blue afterwards and was overheard making comments about how he wasn't throwing well today. "That cowpuncher and I are going to have a showdown the next time we meet," he mumbled. "I'll show him what happens when he messes with old Blue."

Lonnie looked his friend in the eyes with a very serious look before bursting into uncontrollable laughter as he slapped him on the thigh and said, "So now it's Old Blue, is it?" Many of the boys sitting close by joined in the laughter until they had even "Old Blue" roaring with delight.

"We did OK today, Lon. Yes we did, and it's only the beginning! You and I are going places together." For the rest of the trip home the boys sang song after song until their hoarse voices would allow no more.

Chapter Fourteen

As the school year wound down, it became evident to Sara that her services as a tutor were needed less and less. She informed the two Burch boys that Lonnie was well on his way to completing his first year of high school in good academic standing. His grades would not land him on the honor roll, but they were at least good enough to classify him as an average student, although just barely. As strange as it seemed, both Poppy and Lonnie insisted she continue on through final exams. Sara gladly accepted this request for she legitimately enjoyed everything about this tutoring job, not the least of which being the beautiful drive up into the higher elevations of the mountains.

One evening in late May, after wrapping up a review session for the next day's final exam in Algebra, Sara sat in the family room with Poppy as they often did after tutoring sessions, making small-talk. Initially, their conversations had focused almost entirely on Lonnie and his progress in school, but as time went by and the boy seemed to be adjusting better, these conversations turned to other more interesting adult subjects. Over the winter months the two of them had many such talks and were now quite comfortable with each other. The formal air between them had slowly dissipated. Sara was saddened about the prospect of her sessions with Lonnie coming to an end. Although she enjoyed Lonnie's eagerness to do well, the few moments she would spend each week conversing with Poppy had also become important to her. He was quite a man, like none other she had ever met. Sara recognized how deeply Poppy cared for his son and how seriously he took his role as father. She admired this in him. He was not a pretentious man. On the contrary, Sara found him to be humble and modest. When he finally opened up to her, she realized he was quite a story teller as well. On more than one occasion she had stayed late into the evening while listening to one of his fascinating tales.

"Your home is considerably higher in elevation than town," Sara had stated. "Summer is a long time coming up here, I'll bet."

"Yes it is. The ranch is roughly 9,400 feet above sea level. Almost two miles. I love it up here though. The air is so fresh and clean. It really gets to some people if they're not used to it. You know, thin air and all. It's even worse up top."

"What's it like up there, on top? Is the forest real thick and hard to get around in? How do you find your way?"

"I grew up in these ranges so I guess it's easy to find my way about. Although the forest can be very deep and congested at times, it's really amazing at how open and uncluttered it can also be in other places. The entire high country is literally criss-crossed with animal trails, mostly deer and elk. The trails have been used for ages on end. At times a tenderfoot might think he's on a horse trail or even a dirt road, but in fact, the elk are largely responsible. They lead from meadow to meadow and from ridge top to ridge top. At the tree line, it's very open and the mountain peaks above can make it very dramatic."

"It must be very beautiful," Sara added.

Poppy thought for a moment as if he were pondering some great decision, and then asked, "Would you like to take a ride up on horseback with me? Saturday I plan on riding the stream up a ways to un-clutter it. Lonnie usually helps me, but this Saturday he has an early morning track practice. Actually, the stream starts out as an irrigation ditch higher up. About 100 years ago some mountain family put in an unbelievable amount of work digging out an irrigation ditch and lining it with rock. It brings a flow of water all the way across and down from one of the main streams we call Porcupine Creek. In the old days, people worked hard to bring water to their ranches, but they did good because it still flows today and brings water to both my ranch and Maynard's. All it takes for upkeep is a ride up each summer to unclog a few spots where branches and leaves become trapped and stop the water flow. Sometimes I can increase the stream by 50% just by removing old debris. After that, we could continue our ride and you would have a chance to see first hand how beautiful it really is."

"Oh, I don't know. I'm probably not the best horseback rider in the world. I would hate to slow you down."

"Nonsense," Poppy replied. "If you can sit on a horse, you can ride it. There's no hurry, we can take the day. What do you think?"

Sara was tickled to death that Poppy had asked her along. In reality, there was nothing she would enjoy doing more. As for riding the horse, Sara was actually quite a good rider, or so she had been told. However, she couldn't help wondering just where this might lead to. Was Poppy simply looking for company on his ride up the mountain? Was he just being nice to her for tutoring his son? Or maybe, perhaps, he liked her…and if so, was she ready for this kind of relationship again? After a pause she quickly concluded that this was a no-brainer. "All right. I would love to go. It sounds wonderful. Can I pack a lunch?"

"That would be great. We can eat by the falls in the Valley of the Monarch."

"In the valley of the what?"

"I'll explain it to you on Saturday."

Sara wore blue jeans and a button down flannel shirt. Poppy tied her jacket behind Sugar's saddle in case the weather should change and turn cool. By the looks of it though, Saturday was turning out to be a beautiful day. It was already close to 80 degrees when they set out at 9:30 in the morning. The sky was crystal clear and deep blue. Sara noticed how much more striking the blue sky was up here as opposed to back in Denver. The problem with Denver is that it is situated at the base of the Rocky Mountain foothills, and all the dirty air and pollution seem to get trapped in the city by the winds passing by overhead. The smog looms over the city and surrounding area. She was happy to be away from it and congratulated herself for having the initiative to follow through with her decision to move away. They followed the path alongside the stream as it wound its way up the mountain. It looked more like a stream than an irrigation ditch, Sara thought. It was difficult to imagine how a person could dig something like this so long ago through the rock without the help of heavy machinery.

Three or four times on their way up, Poppy stopped to unclog a bottleneck in the slow moving stream. When they finally reached the junction of the irrigation ditch and Porcupine Creek, Sara could see how the original engineer had skillfully tapped into the larger stream to divert a small portion of the water flow into his new stream bed. Poppy explained to her how it was important not to divert the entire stream as it would undoubtedly cause trouble with some other rancher further down the mountain when his creek would run dry. In the old days men were killed for such things. As long as the water flowed consistently, it wasn't necessary to divert too much because it would run twenty four hours a day, 365 days a year. In the spring, it ran fast and full from the snowmelt, but as summer approached the volume would decrease to barely more than a trickle. Hence, the reason for Poppy's annual trek up the mountain in order to keep the stream beds clear and the water running.

Shortly after leaving this spot, Sara began to have trouble with her horse. It seemed that Sugar had it in her mind that it was time to head back down the mountain. No matter how hard she tried, Sara could not get the stubborn horse to move forward. In a desperate attempt to get started, she kicked the horse's flanks mercilessly and hollered, "Giddy up you old sod!" but to no avail. Sugar only sidestepped and got antsier. While looking back to check on the commotion, Poppy could see her dilemma so he slowly turned his horse, Junie, around and came back.

"What seems to be the problem here, cowgirl?"

An embarrassed and frustrated Sara replied, "It seems that your horse doesn't want to go any further up the mountain! Maybe she's protecting me from something up ahead, eh cowboy?"

"Nah, I don't think that's it at all. Typically, when I ride up here by myself, we head back after reaching this spot. Sugar is just used to heading home from here. Try dismounting and leading her a ways. That should do it."

Poppy watched as Sara swung her leg over Sugar's back and hopped to the ground. Her tight jeans and flannel shirt accentuated her shapely figure in a way that he had never noticed before. When Sara looked up and caught him staring, he blushed and quickly turned back around in his saddle. After walking Sugar for twenty yards or so, Sara climbed back up on her back and was finally able to get the headstrong horse to follow along behind her mother. They continued to ride for almost another hour before being forced to dismount and walk the horses due to fallen down trees blocking their path.

"Just over the top of this ridge is an area we call Baldy. It's a large plateau that has no trees on it and sort of looks like a man's bald head from below. When I was a boy, Maynard and I used to camp up here. Now it's one of Lonnie's favorite spots. We try to make it up here at least a couple times a year. It's good for the soul. We're not really church-going people, so I sort of taught Lonnie to get his religion out here. You'll see what I mean in a few minutes."

As the two of them walked their horses up an old elk trail, they eventually came out on top, or rather at the bottom, of Baldy, for it extended almost half a mile onward and upward. Where the open plateau seemed to end, it backed up to a small patch of spruce trees. These seemed to level out for a bit. Above them was the most magnificent view Sara had ever seen in her entire life. A snow-capped peak, awash in sunlight, stood at just over 14,000 feet directly behind it. Sara could see where the timberline stopped and the rugged 'no man's land' of the upper peak began. She was stunned into silence and awe. "I see what you mean, Poppy," she whispered. "This could easily be God's own cathedral."

"Let's ride on up from here," he said. "There's more."

Sara looked left to right while they made their way steadily up Baldy. She could see how the rocky terrain was infiltrated with patches of lush green grass. Off to either side of the plateau which was almost 400 yards across, the elevation dropped dramatically into a heavily forested sea of green pines. There were no deciduous trees at this high elevation as they could not deal with the thin air or the severe winter conditions. She marveled at how small and insignificant they were with respect to these grandiose surroundings.

Upon reaching the top of Baldy, Poppy wound his horse down a small incline into a depression hidden from below. Here he picked up a small stream which was created from the melting snows that lay carpeting the peak 3000 feet above them. He followed it into the timber. In a matter of minutes, they came out into a clearing which was surrounded by trees. It backed up to a spectacular cliff where the stream was fed from a small crystal clear pond. Rising above it was a cascade of water which ran down the smooth rocky surface and ultimately fell the final thirty feet into the basin. Once again, Sara looked on in awe. The splash of falling water hitting the pond sounded like the applause from thousands of people. She looked at Poppy, who had now dismounted from his horse and said, "It's so beautiful. How do you find such places?"

Poppy walked over to her horse and replied, "I'm glad you like it. This is one of my favorite spots." He reached up and placed his calloused hands on her hips and effortlessly lifted her 125 pound body from Sugars back. As he set her feet onto the soft earth at the edge of the pond, their faces came very close momentarily and for the first time, they looked deep into each other's eyes. The contact lasted only an instant, or perhaps a bit longer. Neither of them could say for sure. Poppy's peripheral vision blurred as he focused first on her large blue eyes, then briefly on her nose, cheeks and finally her almond shaped lips and mouth. Sara was silent. She stood there oblivious to her surroundings, mesmerized by his intense gaze, and barely cognizant of his hands still on her hips. At this moment in time she was absolutely helpless, and delightedly so. The magic was interrupted when an impatient Sugar let out a loud whinny and stomped her foot several times.

"Whoa there girl. Settle down now," Poppy spoke softly to the horse. He let go of Sara and immediately began to unpack her saddlebags. Sara awkwardly stepped backward and tried to catch her breath. She had flushed a deep red, and though she could not see it, the warm tingling sensation in her face was proof enough. In an effort to keep Poppy from noticing, she went over to Junie and unpacked the picnic lunch she had prepared earlier that morning.

"Where would you like me to spread the blanket?" she asked.

"Let's put it over there to the right on that grassy area in the sun."

"It's as good as done. If you're as hungry as I am, we can eat right now."

"Then eat we shall. I'll fill up the thermos with some nice ice cold H_2O and then we can have some pure Rocky Mountain spring water with our meal."

"Is it all right to drink this without boiling it first?"

"There is no safer water on the planet, my dear. What's for lunch?"

"Cold fried chicken, deviled eggs, potato salad, and brownies for dessert. This old bottle of Chardonnay may be good to sip on if you're up to it."

"Is there anything you didn't think of?"

"Only napkins."

Over the next hour the two of them had a delicious lunch. Poppy retrieved the bottle of wine from the pond where he put it to chill, and they each had a couple glasses as they lounged in the

The Song In His Heart

sun and took in the spectacular scenery. Sara's talk ranged from early high school days to job opportunities while Poppy told story after story about the old days and growing up with Maynard as his surrogate father.

"He must be quite a man, Maynard," said Sara.

"I reckon he's about as good as they come. After he finished raising me, he started on Lonnie. The boy really loves him. Once when he was just a pup, Maynard and I brought him up here and taught him how to swim. That was some day. I don't think any of us will ever forget it."

"You went swimming right here? Is it deep enough?"

"It's deeper than you think, maybe eighteen or twenty feet under the falls. Cold too!"

"I wouldn't mind going for a swim. Do you think we could?"

"Sure we can, but I'm telling you, it's cold!"

"Maybe just a quick dip to cool down and wash off some of the dust from the trail. Will you join me?"

"If you don't mind seeing me in my shorts."

"I won't tell if you don't," she said with that now familiar twinkle in her eye. "But you have to turn your back until I get in."

By the time Poppy got his boots unlaced and off his big feet, Sara had stripped down to her bra and panties and made a dash for the water. She quickly swam the fifty feet to the other side and pulled herself out of the water onto a large boulder that sat partly submerged along the shore. The water was bitter cold and took her breath away, but it felt good on her skin. She watched Poppy shed his clothing and walk down to the pond's edge. This time, it was he that took her breath away. His long limbed body tapered downward from a pair of shoulders so broad that Sara could scarcely take her eyes off it. The muscles beneath his skin were rippled and hard and told of an incredible strength and energy that might never be controlled. He looked like a Greek god standing there at water's edge, perhaps Neptune without the beard and trident, but instead, wearing a striped pair of purple boxer shorts.

"Just dive in," she called out. "If you do it slowly you'll never make it."

With the grace of an Olympic swimmer, he dove into the water and swam the entire distance across the pond under water to where she sat perched on her rock like the Little Mermaid of Copenhagen. Then, with no warning at all, he shot upwards out of the deep and grabbed hold of an ankle in an iron grip and pulled her back into the water. Letting out a startled yelp, Sara once again entered the freezing water. She climbed onto his back and tried with all her might to dunk his head under. Eventually she succeeded in this, but it took some doing. They splashed about like a couple of teenagers for several minutes before Sara finally broke away and swam back to shore. She carefully made her way up onto the rocky shoreline and then made a beeline to the blanket, which she immediately wrapped around herself, before sitting back down in the warm sun.

Poppy cautiously made his way out of the pond and walked up the gentle slope to where Sara sat wrapped in her blanket. He stood there for a long moment gazing down at her smiling face. She shamelessly looked back up at him. Never before had she seen such a man. His massive chest was highlighted by pectoral muscles that could have easily passed for Roman armor. It was covered with a coat of black, curly hair that extended all the way down his flat belly and beyond. Seeing this demigod standing before her was almost too much. Sara began to melt inside. Never before had she felt so awakened or aroused. She wanted him. Slowly Sara opened the blanket without breaking eye contact. Poppy could see his own desire mirrored in her eyes. He dropped down beside her and accepted the blanket and warm wet body she offered. With one arm encircling a trembling shoulder, he laid her back down onto the ground, even as their lips touched for the first time. Their kiss was long and exploring. Poppy removed her bra and panties with one hand while cupping her full breast in the other. In the following moments, as the two of them became one, she gasped as Poppy's urgency took her to a place she had never been before.

Late that afternoon, as Poppy led the way off the upper ranges of Baldy, Sara questioned him. "Why do you call this the Valley of the Monarch? Does it have a religious connotation?"

"No, nothing like that. Actually, it refers to a large bull elk we have spotted up here over the years. In fact, it could be the largest bull elk ever seen in these parts, if not the whole Rocky Mountain range. Maynard named him Old Ivory Tips because the tips of his antlers are so white from rubbing them. We figure that the valley next to the falls, and this whole mountain top for that matter, sort of belongs to him. He is a real giant, a monarch. Shortly before I broke my leg with Lonnie last fall, we spotted him. Lonnie had an opportunity to shoot, but passed because he felt something that exceptional should not be hunted, and rightfully so. Instead he shot a wounded, lesser animal that was rutting with Old Ivory Tips. I made matching necklaces from its ivory teeth for each of us to wear as a reminder of our hunt together, and for luck. Afterwards, the three of us agreed on a hunting moratorium for the old bull. We all promised to never hunt him and to protect him in any way we could. Because this whole area is so spectacular, we just sort of named it The Valley of the Monarch. It seems to fit."

"I would like to see such an animal one day."

"Perhaps one day if you're very lucky, you will, but for now, we had best be making tracks if we want to make it back before dark."

That evening while the two of them rode the final quarter mile back to Poppy's ranch, Sara made an odd suggestion. "How would you like to race me back? The loser has to cook dinner."

"You're on, young lady!"

Before Poppy could finish his acceptance of the challenge, Sara dug her heals into Sugar's flanks hard, swatting her on the rear with the long leather reins, while at the same time letting out a very guttural and unfeminine 'EAAHH.' The already high spirited horse bolted like a thoroughbred on race day. Sara squeezed hard with her legs while leaning her upper body forward toward Sugar's neck. Her body immediately went into a synchronized motion with that of the horse. She could tell earlier the animal liked to run, but had no idea it would be as fast as it now proved itself to be.

The quick start from Sara caught Poppy unprepared. Before he could react, she had almost two full lengths on him. While chuckling to himself, he gave Junie a swat with his reins and held on as she exploded into motion. Being the other horse's mother, Junie had always been the faster of the two animals. At this point, Poppy was still mildly amused. He was confident that between his own horseback riding skills and his naturally faster steed, he should be able to win the race hands down, even if Sara did have the jump on him.

The two riders rode like the wind on their mountain horses. Poppy soon became aware of the fact that Sara was a far better rider than he had given her credit for. She not only held her initial lead, but was quickly able to build upon it. As they rounded the final bend in the road, Sara let Sugar have all the reign she required. It was almost as if the younger horse was consciously trying to set a new precedent with its mother. As of this day, she would now be the faster of the two.

Once Sara and Sugar crossed over the gravel driveway marking the beginning of the ranch property and the end of the race, she pulled up hard on the reigns. It took all the might she had in both arms in order to bring the animal under control. Moments later, Poppy fought his horse to a stop as well. He gave the victor a congratulatory nod and smile, even though his manly pride was somewhat tarnished, and then proclaimed, "I can see that I have been taken advantage of. Where did you learn to ride like that? I've never seen anything like it. Sugar has never beaten Junie in a race, and I've never lost one. My dear, you never cease to amaze me."

"Maybe the extra one hundred pounds your poor horse had to carry all day had something to do with it," she called out while gasping for air.

"Well, it looks like dinner is on me," Poppy laughed. After walking the horses over to the fenced-in pasture which he and Maynard shared, the two of them unsaddled the exhausted animals and watched as they ran off together. Sugar used her head to rub up against her mother's side while running as if to say, "Well mom, I beat you that time, didn't I."

Chapter Fifteen

April and May proved to be the busiest and perhaps the most satisfying time in Lonnie's life. He worked diligently with Sara twice a week pouring over his subjects one at a time until she was satisfied that he understood the material well enough to ace his finals, or at least to score well. The rest of his time, when not in school, was balanced between doing his daily chores at home, helping Maynard put up a new worm fence, which he was paid generously for, and running mile after mile both at home, on the country roads and with the track team at school.

Lonnie's workouts were hard, but he loved the competitive nature of track. As the season progressed, Coach Trapp's aspirations for him rose steadily. After the second meet Lonnie had been taken out of the hurdles and reassigned to the 200-meter dash and the long jump. He also continued to run the 800-meter. This was no longer his preferred race, but due to the fact that Silvertown High had an abundance of upperclassmen distance runners, Lonnie had to settle for the half mile sprint, as he called it, instead of the mile run which he would have greatly preferred. The coach told him that if he still desired it next year he would let him try out for the spot. Regardless, the youngster seemed to excel at every race he attempted.

When not working on his own events, Lonnie showed a great desire to perfect those of his team mates. He spent so much time in the pole vault pit that eventually he was banned from it until after the regular vaulters were done for the day. No sooner had he heard that than he immediately gravitated toward the other field events and his old buddy Blue. Blue laughed as Lonnie struggled with the twelve pound shot put. Try as he might, the boy was barely able to reach the first measurement arc outside the throwing circle. His skills were better when it came to the discus throw, however. Lonnie's long arms, smooth approach, and twirl enabled him to hurl the four-pound orb considerably further than most other participants on the field event team, with the exception of Blue and Billie Duncan, who was the #2 man in the event. Blue and Billie worked with Lonnie perfecting his style in the hope that Coach Trapp might let him enter into the event in the coming sectional meet as the #3 man; however, Coach would not even consider it. Lonnie was too valuable a runner in his other events to waste his talents and energy as the #3 man for the team in any event.

The sectional meet was the largest and most important competition of the year next to the actual state championships. Coach Trapp had honed his entire team throughout the season to be peaking physically for these two events. He would need the best performance from every athlete in every event if Silvertown High was going to do well in the state championships which followed two weeks later.

Lonnie was excited like never before on race day. He had had a wonderful season so far. Although he had not been able to improve upon his 800-meter time which he ran earlier in the season against Sam Costa and Brian Pellitier, he did manage to come close a couple of times. The good news was that after that race, he had gone undefeated in the event up until this day. Now, once again, he would be racing against Costa and Pellitier who were both battling it out to determine which of them would be the number one 800-meter runner in the state.

Lonnie had also done well in the 200-meter sprint and long jump. His long legs and powerful frame gave him the ideal physique for excelling in both events. Even though Coach Trapp considered the 800-meter to be Lonnie's best chance at qualifying for the state meet, he still held out hope for the boy in the other two events as well. If not this year, certainly next year and the following two. What a specimen this young athlete had proved to be.

Lonnie was especially excited today because for the first time all season, Poppy would be attending the meet. This would be his first time ever that he had the opportunity to see his son perform in track. Things were going well. The weather was nice, not too sunny or humid, and the track was fast. Lonnie knew that the competition would bring out the best in him. Shortly before the race, Sam Costa once again approached him during a warm-up lap to wish him luck. "You have had a great season Lon, but today is the day to put it all together. Take it easy on me. Remember, I'm a senior and you still have three more years to go!"

Lonnie laughed good naturedly and replied, "Yea right. I'll be reading the back of your shoes for sure. Good luck though, anyways." The two friends parted and continued their warm-ups individually. Shortly thereafter, Lonnie had the occasion to speak with the Pellitier boy. Being under the false and naïve impression that all runners were as friendly and personable as Sam, he was taken by surprise when Pellitier actually snubbed him. "Hey, I'm sorry to bother you. All I wanted to do was wish you luck."

"I don't need you to wish me anything, kid. As far as I'm concerned, you're a nobody in this race. Now get lost and stop bothering me. You'll be lucky to finish in the top ten today."

Lonnie walked away visibly shaken by the encounter. He was more hurt than anything else. After all, who did the kid think he was, talking to someone like that, especially when they meant him no harm. Just as he was getting up the nerve to go back and give the ornery kid a piece of his mind, he spotted Poppy and Sara sitting together in the grandstands. They were waving frantically trying to get his attention.

Over the past few weeks, Lonnie thought he noticed a gradual change in their relationship. The sight of them sitting together in the stands made that more apparent. Many kids might be upset by their single parent taking a liking to a member of the opposite sex, but not Lonnie. He liked Sara a lot. She had come into his life during a time when he needed somebody. Her past experience as a runner and coach initially warmed him to her, but it was her sincere desire to help him out both in school and in sport, that really made him like her. She was fun to be with and made learning enjoyable. He felt that he was on the inside track when his Algebra teacher was his own private tutor and part- time coach. She was even kind of attractive, in an adult kind of way. Not like his mother of course, but then no one was that pretty.

"Good luck!" Poppy called out. "Show us what all that training has done for ya."

Lonnie gave an exaggerated laugh and then a thumbs up as the final call for the 800-meter run was announced. He reported to the starting line and this time was assigned the #3 spot in the front row. Looking to his left, he nodded to Sam who had the pole position. Next to him, with a scowl on his face, was Brian. Lonnie wondered what made these two exceptional runners so vastly different in personality. He was past being hurt or angry now. It was best to not even acknowledge the kid. "The way to get even with people like that is to beat them at their own game," Poppy had once told him.

Prior to the sounding of the gun, Lonnie reached into his singlet and put the elk tooth talisman he wore around his neck between his front teeth. Then all was silent as the hopes and dreams of fourteen young boys played itself out over the next two minutes. The crackling report of the starting pistol released a flood of energy and adrenaline that had been building in each boy for several weeks. They charged off the line in a headlong sprint in an attempt to re-establish themselves as close to the pole position as possible and as near to the lead as Sam Costa would allow. Just as informed coaches had predicted, it was Costa, Pellitier, and Burch going into the first turn. They held these positions for most of the first lap. During one brief moment on the back straight-away, the Pellitier boy took the lead as he made a bold challenge against the leader. Within seconds, Costa regained his lead and was soon followed by Lonnie who was now running a strong second. After the first lap, the leaders were on a record setting pace. Sam clocked a .56 flat. He was followed closely by Lonnie at .565 and Pellitier at .57. The three leaders had long since broken away from the rest of the pack. All they had to do now was maintain their positions, and all three would make the state meet as the top five were given the opportunity to advance.

Poppy, who had never before experienced such excitement while watching his prodigy, hollered uncontrollably from the stands. Sara, not to be outdone, was jumping up and down and yelling every bit of advice she could think of. Other spectators sitting nearby were also caught up in the frenzy. Those who weren't simply watched the exuberant parents and were amused. Unfortunately, as much as everybody cheered, the runners were oblivious to their shouts. All three competitors were in that state of mind where everything seemed to be going in slow motion. During important events when athletes give it their all, time seems to almost stand still. Background noise and commotion is blocked out of the conscious mind as every fiber and muscle of their body strains to continue on, and to compete! Movement seems to come at an agonizing pace, and every precious yard purchased comes at a physical cost that is exhausting and a mental cost that is almost unbearable. Only through conditioning can a fine athlete pass through this phase of competition and come out on top.

As the elite three rounded the final turn in the final lap with less than a second separating them and a full six seconds before the fourth runner, they each made their final push simultaneously. Costa, who had been running almost shoulder to shoulder and step for step with Lonnie for most of the final lap slowly began to pull away in the last one hundred yards. Pellitier, who was a more experienced runner and somewhat prone to less than good sportsman like tactics, put on a burst of speed that was enough to bring him abreast of Lonnie. Without looking over or acknowledging him in any way, the younger boy tried to double his efforts. He was running his heart out. In the next instant, Pellitier slowly passed him by and then quickly cut over in front of him, effectively altering his stride. Lonnie's right foot came into contact with the outstretched foot of Pellitier and it caused the younger boy to go down. When he tried to stand there was a severe pain in his foot that would not allow him to continue. Once again he fell to the track, this time not to rise again until every boy in the race had passed him by and only then with the help of Blue and Billie who had been watching and cheering him on from the sidelines.

Many spectators let out a collective gasp as others called out "foul!" Coach Trapp immediately protested the finish, claiming that the Pellitier boy deliberately cut Lonnie off, thereby causing the accident and changing the outcome of the race. Race officials gathered at the finish line in an attempt to make a ruling. Coach Trapp tried to get himself involved with the process, but was unceremoniously ejected from the group. While Lonnie was helped over to his team area, an announcement and ruling came over the loud speaker at last. The race results would stand as they were. Lonnie Burch was officially declared as a DNF-did not finish!

Frustration and rage welled up in poor Lonnie, but he remained silent. In addition to being disqualified from the race, he had a severe sprain in his ankle which was bad enough to keep him out of any further events. This effectively eliminated him from the meet and, worse yet, prevented him from qualifying to compete in the state finals in two weeks. His whole season came to a crashing halt through no fault of his own. Sam Costa and virtually every other runner in the race came over to him and expressed their sorrow, but there was one conspicuous absence--that of Brian Pelliter, who never even bothered to apologize or to say words of any kind. Later, in the distance, Lonnie caught him laughing with his team mates as if at some hilarious joke. He could see them sneaking glances over in his direction and smirking as the team nurse wrapped his foot with an ace bandage. It took all the self control he had in order to keep from going after the villainous runner. At times, Blue had to be bodily restrained by the rest of his teammates lest he, too, be disqualified from the meet. Eventually Coach Trapp seemed to put it behind him once the announcement was finally made and turned his attention towards the rest of the boys and their upcoming races. There was no doubt in anyone's mind, though, that he was one angry coach. "Best to control your anger when an injustice is dealt to you and try to find some other way to get retribution," he later explained to Lonnie. "You have a good solid track career in your future, son. As difficult as it is, try to accept this, but make sure that you learn from it and don't ever let it happen again." Lonnie vowed that he would never in a million years forget this day, and then using a pair of borrowed crutches, moved on to support his team mates.

By meet's end, several of the boys qualified to move on to the state finals. As a team, Silvertown High placed second overall in the meet. They would have placed first if Lonnie had not been disqualified. Blue was happy to capture second place in the discus and third in the shot-put. He dedicated his efforts to his best buddy and tried to give his second place medal to him but, Lonnie gratefully declined the generous offer. "After all, what would I do with a second place medal with a picture of a discus on it!" he said.

"Well, I want you to know that we all feel you were robbed, and in our eyes you took second place honors in that race."

"Thanks Blue, that means a lot to me, but damn, I wish there was something I could do to get even with that kid, short of having you snuff him out."

"Maybe one day you'll get the opportunity," replied Blue.

That afternoon Lonnie decided to skip the ride back with the team. He just didn't feel in much of a celebrating mood, and he knew that there would be a festive atmosphere on the bus ride home. Instead, he rode back with Poppy and Sara, who had driven down together in Poppy's truck.

"I'm sorry I let you down, Poppy," Lonnie stated with downcast eyes as his father slowly drove his pick-up out of the parking lot. "I should have been prepared for that guy's dirty tricks."

Sara, sitting in between the two of them, immediately responded even though the remark was not directed towards her. "Lonnie, there is no reason for you to apologize. You ran better than anybody could have expected or even hoped for. Sometime things don't turn out the way we would like them to, even though we do everything within our power to try and make it happen the way we would like."

"Sara's right, son. Today you showed yourself to be more of a man than anyone out there. After the foul, and that's exactly what it was, you kept your cool and didn't let your anger take over. I don't know how many other boys would have been so controlled. Sara and I knew you were devastated and nobody knows more than us how hard you worked and prepared for that race. Don't let the ordeal put out your fire though. Remember it and use it as fuel next time you race. We're all very proud of you--Coach Trapp, Sara, your teammates, and especially me. There will be plenty more opportunities to race in your lifetime, but one doesn't very often get the chance to show his character and what they are made of the way you did today. You had a great season son, and now I think it's time for you to slow down a little and enjoy your summer vacation."

"I do have some good news for you, Lonnie," said Sara softly. "You aced your final exam in Algebra which gives you a 'B' for the semester. Good job!"

Lonnie looked up with a gleam in his eye and for the first time ever put his arm around Sara's shoulder giving her a squeeze. "Aw, that's good news. Thanks, Sara. I couldn't have done it without you. You're really great, and thanks for coming to the meet, too."

Sara blushed noticeably. "I wouldn't have missed it for the world," she replied.

Poppy looked over and recognized a bond between the two and smiled to himself. "Hey, anyone up for burgers and a shake?"

Chapter Sixteen

That summer and the following two were perhaps the most memorable times in young Lonnie's life. He enthusiastically worked cattle with Maynard and some of the other neighbor ranchers. Each day he kept himself occupied running cows to fresh pasture, branding them, castrating the yearling bulls, riding the fence lines, and repairing them when needed. He was a busy young man rapidly approaching manhood.

At age seventeen Lonnie had grown to almost 6'1". The hard work he did daily as a ranch hand helped to fill out his chest and shoulders. He was almost the spitting image of Poppy in stature and coloring but, rather than having the strong jaw and heavy brow of his father, he carried the more delicate features of his mother, Anjuli, with high cheekbones and a smaller nose and chin.

When the weekends came and Poppy was able to get off work, they managed to ride up into the high country for long days together spent fishing, tracking wild game, or swimming in their favorite pond. Once in awhile, it was fun just riding to the top and then taking a nap in the sun on a lazy day. Sometimes they would go alone; other times they would bring Sara along. Lonnie found where he used to be a bit selfish with the time he spent with his father, especially when they went to their special places in the rugged upper ranges, now he actually enjoyed it when Sara came along. She spent a good deal of her time with the two of them. Sara was an accomplished horseback rider who loved to gallop along the mountain trails at what most people would call 'break-neck' speed. In addition to this, her physical conditioning and stamina did not hinder the men when they wanted to climb and explore new places. Sara was a lot of fun to be with, and her femininity was a welcome change from the company of Poppy and Maynard all the time.

Although his days were long and exhausting, Lonnie always found time for his track workouts. As he approached his senior year in high school, there were very few records at Silvertown High that he did not hold. The versatile nature of Lonnie's physical prowess enabled him to excel at any event, or for that matter, any sport he chose. His old basketball coach practically begged him to come back out for the team, but Lonnie's heart was still with the track team. During his junior year he managed to take first in the state in the mile run, posting an amazing time of 4:12. Coach Trapp had finally capitulated in the boy's desire to run the mile race. Lonnie also took second in state in the long jump and second in the 200-meter dash. All things considered, he had set himself up well for his senior year. Numerous colleges and state universities around the country had already expressed interest in having him apply. Lonnie had mixed feelings about this, however. On the one hand, he certainly enjoyed all the attention and prestige he was getting as a result of the collegiate overtures, but on the other hand, he truly loved living at home in the mountains. His grades had ceased to be an issue over the past couple years. In fact, some semesters he even made the Dean's list. It was just the thought of spending another four years in school away from home, and for what? To learn how to be a rancher? He already knew how to do that. College still looked to be a waste of time in his eyes. When the subject would come up with Poppy, Lonnie still only listened with half an ear. He knew, however, that the time was rapidly approaching when a decision must be made. He loved Poppy more than anyone alive and didn't want to go against his wishes or hurt him in any way, but certainly his own wishes and aspirations had to be considered. After all, it was his life. As time went by and he got older, these feelings only became stronger.

One Saturday morning, late in July, Poppy asked Lonnie if he wanted to take a ride up to the Valley of the Monarch and go for a swim. This was a no-brainer for Lonnie for he always wanted to take a ride up the mountain and go for a swim, especially in the pond at the Valley of the Monarch. This was his favorite place in the whole world. Who knows, maybe they might even see Old Ivory Tips again. Only once had the two of them seen the giant elk since their great adventure three years before, and that was but for a moment. From time to time, they would still hear what they thought must be his bugle. It always made them stop for a moment and gaze up into the dark forest to wonder at the majesty of the creature that lived within.

The ride up the mountain was relatively uneventful. It was a beautiful, hot summer day with not a cloud in the sky. A lone raven made its caw as it drifted over head on an updraft just above Baldy. When they reached the pond below the waterfall where Lonnie had learned to swim years before, they untied a blanket from the back of Junie's saddle and spread it out on the ground before undressing to their shorts and braving the frigid water. It was as fresh and invigorating as ever. Lonnie swallowed several gulps of water as he swam beneath the surface. The old pond brought back many memories to him, all of them good. One of his earliest recollections of being with his parents in the mountains was at this pond, sitting along the shore. It was here that his mother taught him how to skip rocks off the surface of the water.

After several minutes of solitary swimming, they each gravitated back to the blanket which lay on a grassy area in full sun. For some time neither spoke until finally Lonnie broke the silence and asked, "What's on your mind, Poppy?"

The boy's father sat for awhile longer staring at the water as it made its way down the rocks before going air-borne and splashing into the pond. Turning his attention to his son, he couldn't help but notice how much the boy had grown. Indeed, he had become a man. Why, in a few short months he would turn eighteen years old. Poppy thought back to when he himself was eighteen and how uncomplicated his life was back then. That was many years ago, and how fast time had gone by. So much had happened since then. His beautiful wife had come into his life and then left him, changing him forever, but leaving him with a son, with their son! As he looked at his boy's face, he could see Anjuli staring back at him. Over the years, her facial features had become more pronounced in the lad. Many of his more subtle mannerisms were hers as well. At times, Poppy felt waves of emotion swelling over him when he became cognizant of this. For the moment though, he tried to put it out of his mind.

"Lon, son, the reason I asked you up here today is because I need your advice. Well, the fact of the matter is, I have made a decision. Because it's such an important decision and one that will affect us both for the rest of our lives, I wanted you to be in on it."

"Does this decision have to do with Sara?"

"Yes, it does. I love her, and I would like to marry her if she will have me." Lonnie stared at his father without blinking or reacting in any way. "When we first started seeing each other, my intentions were to bring a female influence into your life. You were young and needed a mother, someone to give you the kind of affection I couldn't. When I saw the way the two of you hit it off so well, it made me realize that perhaps she was the right woman. Unfortunately, it took me so much time, three years, to realize that I really do love her. For so many years after your mother died, I couldn't look at another woman. No person on earth could take her place. I was being selfish though, thinking only of myself not you, and what you really needed. Now, when I'm finally ready to make this move, you are a man already, and I don't know how much this will benefit you anymore. But, son, once again I'm being selfish because it will benefit me. I need her. She has helped me to stop living in the past and to look to the future. I'll be honest. It is still very difficult for me to be with another woman. I feel that somehow I'm betraying your mother's trust. There is not a day that goes by that I don't think about her. How do you feel about this?"

"Dad, I believe that you should do what you think is right. Don't make a decision like this because of me. Do it for yourself. All my life you have been there for me. For the past nine years you have been both my mother and father, and I know it has been hard. Probably harder on you than me. For what it's worth, I like Sara a lot. In fact, she's great and she would make a swell step-mom. But no, she can't ever replace mom. We all know that. Do you want to know how I think about mom? She is like music to me, so beautiful and so special. I know it's there, but I just can't touch it or see it, only feel it inside. It never goes away and it never changes. It only gets better with time. When I was younger, she used to sing me a song. It made me not afraid any more. This is how I remember her- - with a song in my heart. It helps to keep me going when things get real tough. Maybe that's why I run so fast. Yea, I think Sara would make a great addition to our family, and you know what? Mom would approve too!"

Poppy could only stare at the young man sitting next to him and marvel at his attained wisdom. It was all he could do to hold back the tears that were building inside him. Rather than risk speaking and losing it completely, he reached out and hugged his son and squeaked out a feeble "Thank you son."

"How does Sara feel about all this? Have you two discussed marriage?"

"Well, not exactly," Poppy replied. "But, sometimes a man can tell when a woman wants to be with him. We have spent a lot of time together over the past three years and have become pretty close. She knows that I think the world of her and she also understands when I need my alone time. Sara is also approaching the point in her life where she is thinking about settling down and establishing roots. Maybe even starting a family."

"Whoa, Poppy! Are you saying that you would consider having more kids?"

"If that is what she wants. Kids are a lot of fun, and they add something special to a marriage that is hard to describe. Wouldn't you like to have a little brother or sister? Someone you could teach how to hunt and fish and ride a horse?"

Lonnie looked off into space for a moment with a faraway look in his eyes before he spoke. "Sure, Poppy, that would be great. I just never ever considered having any brothers or sisters. It will take a bit of getting used to, I guess. When do you plan on popping the question?"

"Tonight, if all goes as planned. I asked her to have dinner with me in town at the Hole in the Wall restaurant. She wanted to make dinner for me at her place, but I told her it was a special occasion and it would be better if we went out. I don't think she suspects anything though."

"Jeepers Pop, you are full of surprises today. I wonder what we'll be talking about tomorrow - probably making wedding plans. I don't suppose that I'll ever hear the end of that one at school. My old man marrying my Algebra teacher. Whoa, that may take some getting used to! I may have to crack a few heads in the hallway. You know she flunked Old Blue in math, don't you? He had to spend almost his entire summer vacation making it up."

"Lon, I have a lot of thing to consider in making a proposal like this, but the fact that Tony Bleuson flunked Algebra is certainly not one of them." Father and son both laughed good naturedly as they each started to get dressed and prepare for the ride back down the mountains.

Later that evening, Poppy and Sara were sitting at a very romantic spot towards the back of the Hole in The Wall, the only Italian restaurant in Silver Town. The place was packed, and there was a line of people already waiting at the door to get in. The charming little eatery was now owned by an old high school buddy of Poppy's, Mauricio Feo. He was known as Dino to his friends. Dino had taken over the restaurant from his father, Paulo, when he could no longer manage the business. Over the years, it had grown from a small trattoria in an old mining town into a four star restaurant, largely due to the exceptional food they prepared, but also the diligent efforts on Dino's part to advertise and market the establishment in nearby towns.

When making his reservations for the evening, Poppy had informed Dino that he intended to propose over dinner. As a gesture of friendship, Dino had given him the best table in the house and a bottle of complimentary Merlot to start off the meal. He also directed his accordion player, who played each Friday and Saturday night at the restaurant, to hang around Poppy's table playing romantic music and serenading Sara.

They were already into their third course and second bottle of wine by the time Poppy finally got the nerve to ask Sara for her hand in marriage. There was a nervousness about him that made him feel awkward. How happy he would be if she accepted his proposal, but how devastated his life would become if she declined. As he spoke the words while looking deep into her blue eyes he could feel a part of his life, almost forgotten, blossoming once again. "Sara," he spoke, "You have reawakened a feeling inside of me that I feared was dead. When you came into my life, I never dreamed that it would make such a difference. I can't go for more than a few minutes without wondering about you--wondering where you are, what you're doing. I don't want to spend another day in this life without you being there by my side. If you consent to marry me, I promise that I will love you and will be loyal to you and will take care of you for the rest of our lives." As he finished speaking, there was a look of sincerity and anxious anticipation in his eyes that would have broken up Sara even if he hadn't spoken the preceding words.

When he had turned down her offer for dinner and suggested the restaurant because it was a special occasion, Sara had a funny feeling. What could be the special occasion? Did she dare to contemplate that he might propose? Oh, if only that were so. Poppy had come along at just the right time in her life. Since getting to know him, her love had grown steadily for the man. Now, as she listened to her heart's desire, it was more than she could take and still keep a dry eye. The tears streamed down her cheeks as she slowly nodded her head up and down and replied, "Oh Tyler. I love you so much! Yes! Yes! Yes!"

Poppy beamed. He took a big breath, his eyes lightened up, and he got a big grin on his face with his big jaw; and before he knew it, he had risen and crossed the table, lifted Sara off her chair, and embraced her madly. The patrons in the restaurant collectively stared in wonderment at the proceedings before Dino came out and lavishly announced to everybody that, "It looks like Miss Sara has just accepted a proposal of marriage!" Everyone applauded enthusiastically as the accordion player immediately went into a rendition of 'Here Comes The Bride.' After that, it was difficult to concentrate anymore on their intimate dinner together. People, mostly strangers, came over to congratulate them throughout the rest of the evening. As the night wore on, the happy couple finally tried to make their escape but not before Dino picked up their entire dinner and hugged each of them in that old Italian way.

Afterwards, while they rode over to Sara's place in the pick-up, they were like two kids again, laughing and talking about things that only hours ago might have been a bit awkward. When Poppy asked her where she would like to get married and have the reception, Sara hesitated for a moment before answering, "I would like to be married in the Valley of the Monarch. Could we do that? We could invite just a few very close people, and then later in the day return to your place for a larger reception."

Poppy simply replied, "I like it."

Chapter Seventeen

The Wedding

Two weeks later Poppy, Sara, Lonnie, and even Maynard all found themselves with a million things to do. All Sara wanted was to get married on a mountaintop, near a waterfall, with a beautiful vista. This should be a simple task in itself, but when one contemplates the logistics of at least a dozen people, including the minister, one romantic accordion player, a restaurant owner, horses, saddles, food and refreshments, the planning gets hectic. Of course after the ceremony, which was to be held at 10:30 am, there would be a reception at Poppy's home. This meant that everyone would have to start caravanning up the mountain no later than 5:00 am--in the dark! It also meant that within an hour after completion of the vows, everyone would have to start back down the mountain in order to attend the reception at six. There were people to call, family members to contact on Sara's side, and good friends to invite. All totaled, they figured on close to fifty people at the reception.

When the day finally arrived, Sara showed up at the Burch ranch at 5:30 am exactly, accompanied by her parents and brother. Her parents were easy going folks who took an immediate liking to Poppy and his boy Lonnie when they first met the previous year. They were retired now and lived in Arvada, Colorado. Sara looked stunning. She wore a white satin blouse with a V-shaped yoke trimmed in rhinestones. It fit her perfect body like a glove. She chose tan suede leather pants, again with colored rhinestones trimming the front and back pockets enhanced by a matching rhinestone studded belt. Her pointed toe boots were made of soft calfskin leather, which were also tan to match her snug fitting pants. Complimenting her wedding attire was a western hat, tan with white satin ribbons that graced the air in the gentle morning breeze. Poppy had given Sara the loveliest pair of earrings she had ever seen as a wedding present. They were simple drop pearl earrings that enhanced her natural beauty. She was the most beautiful bride anyone had ever seen, but it wasn't her very shapely figure and stunning outfit that made people look twice. It was the twinkle in her eye. There was a gaiety about her as she almost danced over to each guest, hugging them in turn. This was the happiest day of her life. The crisp clear morning promised another spectacular Colorado fall day. It was September 28th, her birthday, soon to be her anniversary. This day would be the beginning of a new life together with the man of her dreams.

Poppy was busy at work with Maynard adjusting everyone's saddles and stirrups. He barely had a moment in the darkness to look up and notice his future bride. When he did he felt a warm sensation throughout his body. She was so right for him. For many weeks he had agonized over whether this moment would ever come to pass. Now that it was here, he could hardly believe his good fortune. As he finished up with Dino's saddle, he excused himself so that he could welcome Sara and her family.

"Welcome, Tom. Good morning, Dottie," he said to Sara's parents. "Did you ever expect your only daughter to be getting married on top of a mountain?"

"We hear that it is a very special and beautiful place," replied Dottie. "Do you have enough horses for all of us?"

"My good friend Maynard was kind enough to offer us the use of a few of his. He's the fellow over there working with the pack horses wearing the tails and top hat."

"We were not aware this was going to be a formal event," interjected Tom, "Otherwise, I would have worn my suit."

"Oh, don't worry about that Tom. You're dressed just fine. Maynard is wearing his father's old suit; says he only wears it for weddings and funerals. Let's hope this is the last time he gets to wear it." They shared a laugh together as Lonnie walked up to Sara and her mother.

"Good morning, Sara. You look just great today. Are you nervous?"

"More than I would like to admit, Lon. You remember my mother, don't you?"

"Sure. Hello, Mrs. Evans. Welcome to our home. When we get back later today you won't recognize the place. I've spruced it up a bit."

"Why Lonnie, how much you have grown! You must be over six feet tall."

"Well, actually 6'1"

"Mom," said Sara. "He's almost as tall as his father. Lonnie, I want you to meet my brother, Tommy. If it weren't for him, I might never have become a school teacher."

"How so?" Lonnie questioned.

"Well, when you were probably a very little boy, I was tutoring my younger brother here so much that after a time my mom started to pay me by the hour."

"What did she tutor you in, Tommy?" asked Lonnie.

"Algebra."

"Now how did I know that," the boy smirked.

Even though Maynard was not the man of the hour, there was certainly no doubt in anyone's mind that he was definitely the man in charge. Privately, he had mixed feelings about bringing all these folks up the mountain to the Valley of the Monarch. On the one hand, Poppy and Lonnie were the closest to family he had ever known. They had spent years going up to this hidden place of theirs. In fact, when Poppy was a small boy of six years old Maynard had brought him up the mountain for his first time to this very spot. Maynard felt as if he had discovered the small waterfall and lake and to a certain extent felt as if he were the caretaker. The two Burch boys were the only people he had ever shown this place to. Now, on the other hand, here he was leading a party of over a dozen tenderfeet up to one of his most private places. Poppy had to do a bit of persuading to get Maynard's approval for the event, but in the end, the old mountain man was delighted to be a part of it all. He had warmed up to Sara as if she were his own long lost daughter, and if this spot was so very special to her and she wanted to get married there, then by golly, this would be the spot. The fact that he wore his father's old tails and top hat were a sure sign to Poppy they had his approval once and for all.

When the wedding party finally set out, Maynard rode in the lead followed closely by Lonnie and his old buddy Blue, who was also making the trip for the first time. Poppy rode at the back of the group with Sara so that he could keep an eye on everyone. Sara's parents surprised her when they insisted on making the trip up the mountain on horseback. "Why, your father and I were riding horses together in these mountains long before you were born," Dottie had told her daughter. "There is no way on earth we are going to miss our only daughter's marriage ceremony, no matter where it is." When Poppy heard of this, he developed a new respect for Sara's folks and felt a bit lonely that he couldn't have had his own parents along. Try though as he would, there was not one lasting image in his memory of his parents, who died so tragically many years before. Well, perhaps they were looking down on him on this special day. Everything was turning out just fine in his estimation, although it was still quite cool and Sara had to finally capitulate and wear one of Lonnie's heavier jackets in order to keep warm on the ride up. The clear sky and still winds, nevertheless, were a sign of a beautiful day to follow.

Enthusiastic chatter filled the morning air as they meandered their way up the ever climbing slope. The few wedding guests invited to attend the ceremony were excited to be included in this special event. They passed the time away talking about many different subjects, not least of which was how fortunate the two, soon to be newlyweds, found one another, and the role that Lonnie had played in bringing them together. The Catholic priest, Father O'Brien, who had been asked by Sara to perform the ceremony, had accepted the request with the words, "The House of the Lord is not merely mortar and stone. I would be delighted to ride with you and Tyler to your special mountain top to conduct the wedding vows, for surely our God resides in the chapel of nature as well as in the chapel on Main Street."

Father O'Brien was an amusing little man who brought a bit of the old Irish to the city of Silvertown. He was a powerfully built individual with unusually large biceps and broad shoulders, but it was the combination of his thick black mustache and completely bald head that really made him stand out in a crowd. He had a very deep baritone voice and rarely was inclined to use a microphone while giving his sermons. Many of his parishioners were hard-working blue collar people that were known to visit the local pubs from time to time. It was here that he concentrated on gathering his flock, for although it was no great secret that Father O'Brien liked to take a nip of brandy on occasion and wash it down with a pint of Guinness Stout or two, he did realize how the evils of alcohol, if left unchecked, could ruin a man. Father OB, as he was called, was well respected and liked by everyone. Although he had only known Sara for the few years since she moved to Silvertown, he had known Poppy since he was a small boy and came to regular Sunday services with his Auntie Rose. It was his hope now that perhaps he might be able to persuade Poppy to come back once again to the church which he seemed to abandon after the death of his wife.

Soon after the sun rose the temperature began to rise a bit and before long it had taken the chill out of the air. Just about everyone thoroughly enjoyed the horseback ride up the mountain, everyone that is except for Dino, Poppy's old high school friend and now restaurant owner. Dino had never ridden a horse before. He was more of a city kid growing up. When he got his first job, it was waiting tables in his father's restaurant. On this day however, his fear of riding horses was overshadowed by his desire to attend the wedding ceremony. While his ride started out well enough, it wasn't too long before his horse, Old Pokey, figured out that his rider didn't know the first thing about riding. Not much later, Pokey was in complete control of the timid rider, stopping at every clump of grass along the trail to feast on the sweet greens. Many times the old horse simply refused to walk at all, and when it did, it moved so slowly that an ever- larger space was being created between him and the next horse farther up the trail.

"Just go ahead and give Old Pokey a kick in the ribs and let her know who's boss," Poppy called out to his oldest chum, "Otherwise, he'll walk all over you,"

"That's what I'm afraid of," replied Dino. "I think maybe this horse is a bit too frisky for me. He keeps trying to bite me when I say giddy-up."

Poppy and Sara both let out a good laugh at that one. "Dino, Old Pokey is the calmest, slowest, most timid horse on this side of the Great Divide. If he were any less frisky, we'd have to carry him up the mountain."

"What if I just get off the horse and lead it by the reins. That would be all right, wouldn't it?"

By this time half the troop was laughing so hard at the poor, unfortunate man that finally Dottie had pity on him, came back, took his reins, and led the stubborn old horse while Dino held on to the saddle horn. After a little while he said, "This isn't so tough."

"Would you like the reins back," Dottie inquired

"No, not just yet. Maybe in a little while though."

Once Maynard led the group up over Baldy, there were a lot of "oohs" and "ahhs" as everyone took in the spectacular scenery, both in front of them and to the rear. The upper peaks were all snowcapped, but there were only small patches of snow here and there in shaded areas about them. At this time of the year, in late September, the weather could be very unpredictable. The day prior to their leaving Maynard and Poppy got together and made a determination on possible bad weather affecting their plans. According to the reports and maps on TV, there didn't seem to be any significant moisture in the area that might bother them, so they went ahead as planned. As they rode the final distance to the hidden waterfall, Poppy knew by the blue, cloudless sky and the smell in the air they had made the right decision.

"I do believe this is the most beautiful place that I have ever seen, Sara," stated her father, Tom. "What a wonderful place to be married!"

Maynard and Poppy immediately went about setting up the preparations. Sara took it upon herself to show Father O'Brien where she wanted the altar to be. She chose the grassy area off to the side of the small pond where she and Poppy had first made love three years before. They would face the priest with the waterfall in the background so when the vows were complete and they turned to face the guests, the breathtaking view of the valley below would be visible.

Exactly at 10:35 in the morning, the ceremony began. Tom Evans walked his daughter up to the makeshift altar beaming with pride and kissed her before returning to his seat, which was an old log round that Maynard had come up and cut the week before with his chain saw. Lonnie stood by his father's side as the best man. He winked at Sara as they caught eyes. Father O'Brien thanked everyone for making the long and sometimes dangerous trip up the mountain to this very beautiful spot that was so special to Sara and Tyler. He explained how people can find God in many places, and evidence of his existence was all around them. One simply had to take the time to notice. At intervals throughout the service, Bernard, the accordion player, mesmerized the attendees with his music. The soft melodious notes of Ave Maria echoed off the stone cliffs behind them and created a sensation of feeling in all present that must have been very close to heaven itself. During all this, Poppy leaned forward and kissed his future bride on the forehead.

When it came time to exchange the vows, Poppy and Sara stood facing each other with Father O'Brien presiding over them. "Sara Jane Evans, do you take this man standing before you to be your lawfully wedded husband, to have and to hold, through good times and through bad, through sickness and in health, until death do you part?"

As Father O'Brien spoke the words, Sara stared intently into Poppy's striking blue eyes. She could see a warmth and kindness in them that made her feel like she was the luckiest girl in the whole world. All her life she had been searching for a man such as this, a good man, one with whom she could grow old and never regret a single day. There were times before meeting Poppy when she honestly felt that perhaps her ideal soul mate didn't exist. When she reflected back to the first time they met and recalled the strange sensation in the pit of her stomach, she realized then how hopelessly in love she had become.

"I do." She said ever so softly.

"Tyler James Burch, Poppy, do you take this woman standing before you to be your lawfully wedded wife, to have and to hold, through good times and through bad, through sickness and in health, until death do you part?"

Poppy too was lost in a stare. He looked into Sara's eyes and looked at her cheeks, nose, chin, lips, hair, and everything else about her. Yes, she was beautiful! Not beautiful in the same way that Anjuli was, for they had very distinct differences, but beautiful nevertheless. As he listened to the words of Father O'Brien, his thoughts went back to the day when this very same priest married him and his first love. When the words "until death do you part," were spoken, Poppy winced ever so slightly. "Please Lord," he thought to himself, "Do not take this woman from me, for as long as I live, I will cherish her. If I should ever lose her, it would surely destroy me. If you must ever take one of us, make it be me first and I swear to you now, I will become a better person, a better Christian."

"Yes, I do," he spoke with love in his heart.

"May I have the rings please."

Lonnie reached into his pocket and took out both rings. At the last moment, Sara's maid of honor had to cancel her plans of attending the service due to an adult case of the chicken pox. While the priest blessed the rings, Lonnie also had a moment to reflect on events. Sara was a wonderful person whom he liked more as a friend than anything else. She had helped him at a very difficult time in his life get his act together and for this he would always be grateful. Although he didn't look upon Sara as a mother figure, and didn't love her in that way, he most definitely had strong feelings for her. Why then, was he feeling so strange today, so mixed up about all this? Ever since the day when Poppy had informed him of his desire to wed Sara, Lonnie had felt confused. He recalled stating to his father that he believed even his mother would approve of Sara, but if she was able to look down, would she really? Deep inside Lonnie was frightened that his real mother might somehow feel as if she were being replaced, slowly being forgotten. When he tried, he could still remember the sound of her voice singing to him. Lonnie did not realize it, but he was feeling guilty for liking this new woman his father was marrying and not knowing for sure whether his mom would really approve.

Sara was somewhat controlled when she put the ring on Poppy's finger and repeated the vows, but what little control that remained afterwards soon evaporated when Poppy held her hand and repeated his vows. By the time he finished and Father O'Brien pronounced them husband and wife, tears were streaming down her cheeks like gentle raindrops on rose petals. After Poppy kissed her gently on the lips she clung to him in a hug that made all present realize the depth of her feelings for the man. Bernard finished the ceremony with "On Eagles Wings."

It wasn't until the last note of the song was played before Poppy and Sara turned and started to walk away from the altar when suddenly Lonnie spotted something less than 200 yards away, down the valley. There stood the most magnificent bull elk that anyone had ever seen. Lonnie quickly grabbed Poppy by the elbow and motioned with his other hand in the direction of Old Ivory Tips. As he did this, and the guests noticed the look of excitement in his eyes, they all turned in time to see this magnificent animal bellow out the most incredible sound any of them had ever heard.

"The bull elk bugles!" called out Maynard. "Old Ivory Tips has blessed your wedding ceremony himself. I never would have believed it if I hadn't seen it with my own eyes." Shortly thereafter, a group of cow elk were slowly herded across the Valley of the Monarch by the reigning king of the mountain. Lonnie had the biggest grin on his face he ever had as he thought to himself, "Thanks, mom, thanks for your blessing."

Chapter Eighteen

Lonnie was already aware of the fact that he had been offered a full ride scholarship in track and field at Montana State University in Bozeman even before he won the final three races of his high school career in the state championships. For so many high school athletes it is difficult to keep interest level and motivation intact as the years go by, especially when there are so many outside influences such as girls, parties, and the inevitable freedoms that a car can provide. Lonnie, however, never seemed to let his fire die out. His love for track and field and his competitive spirit was fueled to greater levels by his incredible performances, one after another. Some boys with exceptional talents are content to merely win their events with no greater desire to excel beyond that point. But Lonnie seemed to be looking for something beyond winning. For every race, every event he participated in, the boy seemed to reach inside himself to such an amazing extent that he surprised even the people who knew him the best. He attacked his sport with all his heart and soul as if he were trying to discover some new place where no one had ever been before. Only by repeatedly pushing himself past his maximum could he find release from the pressures he heaped upon himself. Early in his senior year while being interviewed by a local paper, he was asked the question, "How do you stay so focused when you run, and what makes you push so hard?" Lonnie merely replied, "When I run competitively, there is this feeling that builds up inside of me like a great dam that is about to burst from the pressure of holding back all the water, but it doesn't. With each race the dam seems to get larger and larger. When it breaks I will stop running."

As Lonnie prepared to enter the next phase of his life, he had two goals that were paramount in his mind. Scholastically, he intended to finish college, majoring in any curriculum that appealed to him after his first year of compulsories. This goal had little to do with his own desires, but rather to appease the always constant urging of his father, who wanted no more for his son than to graduate from college. Lonnie felt he owed him at least that much, even though he still had it in his adolescent mind to become a rancher and run cattle with Maynard. This part of his dream would have to wait. His second goal was to run in the Olympics. This thought had been building in his mind for almost two years. Secretly, the main reason he decided to go on to college was so he would have a better chance at qualifying for the team. Late in his sophomore year, when he and Blue were dominating every event they entered, Blue made the mistake of mentioning to Coach Trapp he had pretty much accomplished all his goals in track, and after all, what else was there for a high school athlete. Lonnie, not adding much to this, merely nodded in agreement. There were times in his young life when he too questioned all the rigorous training he put himself through- and for what, to beat everybody by an extra 100 yards?

Well, Coach Trapp set the minds of his two all time finest athletes straight in a heartbeat. "Boys, what you two have accomplished here so far has nothing to do with high school sports. It has to do with who you are and what you want to become. If you allow yourselves to stop here, then you will never know what could have been. I'm talking about the Olympics boys, the greatest sports competition of all time. Each of you has the ability and the God-given talent to make the team. Are you telling me you want to give up that possibility? Allow me to train you. Give me your hearts for two more years and we won't just win track meets, but together we'll set you two boys on a course where you will compete against the finest in the world---and win! Now that is something that you will carry forever. Blue, you have not accomplished all your goals in track yet; you just need to set your goals higher and raise your standards." This was perhaps the best advice that Herbie Trapp had ever given a boy.

Each boy was noticeably moved by Coach Trapp's speech. More than anything, they were impressed by his sincere belief that they could actually make it to the Olympics. This opened a whole new world to each of them. For the following two years, Lonnie and Blue did everything that their coach asked of them and more. Neither took any place less than second over the two remaining years of high school in any event—unprecedented in Colorado history. When the talent scouts came to watch them perform and would later make their offers, the boys made it clear with whomever they spoke that they intended on being a package deal. After their conversation with Coach Trapp, they had made a vow to stick together through college and all the way to the Olympics. They vowed to push each other to accomplish this new goal they had set together.

In mid-August following graduation, Tony Bleuson and his little sister Mary, along with his parents, joined with Sara, Poppy, and Lonnie for the ten hour drive to Bozeman, Montana, for early registration. They drove in Knute Bleuson's conversion van. The ride was a lot of fun. Over the years, the two families had become friends while attending the various meets together. The parents were happy their boys were sticking together and were encouraged by how much each pushed and supported the other. Poppy and Sara were especially encouraged by Blue's scholastic influence on Lonnie. He was a straight 'A' honors student, while Lonnie still had to struggle to make his 'B' average. College was going to be different though. No more would he have to study Algebra, Biology and Physics. Now he could take courses that actually interested him. Maybe he could study to be a forest ranger.

The boys had pre-arranged to be roommates. Their dorm room coincidently looked out over the mountains. This gave Lonnie a warm feeling for he had never been away from home before, and now that he was, at least he could be reminded that he was still in the mountains. After unloading personal effects and getting established in their room, they made a tour of the campus together. The various coaches made themselves available for all the early scholarship recipients. When Coach Taggert met the boys, his weathered face lit up. "Well, if it isn't the titanic twosome from Silvertown, Colorado. It's good to see you both again. We're looking forward to having a successful year, and I can't tell you and your folks how happy I am to have you with us. I owe old Herbie Trapp, who, as you know is an old friend of mine, a debt of gratitude. When he told me to get my behind down to Colorado last year to check you boys out, I took him for his word and made the trip myself rather than sending a scout. I must say that it was time well spent."

Poppy took the occasion to say, "It's good to see you again Coach Taggert. I hope you will take good care of our boys. They mean a lot to us. I've never been to college myself, so I realize how great of an opportunity this is for them. Give them good council and remind them from time to time why they are here. They're already fine athletes and I know that's your major area of concern, but we as parents want our boys to succeed when they get out of college too, not just on the playing field." Knute Bleuson nodded in agreement as the boys fidgeted in embarrassment.

"Mr. Burch, Mr. Bleuson, you have my personal guarantee I will do everything within my power to continue making fine young men of your sons and that my door will always be open to them not only as a coach, but also as a friend and counselor." He then turned his attention to his newest recruits and said, "Believe me when I say my door is always open to you at any time for any reason. We work our athletes hard around here, but we also realize that sport is not your major reason for being in college. Yes, I want you to excel and bring pride unto yourselves and to your school, but my real goal is to see each of you turn into the finest, most well-rounded men possible. I also teach Algebra. Perhaps I might even have one of you in my class." Lonnie rolled his eyes and said under his breath, "Oh God, I hope not," at which point Sara elbowed him in the ribs to keep it to himself.

"Why I teach Algebra myself Coach Taggert, and if you should ever find Lonnie in your class I am sure that you will find him a most willing student." She smiled at Lonnie and all the parents and kids shared a personal laugh while Coach Taggert looked on in bewilderment.

Later that day, when it came time to say goodbye, Poppy walked his son off to a side and said to him, "Lonnie, I'm so proud of you. I wish that your mother was here today to see this. She would be so happy. It was always our goal to see this for you, COLLEGE! Lon, this is so good! Do us proud. You have a lot on your agenda now and Sara and I won't always be there to help you. Do your sport as I know you will, and I hope you are successful in reaching your goals; but please son, concentrate on your schoolwork as well. What you learn here will help you for the rest of your life. Good luck! Stay in touch, and remember, I love you. Do you still have your elk tooth?" Immediately Lonnie reached up to his neck and pulled out the original leather string, which had the ivory tooth from his first elk kill attached. Poppy pulled out the identical mate to his son's necklace and they smiled at each other. "We will always be together Son, even though at times we are apart. Why don't you say good-bye to Sara now."

Lonnie walked over to Sara and stood for a moment awkwardly in front of her before she finally reached out and hugged him vigorously. She whispered into his ear, "Remember what I told you, Lon. You're the best, and you can do anything you set your mind to. Work hard and don't forget to call, or at least write and let us know how you're doing."

As they broke from their embrace, Lonnie said, "Sara, I'm glad you came into our life when you did. Dad and I were floundering and needed you to set us straight again. Take care of him for me. He really loves you. Don't worry about me, I'll be fine, and of course I'll be in constant touch." Sara had tears streaming down her cheeks when she finally let him go. Poppy walked over and gave his son a firm handshake before saying farewell one last time.

Blue was a bit less emotional with his parents in his goodbyes. Although they each hugged him in turn and tried to kiss his cheek, he shyly turned away thinking it was less manly to show emotion. It was only when his little ten year old sister Mary hugged him and started to cry that the giant of a man Blue broke down and cried. "Aw, stop that blubbering now, Mary," he said with a frog in his throat. "You know that I'll be home again soon enough, and when I am, you'll be all grown up and pretty. Why, I'll be seeing you again at Christmas time, and you know what?"

"What?" she sniffled.

"I'm going to bring you a great, big present, something really special. You just wait and see."

As the parents drove away, both boys immediately went back into their macho mode and Lonnie said, "Geez, I thought that would never end."

"You can say that again. All this mushy stuff is for the birds. What do you say we walk around and check this place out and try to meet some of these pretty ladies? Why, there's no telling how much these beauties are starved for a real Colorado man." With that, they each strutted away in their own particular manner and unknowingly embarked upon the next phase in their young lives.

Chapter Nineteen

The following three years were a period of growth for Lonnie. He matured considerably both physically and emotionally. Shortly after being dropped off at the University, it became evident to him that college life would be very different from what he had been accustomed to. He welcomed this independence suddenly thrust upon him with enthusiasm and zeal. His academic schedule actually proved to be less demanding than the old high school curriculum. Whereas previous school years were very regimented, college was quite the opposite. Lonnie finally was able to study courses that were of interest to him such as Geology, Astronomy, and Forestry. In fact, he had taken a major in Forestry. His grades were good as he was able to balance his academic life well with the rigorous track workouts that he and the rest of the team were subjected to.

Many of his college friends took long weekends and headed up into the mountains for camping trips. Whenever possible, Lonnie and Blue accompanied them. They would go fishing for brook trout and rainbow trout in the fast moving streams while they hiked the heavily forested Bob Marshall Wilderness Area. Lonnie truly loved this period in his life, especially when he was able to be with his friends on these outings. Although many of their friends partied and reveled unchecked, Lonnie and Blue were somewhat constrained by their commitment to track and field. They would on rare occasions let themselves be corrupted by their wilder friends, but the majority of the time would adhere to their higher calling and pledge to each other to make the Olympic team.

Coach Taggert was looking forward to the next summer Olympics almost as much as the boys, but they were still almost a year away. Much would have to happen in that time if the two boys from Silvertown were going to make the team. Many competitions would come and go before any athletes would have the opportunity to make a qualifying attempt during the Olympic trials at the Northern Rocky Mountain Track and Field Invitational. It was his job as head coach to make sure that his team prepared for each meet up until then individually, and to constantly build towards that final meet where they would be at their physical peaks. Coach Taggert had discovered years before that by looking too far into the future was not a good thing. "Take one day at a time. It's nice to have a long-term goal, but one must follow a very detailed road map in order to accomplish something truly great," he would say.

Coach Trapp had recommended that when Lonnie get to college he specialize in the decathlon. As a high school athlete, Lonnie was gifted in that he was a great distance runner as well as an accomplished sprinter. In addition to this, he excelled in most field events, especially the long jump. It was the coach's feeling that Lonnie would be better able to compete in the decathlon at the college level. Although he was a state finalist in the 200-meter dash, Lonnie nevertheless lacked the innate speed to become a world champion sprinter. The same was true with his other events. It was only by combining and utilizing all of his multiple abilities that Lonnie would be able to compete on the world stage. Coach Taggert agreed and it was predetermined that this would be his major event in large meets.

The decathlon consists of ten track and field events, performed over two days. Points are accrued after each event and ultimately the contestant with the highest number of points is the overall winner. The order of events were the 100-meter run, long jump, shot-put, high jump, and 400-meter run. The second day brought the 110-meter hurdles, discus throw, pole vault, javelin throw, and finally the 1500-meter run. This final race was Lonnie's strongest event; in fact, he had run a 4:02 by the end of his freshman year, and now he was hoping to improve upon that.

Lonnie's first big competition of his college career came in the early spring of his freshman year at the Laramie Open in Wyoming. For this meet, the coaching staff decided to enter him in the 1500-meter run and the 1600-meter relay. The relay event consisted of four runners: each sprinting 400 meters and passing a baton between them. As the most inexperienced runner, Lonnie was assigned the first leg. By the time race officials had them lined up in stagger formation on the track, Lonnie had butterflies in his stomach, the likes of which he hadn't experienced in some time. However, with the report of the starting pistol, he exploded off the line in a manner consistent with many of his greatest races. His assigned lane was lane #4, so roughly half of his competitors were in front of him to his right while the remaining contestants were behind him on his left. He moved out with the grace and speed of a cheetah on the attack. As Lonnie sped his way once around the track at full sprint, his mind simply put the pain aside. He was now entering a new phase of his sporting life and nothing was going to get in the way of him and victory. When it finally came time for him to pass the baton less than 48 seconds later, he was indeed in first place. Now it would be up to his teammates to either increase the lead or surrender it to the next in line. On this particular day, luck was with them and his squad prevailed. It was his first of many top finishes that he would enjoy in college. For the first time ever, he was actually running relays as the weakest link. While he savored the taste of victory, Lonnie made a mental note to himself that he would one day become the strongest link on this squad.

The 1500-meter was a different story. He was ranked third entering the race, but when all was said and done and the runners had all crossed the finish line, Lonnie had placed a distant fifth. It had been a long time since he had placed this far back in the pack and he did not like it. The veteran runners simply went out and ran faster than he did. Never had he seen such talent in a single race. Lonnie thought back to what Coach Trapp had once told him. "Son, it's hard to learn something from a win. You don't really get as good as you can be unless you actually lose once in a while. Sometimes this can be a hard pill to swallow, but we do learn from our losses, and they do help to make us better."

"I will get better," Lonnie promised himself. "Yeah, I took fifth place, but my time was 3:41, and that's the fastest 1500-meter I've ever run." He nodded to himself as if to confirm his thoughts. "I am heading for the top and on the way, there may be some times when I lose, but I will get better because of it, and when my time is here, I will win big!" This was the driving impetus that kept him going when things got tough.

Tony Bleuson also found it more difficult in the early going. He had become so accustomed to winning that it was now difficult for him to come to grips with the fact that he was no longer the #1 man for his event. In reality, he was the #3 man for both the shot put and discus his freshman year. To have two people better than him on the same team was intolerable to Old Blue, but try as he did, he was still no match for the stronger and more experienced upper classmen on this powerhouse university team. During workouts, the veterans shared their knowledge and tricks with the newer boys and future stars, and Blue was happy to accept the offers, but he still had a hard time dealing with the situation.

As an incoming senior, Lonnie had quite a lot going for him. He was now the co-captain of the track team along with his oldest buddy, Blue. Over the previous three years, the two of them had improved steadily and were now serious contenders for making the Olympic team; Blue in the shot put and discus, and Lonnie in the decathlon. Training for the duo had been nothing less than rigorous over the preceding years, and it only looked to get more intense as this final year leading up to the trials got underway. Coach Taggert figured they had a more than even chance at making the cut, barring any serious injury or accident that might interfere with training. Life had once again become regimented for Lonnie. In addition to his studies, he had practice twice a day, six days a week. It had been a long time since he was able to take off for a long weekend in the mountains with his friends, and at times he felt himself wearing down. Coach Taggert seemed to notice when his boys were running low on gas. A week before Thanksgiving he asked Lonnie what plans he had for the long weekend.

"Oh, nothing special I guess. Blue and I just kind of thought we would hang around here and work the javelin."

"Why don't you take four or five days with a couple of your friends and head up into the high country for a camping trip or some other type of recreation. I feel both you and Blue need a break. Too much training right now isn't what you boys need. I want you both to take some time off and come back to me refreshed and raring to go. We're coming down on our final lap in this marathon, so I don't want either of you to burn out and get stale on me before we have accomplished what we have set out to do. Will you appease me on this?"

"Gosh Coach, I don't know what to say. Yeah, I have been kind of feeling a little burned out lately. Maybe a nice little adventure into the mountains will recharge my batteries. I'll mention it to Blue and see if we can't get something going. It's a bit far to travel home."

By the next day, Lonnie and Blue had themselves set up with two of their more adventurous buddies to go on a raft trip down the middle fork of the Salmon River over in Idaho. In old days, people called this stretch of the Salmon the "River Of No Return." It can be treacherous beyond belief in the spring when the snow melts, but at this time of the year it should be fairly low and not quite so dangerous. Only one of the boys had ever been on a raft trip before, Jack Dillon. He was a muscular, former high school football player from Denver who made it a point in college to never play another organized sport again. He was a classic case of the burned-out high school athlete. Jack did have his attributes, however. He was perhaps the finest Frisbee player in the school. Many a day over the past three years, Lonnie had supplemented his track practice by playing a few rounds of "ultimate" with Jack. They were good friends. Neil McDermott was the other boy in the group. Neil was not into athletics. He had one leg shorter than the other and walked with a slight limp. During high school he was self conscious about the limp so he never tried out for any team, although he too, was quite a Frisbee player. Among the four of them, they were a typical group of college kids heading off campus for a few days of adventure and excitement.

It was almost a six hour drive to the drop off point in Idaho alongside the river. They had driven two cars out of Bozeman so that it would be possible to leave one vehicle down river and use the other to transport them all sixty miles back up river to where they intended to embark. Afterwards they merely had to reverse the driving in order to have both cars once again for the drive back home. The raft that Jack had acquired from his older brother was an old army surplus piece that could very well have been a holdover from D-Day. It held four people comfortably with all their gear. The only problem in anybody's mind was whether the old rubber raft could make the journey down river for over sixty miles without getting shredded on the rocks. "Never fear, my good fellows," sang out Jack. "I also have a rubber raft patch kit, complete with over twenty-five patches. Some of them are pretty big!"

"Let's hope we won't need them," groaned Blue. "I don't fancy seeing myself hiking down this river for the next three weeks."

Shortly before two o'clock, the boys had their waterproof river bags stowed aboard along with life vests, paddles, fishing poles, and a couple cases of beer. The plan was pretty simple. They would float down the river for three days, or for as long as it took to come upon their car. Each night they would camp alongside the river and laugh and party around the campfire until wee hours of the morning. When the new day would arrive, they could get a leisurely start after a huge breakfast. Jack figured they should easily be able to make twenty miles a day out of the river current, and no telling how much more if they were forced to paddle. He had never floated this particular segment of the Salmon before, but he had done it further south. "The rapids are what it's all about boys," Jack said. "I guarantee that by this time tomorrow night we will have met the river-god, and who knows what surprises he has in store for us!"

"Would you stop talking like that?" Blue spoke out rather loudly. Lonnie could tell that the big fella was nervous. He never had been a strong swimmer as a boy, but was too proud to admit it. "How do we know what kind of rapids are up ahead, and how do we know that our raft is even capable of handling it when we do find them?"

"Not to worry, my good man. This is a popular float route from here on down the river to the car. At this time of year, in November, the rapids are no higher than a class four, and there are only three or four of those. The weather has been fairly dry over the past few months, so those class fours are probably now more like class threes."

"What is the most difficult class?" asked Blue.

"Class five, and come spring this river will be full of them. Don't worry though, Blue. If the floating gets too rough, we can always pull up along the bank and walk around the hot spots. That is, if there is a bank. Sometimes on this river there are some pretty steep sides. Well, if we get wet, we just get wet! That's why I brought along these wet suit tops. If we dump, they'll help to keep us afloat, but I can't make any guarantees about a big feller like you." Jack said this with a big grin on his face. He enjoyed playing on Blue's trepidation. Whenever the shoes were on the other feet, Blue was always the first to antagonize his friends. Jack knew that for the next three days he would have Blue at his mercy, and he intended to savor every last moment of it. Even now he could tell how the poor guy was battling between his desire to stay ashore and his macho pride which wouldn't allow him to back down on the trip.

"Blue, we're sure to be okay. These wet suit tops and the life preservers will be plenty of protection for us. Don't worry about a thing, I'll take care of you buddy." Lonnie said this with all the reassurance that he could muster, and when Blue nodded in the affirmative and looked away Lonnie gave Jack a hard look which said, "Lay off the guy." Jack nodded good naturedly and went about making final preparations before they shoved off.

Jack had the most experience river rafting, so he was naturally elected as team leader. "We have almost three hours before dark, so let's get a move on," he called out. Lonnie pushed off from the rear of the raft next to Blue while Neil and Jack started to paddle up front in order to gain access to the wider part of the river as quickly as possible. The water rushed by like a fast moving carpet with little agitation. At this particular spot, the Salmon had a width of close to fifty yards. This distance across varied dramatically at times depending upon the grade of the land. As a rule of thumb, the wider the river the slower it moves. When it narrows, there is more water moving through a smaller space so the pace of the river naturally quickens. These were the areas that Jack would keep an eye out for as he rode in the front of the raft. His intent was to have an exciting trip, but he also wanted to have a safe one as well. The river had to be constantly monitored up ahead for dangerous rapids, falls, and other obstacles. Even if a person came down this same stretch of river the day before, it could easily change its demeanor overnight. One fallen tree lodged between a couple of rocks could create a hazard that might become life threatening if they allowed the river to move them into it.

After an hour of easy drifting, Jack started to give some pointers on raft handling. "When we come to the rapids, it's important we all work together. I will give the commands. Sometimes I'll say paddle right. This means the people on the right side of the raft paddle only. Paddle left means the same thing only for the left side of the raft. "All paddle" is self- explanatory. The basic strategy here is to stay out in the middle of the river as much as we can. If we do that effectively, it will be easier to react and maneuver the raft into position for the rapids, no matter which side they're on. Every so often while riding a wave, we may take a deep plunge into a hole. It's very important that when this happens that Neil and I both grab hold of the rope liner in the front of the raft and pull up on it. This will help to prevent us from swamping. We always keep the front up when we go down the swells. If we should ever find ourselves spun around backwards, I'll call out "reverse paddle." This means that the people on the left paddle forward and the people on the right paddle backwards at the same time. I will always try to direct us to the safest part of the river, but we aren't wimps here. It can become dangerous, and it can get confusing. If it gets too rough for you, hold on and try not to let yourself get washed overboard. If that should happen, keep your feet out ahead of you so that it is easier to fend off rocks. Hold on to the raft if you can and we'll get you back in when it settles down a bit. Under no circumstances are you to lose your paddle, Blue. It's the most important piece of gear we have. One last thing, always be listening for a roar. The most dangerous part of this business is when big rapids and falls sneak up on us. A good thing to watch for is the pace of the water- flow. When it picks up, there's a pretty good chance that we might find a surprise around the next bend, so stay alert. Whenever possible, we can pull over and check out the rapids from shore before we attempt them. Does anyone have any questions?"

"Yeah, how did I ever let you guys talk me into this? I'm supposed to be on an R&R weekend, not some death defying cold water river cruise!" said Blue.

"Blue, I guarantee that by the end of the first couple of rapids you're going to be a convert. This kind of stuff gets into your blood," replied Jack.

For the next couple of hours, the four adventurers floated slowly down the meandering river. On a few occasions they encountered some small class one and two rapids, which they easily rode out with little fanfare. It was nice to start the trip out slowly on an easy stretch of the river, Lonnie thought. He looked forward to the next few days and the excitement that was sure to follow. As they floated along, Lonnie thought about home and what Poppy and Sara were probably doing. He kept up a pretty good line of communication, but had neglected to inform them of his plans for the holiday. Earlier in the month Sara had suggested that maybe he might like to come home for the long weekend. Lonnie had declined stating that it would be too difficult to get the time off with studies and training and all. In reality, he wasn't up to the long car ride. Over the previous summer he had bought a third hand Volkswagen from one of Poppy's mining buddies. It had over 90,000 miles on it, but still seemed to run well. The previous owners probably were good on changing the fluids, he figured.

Lonnie felt a tinge of guilt for not keeping them better informed. He promised himself to drop a line when they got back to school providing the highlights of the trip. Sara was feeling a bit depressed recently as a result of an early term miscarriage. She and Poppy had waited awhile before trying, but finally realized they weren't getting any younger. The doctor had informed her it was just one of those things, and there was no reason why the next time things wouldn't turn out better. Sara would make a great Mom, he thought. Perhaps by spring she might have a new announcement to make. Poppy was very supportive. He didn't seem to be so stressed out anymore. Perhaps it was because of himself, finally completing his last year in college. It had been a real struggle at times. Poppy was proud of him; he knew that for certain. Once he stopped talking about being a rancher and living off the land and started paying more attention to his college major in forestry, it seemed like a great load was lifted from his dad. He really didn't want his son to work in the mine. Well, Poppy would get his wish on that score, Lonnie thought.

"This looks like a good place to camp for the night," Neil said. "What do you say we stop here and pitch our tents before it gets dark?"

The boys agreed to stop for the day, and after putting in to shore went about setting up camp. Blue, in a surprisingly good mood once he got his feet back on dry land, offloaded the river bags from the raft before settling himself under a large pine and popping a cold can of Budweiser. Jack and Neil looked on in disgust as they reconnoitered the area for a suitable place to pitch their two-man pup tents. Lonnie took it upon himself to gather wood and build a fire. Within half an hour they each had their sleeping bags unrolled and laid out in the respective tents and were sitting around the campfire wondering what to eat for dinner.

"Ah, pork and beans," Blue said. "My favorite!" As he moved himself over to the fire with an extra large can he was claiming all for himself, he let loose with a disgusting belch that got everyone laughing and shaking their heads.

"I'm glad he's in your tent, Neil! Something tells me it's going to be a long night," Jack said. "How about the rest of you? Does anybody want a freeze-dried pasta meal? These things are great. All you have to do is add boiling water and five minutes later, presto!"

"Sure, it sounds good to me," voiced in Lonnie. "I've never seen so much food for a three day camping trip before. I suppose that when Blue cleans us out we can always catch fish and boil snails. Pass me a brew, will ya, Jack."

The boys spent a fun evening sitting around the campfire telling story after story and generally giving each other a hard time. The sky was clear, but as soon as the sun set, the temperature started to drop. Earlier in the day the mercury had hit sixty degrees. It was supposed to do it again tomorrow, but the night could easily slip below freezing. Sometime before midnight Jack suggested they turn in before Blue drank all the beer. "We don't want to have too much fun tonight guys, or we may have a hard time tomorrow when we hit the river. It would be a shame if Blue got seasick all over everybody when he gets a look at what's in store for us down the river," Jack winked at the others.

"Now there you go again, Jack."

Chapter Twenty

"Paddle right! Paddle right!" shouted Jack. "We have to make it in between those two rocks up ahead!"

Lonnie wedged his feet under the inside wall of the raft and leaned far over the side so that he could plunge his paddle deep into the frothing water without losing his balance. The river had started to narrow a few hundred yards back as the level of the land started to drop. The results were clear for all to see. Turbulent water suddenly appeared when only moments before it had been calm. Large rocks were everywhere, both above the surface, and more precariously, just below the surface. Jack looked down river and could see a long stretch of white water rapids. There wasn't anything in his estimation that might compromise the raft so he hollered at everyone to dig in and paddle for all they were worth. As they moved through the two large rocks on the far side of the river, the narrowed space greatly increased their speed. The raft rode high through the opening for just a moment before it took the first plunge. Jack and Neil both pulled up on the front of the craft as it hit the bottom of the trough allowing a rush of frigid water to come pouring in. In a heartbeat, the rapid pace of the river carried them past the hole, only to subject them to a new and more furious onslaught. Blue and Lonnie bailed the water out as best they could, while Neil and Jack continued to maneuver between the obstacles. Seconds later they were all paddling once more. The pliable nature of the rubber boat allowed it to bend its shape to conform to the changing surface of the water. This undulating motion helped to release a surge of adrenalin in the boys. Blue hollered out in excitement, "Yee ha!"

A quarter mile down stream things started to settle down once again. The river widened and the pitch leveled out. This lull in the action gave the boys a chance to recollect themselves. They were all laughing and shouting and pointing at each other and generally having a good time. "What a rush," Blue called out. "I thought we would capsize for sure."

"No, not in those measly little rapids," Jack answered.

"What do you mean 'little' rapids?" retorted Blue.

"I mean, that while those were a real gas, they will get bigger. We did all right though, especially you, Blue. I'm proud of you. As long as we keep working together like that, things will go just fine." He gave the big guy a nod of approval before turning his attention back to the river. "I reckon it will continue on like this for the next few miles. Those were class three rapids. When the big ones come up, we'll pull over and check them out first."

For the rest of the day, while floating down the river, they experienced intermittent periods of rushing rapids and then calmer waters. During the easier stretches, they lunched on cold cut sandwiches and soda pop. Jack would not allow any of them to drink beer on the river. "That's an extra hazard we don't need on this river," he said. By early afternoon they were exhausted and decided to pull over and make camp with a few hours of daylight remaining. It had been a beautiful day with temperatures rising close to 70 degrees.

"That looks like a good spot to pull over," Neil said. He pointed to a long sandbar peninsula that jutted out into the river. On the right hand side, there was a small bay created where the water was very calm. Along the sandy shore it was fairly open for a ways up into the pine forest. The trees along this stretch of the river were quite large and very old. They covered the rocky faces of the surrounding mountains like a giant green blanket. Most of these forests were still virgin timber. This territory along the Salmon was known as the primitive area of Idaho. It was basically uninhabited national forest land that extended for literally thousands of square miles. Every year there were reports of hikers or campers wandering off into the wilderness and getting lost, sometimes never to be heard of again. If the wild animals didn't get them, hypothermia usually would.

Once establishing camp along shore was complete, Lonnie and Blue decided they would go for a hike and check the place out. They followed the river for a while keeping to an old animal trail along the bank. "This is an elk trail we're on," Lonnie stated as a matter-of-fact. "In these deep forests there aren't a whole lot of deer. If we keep quiet maybe we'll come on something. Who knows, we might even find a moose."

They meandered their way along the river following the trail for almost thirty minutes. At a junction in the path, Lonnie paused for a moment, and then took it to the right. There was a clearing up ahead they could see through the trees and he wanted to check it out. Walking along, they came upon a beautiful meadow, which was carpeted with long grass and had a small pond. It was a couple acres in size. Large boulders were strewn about haphazardly. "Now this is a place I would like to come back to some day and build me a log cabin," Lonnie said. "I wonder how many people have seen this spot in the past fifty years."

"Not too many, I'll bet. We're way the hell out of the way in this place. But, I could see a nice cabin over there," said Blue, as he plodded over to a flattened area which bordered a group of humongous spruce trees. "We could put the pool right here." While he spoke, a slight breeze blew in his face. "Say, what's that

God awful smell? It stinks like shit; worse, it smells like something dead."

Lonnie had been following him a few steps behind. "It is something dead. Something big!" he said.

"Lets check it out."

"No, Blue, let's not. In fact, let's get out of here. I don't feel good about this all of a sudden." Lonnie spoke the words as he walked up close to his buddy and reached out to put his hand on his shoulder. Before another word could be spoken, the two boys were confronted by a large brown colored bear which suddenly appeared from behind one of the spruce trees. It rushed at them on all fours until it was less than a hundred feet away. Here it stopped abruptly and rose up onto its hind legs. The bear was an exceptionally large male Grizzly. It easily stood nine feet above the ground. The animal had a huge head with a great protruding snout. It stared directly at Blue and Lonnie with its pig-like eyes while clashing its jaws together repeatedly in a demonstration of intimidation.

"Ho-ly shit, what did we go and get ourselves into, Lon" Blue whispered softly. "That's the biggest God-damn bear I've ever seen---on this side of zoo bars. What do you reckon we should do?"

"Just stay real cool, and whatever you do, don't look him in the eyes." The large carnivore continued to snap his jaws at the terrified boys. He twisted his head from side to side while pawing the air with his feet and stomping the ground. Blue could see the sun shine off his long sharp claws and realized for the first time that the creature had blood smeared about its face. The gentle breeze could be seen blowing the bear's heavy coat of fur. If he weren't so terrified, Blue might actually have thought it amusing. Ever so slowly, Lonnie lowered himself to one knee.

"What are you doing, Lon?"

"Just stand real still and don't do anything." With that said, Lonnie reached down and picked up two medium size rocks he found laying at their feet. As slowly as he could possibly move, he raised himself back to an upright position never turning away from the bear. With a steady nerve Lonnie steeled himself to the task ahead and tried not to think about the consequences if he failed. SMACK--- SMACK--- SMACK. With all his might, but with as little movement as humanly possible, Lonnie crashed the rocks together in his hands. When the bear would snap his jaws shut, releasing a loud popping sound, Lonnie responded by crashing the rocks together. This went on for a few unchecked moments with little results before Blue finally looked over at him and said, "What the hell are ya doin, buddy?"

"Bark like a dog," Lonnie replied.

"Say what?" Blue's response was a bit louder than he had anticipated. The bear continued snapping its bone crushing jaws as it took a few more steps closer to them.

"I said, bark like a dog," he said with intensity.

Blue thought for a brief moment about how his hero buddy had finally lost it when the chips were down. The guy is freaking out right in front of me, he thought; and worse yet, he's freaking out in front of the bear. Before Blue could conceive of any plan of action, Lonnie started to bark loudly at the angry monster confronting them. He continued smacking the rocks together and barking with all his might until finally, the confused bear stopped snapping and stared at them in bewilderment. It shook its head back and forth as if to make better sense of what it was seeing. Blue, noticing the effect his friend was having on the bear, immediately started barking for all he was worth. Unfortunately, for the big guy, his first few yelps were little more than what a frightened Chihuahua might have made. In the horrifying position they were in, Blue was so afraid that his voice naturally came out a few octaves higher, even in his bark!

The bear continued to look on in confusion. After shaking its giant head a few more times it finally spun around on its hind legs while dropping to all fours, and scampered back behind the trees from where he had appeared in the first place. At this point Blue looked at Lonnie wide-eyed and said, "Now what?"

"RUN!" he cried.

If Coach Taggert had a stopwatch on Blue that day, he would certainly have moved him to the 800-meter run. The two explorers put so much distance so fast between themselves and the Grizzly, that it amazed even Lonnie. Only once did they stop on the way back to the landing, and that was to make sure the bear wasn't following.

"Hey guys, you look out of breath. Where have you been?" asked Jack.

"You are not going to believe this," started Blue, "but we just had an encounter with the biggest bear that lives in these woods. Jesus, if I hadn't seen it with my own eyes I wouldn't have believed it." He turned his attention to Lonnie who was panting by his side and said, "Will you kindly tell me what just happened? What were we doing back there?"

Lonnie laughed for a moment, and then without saying a word, he went over to where the Budweiser was sitting and poured down a cold one. After letting loose with a belch that even Blue would have been proud of, he popped another before attempting to explain to everyone what just transpired. "The reason the bear was snapping his jaws is because he was trying to intimidate us. He obviously had a dead elk or something behind the trees he was protecting. The bear didn't want to fight us. All he wanted to do was scare us away so he could go back to eating dinner. When I smashed the rocks together, the bear heard a louder sound than he was able to make. We were standing our own ground, but at the same time not advancing on his dinner."

"Ok, I can understand that. But why were we barking like dogs?"

"Barking," Neil blurted out and then started to laugh along with Jack.

"Well, that grizzly has probably never seen a human being before living way out here in the forest and mountains and all. At least I'll bet it never spoke to a human. Anyway, if we yelled and screamed at it, it probably wouldn't have recognized our sound. Certainly it wouldn't have been afraid of it. By barking at the brute, we gave him a sound to hear that he probably did recognize like the sound of a wolf or coyote. If he pursued us, for all he knew he would get bitten up. When he realized we weren't moving in on him or his meal, he retreated back to the kill. If we had followed him the next attack would have been fatal. The initial charge of the bear is called a mock charge. When you're lucky, that's what the bear does. When you're unlucky, he keeps coming and then eats you. We were lucky!"

"Yer God-damn right we were lucky! Where did you ever learn all that, Lon?"

"Well, I kind of made it up as I went along," he laughed modestly.

"Should we be thinking about moving camp farther down river?" questioned Neil.

"No," Lonnie replied. "I think we'll be all right if we stay here. That bear has already had his dinner. He probably won't stray more than a few hundred yards from that spot until he's eaten everything edible, and that would be everything. Let's be real careful about leaving any food out though, no sense pushing our luck." That night the boys built an extra large fire as a bear deterrent while they sat around camp. Jack and Neil had to listen to Blue's rendition of the story all evening. They rolled their eyes collectively when he talked about how he thought Lonnie had lost it and about how he was going to have to save the day all by himself. Lonnie only let his old buddy embellish on the account so much before finally asking him to give everyone a demonstration of his Chihuahua bark. This shut Blue up real quick, but only momentarily, until he started laughing hysterically at himself.

"Yup, I was one mad dog back there. Maybe just a little dog, though." Everyone joined in laughing with him and continued on until late into the evening before finally turning in when all the beer was gone.

Chapter Twenty-One

The following day they weren't on the river until almost 11:00 am. Once again, the weather seemed to be cooperating with an unobstructed sun shining down upon them. Jack suggested everyone remain in their original positions because they did so well the previous day. No one disagreed. Although the river started out calm for the first few miles and everyone got plenty of exercise paddling, it soon started to pick up at a substantial chop. This continued for some miles until they encountered a set of more challenging rapids. With little hesitation, they paddled into it aggressively following the orders of Jack. These class three and sporadic class four rapids were considerably more demanding than anything they had encountered the day before. The raging water drenched them time and again. Lonnie was thankful Jack had insisted on the wet suits. Occasionally the small craft would get caught up in obstacles on the river such as trees and rocks. This can be very dangerous as the force of the water coming up behind them can sometimes cause the raft to be swamped or even spun around backwards. Tree branches have a nasty habit of punching holes in rubber rafts, so Jack would always try to avoid them at all costs. On this day the river was very powerful, but the little raft persevered and continued down the river with its crew of now veteran river rafters.

"We had a good day today, guys," Jack started. "If I had to guess, I'd bet we traveled over twenty miles. That would put us two thirds of the way to the car and the finish line. Our experience over the past two days has been good. We're gonna need it tomorrow. The last ten miles or so will be the most treacherous. Last year, some friends of mine floated this section of the river in the spring and ended up fording around almost two miles of rapids. The water isn't so high now, but you can never tell until actually seeing it how passable it will be. If we need to, we can pull up and check it out. The elevation drops pretty significantly between here and where we're going, so be ready for a good one tomorrow."

The following day Jack was right on the money, as usual. Things started out calm enough when they embarked on the last leg of their journey, but pretty soon things began to get rough. Within a mile of their campsite, the boys came upon the first sustained set of rapids of the day. The roar of the river alerted them to the turbulent conditions up ahead long before they were able to see it. At first glimpse, Blue swallowed hard and suggested that perhaps they might want to pull over and check out the situation before entering into something they might have a hard time getting out of. The others agreed.

Single file they made their way along the banks of the river. It became increasingly difficult to stay at water level along the rivers edge because the cliffs on either side had encroached right up to the shore in many places. Nevertheless, with a bit of hiking determination they were able to climb up to a vantage point where it was possible to look down the river for almost a mile and check it out. Things looked wild indeed, significantly more so than anything they had encountered up to this point. After a bit of quiet reflection by everyone, Jack broke the silence by saying "This is why we came here, boys. If it were easy, it wouldn't be any fun. My vote says we go for it, there's nothing down there we can't handle." After a little more discussion, the four of them agreed to make the attempt, but only after examining the river and shoreline in great detail. The major concern was once they committed to the run, it would be nearly impossible to pull up alongside shore and abandon their attempt. They would be in it for the duration no matter what the river threw at them.

"Remember, we want to stay in the middle as best we can. If we dump, hold on to your paddles and try to stay with the raft." Jack looked at each of them as he gave his final instructions while the swift current carried them along. He could see hard determination in each of their eyes, but it was coupled with a lingering fear that no one was willing to admit. "It's OK to be afraid, Blue. Hell, I'm scared shitless!" he laughed nervously.

"You look shitless, from where I'm sitting. I'll see you on the other side," he replied.

Lonnie tightened the straps on his life vest without even knowing it. As he looked about, he quickly realized they had gotten into something much more intense than anything they had rafted so far. Nevertheless, each of them paddled hard and tried as best they could to work together. They shouted out in excitement every time the river would throw them a scare. The sensations were exhilarating while water was pushing and splashing in every direction. The force of the river was just incredible. It seemed to be a living entity, which was content to merely play with these intruders for the time being, at least until it was able to get them deep enough into its grasp to where there was no escape. The Indians called this river "The River of No Return." Lonnie was very quickly beginning to see why. The farther they moved down stream, the steeper the sides got and the more treacherous it became. Eventually, what had started out as an exciting ride, soon regressed into a maelstrom. Giant waves picked up the small craft and carried it along precipitously on their crests, only to then disappear, causing it to then plummet into the boiling cauldron below, swamping the occupants time and again. The boys were thrown about violently inside the raft repeatedly as they tried to negotiate the angry rapids. Every time they would get themselves reoriented, another wave would then hit them from a different direction sending them tumbling into each other once again. Rocks were a constant hazard. They must be avoided at all costs in dangerous rapids such as these. While it was a natural instinct for the boys to hunker down when they came upon really serious water, it could also be quite dangerous if the raft were to come crashing down on a jagged rock under the surface.

"Paddle left! Paddle left!" Jack cried.

"No! No!" shouted Neil. "There's a big rock underneath."

"Here, too!" called back Jack.

This brief moment of confusion caused the boys to hesitate. Instantly the rapid current of the river carried the helpless raft up onto the concealed rocks where it was then spun around backwards by the force of the onrushing water. All on board immediately recognized the peril they were in. Jack shouted out commands to reverse paddle, but it was too late. The hole immediately behind the rock sucked them in and set them up perfectly for a cross wave that struck from the side. This caught Jack completely unprepared as he was leaning over the side trying to turn the raft by wedging his paddle into the rocks they had just caught on. He was washed from the boat instantly. Blue made a valiant attempt to grab him as he went by and would have been successful if it weren't for the next wave that hit them and completely capsized the raft. Lonnie managed to grab the side rope as he flew through the air and only held on to his paddle by shear luck. As they were washed violently down river, Neil was able to catch hold of Lonnie's extended arm and pull himself to the opposite side of the raft where he held on for dear life. The next five minutes were an eternity for each of them. Jack was bobbing above and below the surface as he was swept along not even twenty feet away. The sudden plunge into the ice- cold water took his breath away as he struggled to survive. He concentrated on trying to keep his feet out in front of himself to protect against rocks, but the rushing water took complete control. Lonnie tried to keep him in sight so he could help guide him to the raft if it became possible, but after a minute or two, Jack was nowhere to be seen.

Blue was directly in front of the capsized raft. He also was struggling to maintain his position in the rapids, but there was no fighting against the stronger will of the river. Its waters carried the helpless adventurers downstream with little regard for personal safety or even life itself. Lonnie called out to Blue so he could get his bearings on them. If somehow he could slow his rate of speed, perhaps the raft could catch up to him. "Stay in the center!" called out Lonnie. "Too many rocks on the side! Up ahead it's calmer; we'll catch you there!" Lonnie had to scream at the top of his lungs to be heard over the deafening roar of the rapids.

Finally when the white water began to subside, Blue was able to make his way to the raft. Among the three of them they were able to right it while continuing to float down the center of the river. "Where is Jack?" gasped Blue, as he pulled himself up and into the now empty raft.

"The last we saw of him, he was moving over towards the right," answered a very shook up Neil. "We've got to get over to the side and pull up. If he's upstream, we'll have to backtrack along the shore and find him. I lost my paddle."

"So did I," said Blue.

Lonnie shook his head while handing Neil his own paddle and said, "Here, you paddle while we push." With that said, he and Blue lowered themselves over the back end and began to push the raft toward shore. Two hundred yards downstream they finally succeeded in getting a foot hold on the far side. "Blue, you check downstream. I'll go upstream. Neil, stay with the raft after tying it off. Get a long stick and watch the river in case Jack comes floating by. Keep an eye out for any of our gear, too." Lonnie automatically took control of the situation. There was no time to stop and decide on a game plan. They had to act and act quickly.

Lonnie moved quickly up the riverbank. When the shoreline would not allow him to pass by, he took to climbing the cliffs. As precious minutes ticked by he called out repeatedly, but with no luck. It took almost thirty minutes before reaching the spot in the river where he had last seen Jack. There was no evidence of him, either in the water or on shore. He prayed that Jack did not strike his head or get sucked down into a hole and drowned. At this point, the only other option was to head downstream and check with the others.

When Jack was thrown from the raft, he had to struggle to keep his head above water. He got into a rougher section of the river, which ultimately carried him off to the right more. While trying to reach shore he struck an underwater rock full in the chest and shoulder. The ensuing pain was acute. It knocked the wind out of him, and if it weren't for one of the river bags he managed to snag while floating by, he very well may have drowned. Jack wrapped his arms around his new lifeline being careful not to let go of his paddle. In this manner he floated down river for almost a mile before he was finally able to reach shore. When he did, it was all he could do to pull himself out of the water before he collapsed in pain and lay there.

Blue could move quickly for a man of his size. Following the shoreline, he made his way downstream at a trot. When he came to sections that were not passable, he walked out into the river and floated along until once again it became clear enough to travel on land. After fifteen minutes, he spotted the orange of Jack's life vest one hundred yards up shore. "Hello, Jack, can you hear me?" The river had settled down considerably from where they had capsized further back, so the deafening roar of the rapids had abated somewhat. After calling out a second time, Jack rolled over and waved his arm feebly. Blue could tell that Jack was hurt and doubled his efforts to get to his injured friend. "Jack, are you ok? Speak to me buddy."

"Yeah, I'm still kicking, but damn, I smashed into a rock and screwed up my shoulder and maybe some ribs. It's real hard to breathe; it hurts. What about the others? Did we lose anybody?"

"No, everybody is present and accounted for, now that I found you. Yeah, it's good to see your ugly face. I never thought I'd miss it until now." Blue checked him over to make sure that his injuries were not life threatening. When he was assured of that, he said, "Let me head back up river and let the others know you're all right."

"I'm not all right, that's why I'm laying down here in the muck," Jack said pitifully.

"Well, let me at least tell them that you're still alive."

"Hurry, I'd hate to make a liar out of you."

Blue headed back up river to retrieve the others. By the time he reached Neil, Lonnie came trotting into camp. He explained the situation to their great relief, and they decided the best course of action would be to float the raft down river leading it from shore with a line. It took them another forty-five minutes before reaching a very pale and shivering Jack, who was now sitting with his back perched up against a fallen tree.

"You gave us all a scare, Jack," began Lonnie. "I guess we need another lesson or two on the finer aspects of negotiating class four and five rapids. That was some heavy stuff back there. We're lucky we made it through as well as we did. It could have been worse. Thank God you didn't lose your paddle or we would really be up a creek. Now we have two."

"Who lost their paddles?"

"I did," said Blue with downcast eyes.

"So did I," added Neil.

"I warned you guys to hang on to them. Imagine going down this river with no way to steer. It would be suicide. We're still a long way from the car and I don't fancy myself walking the rest of the way. Keep a sharp eye and maybe we can find them caught up farther downstream."

By outward appearances, it looked as though Jack had probably cracked a rib or two. His side was very tender and already showing the black-and-blue coloration of a deep bruise. In addition to this, he had banged up his shoulder pretty bad. It looked to Lonnie as if he had also broken his collarbone. "Jack, there's not a whole lot we can do for you at this point. We lost most of our supplies when we capsized. The river bag you managed to latch onto has our sleeping bags in it and the tent, but no food or first aid. We can tie up your side with our belts and immobilize your arm so that the movement on the river shouldn't be too bad, but I can't guarantee you won't feel it. It's almost 1:00 p.m. now. I recommend we continue on and make it as far as we can today. Before too long we're going to start getting hungry if we waste a lot of time around here."

At this point, Blue made an attempt at humor to lighten things up a bit. "If things get really bad as far as the food is concerned, we can always eat Jack. You would be agreeable to that in order to save the rest of us the inconvenience of having to starve for a few days, wouldn't you, Jack, old buddy?" He looked at his incapacitated friend with an exaggerated gleam in his eyes.

"You just keep your distance from me, you moronic cannibal, or I'll give you this paddle to chew on." The others laughed at this, but Jack gave Blue a mighty strange look while shaking his head.

As quickly as they could, the boys were back on the river. Neil and Lonnie rode up front with the paddles while Blue and Jack sat in the back. Before pushing off, Blue grabbed himself a long pole to help navigate. They were lucky in that the next few miles were fairly easy going. The whitewater continued to appear and disappear, but the severity had settled down since the early morning debacle. When they finally did come onto a more challenging stretch of water, Jack insisted they pull over and check it out first. It took a good forty-five minutes to scout the rapids. "We can do it, but it's going to be uncomfortable, Jack," Lonnie said.

"How far down do the rapids extend?"

"At least a mile. There are mostly class threes and maybe a class four or two coming up. What do you think?"

"I think we should set up camp right here and attempt it in the morning. If we try now and dump on the river, we may get separated going into the night. It's better to try when we have a whole day to regroup, just in case."

"Ok, tomorrow it is then," Lonnie announced to everyone. "Let's make camp."

The night played out to be a cold one. All their dry clothes were in the other river bag, which was lost when the raft capsized. Lonnie was able to build a fire with some matches he had squirreled away in the bag, but it only served to take the chill off. With no food to eat as they sat around the fire and no enthusiasm about the day to come with its inevitable dangers, the boys called it an early night.

It started to rain shortly after midnight. Lonnie lay in his sleeping bag dozing as he listened to the sounds of the raindrops gently hitting the walls of his tent when suddenly a loud crack of thunder startled him. He heard Neil mutter some obscenity from the next tent. As the night wore on the wind picked up considerably, and the intensity of the rainstorm grew. Flashes of lightning could be seen through the thin nylon sides of the tent. The deafening sounds of thunder continued on unabated late into the night. "This is a hell of a storm, Lon," Jack said. "I wonder what it will do to the river."

"We'll know in a few hours," replied Lonnie.

The next day brought overcast skies and continued drizzle. When Lonnie crawled from his tent he immediately noticed how the river had risen during the night. Water rushed by not ten feet from where they had set their tents, whereby the previous night there had been a good thirty feet. Before anyone else woke up, Lonnie took the hike downriver again to see how things might have changed during the night. He was not encouraged by what he found. The turbulent white water had grown substantially and the accompanying roar of the rapids was quite intimidating. In addition to this, there were trees and other debris floating down the river. The danger factor had increased many times over.

"We've got problems, boys. This has turned into one ugly river. I can't imagine running it with Jack rolling around on the bottom of the raft. If we stay here and try to wait for it to go down, it could take days, not to mention the fact it will probably get worse before it gets any better. Jack, how do you feel about trying to make it by this next stretch on foot? I'm figuring Blue and you could walk it while Neil and I take the raft. As quick as we get through this section, we'll pull up and wait. The only other alternative is for all of us to walk it, but this might be a problem down river if walking becomes impossible and we don't have a raft to ride in."

As much as no one wanted to admit it, Lonnie was right. After some discussion, it was finally agreed they would proceed as he had laid it out. Blue and Jack started out immediately. The plan was for them to get a good head start. If Lonnie and Neil got into trouble, they might be able to better help by being downstream. Jack was obviously in pain, but he kept it to himself for the most part. One hour later Lonnie and Neil pushed off for the ride of their lives.

Lonnie rode in the front of the raft on the right side while Neil rode in the back on the left. They kept to the center of the fast flowing river as much as they could, always opting to take the easiest route whenever possible. In a matter of minutes, both of them were completely drenched and they were sitting in a pool of water. If it weren't for the wetsuit tops, they would surely have been susceptible to hypothermia. Whenever possible, each would bale the best he could. Rather than risk being swept overboard, both of them squatted down low inside the raft and tried to paddle from there even though it wasn't nearly as effective. Large waves, one after another, hit them from every direction. Sometimes they would ride high on a swell for a brief moment only for it to disappear in the next instant and they would come crashing down. Large rocks were everywhere and floating hazards constantly threatened to scuttle their craft. Once, when they got caught in a backwash behind a large boulder, the raft spun around backward. Within seconds, the two of them, working in concert, managed to complete a 360 degree revolution.

"Try not to do that again!" Neil shouted out trying to be heard over the rushing noise of the river. As frightened as they were, each of them had feelings of exhilaration every time the raft made it by a seemingly impossible obstacle. Lonnie actually felt thrilled to be riding the river in this manner.

"There. Up ahead. It's Blue and Jack," called out Lonnie.

Jack had positioned himself at the end of a narrow point protruding out into the river. He was waving frantically with one arm for them to pull ashore. They made a valiant effort to reach him, but in the end went sailing by. As they did, Neil heard him call out, "Waterfall ahead, get to shore." The roar of the river suddenly got louder. Lonnie could see up ahead that the drop was considerable. Stretching out for as far as he could see was a rock strewn, no-mans-land of danger and destruction. Broken and fragmented trees caught in the rocks protruded out in every direction and presented a picture of impending doom. They paddled for their lives as the river carried them on to almost certain death. When it appeared as if all was lost, Lonnie looked back to Neil and saw terror in his eyes. He shouted, "Try to swim to shore. It's our only chance." Simultaneously, they both dove out of the water filled raft, which had become almost impossible to maneuver because of the weight inside, and swam for shore.

As if out of nowhere with no regard for his own safety, Blue suddenly appeared wading chest deep into the water. He was toting a large staff which he thrust out for his friends to grab as they floated by. Once Lonnie got a grip on it, he managed to lock hands with Neil before Blue wrestled them both onto shore. The raft continued down its fated path and within moments had completely disappeared in the turbulent river ahead. When the three of them reached shore Lonnie gasped, "What a ride."

Chapter Twenty-Two

The night was miserably cold and damp. If Lonnie hadn't thought to tuck away some matches in a waterproof container and place them deep inside his wet suit, they would surely have succumbed to the elements. All four huddled closely around the campfire in an attempt to ward off the nights chill which mercilessly attacked them from every side. Each of them slowly drifted in and out of consciousness throughout the long evening. They retreated into their own private worlds where they might seek solace by remembering happier times. Lonnie couldn't help but think about the time years earlier when he was forced to spend the night inside a snow cave deep in the mountains. He had been able to pull through then, and he was certain they would be able to do so now, but there were still many dangers that lay ahead. Lonnie remained awake long after his comrades dozed off. As he fed the constant appetite of their life saving campfire he looked over at Jack and felt a twinge of pity for him. Here was a young man in the prime of his life. All through high school, he had been a top athlete and overachiever. Lonnie had a tremendous amount of respect for him and his accomplishments; but now, as his friend lay shivering on the damp ground with his broken body, Lonnie realized that it would be up to him to lead Jack and the rest of their hapless party to safety. These thoughts and many others clouded his mind late into the night until he, too, faded off into a restless sleep which was plagued by nightmares brought on by the day's events.

The following morning, it was Blue's animal like snoring that finally aroused everyone. He was sprawled out on the ground with the back of his head perched on a rotten log, the exact same position he was in nine hours earlier. "Leave it to Blue to make the best of a miserable situation," Lonnie thought. He had slept right through the evening without stirring once, not even to feed the fire. The fire had been kept up all night by the others, whomever was awake and cold enough to make the effort to pile wood on. Fortunately, the weather had cleared during the night and now the sun shown brightly in the eastern sky. As the boys moved around camp and talked about the day to come, Blue finally started to stir. "Good morning all. I trust you slept well."

"No, thanks to you, ya big lunk. Your snoring kept me awake all night," responded Jack testily.

"Oh, don't be such a complainer, Jackie boy. I had to get my beauty sleep so that I could carry your sorry ass off this river bottom. What's for breakfast?"

"No breakfast today, Blue. I'm afraid we've got a long hike ahead of us before we'll be able to eat anything. It's best we get a move on though. No telling what lies ahead," Lonnie said. "How are you feeling, Jack? I wish there was something we could do for you, buddy, but other than giving you a hand, I don't know what."

"I'll be all right. I'm not too excited about doing much climbing, though. It looks like we're going to have to walk out after all. The raft took the plunge over the falls. It could be miles downstream by now or else it got torn to shreds by all the debris caught up in the rocks. I'm not very hopeful one way or another."

After putting out the fire, the four of them got under way. Their first hurdle was to negotiate a path down the side of the falls that very nearly ended their river odyssey in tragedy. The force of the falling water was tremendous. Little could be heard over the thunderous roar created by the urgency of the river struggling to once again find itself on level ground. Neil came close to Lonnie and said, "You know, we probably owe our lives to Blue. There's no way we could have come out of this alive. Check those rocks down below." Lonnie looked down to the bottom of the falls almost a hundred feet below them. In addition to a killing zone of jagged rocks, there was a collection of broken and splintered trees and other debris that had been collecting there for ages.

Lonnie nodded to his friend and replied, "That's for damn sure."

"Blue, yesterday you saved our lives by keeping Lon and me out of this, and I want to thank you. You're OK in my book no matter what anyone else says about you." Neil shook his friend's hand and patted him on the back. Blue swelled with pride as he looked Neil in the eyes. Even Jack came over to him and nodded his approval.

"It's about time somebody recognized me for my contribution," Blue said. "I've got lots of good qualities."

"Don't let it go to your head, Blue. We're just trying to be nice," said Jack who immediately shifted back to an antagonistic attitude towards his friend.

It took some doing and plenty of hard climbing before the four of them were able to get to the bottom of the falls. At times they were reduced to sliding down the embankment on their butts, lest they slip on the wet rocks and tumble over the side. Upon reaching the bottom, they searched the area in an effort to locate any remnants of their raft or provisions but were unsuccessful. Lonnie led as they worked their way along the shore. The going was slow as the ground was rugged and covered with boulders. Many times they were forced to climb up the sides of steep walls that came down to the water's edge. Other times, they had to backtrack in order to find an easier route. During this whole ordeal Jack never complained once even though it was evident he struggled to keep his composure. Onward they trudged as the day passed from early morning to early afternoon and then to late afternoon. There were few rest breaks and little talking among them. On occasion they came upon small impressions in the rocks where water had collected from the previous storms and were able to slacken their thirst; nevertheless, hunger gnawed at them continuously.

Once again, the weary group was forced to spend another night out. This time they were able to move away from the river and seek shelter in the forest. Here Lonnie put his camping skills to good work and built lean-tos for everyone to sleep in. While sitting around the campfire that evening, the boys talked about what they were going to eat when they finally made their way back to civilization. Pizza and greasy cheeseburgers were at the top of the list for everyone. Ultimately, Jack had to threaten to muzzle Blue if he didn't stop fantasizing about various things to eat. Their constant jabbing at each other never went further than that as they had actually become quite good friends over the past few days. Hardship and danger shared by companions have a way of bringing people closer together. Antagonism directed at one another soon disappears, and is replaced by respect, even if it is begrudgingly. In the case of these two, it turned into a lifelong friendship.

"Am I hallucinating from lack of food or is that our raft up ahead caught on that sandbar?" shouted Neil excitedly the following day shortly before noon. Sure enough, less than fifty yards downriver, sat an old yellow raft marooned on the shore of an exposed sandbar in a protected inlet. It turned out to be none the less for wear as it sat face down where it had beached itself some time in the past day or so.

"What a stroke of luck," Jack said. "If we can find some long wooden poles to guide the raft, we can float down the river. I'm pretty sure the worst is behind us. It can't be more than a few miles left to the car anyway."

Within a half hour, the four boys were floating down what had turned into a very wide and easy flowing river. Their morale had picked up considerably as they rested lazily and watched the shoreline passing by. To the great relief of everyone, now that they had the raft back, they wouldn't have to make their way across the river when finally reaching the car. When their troubles began above the falls, they found themselves on the opposite side of the river. No one really spoke about it much over the past couple days, but it was always on Lonnie's mind. Crossing this river without the help of a boat would certainly have been an ordeal, especially for Jack.

"I do believe I see your marker hanging on that tree up ahead Jack," announced Neil. Before they left the area where the car was parked, Jack had tied an orange ribbon to a branch of an overhanging boxwood tree. It was now clearly visible for all to see as the small raft floated along. Simultaneously, the four weary river rafters all let out a shout of joy and triumph as they realized that their trip had finally come to an end, and not a minute too soon. Not a moment was wasted as they pulled up to shore, tied the raft to the top of the car, and got underway for the sixty-mile trip back up river to pick up the other vehicle. Normally this ride would have taken just under an hour, but Blue took the first exit he saw that advertised a restaurant. Over the next two and a half hours, the four fast friends enjoyed one of the finest meals of pizza and greasy cheeseburgers that any of them had ever had. Even an injured Jack insisted on getting a good meal and a couple of beers before heading back to college where he would ultimately seek medical attention

"What do you say we try this trip one more time in the spring when the water is higher?" Blue teased Jack as they made their way back to school. "Now that we have all this experience, it should be a piece of cake."

"Talk to me then," answered Jack before dropping off to sleep.

Chapter Twenty-Three

When they returned back to school after their wild river adventure, Blue and Lonnie each went into a work hype that carried them right through winter and into spring. The two Olympic hopefuls trained like never before with the ultimate goal of qualifying for the Games, which were to commence the following July. In order for any athlete from any country to be eligible for participation in the games, they first must qualify at a meet sponsored by the Amateur Athletic Union (AAU) or its equivalent, depending upon the country they are from. These meets are held around the country starting in early spring. The meet Coach Taggert had chosen was the prestigious Northern Rocky Mountain Track and Field Invitational, held in Boise each May.

"Nice throw, Lon! It appears that the weight training is finally starting to put a little muscle on those scrawny arms of yours!" called out Blue. He was standing well out from where Lonnie had just thrown the javelin. "It looks like you're just a frog hair over 210 feet. It won't break any world records by itself, but when you combine it with the rest of the events in the decathlon, it should be one of your strongest events." Lonnie made a couple more tosses before heading over to the shot put pit.

"Blue, this is still my weakest event. I need to add a good eight or ten feet if I'm going to have a chance at qualifying next month. How do you get the push off so well every time? I'm just not consistent."

"Lon, you just hit it on the head. How many times have I told you over the past few years that when throwing the shot, you must do everything exactly the same from the moment you enter the circle until letting go of the ball. Think about the same thing every time. Do the same thing every time. Keep your focus on the ground or else the sky. Don't look around to see who's watching; just concentrate. When I tuck the ball under my chin and get ready to go into my spin, I imagine that it is covered with spiders, and for me, that gives it that extra little boost to send it flying. Remember, when you toss it, breathe out. Don't hold your breath. Let out a good yell every time and that will help you, but yell the same thing. Take the same number of breaths, spin the same way, spit, and think about spiders. Consistency, my boy, that's what we want. Now, try it one more time."

As Lonnie and Blue worked late into the afternoon, Coach Taggert stopped by while making his rounds and watched from a distance before finally approaching the boys. "How is it going fellas?" asked the coach.

"Not so good, coach," replied Lonnie. "I can't seem to get any distance with this blasted piece of iron. Blue has been helping me with it for years, and it's still my weakest event. Weight training has helped me a ton with the javelin, but it doesn't seem to help much with the shot." Blue stood there and bobbed his head sadly in agreement.

"Why don't you stop by my office later on after you shower, and we can go over some numbers together," said the coach. Lonnie nodded in the affirmative. Over the past few years Coach Taggert had become like a second father to him. They spent many a long hour discussing everything from weather patterns over the Rocky

Mountains to the plight of the spotted owl. Today, however, Coach Taggert had something else on his mind. He had been monitoring Lonnie's progress carefully over the past few months, analyzing his times and distances relative to the competition for this year's spot on the Olympic team. Although the lad was perhaps the finest athlete he ever had the good fortune to coach, and his decathlon scores were incredibly good, it had slowly become evident he still did not quite have the scores that it would take for him to make the team.

"Lonnie, I've been giving this a lot of thought over the past few months, and I've come to the conclusion that if you want to make the Olympic team, we are going to have to change your focus."

"What do you mean, coach? I thought that I was plenty focused."

"Son, I don't mean focus relative to your commitment to track, but rather which event you have the best chance of qualifying in."

"Oh, I see," said a suddenly disappointed Lonnie. "You don't think I can qualify in the decathlon?"

"No, I don't. This year's field is just too strong. You are one of the finest athletes to ever compete in this event, and God knows, you have never even been beat in it, but I just don't feel you can overcome your deficit in the shot put and high hurdles. We have been competing locally here for the past couple years. The top decathletes in the U.S. haven't even participated yet. When they do, come May, I fear we will encounter a whole new level of competition. It's my feeling that your best chance to qualify will be in the 1500-meter and the javelin. If we concentrate on those, I'm confident we can get you a spot on the team. On the other hand, if I let you try for the decathlon and you get edged out, then you're nothing but a spectator for the games, and I don't know if you or I could face that. It's my responsibility to get you into the games. I'm sorry, son. I know how hard you have worked for this and how much it means to you, but you'll see. It will work out. Trust me."

That night Lonnie walked back to his dormitory in a daze. Suddenly his whole world seemed to be falling in around him.

Granted, he was not satisfied with his performance in the shot or the hurdles for that matter, but that was no reason for the coach to give up on him. Not now. Not when everything was so close to becoming a reality. He could make up on his scores in his strong events. After all, isn't that what everyone else does? The more he thought about it, the worse it seemed. Shortly after midnight, after tossing and turning in bed for what seemed like hours, Lonnie made a phone call.

"Hello, Poppy, it's me," said Lonnie in a voice so low that his father almost didn't recognize it.

"Lonnie, is that you? Is everything all right?"

"Yeah, everything's OK, I guess. I'm sorry to call so late, but do you think I could speak to Sara for a little bit?"

"Sure, son." Poppy handed the phone over to Sara who lay by his side. "It's Lonnie. He wants to speak to you."

Sara took the phone and said softly into the mouthpiece, "Hello Lon, are you all right?"

"Yeah, I'm all right. I'm a little mixed up and thought you might be able to give me some advice. Coach Taggert doesn't want me to compete in the decathlon next month at the Olympic trials. If I do, he says my scores aren't good enough to qualify for the Olympics. He wants me to run the 1500-meter and throw the javelin instead. I don't know what to do, but there's one thing I do know. If allowed to compete in the decathlon, I will make it. Somehow, he has lost faith in me. What do you think? What should I do?"

Sara listened to Lonnie for almost an hour. Ever since he was a young boy, and she first tutored him in Algebra, he had the ultimate confidence in her advice, especially when it came to matters of sport. She knew him and his abilities like no other. "Lonnie dear, I've told you this before. You're the best, and you can do anything you set your mind to. If the decathlon is your event and that is where you think you will make your mark, then by all means do it. Coach Taggert is just trying to play it safe. He doesn't want you to be hurt if things don't go right. I know if you set your mind to winning the decathlon at the trials, that is exactly what you will accomplish. Think it over tonight and then tomorrow when your head is clear, make your decision. Perhaps the coach just wants you to reconfirm the fact that nothing will stand in your way of winning next month. Whatever you decide, we will support you on it. Good luck."

Lonnie felt better after speaking with Sara. She always knew just what to say. Maybe this was all about the coach wanting Lonnie to reconfirm in his own mind the decathlon was his event. One way or another, he intended to let the coach know tomorrow he would be competing in the decathlon; and if he didn't make it, well, at least he would have given it his all. Sara seemed to think that would be good enough. As a matter of fact, so did he. With this now confirmed in his mind, he rolled over one last time and dropped off to sleep.

The following morning at half past five, Coach Taggert discovered Lonnie out on the track oval working the high hurdles. He watched in bewilderment from his office window for close to two hours as Lonnie moved from the track to the long jump pits, the high jump bar, and finally, over to the shot put area. No one else was around this early on a Sunday morning, especially when it was typically a day off from practice. If it weren't for some class-related work, he too, would not have bothered to show up. Finally, at a little past eight, Coach Taggert made the long walk across the field that separated his office from the track and took a seat on the bleachers directly in front of where Lonnie was working on the shot. Neither of them spoke for several minutes as Lonnie went through his motions again and again. Each time while making the final push off, he would let out a deep growl which seemed to resonate from deep within himself. Coach recognized this as a completely different sound from what he was used to hearing during past workouts and performances. He understood that it was the boy's way of showing his new determination and conviction in himself.

"You seem to be getting more distance today," he said to the young athlete while approaching the pit.

"I'm just past 46 feet for the first time in my life," responded a very determined Lonnie without looking up. "That's an improvement of almost two feet since yesterday."

"Good, because your going to need it, and then some--next month."

Lonnie looked up immediately and locked eyes with his coach and friend. "I can do it coach; all I need is a chance."

"I know you can, lad. I just wanted to be sure you knew the score. Why don't we work a bit on the pole vault? I'd like to see if we can't raise the bar on that one a bit as well." Lonnie smiled as they moved across the infield together with Coach Taggert's arm around his shoulder. They worked together for another good couple of hours before finally taking it inside and watching some old tapes of past performances from Olympic champions. Lonnie knew he had made a major decision and his coach was supporting him in it. He only hoped that he would not let him down.

Chapter Twenty-Four

The next five weeks passed by very quickly for Lonnie and Blue. Each had signed up for a reduced class load this semester so they could devote more of their time to training. While Blue's parents were agreeable with this, it took some persuading by Sara to get Poppy to go along with it. He still wanted his son's main emphasis to be on completing his education and was leery of anything, including the Olympics, which might hinder it. Ultimately, Sara's gentle persuading prevailed. Even though Poppy didn't always show it on the outside, he was tremendously proud of his son's athletic accomplishments. In fact, he was even planning to attend the big meet in Boise with Sara, Maynard, and Blue's folks. Their intent was to drive up all night the evening before so that Poppy wouldn't miss work.

On the Friday they were to depart, Poppy reported to the mine as usual to put in one last day of work before leaving. He intended to take a few days off the following week after the track meet and spend some time with Sara and Lonnie in the mountains of eastern Oregon fishing for rainbow trout. It was to be a week of total relaxation for all of them after the rigors of constant training for Lonnie and almost six months of straight work for Poppy. The devotion to his job and dedication to the miners he showed was admirable to Sara, but there were times when she wished he would take it a bit easier. His response to this was, "When Lonnie is done with college and he is well on his way to becoming an independent person, then perhaps I can slow down and think about taking my pension. In the meantime, though, it's work as usual."

Over the past eight years, Poppy had made a difference in the mine. As safety officer, he was ultimately responsible for the well being of every miner who donned a hard hat and entered the mine. During his tenure in this critical position, serious injuries had declined over thirty-six percent. Fatal mining accidents were reduced to one, that being the 23-year-old Andy Manion who had been crushed while working the long-wall during Poppy's first few months on the job. He had been so shaken up by that mishap that he pushed for, and received, a commitment from management extending the above ground training for every new miner by an extra week. Over the years, this would cost the mine many hundreds of thousands of dollars in lost productivity and wages, but in the final analysis when the incidences of major accidents were reduced, the mine would come out way ahead of the game.

This Friday started out just like any other, with Poppy riding one of the large diesel trucks through the front portal down into the mine. He enjoyed talking with the men on these trips as they descended into the lower bowels where the bulk of the work was being conducted. Poppy was a firm believer that if he was ever going to learn anything about improving mine safety he had better have a good line of communication set up with the men he was supposed to be helping. Once they reached their workstations, conversation became difficult due to the loud noise of the heavy equipment and the protective ear covers they were required to wear. Poppy got out with some of the men at sub-level six and immediately began to make his rounds. Today he was paying particular attention to one of the more remote collapsed locations or "gob" areas directly behind the long-wall machine on that level. He planned to install a digital gas detector, called a canary, for sentimental reasons. It had an automatic alarm set to activate in the event CO_2 or carbon monoxide levels passed the safe threshold. Things were quite noisy. The string of overhanging light bulbs put off an eerie glow. Everything seemed status quo, he thought to himself, while making his way back to the farther recesses of the chamber.

He wiped the sweat from his brow with the hanky he carried in his upper pocket. There are many things about working in a coal mine that one gets used to over time, but one thing Poppy could never get used to was the always present stifling heat. Today it seemed worse than usual. Sweat continued to pour off his forehead, and he could feel it dripping down onto the small of his back. This uncomfortable feeling made him think about the mountains and how great it always was whenever he was at altitude. There is nothing like the fresh air that comes off the upper peaks of the Rockies in late spring, he thought to himself. Suddenly, Poppy froze. His mind had been in a far off place and he had not been paying attention to the warning signs. It was hot in here. Too hot! He immediately checked the dosimeter used to monitor the air and found, after a moment, that the elevation of carbon monoxide in the surrounding area was indeed elevated. This could only mean one thing, and that was bad. Very bad! When higher elevations of carbon monoxide in the mine are present, in addition to being deadly, it is also a sign of combustion. That means fire. Somewhere deep down in all this debris, the heat had become so intense that it had actually ignited the surrounding coal.

Poppy didn't hesitate for a moment. He clicked on the hand-held radio he carried and quickly alerted his level supervisor there was a spontaneous combustion, or a 'spon-com' situation on sublevel six. He instructed that all electrical machinery be shut down immediately. All mine personnel were to evacuate the mine while using their SCBA'S, or self-contained breathing apparatuses. These life-saving devices provide one hour of oxygen to the wearer in the event of emergency situations where the air becomes unbreathable. As soon as this was completed, he retraced his steps back and found, to his dismay, the long-wall operator on this very level continuing to operate as if nothing had changed. Poppy motioned frantically for him to stop. At the same time he instructed the miners in the immediate area to vacate the mine, post-haste. Men from all levels were now streaming in an orderly fashion through the dark tunnels in an attempt to make it to the surface on foot. Most did not bother waiting for a ride, as it would certainly be more expeditious to haul ass rather than waiting around for a lift which might take more time to arrive than anyone was willing to spare. A loud siren and strobe lights were activated to alert anyone who might not be aware of the situation.

Usually in a 'spon-com' situation, an orderly evacuation of the mine is undertaken. It does not necessarily mean there is an impending disaster about to happen, but for safety reasons, all mining operations must come to a stop in the immediate vicinity until a Kennedy Stopping is built. The purpose, once again, is to effectively seal off the combusted area from its' supply of air, thus starving it of the main ingredient it needs to thrive, oxygen. If ample supplies of oxygen are present and there is an abundance of coal dust suspended in the air, this can lead to an explosion. It was for this reason that Poppy acted with such haste. The proximity of the operational long-wall machine in such close quarters to the spon-com area posed a significant danger in his mind and it justified his radical response.

In a coal mine, there is one ingredient when added to a spon-com situation that can exacerbate the event beyond belief. Methane gas! This is the nightmare scenario of every subterranean coal miner. Methane is a colorless, odorless, and highly explosive substance. It forms naturally when plant material decays and there is very little air. Unfortunately, coal mines are a perfect environment for its formation, coal being produced by the compression of plant material over thousands of years.

Finally, the long-wall operator, a fellow named Lucas Padilla, happened to look over in Poppy's direction and realized that something must be amiss. Poppy was making a "cut the throat" motion with his hand in an attempt to communicate his desire for the machine to be shut down. Lucas complied without hesitation, but not before the large cutting machine sheared off a final mass of wall face which exposed an open crevice extending deep into the coal seam. This crack in the earth's structure formed millions of years ago during a period of time when the western United States was prone to higher amounts of geologic activity. Over the eons it had served as a collecting place for the naturally forming methane gas that was produced by the aging coal.

As the third generation Mexican American and long time friend of Poppy's disengaged himself from the heavy piece of machinery and walked over to his old friend, a hissing sound could barely be heard escaping from the wall face where the cutting tool had finally come to a stop. It went unnoticed, not being a common sound in the mine. Poppy explained to Lucas how there were elevated levels of carbon monoxide emanating out of the gob area behind them and how it must be a spon-com. He indicated that the mine was being evacuated as a precaution, at least until they had a chance to get to the bottom of it. Lucas nodded in agreement and wasted no time in moving out. He headed away in one direction towards the surface, while Poppy went off in another to check on whether his message had been received in other parts of the mine and to ensure that it had been complied with.

Fifteen minutes later, satisfied that everyone had vacated the level, Poppy started to retrace his steps back to where he had left Lucas. Lucas, on the other hand, realizing he had forgotten his lunch pail had returned to his workstation to retrieve it. The two unsuspecting friends entered the chamber from opposite sides almost simultaneously. It was dead quiet in the mine, a sound not very often heard at this time of day. When Poppy detected Lucas on the other side of the chamber moving towards his lunch pail on a makeshift table, he hollered at him to get the hell out of there. Lucas looked up and answered, "Sorry boss, forgot my lunch bucket." In the next instant a very powerful explosion ripped through the mine. The concussion of the detonation was mind-boggling. Tons of overburden collapsed down into the once large chamber and covered the entire area in rocky debris while filling the air with a fine dust. The entire mine was thrust into chaos and darkness. Men from every level suddenly found themselves disoriented and afraid and on sublevel six, there was silence.

Chapter Twenty-Five

Early Friday morning, Coach Taggert departed via bus with the entire boys and girls track teams for the long trip to Boise, Idaho, where the Northern Rocky Mountain Track and Field Invitational was held each year. It was a two-day event, which commenced on Saturday morning at 10:00 and ran through Sunday until 5:00 pm, concluding with the finish of the men's marathon. This prestigious track meet, sanctioned by the AAU, was also open to unaffiliated individuals who were attempting to qualify for the Olympic team. Once every four years the list of invited teams was supplemented by a number of elite athletes who were past their college years and needed a forum in which to compete. These elite athletes always raised the competition level to new heights not normally seen throughout the earlier season meets. The coach had been preparing his team for many months to meet this challenge. For some seniors it would be the last track meet of their careers, but for a lucky few it could become their opportunity to move on to the most famous and sought after track meet of all, the Olympic Games.

The Song In His Heart

Lonnie had high hopes that Saturday morning as he sat in the infield stretching. Looking around in the spectator stands, he tried to spot the Silvertown contingent but as of yet, they were nowhere in sight. It was still early, though, and there was plenty of time before things got underway. He could see all around young men and women competitors not only from the Western states, but from throughout the United States at large. There were some he recognized from earlier competitions in his career and others he recognized from photographs. This was indeed a Who's Who of the track and field community. While conversing with Blue about the perfect weather they were having, an old acquaintance walked up in blue jeans and reintroduced himself. "Hello, Lonnie. Do you remember me? I'm Sam Costa. We raced eight years ago in the Colorado state meet."

Lonnie blurted out, "You bet I remember you, Sam! How the hell are ya? Gosh, it's good to run into you here."

"Well, it's no accident. I've been following your career since high school. I knew you'd do well, Lon. There was a hunger in your eyes back then, and I can see it's still there."

"Sam, I owe a lot to you. Probably more than you realize. That day back then was a real scary experience for me, and you made it a little bit easier by being nice. Heck, I was just a kid, but watching you float around that track was an inspiration. I never forgot how easy you made it look. Did you continue on after high school?"

"I wanted to, but I broke my leg in a skiing accident and was never able to make it back after that. Perhaps it was never meant to be. Today, I can say I beat Lonnie Burch in the half mile and he never beat me back." They all laughed for a moment before he went on. "Lonnie, I would like you to meet a friend of mine who was an inspiration to me when I was a freshman in high school." He nodded over to the well-dressed man who had approached with him. "This is Mike Dorazil. Maybe you've heard of him."

"Good God, Mike Dorazil! Yeah, I've heard of you. Who hasn't? You were the greatest cross-country star in the whole country for awhile, and before you, it was your two brothers. Gee, I'm real pleased to meet you."

"The pleasure is all mine, Lonnie. I, too, have been following your career over the years. You have made quite a name for yourself. When Sam told me he had raced against you once upon a time and the two of you were acquaintances, I asked if he would introduce us. I just want to wish you good luck. The decathlon field is strong this year. Give it your all and don't hold back a bit. Take one event at a time, and don't even think about the next one until you're finished with the first one. We'll be rooting for you."

After a bit more small talk Sam and Mike moved on, but not before Sam added, "Oh, by the way, are you aware that one of our old nemeses is competing against you in the decathlon?"

"Who would that be," Lonnie asked?

"Brian Pellitier. He's been competing in California since he moved there after high school. I understand he's been working hard to make the Olympic team in the decathlon. This is his last hurrah I'm told. Maybe a bit of payback is in order. The guy never was quite right. Well, good luck again."

If Lonnie didn't show it while speaking to Sam, it was hard to conceal now from Blue. "Brian Pellitier, that son of a bitch. Our paths have finally crossed once again, after all these years." He stared off into space with a faraway look in his eyes as if he were reliving something from the past.

"Who is Brian Pellitier," questioned Blue?

"He's the dude who cut me off in the state meet our freshman year and caused me to trip. I've never forgotten that guy. Afterwards, I saw him laughing about it with some teammates."

"Now I remember," said Blue. "Well, this is good news. If you ever needed an extra push in the motivation department, this is certainly it."

"Yes sir. It certainly is. Say, I wonder where the folks are at?" Lonnie said, changing the subject.

At 11:15 am Lonnie was on the line for the 100-meter sprint, the first event of ten in the grueling two-day decathlon. He had given up searching for Poppy and Sara in the stands almost an hour earlier so that he could concentrate on the task that lay ahead. Lonnie was confident they would be somewhere out there watching, but with over ten thousand people in attendance, it was better not to concern himself with trying to pick them out. After all, Poppy had told him just two days ago they would be there come hell or high water.

Pellitier was not in this particular heat. With over thirty entrants in the decathlon, it was not possible to line everyone up together for each event. For the 100-meter, there would be five heats. Runners would be competing against the clock. Because of the complicated point system awarded for each event, it is difficult to tell which athlete is actually in the lead until the final times and distances are tabulated. There are six field events and four running events in the decathlon. Each field event has a designated number of points that are awarded for every inch attained by the contestant's effort. In the running events, points are awarded at time intervals, the lower the time the higher the point total. This point system is universal from meet to meet. In order for Lonnie to be assured of qualifying for the US Olympic team, he must post one of the top three scores registered in a sanctioned meet in the entire country. Due to the fact that this was the last sanctioned track and field event in the US where the decathlon was being held prior to the Games, there would be a definitive answer as to whether Lonnie would qualify by the end of the day on Sunday. The third highest score attained so far this year in the USA was 8350. If Lonnie topped that and placed first in this meet, he would be on the team. If he did not surpass that score, his collegiate track career would come to an end tomorrow. Placing anywhere less than first here would also complicate matters unless at meets end, his final score was in the top three nationally. Coach Taggert made it simple--win this meet with a score of 8351 or better and mission accomplished.

Lonnie had long since stopped being nervous prior to a race. While the official held up the starting pistol, Lonnie was a picture of perfect concentration. He focused on the finish line 100 meters down the track. As had become his usual custom prior to race start, he held the elk tooth talisman given to him by his father so many years before between his front teeth until the gun went off. When it did, he exploded out of the starting blocks like a finely tuned machine. In exactly 10.84 seconds Lonnie crossed the finish line in first place. His score for this was 897 points, a brilliant start. He continued running around the track as he slowed his pace to a walk. Looking around he still could not spot any familiar faces in the crowd. After returning to the finish line and registering with the race officials, he shrugged his shoulders a bit and jogged over to the long jump pit where he would prepare for his next event.

While awaiting his first jump attempt, he watched the next few heats of the 100-meter. In the third heat he saw Pellitier cross the line in first place. The loudspeaker shortly thereafter confirmed his winning time at 10.95. "Ha, I got you on that one," he thought to himself. In the fourth and fifth heats, however, the times reported were faster than his own. Lonnie turned his attention away from this and tried to focus on the long jump. He had learned from earlier competitions not to get caught up in the point games. The strategy here was to do the best he could on each event and not to get distracted by what everybody else was doing. This was one of his best events. On a good day he could clear 23 feet.

Lonnie took the two practice jumps that were allotted to him. He stepped off the distance from where he would start his run to where he would actually go airborne to make sure of his footing and stride interval. There is a board just before the sand pit that serves as a launching platform. Jumpers are not allowed to cross the plain of the far side of the board nearest the pit or it is considered a scratch jump and does not count. In order to maximize on distance, it is desirable to jump from as close to this edge as possible, because that's where the measurement starts. To jump too soon is to lose distance. Each participant is allowed four attempts.

Lonnie approached the pit at full sprint and went airborne with less than an inch to spare. When he landed in the sand, he made sure to let his momentum carry him forward so as not to make any impression in the sand behind where he first landed. The measurement is marked from the closest impression in the sand to the edge of the board. His first jump cleared 22'10"--- not bad for a first attempt. Unfortunately, his next two jumps were a scratch. After waiting his turn for what seemed an eternity, he made his final attempt. As luck would have it, Lonnie did everything picture perfect and scored his greatest jump distance ever at 23'6". This gave him a score of 852 points. He was beside himself with joy. Every athlete wants to perform his very best on competition day, and today he was off to a rousing start.

Once again, Lonnie looked long and hard in the stands for his people before finally spotting Blue talking to his folks and Maynard down near the edge of the infield. This was somewhat strange since the infield was an off limits area for spectators. As Lonnie made his way over to them, he realized that Coach Taggert was also standing there. They seemed to be listening to Maynard who was speaking with his hands in his pockets. "Hullo, Maynard," he called out as he got nearer. "Where have you guys been? Did you see that last jump of mine? Where's Poppy and Sara? I haven't been able to spot where you're sitting." Before he could detect anything was wrong, Maynard walked him off to a side with his arm over his shoulder while the rest of them remained behind.

"Lonnie, your father and Sara aren't here yet. There's been an accident in the mine, an explosion. It happened yesterday at about 4:00 in the afternoon. As of last night at 10 pm, they were unable to get Poppy out, so Sara asked me to come up here with Blue's folks to reassure you that everything is gonna be all right. He was down on one of the lower levels. I don't really know much else other than as quick as they get him out, he and Sara will be high tailing it up here to see you win this thing. The brass at the mine said they would fly them up in the company plane. Can't get much better service than that now, can you?"

Lonnie was dumb struck. He didn't know what to say, but at the same time had a million questions, none of which he was able to articulate. Maynard put a reassuring hand on his shoulder and said, "They're doing everything humanly possible to get them out, Lon. A total of eight men are unaccounted for. As quick as they can get through the rubble blocking the shaft, rescuers can get in there and haul them out. There's no reason to think the worst; your old man is as tough as nails. He'll be here by late today or early tomorrow at the latest. Sara said she would give me a call as soon as something came up. She and some of the other women folk are keeping a vigil at the mine."

"What am I supposed to do now?" asked Lonnie. "How can I go on as if nothing has happened?"

Coach Taggert approached the two of them from behind and took the liberty of answering for Maynard. "You must continue on, Lonnie. These meets don't stop for any reason or anybody. Your parents would be devastated if you dropped out now after all your work and training. I truly believe this. Try to tuck it away in your mind for the next few hours or so, and use it as fuel. Later, when they arrive, you'll be happy that you did, and so will they."

Lonnie nodded in agreement. "You're right, coach. Let's get this thing done." Before moving on to his next event, the shot put, Lonnie exchanged greetings with Blue's parents who both wished him well. Blue then walked with his friend as they moved on.

Knute Bleuson made the comment, "Poor Lonnie. I hope this doesn't take him out of his game today. He's going to need everything he's got to do well, I'm told."

Maynard replied simply, "It's this type of thing that brings the best out in the boy. He'll do his best, of that I am sure." The three of them slowly walked back up to the stands where they planned to spend a long afternoon watching the meet and shuttling back and forth to the telephone in order to keep abreast of the situation back in Silvertown.

Lonnie stood in the circle getting ready to make his fourth and final put, the shot tucked tightly under his chin. His first throw had only cleared 43', a far cry from where he had hoped to place it. Unfortunately, his second attempt was a scratch. After lofting the

16-pound metal ball, the momentum from his circular rotation had carried him outside of the throwing circle. If he were going to have any chance of succeeding here today, he would have to score big on this, his final throw. Lonnie bit down on his talisman as he tried to think of spiders or anything else which might give him a few extra inches. With all his might, he pushed off one last time. The shot flew through the air and landed with a thump. Lonnie looked on in disappointment as the measurer called out his distance, 44' 3"; certainly not his best throw, and only good enough for 697 points. He walked away from the pits, oblivious to his surroundings. His anger with himself was apparent as he kicked at the ground. For no reason other than frustration he started running and made two complete laps around the inside of the track at close to race pace before finally slowing to a stop. His pounding heart made him feel better and relieved some of the anxiety he was feeling.

Early in the afternoon, Lonnie reported to the high jump pit where he would compete in his third and final field event of the day. This was a critical stage for him. If he did poorly here, he could pretty much kiss any hopes of qualifying for the Olympic games good-bye. On the other hand, if he did well, his chances would still be alive. In the decathlon, every athlete has his strong events and his weaker ones, but when competing at this level, having more than one low score will most certainly eliminate you from the winner's circle.

Lonnie passed on all jump attempts until the bar reached 6 feet. It was his prerogative to enter the competition at any level but once he started, he must clear each height before moving on to the next one. Three consecutive misses in a row and he would be eliminated. If he failed to clear the six-foot level, his score would be zero and his season would be over. In effect, Lonnie was going for broke. He rationalized to himself anything less than six feet would eliminate him anyway. After one final glance toward the stands, he started his approach to the bar. Lonnie concentrated on putting as much spring in his step as possible. When he reached his take off point, he leapt up as vertical as he could with all the elasticity in his legs, and went head first with his back to the ground over the horizontal bar in a style that has become known as the Fosbury Flop. Once his head and torso cleared the bar, he kicked his feet up and cleared the level with inches to spare. Immediately upon landing in the foam rubber pit, he did a backward summersault and hopped to his feet making a pumping fist motion in the air above his head. Many times over the previous few months he had cleared this height, but to do it now was a real psychological boost for him. On his next two attempts he cleared 6'2" and 6'4" respectively. By the time he finished with the event, Lonnie had cleared 6'8", tying his best ever, and had accumulated 831 points. He wasn't on a winning pace yet, but Lonnie had already participated in his worst event, the shot put, and by all estimates was still alive. His final competition of the day would be a running event, the 400-meter. If he did well here, and it was quite possible considering his previous times, by days end, he would be right back in the thick of it going into day two.

When the announcer called off Brian Pellitier's name and he stepped up to the starting line, Lonnie came into contact with him for the first time. The two young men simply ignored each other as they prepared to run the final race of the day. Sometimes in sport, great competitors are antagonistic towards one another. This is unfortunate as one would naturally think the love and desire each showed for their chosen field would actually give them something in common, and they would show a mutual respect for one another. This was certainly not the case here. It was evident there was a deep dislike between the two. When the starting pistol sounded, the group of six in heat #3 blasted out of their blocks and sprinted for all they were worth once around the 400-meter track.

Pellitier won the race with a time of 49.28. Lonnie came in third with a time of 49.54, not good enough to place him first in the individual event, but nevertheless the best performance of his life by .2 seconds, and good enough for 836 points. It was a good race and even though he lost to Pellitier, he was happy for the point total, picking up more than he had counted on in this event.

Tomorrow, he thought, would be a different story, with his two strongest events to come. "This is not over by a long shot," he said to himself while walking over to his team's congregation area, not bothering to acknowledge the winner of the race, but making every effort to congratulate every other contestant.

That evening before breaking with the team to be with Maynard, Coach Taggert and Lonnie went over his scores for the day. After five events he had a total of 4113 points and stood in third place. Pellitier, currently in first place, had 4195 points, and a twenty-eight-year-old named Ted Deery from Tucson, Arizona, was in second with a score of 4160.

"Lon, you're projecting out at 8226. This is 126 points below qualification cutoff. You're also sitting here today in third place. Tomorrow you have three solid events to make it up on, and if you don't lose too much ground on the 110-meter high hurdles, perhaps we can pull this one out. It's imperative though, that you get a good night's rest tonight. Do you understand?"

"Yes sir, I do. Tomorrow is going to be a big day. Is it okay with you if I stay with Maynard tonight? He's like family to me."

"Sure son. Try not to worry too much. Everything will turn out just fine, you'll see."

Chapter Twenty-Six

Early that evening Sara called and spoke with Lonnie. There wasn't much to report about Poppy, but some good news did come out of the mine. Four of the missing miners were rescued, and except for a few abrasions and some rattled nerves, they were alright. The information they were able to provide along with what had already been learned is that there was an explosion somewhere on sub-level six. This was due to a spon-com situation that Poppy himself had reported. In an attempt to make sure everyone had been warned and were evacuating, he stayed behind. The last report had him moving away from the area where they figured the explosion occurred. It had collapsed the main portal leading into this area, and until they were able to clear it out, there would be nothing new to report. Men were working around the clock in an effort to accomplish this. Considerable headway was being made and they were confident on breaking through at any time.

As the conversation progressed, Maynard realized Lonnie seemed to be the one offering the words of encouragement. He was proud of the boy and how he had grown to be so strong both physically and emotionally. Sara, understandably so, was drained. She had not slept nor left the mine since arriving there the day before. Many of the wives were there to support her and the other women whose husbands were also missing. Each knew it could easily have been their own husband trapped. They also knew as well as every other worker in the mine, both below ground and above, what a difference Poppy Burch had made in mine safety.

"Just as quick as we get word, I'll be on the phone to Maynard; and if at all possible, we'll be there tomorrow, Lon. Good luck. Remember, we're both so very proud of you." Sara said good-bye and Lonnie could tell she was crying. This in turn, created a lump in his own throat. For the rest of the evening the two of them did very little talking as Lonnie feigned fatigue and pretended to sleep. Maynard knew the boy lay awake for most of the night but respected his private thoughts and kept to himself as well.

There was no way of telling how long he lay there when he finally awakened, but Poppy knew it must have been some time for the entire area was covered with a fine dust and the air had cleared somewhat. He was in a complete darkness, one that humans are rarely subjected to. There were rocks and boulders strewn about everywhere, he could tell, even though he had not yet been able to illuminate the area with his flashlight. While trying to sit up he realized he had been lying on his back. Almost instantly he determined his body was not right. Taking stock of himself, he became acutely aware of a severe pain in his left shoulder and arm. Indeed, they had been crushed under a large rock of coal that still sat atop of him. In addition to this, he could feel a pain deep in his chest and side where he obviously had a number of broken ribs. Poppy used his right hand and located the spare flashlight that hung from his belt. The thin beam of light revealed the chaos of the once open chamber. With a Herculean effort and considerable pain, he managed to push the large chunk of coal off his body and to sit himself up. By the looks of the area around him, he was thankful he had survived the blast. If not for the hearing protection he always wore, his eardrums would certainly have been blown out. His movement and exertion caused him to cough, which sent paroxysms of pain throughout his body. Reaching for his self-contained breathing apparatus, he was able to provide himself with fresh air. After a few moments, he felt better and switched it off. The SCBA held a limited supply of oxygen. It wouldn't last for much more than an hour, so he tried to be conservative.

Poppy tried to remain calm and to conserve his energies. He knew at this very moment men were working furiously in an attempt to reach him. Thinking back, he tried to piece together what had transpired immediately before the explosion. After some time, he recalled shouting at Lucas to get out. This was the last thing he could remember. What had happened to his old friend? Was he killed in the explosion? Poppy shined his light over in the direction where he had last seen the man. Removing his earplugs, he called out and tried to listen intently for a response. There was only silence, accentuated by the occasional sound of falling pebbles. With a great deal of pain, Poppy made his way across the littered chamber over piles of jagged rock and boulders to where he hoped to find Lucas. Using his light, he methodically covered the ground but could not find any trace of the man. Exhausted, Poppy sat down and waited for what seemed like an eternity. He focused all his senses on listening for the sounds of heavy machinery digging and men's voices.

At first it was almost too faint to hear, but after a moment, it became more pronounced. There was a whimpering sound coming from off to his left. Immediately, Poppy returned to his feet and tried to locate the source. When he isolated the spot, he started moving rock the best he could. Eventually, a man's trousers became visible. Poppy redoubled his efforts and soon was able to clear the debris from the man's upper body. He lay face down. It was Lucas, and he was alive! The force of the blast had completely buried the wretched man. Poppy put himself through great physical pain and exertion in digging his friend out, eventually succeeding. Lucas was semiconscious and delirious from pain and dehydration. It soon became evident that both his legs were broken. Poppy tried as best he could to administer to the man, but unless help arrived soon, there would be no saving him.

Even if rescuers were able to break through, it might take additional hours to locate them and get proper medical attention. By that time it would almost be a certainty poor Lucas would expire. He thought of the new daughter his friend had been bragging about just last month and pitied the man. With no thought for his own self, the broken and severely injured Poppy hoisted the moaning Lucas up onto his good shoulder and began to walk, and to climb, and sometimes to crawl his way through the mine in an attempt to position themselves where they would best be discovered. There was no telling how long he labored at this task. Sweat streamed down his face and covered his body mixing with the blood that oozed from open wounds he was scarcely even aware of. Thirst gnawed at his stamina and will power, but still, Poppy moved on ever so slowly through the debris-choked chamber until he came to the portal leading out of the big room. When he realized it was still intact, a small feeling of relief came over him and heartened his resolve. This did not last long however, for within a few short yards, they encountered a collapsed tunnel choked to the ceiling with tons of overburdened coal that had fallen as a result of the explosion and now completely blocked their only way of escape.

Poppy backed away a few feet from the blockage and slowly lowered Lucas to the ground. He was not doing well, but had at least regained his senses and was now able to converse with Poppy. The poor man was in a great deal of pain. Realizing there was no going forward anymore, Poppy also lowered himself to the littered floor of the tunnel. He backed himself up to a wall and positioned Lucas so he could rest his head in his lap. As they sat there together deep inside the mine, Poppy explained to Lucas help was on the way. Occasionally, he would be wracked with fits of coughing that put him on the verge of unconsciousness. During these bouts Poppy insisted he breathe the oxygen in his SCBA. When Lucas had consumed all the air in his own, Poppy gave him his. In this manner the two men spent the next few hours totally alone, in constant pain, and with what little hope they had slowly dwindling away.

Poppy reassured his friend everything would turn out fine and tried to keep him from worrying. After awhile though, conversation ceased. Each was so far gone he had retreated into his own world of thoughts where more pleasant memories abounded. Poppy sat in the total darkness and envisioned scenes from his earlier life. He recalled the plump face of his Auntie Rose tucking him in each night and kissing his forehead before going to sleep, and how he came to love her after the death of his parents. Her affection for him was genuine. Even as a small boy, he realized this. Growing up on her small ranch outside of town with the ability to ride horses up into the mountains was everything a boy could ask for. He recalled the many hunting and fishing trips taken with his friend and idol, Maynard. Anjuli flashed into his thoughts and a tear came into his eye. What a shame that she was robbed of her life and the joy of watching her son grow into the fine young man he had become. What might have happened if she hadn't died? How might things have turned out? What about Sara? Oh, how he loved her. She must be in an awful state now. Poppy wished he could hold her and reassure her everything would be alright.

Lonnie, he thought! What pride he had in the boy. All his life, Lonnie had strived to please him, to make his father proud. Even though the boy had very definite hopes and goals of his own, he altered them so they would be more readily accepted by him, his father. If only he had told Lonnie that he loved him. What was he doing at this very second? Perhaps winning his decathlon and going on to the Olympics. He had tried so hard for this. Poppy regretted he might not have let Lonnie know how proud he was of him for his track and everything he had accomplished in it. He had been so stubborn about him getting an education. How he wished he could be there to see him perform.

Poppy coughed once again in the stifling heat. The pain in his chest had become so acute he hardly felt the jagged edges of his shattered rib scraping against his internal organs. He stroked Lucas' head and told him it wouldn't be long now. All the poor man could do in the darkness to answer was to feebly squeeze his arm. Then, as if in a dream, Poppy recognized the sound of men's voices. They were calling out his name. The sound seemed to be coming from inside the blocked tunnel. He tried to answer, but it was just too painful to shout. Soon, the sound of digging became apparent, and then that of falling rock.

"We've broken through," someone called out. Poppy could feel a small breeze blowing in his face. The smothering stagnant air he had been breathing became less so as the sound of struggling men came closer. Poppy turned on his flashlight and tried to signal the rescuers. He could see where they had broken through the wall of rubble. Three men had already crawled through the small tunnel by the time his light was spotted. "Ho, there! We're here to take you out," one man called out as he made his way over to them. Another shouted back through the tunnel, "We have survivors!"

Poppy could hear a muffled cheer emanating from the blocked portal. "Please, help Lucas. His legs are all busted up." One man immediately came forward with water and gave Poppy a drink. With a bit of coaxing, they were able to get Lucas to take some as well. Without a minute passing, another man approached with a stretcher. He tried to get Poppy onto it, but the courageous man would have none of it until Lucas was first safely out. "You're goin home, Lucas. Hang on, Buddy."

"Thanks, Poppy. I'm sorry I was such a drag on you," he whispered.

The three rescuers were able to get Lucas onto the stretcher and somewhat stabilized before moving him over to the freshly dug tunnel. They worked in conjunction with each other as they carefully moved the critically injured man slowly through the small opening, one man backing out with the stretcher, and the other two men bringing up the rear. "Hang on, Poppy, we'll be back for you in a jiffy," called out one man over his shoulder.

"Take your time," he replied. "Make sure you get old Lucas out. He's got a new little girl back home waiting on him." With that said, Poppy took a deep breath and tried to lean back once again against the wall. He was proud of the men for the way they had got in here to rescue them. They were good men, some of them just boys. Poppy thought to himself, "I did make a difference – here, in the mine, didn't I?" He wasn't sure if he had or not, but at this point was just happy that Lucas was on his way out.

Poppy could feel the cool mountain air blowing in his face as he put his head back and closed his eyes. He was proud that young Lonnie had shot the wounded elk rather than Old Ivory Tips. He was also happy that he had met Sara and married her. They had had a good life together. The snows would be coming early this year, he thought. As the mountain breeze blew in his face, he could see the yellow aspen leaves fluttering in the air and falling to the ground. Poppy thought to himself, "What a beautiful place this is, and what a wonderful world we live in." He made a big sigh, and then breathed no more.

Chapter Twenty-Seven

Sunday morning started out with a driving rain. By the time the second day of the meet got underway at 10:30 am, it had tapered down to a light drizzle and promised to clear completely by midday. Lonnie was practicing his start off the blocks just prior to the 110-meter high hurdles. He didn't mind the wet so much; in fact, he rather enjoyed it. First thing that morning he and Maynard had called Sara to see if there was any news concerning Poppy. There wasn't. Sara had spent the entire night at the mine with many other people from Silvertown and the surrounding areas. Whenever a calamity such as this occurred in small towns across America, it brought folks together as a sign of support for one another. Lonnie was nervous today, not so much because of the race or what lay ahead for the day, but rather the absence of any news concerning his father. Surely they must have found something out by now. He strolled back and forth as the loudspeaker announced his name for the upcoming race.

The 110-meter high hurdles wasn't one of his best events, but with his long legs and natural speed he hoped to score well nevertheless. The race was a complete sprint. In order to do well, one must barely clear each obstacle without jumping too high into the air. The elite runners in this event barely jump at all, but rather clear the 42-inch hurdle with an elongated stride. It doesn't matter if the hurdle is knocked over, just so long as the runner goes over it. Prior to the report of the starter's gun, Lonnie, anticipating a fast start, left the blocks early. All runners were called back to the line and Lonnie was credited with a false start. One more and he would be disqualified from the race and would post a score of zero for the event.

As the contestants stood at the line for the next start, the tension was enhanced. A bad start could cost two tenths of a second, and this was unacceptable. Lonnie timed it perfectly this time. With just the right amount of anticipation he charged out of the blocks like a hungry cheetah on the chase. In less than 15 seconds he crossed the finish line in first place. The official time was 14.94. This was huge for Lonnie. Coach Taggert ran out onto the track and hugged the boy. He had just run the fastest time of his life in this race by three tenths of a second. The total points awarded were 857. Lonnie had started the day out like a champion. This was a race that he badly needed. He and his coach both knew in order to win this thing, he must break 15 seconds, something he had never done before.

After the shot put, the discus was Lonnie's weakest event. He had been throwing it with Blue for years and could place in the top three in most meets on any given day. Today, however, the competition was keen. Not only was he competing with athletes at this particular meet, he must also score well against previous competitors to rank in the top three decathletes for the entire country. While waiting his turn in the throwing circle, Lonnie stood off to a side with his elk tooth talisman gripped between his front teeth. He searched the stands for Maynard and realized he was not in his seat. Perhaps he had found something out. The Bleusons were there and waved to him when they caught eyes.

Lonnie waved in return before refocusing his attention on the discus throw.

He was heartened when the sun peaked out from behind a cloud. There is nothing worse than throwing a wet discus. When trying to get the maximum performance, any little slippage can cause a substantial reduction in distance. The technique adopted by most discus throwers is to complete a full spin before flinging the 4 lb 6 ½ oz disc with a sidearm motion out into the field where it is measured from the point of first contact with the ground. Lonnie slipped on his first attempt and thus was credited with a scratch when his body left the circle. On his next try, he did better with a toss of 155 feet even. His following attempts did not enable him to improve upon this, so his final score for the event totaled 814 points---not great, but still in the running.

The field events were tough on Lonnie's mind today as they gave him too much time to think about what might be happening back in Silvertown. He moved on to the pole vault and knocked the bar down on his first two attempts. Coach Taggert came over and chewed him out for not concentrating enough on his approach. In the pole vault, it is imperative that the jumper's body be in exactly the right position when the far end of the pole is thrust into the metal box embedded in the ground at the end of the runway. At this point, the jumper's forward momentum causes the fiberglass pole to bend, thus creating the thrust upward when it straightens itself. Lonnie was not positioning his body in the proper manner to maximize on the upward thrust of the pole. Therefore he was hitting the horizontal bar on the way up, which was set at a mere 14 feet.

Finally on his last attempt at this beginning height, Lonnie got it together and cleared the bar with ease. He was ultimately able to vault 15'6" before finally fouling out. His disappointment was evident with this performance. Just last week he had been clearing 16 feet with relative ease. Where he had been able to capitalize on a superb performance in the hurdles, he now was forced to give back in the pole vault. His points for the event totaled 825.

The pressure was beginning to mount for Lonnie as he prepared to compete in his final two events. He had pulled into second place after eight, but Brian Pellitier held a slight lead of twelve points. More importantly though, if he intended to move on after this meet, he must register a combined total of 1742 points in the last two remaining events, while at the same time beating Pellitier. He could beat the point total if everything went as well as it possibly could. In other words, if he performed better than he had ever done before. Would this be good enough to beat Pellitier? Lonnie did not know. He walked slowly over to the javelin area with an increasing burden upon his shoulders. Where was Poppy? Why no word? What happened to Maynard?

The javelin throw had always been one of Lonnie's favorite events. Even though Blue could handily beat him in the discus and shot, the javelin belonged to Lonnie. Earlier in his high school years, this event was deemed too dangerous and therefore not included as part of the regular track and field program. On his sixteenth birthday, however, Sara had given Lonnie a javelin as a present. Even though he never competed in the event until college, there had been quite a bit of practice going on in his back yard prior to it. Coach Trapp had given him a few basic pointers on how to throw the spear-like object, maximizing on distance. Lonnie was confident he would do well here. Secretly he hoped Pellitier would throw just before him, or at least be on hand to witness the thrashing he planned to give him in the event.

For the first time all day, Lonnie smiled when he realized his vindictive wish had come true. Pellitier would throw just before him in this very critical event. He had grown over the years into a very solid six-foot man, weighing in at 190 lbs. While waiting his turn, he stood off to one side by himself and watched the other decathletes throw. Lonnie also stood off to a side, but directly opposite him, and stared at the man intently. Eventually Pellitier looked over at him and they locked eyes for a moment. There was tension in the air. Each had exactly the same goals by competing in this track meet--- qualifying for the U.S. Olympic team. Based upon the scores already registered around the country so far this year and considering where each of their scores presently were after eight events, there was little chance they would both make it. Pellitier was the first to break off the stare down but only after his name was called out to report.

Even Lonnie was impressed when he witnessed the first throw. With a distance of 224 feet, Pellitier placed himself firmly in first place for the event. Upon hearing the measurement called out, Pellitier looked over at Lonnie with a big smile on his face and made an obscene gesture to him. Inside Lonnie was boiling, but on the outside he remained cool. It was better not to let the arrogant ass know that he rattled him, but rattle him he did. Lonnie's best throw ever was 218 feet, and that was wind aided. Over the next couple throws allotted to him, Pellitier was unable to improve upon this mark. It was a scary moment indeed, however, when on his last attempt, he actually threw the javelin a good 10 feet further. Unfortunately for him, it landed outside the arc and registered a scratch. Lonnie let out a deep sigh of relief as he approached the officials table to check in.

"Two hundred and six feet," the measurement official called out. Lonnie's first attempt did not encourage him. He was upset with himself because he threw too early and did not take advantage of the entire space allotted to him for making the approach. His second throw registered even worse, measuring a good seven feet shorter. On his final attempt, Lonnie hesitated for a moment before starting his approach. He looked over and saw Pellitier and a half dozen other decathletes watching him. Coach Taggert also was there, along with Blue, and some of his own teammates. Looking over to the stands he could now spot Maynard, who once again sat with the Bleusons. Lonnie wondered if there was any news. Surely somebody must know something by now.

Lonnie held the 8' 10 ¼" javelin in his right hand just above his shoulder. He rotated the cord grip in his hand midway up the shaft until it felt just right. Extending his arm straight up and down over his head twice while holding the javelin securely was part of his pre-throw routine. This accomplished, he started down the runway picking up speed as he went along until he was running at a full sprint. Just before he reached the end, 110 feet away, his forward running style changed to a side step motion for the final few steps before he flung the 28 ounce spear with all his might out into the field. Lonnie heeded the advice his coaches had given him over the years---aim high and rotate the shaft slightly as it is being released in an overhand fashion. The spin was always good for a few extra feet if done properly. The javelin flew straight and true. Everyone held their breath collectively as it sailed through the air. When it landed and stuck in the ground tip first, it was obvious this was Lonnie's best throw of the day. The final measurement came after what seemed like an eternity, 222' 6". The attending crowd went into an uproar of applause. It was a bittersweet victory for Lonnie, however. On the one hand, the distance measured 4-½ feet farther than he had ever thrown the javelin before, certainly a throw to be proud of. On the other hand, it was 1-½ feet short of what Brian Pellitier had just done. Lonnie's point total for the event was 826. Pellitier scored 830, increasing his lead over Lonnie to 16 points.

Blue approached his best friend and gave him a huge squeeze around both shoulders with his bear like arm. "Atta-boy, Lon. Way to hang in there tough. It looks like this one is going to come right down to the wire. You can beat him in your best event and take this thing."

"Yeah, his best event, too," replied an emotionally drained Lonnie. They walked together over to the congregating area for his team and accepted congratulations from everyone. Afterwards, Lonnie took the opportunity to lie down and shut his eyes. He had just under an hour before having to report to the track for his final event, the 1500-meter run. This would be the most physically draining contest of the entire two-day meet. Although nothing so far really wore him out, the combination of the preceding nine events carried a heavy toll on his stamina. If he were to have a chance at coming away victorious here, he must beat Pellitier by at least three seconds, and in doing so, run the fastest time he had ever run by two seconds.

Lonnie was confident. He would not allow Pellitier to beat him in this final race, not after taking into consideration what had happened years earlier at the Colorado high school state qualifications. Lonnie had never forgotten the incident and had long since given up any hope of ever being able to race him again. This situation, with the two of them coming head to head once again for the greatest prize of all, seemed to have been devised by some higher being as a way for Lonnie to exact his retribution. He said a small prayer to himself, asking God to give him the strength to prevail over this competitor. "I have come so far to get to this point, Lord, please help me to win." Lonnie continued to lie there shutting the world out for another few minutes until, almost as an afterthought, he said a small prayer for Poppy. He prayed for his father to make it out of the mine safely and still be able to attend his final event. Lonnie wanted Poppy to see him capture the gold medal and qualify for the Olympics in doing so.

When the first call went up for the final event of the decathlon, Lonnie was up and stretching. He jogged around the track a couple times to get his blood pumping. Sam Costa called out good luck as he ran by, and Lonnie flashed him the thumbs up sign. Maynard informed him while passing by there was still no word. Lonnie nodded his head and continued to move around the track. He was completely focused now. Little, if anything, would distract him. With the announcement of the second call, Lonnie began his wind sprints. This would be a fast race and he knew it. Coach Taggert had informed him it would most likely come down to a finish between him and Pellitier. The Deery fellow was expected to start out fast but was not known to be a strong finisher. On coach's advice, Lonnie was to keep pace with Deery, or whoever the frontrunner happened to be, and to set a blistering pace. If no one else took the initiative, then he must be prepared to lead himself. If Lonnie got suckered into running at the slower pack pace, he would never be able to put a distance of at least three seconds between himself and Pellitier by the end of the race. Pellitier was known for finishing strong.

When the gun went up, Lonnie was totally in control of his emotions. He was neither nervous nor excited---just ready. If he ran well here, it would open the door to one of his life long dreams. If he didn't, then it would probably be the last race of his career. Lonnie looked down the starting line from where he stood on the pole. There were twelve runners in this, the fast heat. Pellitier was in lane two. Shortly before the gun went off, he looked over at Lonnie and said, "Try to stay on your feet this time kid, no excuses. I'm goin to whup ya."

Lonnie laughed sardonically, "We'll see ass-hole." Then he turned his attention to what lay immediately ahead of him blocking out everything else. Just prior to the pistol shot, Lonnie felt as if he were frozen in time. Everything seemed to be standing still, and then, BANG! They were off.

The 1500-meter run is approximately 150 yards less than a mile. It is by no means a sprint, but the pace is extremely fast at this level. The pain one feels is intense while running this event, especially after completing the previous nine events of the decathlon in the past twenty-four hours. The race distance is four times around the track. With serious competitors, this breaks down into four separate races. To lose one is to lose them all. This does not mean a runner must be in first place throughout the entire race, but rather, he must form a plan for each lap tailored to his own race strategy and then carry it out. Lonnie's plan was to run the first 3 ½ laps at a one minute pace per lap. If he ran slower, it would open the door for Pellitier to be on his shoulder going into the final lap, and that would be a recipe for defeat. On his final half lap, Lonnie would dig deep and give it everything he had left. As a freshman in college, he had once run a 4:02 in the 1500-meter, but this was when he had only participated in one or two events and trained at that distance specifically. Since his coach switched his emphasis over to competing in the decathlon with his training time spread out over ten events, he had lost some time in the event. In recent years, his best performance was a 4:05. To do that today would be just good enough for him to surpass the third highest overall score in the decathlon, thus achieving his goal of qualifying---but would it be good enough to beat Pellitier?

As expected, Deery shot out like a rabbit, establishing himself in first place going into the first turn. Lonnie fell in close behind as they completed the turns and entered into the straightaway. He concentrated on maintaining his form and keeping his arms and legs in a perfect unison, which he perfected over years of running distance. When they completed the first lap, the official called out their times. Lonnie heard 1:01 as he ran by--perfect! The second lap went by pretty much the same as the first, with Deery leading and Lonnie keeping close contact with him. "2:01," he heard. His second lap timed out at one minute flat---even better! He could hear breathing behind him but was unsure as to who it was. It was not worth it to waste precious energy and break momentum to look behind. This was one of the first fundamentals he had ever learned in track. If you must check, do it on the turns.

Going into the third lap, Deery began to fade, right on cue. Lonnie thought to himself as he blew by, "Thank you sir, you have served me well." He raised his head a bit to keep his windpipe open and took over the lead. Within moments, he heard footsteps coming up along his side. Looking over, he noticed Brian Pellitier had put on a short burst of speed and took the lead going into the far straightaway. Lonnie was perplexed. Should he battle for the first position now or stick to his game plan? At the 2 ½ lap mark where Coach Taggert had positioned himself, Lonnie heard him call out, "Stick to your plan. You're on pace." Lonnie felt relieved. He maintained his one-minute per lap pace and fell in behind Pellitier, who was playing a dangerous game by making an early push in an attempt to draw Lonnie out and exhaust him prior to the final lap. He would then try to out kick him down the final straightaway.

By the time he completed the third lap, the ten-yard gap was slowly narrowing between himself and first place. The timer official called out "2:58." Lonnie was tired, but he kept his focus. In just over a minute, the cards would be played, and nothing would be able to change them. This was now a two-man race. A distance of twenty yards had opened up behind second place. As Lonnie ran by the first turn of the final lap, he heard a familiar voice calling out to him. "Run, Lonnie, Run! You can do it!" In a sudden moment of awareness, he changed his focus from Pellitier's back to the sidelines where he spotted Sara. She was waving her arms and urging him on, like she had done so many times before in the past. Lonnie was elated. He didn't see Poppy right away, things went by too quickly, but surely, he would be there watching as well.

"Thank you, God," he verbally said to himself. "Now the rest is up to me."

With a huge rush of adrenalin brought on by the relief of knowing Sara and Poppy had finally made it and that everything had turned out alright, Lonnie put it into high gear and raced by Pellitier. From that moment on, the distance between the two only grew larger. Lonnie ran like he had never run before. Exhaustion never even entered into it. During the final thirty seconds, Lonnie was in a dream world, beyond pain and discomfort. This is commonly known as the 'runner's high'. Upon crossing the finish line, and looking up to the official time clock, he realized he had just run the fastest 1500-meter race of his life, coming in at 4 minutes flat. A quick glance backward told him that Brian Pellitier was about to take a distant third place behind Deery. When the official times were announced, Lonnie had beaten his arch nemesis by twelve seconds.

Blue, Coach Taggert, and ten other teammates mobbed him as he walked off the track into the infield. "Lonnie, my boy, you have just qualified for the United States Olympic Team. Your point total for the event is 952, which gives you a grand total of 8387. This surpasses the next highest mark of 8350 by 37 points. You are our number three man for the U.S. squad."

"How did Pellitier do?" asked Lonnie.

Coach responded, "His final score is 8319. This places him fifth nationally. His gamble didn't pay off."

"No, it didn't. Good!"

"Congratulations for sticking to your race plan. That's why we make them, son! You sure did hit it on that last lap. For a moment there, I thought perhaps you started a bit too soon. What got into you, anyway?"

"My folks were on the turn. They made it after all. Turns out that was the best boost I could have ever gotten. Pellitier never had a chance after that. Do I have time to run over and see them?"

"Not unless you want to miss the medals ceremony. They're calling the decathletes up now. I'm sure they'll be on hand for that, with cameras too, no doubt." They all started moving over to the center of the infield where the medals were being awarded with much fanfare.

Lonnie turned back and tried to spot Poppy as they moved along, but was unable to catch a glimpse of him in the crowd. He saw Sara talking with Maynard and the Bleusons, but was unsure as to whether Poppy was in the group. "Strange. I'm surprised he wasn't on the turn with Sara," he thought. "Probably telling everyone about the cave in, if I know him. Well, they sure as shootin won't miss this next event."

It ended up taking almost thirty minutes before the officials were ready to present the awards. The top six finishers were singled out to stand on the podium. Ted Deery ended up taking third place and the crowd gave him a warm reception when he took his place on the platform. Brian Pellitier was called up next to receive his second place award. He graciously accepted it and acknowledged the crowd, which was now applauding even louder, for it had been an incredible competition and everyone knew what the stakes were throughout.

"And now for our first place winner and champion," came the announcement, "Lonnie Burch, from Silvertown, Colorado."

Lonnie strutted across the grass and approached the podium with a big grin on his face as the crowd went nuts. Never before in his life had he ever witnessed such an accolade over one of his achievements. While stepping up to the platform, he received handshakes from every competitor. Perhaps the most enjoyable was when Brian Pellitier offered his hand in what appeared to be a sincere congratulatory gesture. While shaking hands he added as an aside, "You were the better man today, Lonnie."

Lonnie was just beaming. He was so proud of himself he could hardly stand it. As he waited for the medal to be placed around his neck, he spotted Sara, Maynard, Blue, and the Coach all standing not fifty feet from the podium, right out in front. How had he missed them? Where was Poppy? This isn't right. He should be here. After all, this was all done for him---to make him proud. Suddenly, Lonnie felt queasy in the pit of his stomach. He locked eyes with Sara and could see she was crying. Looking at Blue, he realized his friend would not even look at him. Maynard was all red in the face and obviously very upset about something. Slowly, Lonnie reached up to his neck where he wore his elk tooth talisman and subconsciously tried to grasp it in his hand. Looking at Sara once again, he recognized a look of pity in her face as she slowly moved her head back and forth in a negative gesture, tears streaming down her face. Lonnie didn't know what this meant. Was Poppy hurt? Worse? Where was the elk tooth talisman? He became very conscious of the fact that the good luck piece was gone and, all of a sudden, he realized that Poppy was gone, too.

Chapter Twenty-Eight

Miners and their families came out from across the state in large numbers to show respect and admiration for one of their own. In saving the life of Lucas, Poppy had proven himself a hero, and the media picked up on it. Family and close friends filled the pews at the local church, people to whom the life of Poppy Burch actually had made a difference.

Maynard and Lonnie sat with Sara in the first pew. She was crushed and had a difficult time maintaining her composure. The poor woman was almost eight months pregnant. Her unborn child would never have the opportunity to meet the man that brought him into the world. If it weren't for the steady support and strong arm of Lonnie, Sara would never have made it through the following days. Lonnie showed great maturity throughout this period. Never once was he seen to shed a tear, although everyone knew of his anguish. Lonnie simply endured. The myriad of thoughts and emotions running through his mind sapped his energy and left him strangely quiet and distant. Although he was pleasant and supportive on the outside, on the inside, Lonnie withdrew into himself.

There is no greater trauma in ones life, other than for a parent to lose a child, than for a child to lose a parent, especially when there is a strong bond between the two. To say that Lonnie was devastated was an understatement. Both of his parents had now been cruelly taken away from him in the prime of their lives. He was utterly and completely lost. Suddenly his whole world was crashing in on him and his purpose in life came into question. He began to examine his own values and the earlier decisions he had made in his younger years. Poppy and his mother Anjuli had always wanted him to graduate from college and find a decent job outside of the mine. Graduation day was less than three weeks away. After that he would finally be finished with his schooling. Now it would be time to find a job and start to work. As much as he hated to contemplate it, the Olympics would not find a place in his future. He just couldn't bear it anymore.

"What do you mean you're not planning on going to the Olympics?" cried Sara. "Is this what you have learned from your father, to come all this way through immeasurable hardships only to stop and quit before accomplishing your goal? He would not agree with this. You would be taking the easy way out. Lonnie, you have made your place and paid your dues. People who you don't even know are proud of what you have done with your life and they are counting on you to represent the rest of us when you compete. I know as a fact that your father was so very proud of you. He was counting on you, as we all are, to go on to the Olympics and to accomplish your goal. Your father wanted this so much for you, Lon. He just had a hard time saying it."

It took almost a week, but Sara was finally able to convince Lonnie to change his mind and to continue training again for his Olympic dream. Coach Taggert supported Sara. He tried to show compassion when he spoke with Lonnie, but ultimately gave the boy the same basic lecture that Sara had, only he added to it a bit about heroes. How some people, by their very nature, are destined to become heroes. They can't help it. "Your father was one of these people," he said, "And some day you will be one as well. It's in your nature. I can see that in you today, Lon."

Lonnie restarted his engines and for the next six weeks preceding the Olympics he trained hard. Each day Blue and he would go through their regular routines. Blue had always good naturedly given his best buddy a hard time concerning the shot-put and his relatively weak throw. After all, his own throw beat Lonnie's, on his best day, by almost twenty feet. Blue realized he was playing an important part in the emotional recovery of his friend. The jesting helped to strengthen their bond. If Lonnie could only manage to pull it together for one last competition, his coaches felt he had a better than even chance to medal in the decathlon.

Lonnie did manage to keep his focus. Over the next several weeks he trained like a man possessed. On more than one occasion Coach Taggert insisted he take it a bit easier, but it was to no avail. The young athlete pushed himself to the limits of his endurance, and then beyond. When his opportunity came to compete in the greatest sporting event of all time, Lonnie performed brilliantly. Although he came in close to dead last in the shot put, he did manage to improve upon his best throw ever at just over 49 feet. It was in the javelin throw, however, where Lonnie finally created the momentum to persevere. He took first in the event with a toss of 232 feet, another personal best. The final event in the two day competition was the 1500-meter run. Prior to the start of the race, Lonnie was in 7th place in the overall standing. His first place finish time of 3:59 01 was enough to raise his final point total to 8485, thereby earning himself a third place bronze medal finish. His coaches, friends, and fans alike, for he had made many over the preceding days, applauded him enthusiastically.

And so it finally came to be. The long journey that the small boy from the mountains of Silvertown, Colorado had set out upon so many years before had finally come to an end. He had reached his dreams and accomplished his goals. As the Star Spangled Banner played for the first place finisher from Illinois, Lonnie stood in awkward silence. Yes, he was proud of himself, and also proud of his buddy Blue who had taken a silver medal in the discus. But still, he couldn't help but feel empty. Throughout his entire life, Lonnie had strived to make his father proud of him. He struggled to earn his father's respect by the only means he mistakenly felt he could, through sport. Now, when everything was said and done, here he stood on the podium, alone. Poppy would never know, at least in this world, of his accomplishment. As the anthem continued to play, Lonnie felt a great lump form in his throat. Before he knew what was happening, tears were streaming down his cheeks. The young man who had come so far finally realized that there was no place else to go, and that the individual he wanted to share it with the most was now gone. Lonnie's head dropped to his chest. Slowly, he went down to one knee, sobbing like the child who had once made a promise not to do so with his father in the mountain blizzard so many years before.

Of course, everyone knew the underlying reason for his tears. The media, always looking for a human interest point of view, had picked up early on Lonnie's loss. In an effort to keep his head clear and his focus intact, Lonnie had refused all requests for interviews upon the recommendation of Coach Taggert. Nevertheless, the dogged tenacity of the press had traveled to his home town and interviewed many locals. The fact that a local boy was going to the Olympics to compete in the decathlon after the tragic loss of his "hero" father was too much of a story to pass up. Every network and newspaper had focused on this unhappy event for the past couple weeks. Even though Lonnie tried to keep himself isolated from the attention, it proved difficult. The stress had been building inside him ever since he and Maynard made the long trip to Olympic Village. With the completion of the decathlon and the medals ceremony underway, Lonnie could just not hold it in any longer. The dam had finally burst. Afterwards, the first place American and the second place Norwegian helped him from the podium with gentle support and kind words.

The watching world ate it up. Even though he placed third and missed the gold, Lonnie had become one of the Olympic favorites

The Song In His Heart

and an instant celebrity. He had overcome the turmoil in his life and come out a winner. Never mind the fact that he had lost his father. When the chips were down, the athlete produced. This is exactly what the crowd wanted. In their rush to congratulate him and to share in his glory, Lonnie found himself even more alone. Perhaps it was modesty or maybe a bit of anger at having his personal life splashed all over the headlines, but shortly after what should have been the biggest and happiest day in his life, Lonnie and Maynard departed from Olympic Village for the long trip home.

Several weeks later as Lonnie sat at the dinner table with Sara and her newborn baby girl, Megan, they discussed his future and what he intended on doing. As luck would have it, the notoriety had followed him home. Lonnie had mixed feelings about this and his instant fame. Nobody from Silvertown had ever won an Olympic medal before. He took great pride in going to see his old coaches, and showing them his bronze medal and thanking them for their time and support in helping him get to this point. When he walked in any public place, people approached him and wanted to hear about how he was doing. Even though their intentions were sincere, it soon began to play on him. People and companies he had never even heard of were coming out of the woodwork and offering him jobs and endorsements. Lonnie had become a commodity, and he wasn't sure about how to handle it.

"I have been doing a lot of thinking lately, Sara. During the last few months of school Coach Taggert pulled a few strings for me, and I was able to get an interview with the Idaho Department of Conservation. Well, last week I received an offer from them to become a ranger. It's only a training position, but it's exactly what I've always wanted to do. It's a pretty good hike from here, but then so was college. If it's okay with you, I think I would like to take it. I'm finding it difficult to be here right now and think that maybe if I got away for a while things might become a bit easier. I guess I need some time to myself; someplace where people won't know me so much."

"Of course it's alright with me, Lonnie. I want you to do anything which makes you feel right. But this is your home. Don't feel that you have to move away because of me. If you need privacy, I could find another place to live."

"Sara, what are you saying? The ranch is as much your home as it is mine. You and Megan more than anyone belong here. Anyways, I won't be moving for good. Just until things settle down a bit. I'll be coming home for vacations and all. Gosh, now that I have a baby sister, you can't get rid of me that easy." They both chuckled as Sara reached over and held Lonnie's hand.

"You have been such a support for me, Lon. I don't know how I could have coped if not for you. But if you're convinced this is what you want to do, you have my blessing. We can get along here fine in your absence. Maynard is always at hand if we need a man's help. Have you accepted the offer?"

"Yes."

"When do they want you to start?"

"Next week."

"Oh, that soon?"

"I think it's better this way. Once I get myself established, I'll be in regular contact with you." Lonnie stared into Sara's blue eyes and thanked her again for all she had done for he and Poppy. She nodded ever so slightly with a tear in her eye and replied, "And thank you, for all that you have done for me. You will never know how much our relationship means to me. When you have found what it is that you are looking for, come home and come home often."

"Of course I will, Sara."

Chapter Twenty-Nine

Six Years Later

Rachel looked out at the twin engine Cessna 421 sitting on the runway and swallowed hard. Flying had never been one of her favorite past times. If it weren't for the fact her best friend was getting married and she was to be the maid of honor, she would never have even considered making the flight in this small private airplane. Even still, it took quite a bit of persuading to talk her into it. Tina and Rachel had met in college at the University of California, Berkeley, where they were roommates, first on campus, and then for the final two years off campus. Tina had gone on after college into advertising, pursuing her goals of a career-minded woman. In the seven years since graduation, she had done quite well for herself, moving up to the position of vice-president in one of the top advertising firms in Spokane. She brought to the table a whole new perspective from the younger generation that the firm's aged management had been quietly seeking in order to realign their image with the fast pace of a changing society. The man she intended to marry, Tom McBride, was ten years her senior. He had started his own business some years earlier designing and installing computer software. Over time, the business had grown into a very lucrative enterprise, making him one of the wealthiest people in Spokane. Tina had met him three years earlier while handling his account. It was his private airplane, or at least one of them, now sitting on the tarmac refueling and getting ready to bring Rachel and her 7-year-old son back to Spokane where the wedding would be taking place in three days.

Rachel had married right out of college to a fellow student from the University. Within seven months she gave birth to a beautiful baby boy, whom she called Rusty, and who now was the pride of her life. After four years, the couple decided to call it quits due to irreconcilable differences. Rusty's father, Don, never wanted to buckle down and go to work after college. He moved from job to job in a never ending quest for that perfect position where he could make lots of money with very little effort. When the marriage finally broke down, Rachel took their son and moved from the Bay Area of California back to her hometown of Salt Lake City, Utah. She had agonized for some time as to whether or not she should move back to her hometown and separate Rusty from his father, but in the end, she figured it was the only way she could get on with her life.

Don had not been a good husband. Over the tenure of their marriage, he had a number of affairs with other women and at times wasn't very discreet about them. The final straw was when she came home early one Sunday morning after spending a long weekend away visiting her parents in Utah with Rusty. She wanted to surprise Don on his birthday by sneaking in and preparing him his favorite breakfast to wake up to. Well, surprise him she did, but not in the way she had intended. Don had been spending the weekend with his best friend's wife at their home, and when Rachel sent Rusty in to check on him, the two were caught in bed together. The poor little boy didn't know what to think. Being only 4-years-old he didn't quite understand what was happening, but from the reaction he got from his father, realized there was something not right. Rachel walked into the bedroom, and rather than confronting an embarrassed and apologetic husband, she was lambasted by a fusillade of verbal abuse and profanity. At that moment, her marriage ended and she never looked back. Even after she moved away, Don never made the slightest attempt to see her or his child. He just didn't seem to care. The responsibility was more than he was willing to deal with. As far as child support, there wasn't any, nor was there any financial assistance of any kind. Don kept the house, all of the furnishings, and most of their personal effects. Rachel kept Rusty.

Upon returning back to Salt Lake, her parents insisted she and her son move back in with them, at least until she was able to get her feet back on the ground. This presented no burden to them as they were quite wealthy anyway and tremendously fond of their only grandson, Rusty, whom they doted upon and spoiled on every occasion. They looked forward to having their only child back once again in their lives.

Rachel got a job working for a local hospital as a laboratory technologist. In college, she had graduated at the top of her class with a major in biology. Shortly thereafter, she had taken a position with the University as a research assistant. When she left California, her boss, a wonderful old pathologist, arranged for her to get a job with one of his past colleagues at Brigham Young University working in the Cytology laboratory. This was a new field for Rachel, but after a one-year training course, she graduated with distinction and now thoroughly enjoyed her new career and profession as a cytotechnologist. Within a year and a half, she was back on her feet and living independently of her parents in her own small home across town.

"We're all gassed up and ready to go," said the pilot Nathan as he walked up to Rachel and Rusty sitting in the lounge area of the private plane section of the airport. "Once I complete the flight plan, we can take off." Nathan was Tom McBride's private pilot. He had learned to fly in the Air Force years earlier. When he finished his stint with the armed forces, he took a position with one of the major airlines and had worked with them for twenty years before finally retiring with a fat pension. As far as qualified pilots went, there were few with more credentials or a higher skill level than Nathan. He was a good-natured fellow who was approaching his 60th birthday. Rusty took an immediate shine to him when the old man let him wear his pilot's hat. He insisted on the boy sitting up front in the co-pilot's seat to help him fly the plane.

"Can I, mom?" pleaded Rusty.

"Are you sure it's safe for the boy to sit up front, Nathan?"

"Why sure it is. He can help me navigate, maybe even help to keep me awake," Nathan said, as he winked at Rachel.

She did not appreciate his humor but kept it to herself for she knew he was one of the best in his profession. Otherwise Tom McBride wouldn't use him. "Ok, young man, but you listen to Nathan and don't touch anything you're not supposed to."

"Ah, come on mom. How can I help fly the plane if I can't touch anything?" Rachael looked at her small boy and smiled.

"Oh, I'm sure you'll find a way."

Shortly after takeoff, Rusty turned around with a set of headphones on and smiled at his mom. This was one of the most exciting events in his life and she was happy she had decided to bring him along. Tina had insisted, especially when Rachel indicated she might leave him at home rather than take him out of school. "He is my godson, and I insist he be present at my wedding and serve as the ring bearer," she said.

Rachel watched out the window as the eight-seat airplane made its way up to a cruising altitude of just 12,000 feet. The turbulence, which is what always made her nervous, was not a factor today. Nathan had said it would be a smooth ride. "At this time of year in late April when the weather is cool, there is very little turbulence if the radar screen is clear," he said. Rachel was thankful for that. It was a clear day. In fact, there wasn't a cloud in the sky. She marveled at the thick forests of pine they were flying over in Idaho. What a beautiful landscape the mountains below made with their thick cover of green. Nathan turned around and spoke to Rachel while the airplane flew under automatic pilot.

"We are heading over the primitive area of Idaho right now," he said. "These mountains are called the Bitterroot, and the forest below is known as the Selway. It's mostly virgin timber, real thick stuff. Down below you would find few roads or signs of human habitat. It's an area where all mechanized machinery, including vehicles or even chain saws, are strictly forbidden. It's about as wild and primitive a place as you'll ever encounter in the lower forty eight. People move around by horseback or by foot, but mostly they stay out, except during hunting season. The land mass is thousands of square miles. Once, when I was a boy, my father took me hunting down there with some of his buddies and their sons. One of the fathers got lost. He wasn't found for three weeks, and when he was, well, there wasn't enough of him left to identify except by dental records and the boots he was wearing. It seems the wolves and bears got him. They never did figure out how he died."

Rachel shuddered and just commented on how awful it was. She liked the outdoors as much as anyone but rarely had the occasion to spend much time in it. During her youth she had learned to ski with her parents outside of Salt Lake, but with the exception of camping once or twice as a Campfire Girl, had never really spent much time in the wild nor at this stage of her life did she intend to.

After awhile and a bit more small talk, Nathan turned his attention back to flying. Rusty soon became either bored or just plain worn out and moved into one of the empty seats back next to his mom. Within minutes he was sound asleep, a look of complete contentment on his young face. Rachel continued to gaze out the window as she thought about the pending wedding and the next few days ahead. She was happy for Tina, and hoped her marriage experience would be happier than her own. Tom seemed to be a great guy. In fact, he was a real catch, she thought. They certainly knew each other for long enough. Good gosh, they had been living together for almost a year.

Rachel thought back on her own failed marriage and how it had gone sour. During college she honestly felt she could not possibly love anybody any more than Don. When she had accidentally become pregnant, he had suggested her having an abortion. That should have told her something right there and then. She had adamantly refused to abort the fetus, and Don, finding no way in which he could convince her otherwise, agreed to marry her. It was a recipe for a failed union from the start. Soon after Rusty was born and she was able to return back to work, the infidelities became obvious. Each time it would hurt her to no end, but for the sake of her child, she tried to live with it and to forgive him. In the end, it was for the sake of her child that she did finally leave him. Did she do the right thing? Absolutely, without a doubt! Still, it was hard on Rusty. When he played with his friends and came into contact with their fathers, he would sometimes come home and ask about his own father and why he didn't want to be with them anymore. These times were especially hard for Rachel as she tried to pick up the pieces from her failed marriage and to move on with no real end in sight. There wasn't even a boyfriend in the picture. Who had time for dating when it was all one could do to make a daily living and still have time to be a full time mother? It had been difficult trying to date after the divorce as her trust in men had become so shattered. Rachel tried to tuck her depression away and to forget the bitterness she still carried for Don. After awhile, the vibration of the airplane engines lulled her into a lethargic state where it became difficult to keep her eyelids open. Sleep followed shortly thereafter.

It was easy for Rachel to sleep in a moving vehicle. She dozed while listening to and feeling the soothing vibrations made by the rhythmic hum of the Cessna engines. When the constant drone from the left engine faltered and then stopped, Rachel didn't even notice it, so deep was she in her subconscious thoughts of the days to follow. Nathan, realizing there must be an air lock of some kind in one of the fuel lines, decided not to alert Rachel as the engine sputtered to a stop. Glancing over his shoulder he made sure each of his passengers was buckled in with their seat belts. Although the situation had suddenly become more dangerous on the flight, it was by no means critical. The Cessna 421 twin engine was fully capable of flying on one engine until they reached their final destination. Protocol, however, dictated to Nathan he change his flight plan to land at the nearest airport immediately, more as a safety procedure than anything else. He called his air traffic controller radio contact and notified them of his change in flight plan and the reason why. They directed him to land at the nearest airport, which was the one at Missoula. Nathan made the necessary navigation adjustments before sitting back once again to wait out the ride. He again considered waking Rachel to let her know of the change in plans but elected not to for fear of scaring her unnecessarily.

Rachel almost jumped right out of her seat when a loud bang came out of the right engine. With wide-open eyes, she looked in startled apprehension at Nathan as he continued to fly the airplane as if nothing was amiss. He was acting so normal she really didn't know if anything was wrong at all. Perhaps the loud bang was only a dream. Something wasn't right, though. What happened to the sound of the engines? Where there had once been the rather loud drone of the two engines, now there was only silence.

"Nathan, what's happening?" She called out in a voice bordering on panic.

"Miss, I'm sorry to say we have lost our engines. Right now we're in a full glide. I'm looking for a place where I can set her down---Mayday, Mayday, Mayday," he called out into the microphone. "Flight number Foxtrot 2867 Gulf declaring an emergency. We have lost both engines and I'm looking for a place to put down. We are 65 miles southwest of Missoula. Miss Rachel, please wake your son and make sure he's buckled in tight. I want both of you to lean forward and grab your thighs in a full body hug and hold tight. It may get a bit bumpy on the way down, but don't you worry, we'll come out of this just fine. The trick is to slow the craft down as much as possible, and then to gently set her down on the treetops. Not to worry, I've done this lots of times."

Rachel tried to take comfort in the soothing tones Nathan was speaking in, but the urgency in his voice scared her beyond belief. Little Rusty whined when he realized what was happening. Rachel put her hand across his shoulder in a protective manner and attempted to console him as the aircraft whizzed through the air in a silent ever-declining trajectory. While risking a moment to look out the window, the powerless mother couldn't help but notice how slowly they seemed to be traveling, but as they got closer to the treetops, it seemed their speed was picking up. At the last moment, before burying her head against her son's side, Rachel actually thought the airplane tilted upwards. At this exact instant, she heard Nathan call out, "Holy Mary," and then all hell broke loose.

Chapter Thirty

"I don't know why Doyle always has us doin all the hiking. Every time these goddamn birds are sitting on top of some mountain. It just really sucks! I would much rather be down in the valley sitting on some bear stand smokin cigarettes like Luther. That lazy fuck! Who the hell does he think he is? I hate him." Lamar had been bellyaching for close to an hour now, ever since they had left camp earlier that morning.

"Ah, shut up, will ya. I'm sick and tired of hearing you complaining all the time. We each got our job to do. They do theirs and we do ours. How'd ya like to be skinning bears anyways? Fuckin things look like humans when they're skinned; gives me the creeps." Grappa spoke in a raspy baritone of a voice that had been violated by over thirty years of smoking Camel cigarettes. He was a large ugly hulk of a man with a huge hooked nose which had obviously been broken a number of times. There was a long purple scar running down the right side of his face he got in a knife fight while working on the docks in Hong Kong some years earlier. Grappa had a full head of dirty black hair he kept pulled back in a ponytail. The whole mess was covered by a filthy wool cap which most people in camp thought he was born with. "Look there, just up ahead, that's what we're after. Now let's get a move on."

Lamar and Grappa moved silently through the woods using tree cover whenever possible to keep themselves hidden from their unsuspecting prey. Upon reaching a small rock outcropping, they were able to view the nest clearly. Sitting atop of it was a large American Bald Eagle. Its white hood and tail feathers were clearly visible with the naked eye. Overhead, they could see its mate circling in an effortless flight pattern maintaining a constant vigil for any food opportunity that might present itself. "Go ahead and pop him one," said Grappa. "Maybe we can then get the other to come in for a closer look, but stay out of sight."

Lamar rested his old beat up 270 Winchester on the rock face concealing him and took careful aim. A few seconds later the rifle erupted with a loud boom and Grappa could see the poor unsuspecting mother eagle rise three feet above her nest in a cloud of feathers before falling lifeless to the ground. "Good shot, shit head," he said. "I'll give you one thing. You sure as hell can shoot!"

"Thanks," replied Lamar. He took satisfaction in the compliment from the larger Grappa. They were by no means friends as there was very little friendship in this dirty business they were involved in, but over the last couple of years working together, they had each formed a grudging respect for the other and their peculiar talents. Lamar was much smaller than his companion, standing just under 5' 7". He was a vicious, evil little man with a temper that sometimes bordered on the malicious side of human nature. At 35 years of age, Lamar had been in trouble for most of his life. He grew up in a shanty-town in Mississippi, where he learned how to shoot as a small boy. He dropped out of school before finishing the eighth grade. After spending a year and a half on a chain gang, he moved out to the west coast where he was arrested and served time for breaking and entering and assault with a deadly weapon. The judge gave him the maximum sentence of ten years for the particularly heinous nature of his crime. After tying up an elderly man and woman, he beat them with a hammer until they disclosed where they had hidden their valuables. Of course, there were no valuables of any significance, but that didn't matter to Lamar. He was enjoying himself.

After prison, he moved up into the northwest where his oddities and temper might go unnoticed. While in Alaska, he met a man named Doyle, no first name, just Doyle. They formed a business relationship together where Lamar would poach wildlife for a bounty. Mostly he would shoot eagles but he had also taken Dahl sheep, brown bears, and mountain goats. When the conservation department caught wind of the operation, the motley group simply moved it down to the primitive area of Idaho. For the past two years, Doyle, Grappa, Luther, and Lamar had been working the surrounding mountains. They picked up and moved camp every few weeks so they might always have fresh game to kill, but more importantly, to keep from being discovered by the DNR.

Doyle used his contacts to sell the illegal body parts and trophies to the highest bidders. He was part of a vast syndicate that had operations all over the world. For the past couple of years, Doyle had been specializing in black bear gall bladders and eagles. The Orientals wanted the gall bladders for aphrodisiac purposes. By the time this highly illegal plunder hit the streets in the Far East, it could bring as much as $10,000 per bladder. Doyle received $1,200 for his part from his contact. After paying his poacher employee $400 for making the kill, he would net $800 profit per animal just for the gall bladder. A bear hide would bring an extra $200. The meat was almost always left to rot, or in some cases, used as bait to lure in fresh bears. The eagle carcasses and feathers, on the other hand, were sold to just about anyone willing to pay the price. Mostly, they were pawned off on unscrupulous taxidermists. They, in turn, would mount and sell them to anyone willing to pay the $5,000 price tag and willing to risk discovery. Penalties for having possession of an endangered animal illegally taken are severe, but this rarely stopped people who had the inkling to collect this type of thing.

"Keep an eye on that other buzzard up there. Pretty soon he just may land and check things out. If we can get him today that will save us having to hike all the way back up here again tomorrow." Lamar didn't like Grappa telling him what to do. He had been shooting eagles for most of his adult life and felt there was little his ugly companion could teach him about it, but he kept his mouth shut. There was no sense in antagonizing the brute needlessly. One of these days, when he decided to take out Doyle and the rest of his group, he just might need him. After all, Lamar thought, he could certainly run this operation on his own. What the hell did he need Doyle for?

"Heh, Lamar. Check that airplane out. She's flying mighty low. Do you think it's the DNR?"

"Hard to tell, but it's comin in mighty low. Keep outa sight."

The two of them watched as the twin engine Cessna 421 approached from the southwest. The altitude of the aircraft was obviously getting lower. Either it was searching for something or else it was having engine trouble. "I don't hear no engines," said Lamar after a moment. "I think that plane's goin down. Looks like right in the valley." They watched as the crippled airplane made one small circle in the sky before finally attempting to land in the canyon below. The only problem was, there was no landing strip down there, only trees, lots of trees.

It took a few seconds before the sounds of the crash reached them. There wasn't any explosion, but the impact of the plane made a considerable amount of noise before it was completely swallowed up by the forest. "Mark that spot while I fetch the buzzard," called out Lamar over his shoulder as he started for his kill. Upon retrieving it, he noticed a set of fresh cougar tracks. They were huge too, he thought--probably a big tom. He returned to Grappa and together they worked their way down the steeper side of the mountain making a direct beeline to where they last saw the plane go in. Grappa marked it on his compass. They needed to head due south and they should walk right up on it. It was important to mark the location, for in these woods it was easy to lose track of things. The Selway could be a formidable place when moving around on the forest floor without the benefit of familiar trails or landmarks.

"There it is," whispered Grappa. "She's all busted up at the base of that tree."

Lamar and Grappa approached the wreckage cautiously. They were in no hurry to let themselves be discovered, nor were they intent on offering any assistance; they had something more important on their minds, plunder! Anyone who could afford to fly in a private airplane must be loaded. This would be easy pickings. Wallets, jewelry, and who knows what else. After a moment of quiet observation, Lamar's greedy anticipation got the better of him and he rushed over to the plane. Looking inside one of the broken windows, he could see the bodies of three people; the pilot, a woman and a kid. Grappa came up behind him and forced the single door open with some effort. As they entered the aircraft, it immediately became clear both the woman and her son were still alive. The boy, found struggling in an attempt to free himself from his seatbelt, didn't seem to be any worse for wear, but the woman had a nasty gash in her forehead going up into her scalp line. Blood covered her face and presented a grotesque sight. She was moaning as she slowly returned to reality.

"Ah, shit!" said Grappa. "Now what are we gonna do?"

"We'll get them out, and then I'll check on the pilot," replied Lamar. The two of them freed Rachel and Rusty from their life saving seat belts and moved them away from the wrecked aircraft. While Grappa tended to Rachel by helping to wipe the blood off her face, little Rusty sat crying at his mother's side. She tried to speak words of encouragement to him, but the gravity of what had just happened overwhelmed her. Lamar returned to the aircraft and made his way up to the pilot's seat only to discover that he, too, was still alive. In fact, Nathan had the radio transmitter on and was trying to radio in a distress call.

"Oh no you don't," said Lamar as he ripped the headphones off the critically injured pilot. "We'll have none of that." Without hesitating in the slightest manner, Lamar picked up a large flashlight Nathan had always kept under the seat for night flying purposes and beat the helpless man to death. He repeatedly and cold bloodedly bludgeoned him over the head until there was hardly a face left to recognize. As the blood lust abated, he collected himself before backing out of the plane, but not before first taking the man's wallet from his back pocket and slipping it into his own.

By the time Lamar returned to the group, Rachel had regained much of her composure. "What about Nathan, the pilot? Is he trapped inside? Is there anything we can do for him?"

"Lady, he's beyond help," was the only reply Lamar put forward. "That man has done gone to see the Maker." Lamar stared down at her with his blood-splattered face and grinned.

Rachel was too shaken up by the news to realize the foul deed that had just taken place, nor was she in any condition to recognize the danger suddenly thrust upon her and Rusty. "Oh my God, what are we going to do?" she cried out in despair. "Where are we? Sir, can you please help us?" she begged Grappa.

"Sure we can, ma'm. We can take you back to our camp and get help from there," he replied. At that moment, Little Rusty decided to let out a wail. It distracted Rachel for a minute while she tended to him. Lamar motioned for Grappa to move away so they could have some words in private.

"We can't bring them back to our camp, Grappa. Doyle will have our heads. He'd kill anyone who compromised his operation. We've got to deal with this here."

"How do you mean to do that?" he asked quizzically.

"We kill them," he whispered. "After we whack the kid, we can have some fun with her first, but then she gets it too. There's no other way." Lamar was starting to get that blood lust in his eyes again.

Grappa thought for a moment before responding. "If we whack em, someone is goin to figure it out when the rescue teams get in here. Then there'll be shit goin down all over these woods. Hell, they're probably already on the way in. These must be real important people, flying in their own airplane, and all. She's probably the wife of some big company big shot. Now, if we save them, maybe there will be some kind of reward or something."

Lamar thought long and hard on that one. On the one hand, there was nothing he would rather do right now than have a little bit of this snotty nose rich bitch, but on the other hand, Grappa was right. Maybe there would be a reward for their safe return. Lamar continued to think with his limited mentality. Finally, greed prevailed over lust, and he agreed to take them back to camp and let Doyle deal with it; if Doyle refused to share the reward, then he would have to deal with him a bit sooner than he had intended, that's all.

Before leaving, they ransacked the aircraft looking for anything of value. Grappa used the excuse they were attempting to remove any personal items so they wouldn't have to return until help arrived. Once they set out on the three hour hike back to camp, each of them had a backpack full of plunder, including the full bar that was kept stocked at the rear of the plane. It didn't take very long as Rachel watched the two of them swigging Jack Daniels on there journey back before she started to realize they could very possibly be in worse trouble now than when the plane was about to crash. The fact that Lamar was dragging along a dead bald eagle, which he had obviously shot, didn't help matters much either; and what about all that blood splattered on the little guy's face?

Rachel didn't want to let on to her supposed rescuers or Rusty she suspected foul play, so she pretended to be grateful for the help and even mentioned on one occasion how grateful her husband would be to get them back safely. "He is a very generous man," she stated, "and would certainly be more than willing to compensate them for any inconvenience they have gone through in rescuing me and the boy." She noticed a furtive look between the two after making this comment but pretended to ignore it.

The forest they were passing through was the most incredible thing Rachel had ever seen. In most directions, it looked impenetrable. The huge pine trees easily rose hundreds of feet into the air and were larger around in the trunk than anything she had ever even dreamed of. Moss covered almost everything on the ground. In places, it was two feet thick. After traveling for the first mile or so, everything looked the same to her. She had no idea how the little guy was able to find his way, but he seemed to be moving along with confidence and purpose. At times, he would be following some sort of animal trail, but then he would leave the trail and cut across large areas.

Before they had gone a mile, Rachel complained about the fast pace they were setting. She had injured her ankle in the crash, but was hesitant to admit it for fear of having one of these goons start playing with her leg. From that point, she shuddered to think what would come next. She used Rusty as an excuse to try to get them to slow down. Rusty had actually come out of the accident unscathed and was completely enjoying himself exploring this virgin wilderness. His innocent mind could not fathom the danger his mother perceived them to be in. Grappa dropped back and offered to carry Rusty on his shoulders, which the little fella gladly accepted. He sat up on the man's broad shoulders, and with a long stick, lashed out at everything within reach, occasionally whacking Grappa on the backside and saying "giddy-up." The big man didn't seem to mind, so Rachel was thankful for the help. Perhaps the man would form some kind of friendship or bond with the boy that might help to protect them later.

Almost as soon as they had left the crash sight, Rachel, bringing up the rear, made a deliberate attempt at leaving a trail. Whenever possible, she would disturb the natural terrain by upsetting piles of moss on the ground or by simply bending twigs from small branches as she walked along. They were minor little things and she had no idea as to whether anyone could even follow it, but it was worth a try. These men were obviously not weekend hunters. They were poachers, and only God knows what else. Anything she could do to make it easier to be discovered was worth the extra effort and risk she was undoubtedly subjecting herself and Rusty to. Certainly, in a matter of time, people would realize their plane had gone down and would send help; but time was a valuable commodity, and Rachel didn't know how much of it she had.

Just before five o'clock and as the shadows were getting longer, Rachel smelled camp smoke. Minutes later, they walked into a small clearing where she immediately spotted two men sitting around a campfire smoking. A decrepit dog, missing a hind leg just above the elbow, looked up and growled as it gnawed on an old elk leg bone. If she had thought the men in her present company were unsavory, these new men were even worse. One man had a full beard that extended down to the middle of his chest. He wore a patch over his left eye. His long, repulsive, unkempt hair was shoulder length and tangled in his beard. This gave him a Charles Manson like appearance. He was a powerfully built man who reminded Rachel of someone she might have seen on late night television.

If the first man gave her the creeps, it was nothing compared to what the second man incited in her. Physically, he wasn't that horrible. In fact, with a good overhaul, he might just be able to pass as a good-looking man. It wasn't his appearance though, that frightened her. It was his demeanor. The man, whom Lamar approached and referred to as Doyle, stood well over six feet tall, with broad strapping shoulders. He rose like a lion getting ready to pounce, very slowly and deliberately. On each hip he had holstered a large caliber pistol worn on a thick leather belt studded with bullets. His eyes were frightening, deep set into his head and overshadowed by a heavy brow. They first took in the sight of Grappa, setting down the child over on the far side of the camp next to where a couple packhorses were tethered, and then Rachel, who rushed over to his side. From there, still without having said a word, he riveted his expression to the now bumbling and obviously intoxicated little man standing before him.

"What is this?" he asked almost in a whisper, not because he was trying to be secretive or anything, but rather because this seemed to be the way he communicated.

Lamar quickly explained how they had witnessed the plane crash and come upon the survivors. While rummaging through the insides, they found the woman and her son whom he figured they could rescue and return for a reward, or maybe even hold them for ransom or something. Doyle didn't say a word; he merely stared at the twitching man in front of him. In an attempt to gain favor, Lamar quickly reached into his pocket and removed the wallet he had stolen from the murdered pilot. "Look, I even got his wallet. It's loaded with dough! We can split it------. You can have it all if you want. I don't need it."

In the flash of an eye, Doyle removed one of the pistols from his hip and struck Lamar hard on the shoulder with it. It was evident the blow hurt, but Doyle was careful not to break any bones, after all, he needed the little man to do his dirty work for him. "You inbred idiot. What do you think is going to happen when rescue teams get to the crash sight and find it's been robbed and the passengers are missing? Do you think they'll just go away and forget about it?" He walked into Lamar who was standing there half bent over rubbing his shoulder and gave him a solid push, which sent him sprawling onto the ground. "I'll tell you what they'll do. Within a couple days they'll have three hundred people out here looking for them, combing every inch of these woods until they find them, and us."

Lamar quickly rose to his feet before the inevitable boot came flying towards his midsection. "Ok, Ok. I'll take them out and bash their heads in and bury them where no one will ever find them," he practically shrieked. Rachel's heart skipped a beat when she witnessed this.

"You're goddamn right you'll bash their heads in, but not until you get em back to the crash site where you can make it look like they were killed in the crash. Maybe that way we can keep half of Idaho from organizing and runnin roughshod through these mountains." Doyle glared at him as he cowered away towards the other side of the campfire. "Luther, get on over there and help Grappa tie them up," he said to the bearded fellow sitting on the log with the toothless grin. "Grappa, you make sure they're tied tight and we don't have to worry about them goin nowhere, and plan on headin back tomorrow morning early, too. Once you're done there takin care of business, I want you both back here keeping watch." As he finished giving orders, he glanced over at a horrified mother who was trying desperately to protect her only son while being hogtied by two rogues. Rusty screamed hysterically as they tied his small hands behind his back. "Gag them if they don't shut up," he called out in an ominous voice before walking back to the campfire.

Chapter Thirty-One

If Rachel thought she might somehow be able to connect with Grappa earlier, it was now just an illusion. He had tied her arms and legs so tight they were losing circulation and going numb with pain. She could only guess at the terrifying state of mind little Rusty was in. The poor child had panicked when he was being tied so roughly, especially by a man he thought he had befriended. When the bearded man put a piece of duct tape over both their mouths with a grin, the small boy looked over at his mother with tears and horror in his eyes. Rachel was distraught that she could not reach over and comfort him. In fact, she too, was completely helpless. How did she ever come from her safe little world into a predicament like this? These horrible men intended to kill her and her son, of that she was certain, and God only knows what else might be on their evil minds before that. Rachel lay there and prayed for a miracle. Her head throbbed where it had been bashed in the plane crash. She thought of poor Nathan, and realized now, that he must have been murdered by Lamar. "If only I had been more aware of what was going on, perhaps we could have escaped before coming to this." So many thoughts came into her mind over the next few hours, and none of them were very comforting.

Eventually, Rachel was able to slip off into a fitful sleep. She had the most horrible nightmares imaginable, dreaming about being chased in a dark forest by ruthless men bent on doing her great physical harm. These villains laughed as they took sadistic pleasure in stalking her and running her down. Fighting them off was impossible as they were heavily armed and powerful men. In a state of panic, she ran wildly through the woods with branches constantly tearing and scratching her in the face. When running further became impossible, she curled up into a fetal position and tried to hide in the thick underbrush. Her eyes were tightly closed in a vain attempt to shut out the evil surrounding her. When the inevitable pressure came to her arm, indicating discovery, she tried to scream, but was unable to utter a sound. Paralyzing fear prevented any sound from escaping her mouth. Only desperate grunts could be heard. Rachel startled in her sleep and was suddenly very awake. She had been thrashing about as her assailant pulled on her arm. It had only been a nightmare, but relief in awakening was not to be had. The pain from the rope cutting into her, and a fearsome headache quickly brought her back to reality and the awful situation.

The dark starry night was brisk and sobering. Rachel shivered in an attempt to ward off the chill, and then once again she felt a squeezing pressure on her arm. This was no dream, but a nightmare in the worst sense. One of these animals in camp had sneaked over to her while she slept and now had intentions she feared to even think about. Well, if this was to be the end game, she would not go without a fight. Better to die in the struggle and rob them of the pleasure of a warm body. Rachel steeled herself for what lay ahead; again, the pressure on the arm. Something didn't seem right, however. Why would one of these awful men touch her arm in a gentle manner, for it was a gentle pressure she felt. Looking over, Rachel was able to make out a dark figure lying on his stomach behind where she lay. He wasn't groping, but was rather trying to awaken her. It became immediately evident this man was not one of the earlier men from camp. He put his finger to his lips in a hush sound, and then slowly crawled up and whispered into her ear.

"Don't make a sound. I'm here to help you. If we're discovered, these guys will kill us all. I'm going to untie you and then we will have to sneak away. It's better to untie your son later and let him continue to sleep right now. I'll carry him." Rachel nodded in the affirmative, daring once again to hope.

The dark figured man used a knife to cut the rope from her hands and arms as the sound of snoring from several men could be heard coming from the two wall tents they were using to sleep in. He slowly removed the tape from her mouth so as not to cause any undue pain or discomfort. "Who are you?" she whispered.

"Later," he said. "Trust me." Next, he slithered up to her feet and cut the bonds restraining them. "I want you to crawl very slowly back towards the woods. When you're safely there, I'll follow with your son." Rachel nodded wide-eyed before crawling away and leaving her son with the stranger. Several minutes went by after she reached the relative safety of the woods before the man joined her with Rusty. The boy was still asleep. Quickly the two of them untied him, but the man wouldn't allow the tape to be removed from his mouth. "Not yet," he spoke softly. "If he wakes up and calls out, we're done for--just a bit longer. Now, please follow me and don't make a sound. Try to step where I step. These are very dangerous men and if we give them the chance, they'll kill us for sure. We have to put as much distance between them as we can by morning."

"Do you think they'll follow when they wake and find us gone?"

"There is no doubt in my mind they'll do anything and everything in their power to catch and kill us before help arrives. Unfortunately, we are all witnesses to their crimes. If we escape, they're very aware of the fact we'll bring the law down upon them. Their survival depends upon our capture and murder, and I'm not going to let that happen. Now, no more talking. We have to move."

Lonnie back-tracked on the path he had taken earlier in the day on his way to the poacher's camp. He had first suspected foul play when he came upon the scene at the crash sight. The pilot apparently had succumbed to massive head injuries, but there was no significant evidence of damage or blood remains on the windshield or steering wheel of the plane. The bloodied and broken flashlight told another story. For some reason, the pilot was ruthlessly murdered and the passengers, apparently a woman and young child, were abducted. The footprints around the crash sight indicated two men, one large, perhaps close to 240 pounds, and one smaller, had led the two passengers away. Certainly, they were up to no good. Lonnie cursed when he discovered the radio to be inoperable. He felt there was no time to return to his camp and use his own radio to call for help and give coordinates because the passenger's lives were obviously in danger. Instead, he immediately set out on their trail.

Lonnie arrived at the poacher camp shortly after Lamar and Grappa did. He was cautious not to let himself be discovered as it was evident these were armed and dangerous fellows. By circling around the camp, he was able to pick up the conversation Doyle was having with Lamar after he struck him with the barrel of his revolver. The orders he gave came as no surprise to Lonnie. The DNR, which Lonnie now worked for, was aware there was commercial poaching going on in the Bitterroot Mountain Range, but they were unsure of just where the culprits were encamped. Over the past few years, the organized thugs and the DNR had played a game of cat and mouse with each other throughout the Selway. The stakes in this game were at times quite high. Two years earlier, two conservation officers were murdered when they got too close to this group and tried to make an arrest without proper backup.

Lonnie was not going to take any chances, especially when the lives of this innocent woman and her son were at stake. Even if he had been carrying a weapon, which unfortunately he had left in camp that morning when he rushed the three miles to the crash sight, he probably would have decided to sneak away after the rescue and call for help before attempting to arrest these guys. This was his intention now, but first, they had to get away. The plan was to head back to his camp from the point where he had first encountered the crash. There, he could radio in a distress call, and also arm himself in the event they were discovered before help arrived. Lonnie took nothing for granted. He knew these were men with considerable skills in the back country, and if anybody could follow a trail, it would be these professional poachers. It would take a considerable amount of luck to avoid these men until help arrived.

When the sound of a barking dog could be heard in the distance, Lonnie knew their escape had been discovered. He had remained hidden outside the camp for almost six hours until everyone went to sleep, and then another hour just to make sure they were down for good. When the mangy old mutt went into Doyle's tent with him for the night, Lonnie thanked his lucky stars, for he wouldn't have been able to sneak the hostages away if the animal were on watch. "They'll be coming after us now," he said. "We had better pick up our pace."

"Will they be able to track us in the dark?" asked Rachel.

"Most men wouldn't be able to, but something tells me these men can, and with the help of a tracking dog, there isn't a doubt in my mind." Lonnie carried Rusty on his shoulders, long since having removed the tape covering his mouth. The boy was afraid, but made a valiant attempt at showing bravado, especially when it came to describing what he would do to those dirty men if they touched his mom again.

"I'll poke them in the eyes with a big stick!" he said. The boy's tough talk made Lonnie feel good. He appreciated the youngster's courage, especially after what he had already been through. Under any other circumstances it could have been almost funny, but today, there was an element of danger that made it seem sad.

"Don't you worry one bit, young fella. Nobody's gonna hurt your ma while I'm around. You either. Your old Uncle Lonnie will take good care of you. I know these woods like the back of my hand, and as soon as we get back to my camp, we're gonna call for help. Then we'll get these guys and put them where they belong, understand?"

"Yup," the boy simply replied.

"But, you're gonna have to help me, son. I need for you to continue to be real brave, you know, so your mom won't get scared or anything. Do you think you can do that?"

"Yup."

"Say, as long as we're going to be spending some time together, don't you think I should know your names? Mine is Lonnie Burch."

"Mine is Rusty, and this is my mom."

"Rachel," added his mother. "We were on our way to a wedding in Spokane when the next thing I knew there was a loud bang. Then Nathan, our pilot, told me we were having engine trouble and going down. I think the little guy killed Nathan. He had blood all over himself. I should have figured it out sooner." She started to choke on her words.

Lonnie stopped walking for a moment and focused his attention on the distraught woman. "Rachel, there is nothing you could have done, except maybe got yourself killed. Don't think about it now. We're dealing with some real bad elements here, and I'm going to need all your strength and endurance to see this thing through. Once we reach my camp and call for help, we're going to have to then hide out until it arrives. Don't you worry though, nothing bad will happen to you or Rusty, on that you have my promise."

Rachel thanked him and touched his arm. "We can be real tough, can't we Rusty?" She gave the child a reassuring pat on his leg as he sat atop Lonnie's shoulders. Already he was starting to doze off once again.

Chapter Thirty-Two

"What do you mean, they're gone?" raged Doyle. "How could the woman possibly get loose?"

"The ropes were cut," answered Grappa. "There's no way she could have untied herself without help. I checked out the area. There's belly marks leading from the woods up to where they was laying down. Somebody must have followed us from the crash and set them loose after we went to sleep. It looks like just one person. All I could find was one set of tracks."

"How long ago?"

"Can't say for sure. Luther got up to take a piss and they was gone. He's out checking around for tracks now. My best guess is they got a half hour to an hour start on us."

"Round everyone up and prepare to leave camp immediately. Plan on being gone until we find them. I don't care if it takes a goddamn week, but we had better find em and kill em before they get the law onto us." Doyle kicked his mutt and spat at him, "Where were you during all this? A lot of help you've been." He grabbed his pack and shoved a few essentials into it, including a couple boxes of 45 caliber bullets for his pistols and a box of 300 Winchester mags for his rifle, which he slung over his shoulder on his way out of the tent.

"What do you know, Luther? Could this hero be from that camp you spotted down in the valley a few days ago?"

"I reckon it must be. It's too soon for a search party to get this far in, and people just don't hang around out here when it's not huntin season. That's the only camp we know of in this entire basin; best I could tell, it's manned by just one dude and his dog. I suppose he could have heard the plane come down just like Grappa and shithead here, and went to check it out. When he got there and saw the wreck, he most likely picked up their trail and followed it here."

"Ok, here's the plan. Luther, you take Lamar and head directly to that camp. Find out who that guy is and if he had anything to do with this. If he did, and if he has that woman and her kid, well, you know what to do. Afterwards, break the whole camp down and bury it along with em somewhere it won't never be found. Understand? No fuck-ups. Lamar, I hold you personally responsible for this mess. Find this dude and finish it, or I'll finish you! Grappa and me will get on their trail from here with T-Bone. He can track down a coon in a rainstorm; don't reckon we'll have too much trouble stayin on their trail. My intention is to push em until they can't go no farther, then we'll catch em and deal with it. The woman will slow him down for sure. There's a good chance they'll head back to his camp, so if he's not home when you get there, plan a reception. We shouldn't be too far behind. If this doesn't work out, plan on meeting at the big meadow on the creek near the old eagle's nest tomorrow night. We got to finish this real quick-like, and then get back here and break camp. There's gonna be a search party comin through lookin for survivors, and I don't want to be in the neighborhood when they do."

Without any further conversation, everyone moved out as they were instructed. Lamar had good enough sense to keep his mouth shut because Doyle was in no mood for being messed with. If he were rubbed the wrong way right about now, he would more than likely settle it with a bullet between the eyes. Although he felt he got the raw end of the deal, it was better to bide his time. For what it was worth, he did appreciate the urgency of the situation. One radio call could bring the law down on them all, putting the kabosh on their entire operation, and the money was just too good to throw away. This wouldn't be so bad. He could hunt his favorite game--people!

Doyle held the rope restraining T-Bone as they picked up the trail outside camp. The hound did have a good nose for following a scent. In its earlier years, T-Bone was a coon dog, but out here he was used to track down bears and when the opportunity presented itself, mountain lions. It was the latter which took his leg two years before. After a few months of convalescing around camp, he began to hobble about until eventually he moved pretty good, considering. Doyle knew he could just let the dog run and he would catch them in no time, even with three legs, but this could prove risky. If the hero had a gun with him, and there was no reason to think why he wouldn't, he would make short work of the dog, and then they would be left to tracking the old fashioned way. It was always better to stay with the hound. He could protect him and at the same time use his nose to close the gap. When they got real close, they would know it. Grappa was moving shoulder to shoulder with Doyle. "The dog's taking us back to the crash. Why would that guy head back there?" he questioned.

"I dunno," responded Doyle. "Maybe that's the only way he knows how to get back to his camp. If that's the case, we got em. Luther and Lamar will be waiting. I don't figure any rescue squads will be in here yet, but they will be soon. They'll probably drop in rangers with a helicopter some time after daylight. If we see them, all bets are off and we get back to camp and clear out. The way I see it, we got a couple days."

"Maybe longer," said Grappa. "The plane went down in a thick forested area and there was no fire. I can't imagine anyone seeing it from above. They'll probably get in here somewhere in a twenty-mile radius and begin working a grid pattern. As long as we stay out of their way, we could buy some extra time. Once they find the plane though, the shit is gonna hit the fan. Lamar bashed the pilot's brains out with a flashlight. I can't say for sure, but it may not look like part of the accident."

"Goddamn it. Have you got any more secrets you want to let me in on?" Doyle was fit to be tied. "If that bloody Lamar weren't such a good hunter and tracker, I would have gotten rid of him long ago. He's a time bomb waiting to happen, and I'll be damned if I'm going to let him take me down with him. We'd best check on the plane and make sure everything looks like an accident."

The two men and barking dog continued to push on towards the crash sight as dawn approached. It looked like it was going to be a clear day with no rain or late snow falls in sight. The ground was damp and spongy with deep moss in many places. When the sunlight was able to penetrate the overhead canopy of spruce and fir, it danced across the ground in a shadowy display of ghostlike apparitions. It was obvious where people had moved through the area earlier by the disturbed ground cover. Doyle recognized how they were keeping to the exact same trail as when Grappa and Lamar had first moved through on their way to camp the previous day. He was keeping a keen eye on the trail in the event they broke off and headed in a different direction, something the dog may not immediately pick up on. Doyle knew the barking of the hound would be heard by the fugitives as they tried to make good their escape, and he also realized the psychological effect it would have on them. Animals being pursued by a hound tend to run blindly as if in a panic. They don't use their intelligence, only their instinct to escape. People were not much different, he figured. When they could hear the sounds of pursuit getting closer, their thought process becomes corrupted, and they make mistakes. It would only be a matter of time before this hero made his mistake, and when he did, it would be his last. Doyle found, after some time, he was actually enjoying himself on this early morning chase. He chuckled to himself so as not to let his companion recognize his mirth for he had a role to play, and that was one of strict and uncompromising leader.

"Looky here," Doyle said. "This is where they broke off the trail. Our hero tried to walk on a series of rocks to cover his escape. Unfortunately, he, or more likely she, turned one over and then back again. It left a disturbed area. See further up the way there, the moss is squashed down. I do believe our friend has made his first attempt at shaking us. This way." They turned off the trail and began to follow the new, much more difficult to see trail. Doyle kicked T-Bone and called out, "Come on, dog, let's hear it." The animal immediately began to bark and yelp once again as they changed direction towards the stranger's camp down lower in the basin.

The forest area they were in seemed to be completely devoid of life. Although the Selway area was home to many species of wildlife including elk, deer, bear, moose, mountain goat, wolves, and cougars, they tended to congregate around areas where food was more plentiful, such as burn areas. These heavily forested spots served more as a place of shelter for the animals when they were bedded down. Due to the dense nature of this primitive wilderness area of Idaho, it was extremely difficult to spot wildlife, even though the animal sign was thick. Elk trails and bear pathways from countless generations crisscrossed the forest floor going in every direction. Only the animals seemed to know for sure where they went. Doyle noticed his quarry was sticking to these trails whenever possible. Although it made the chase easier, it also allowed for them to move more quickly through the forest. "That's OK, my friend. I'm not trying to catch you, only move you into my trap," thought Doyle. He paused for a few moments to let Grappa catch his breath. If the fat guy hadn't been his ex brother-in-law, he wouldn't have allowed him to be part of his outfit. He looked to be a miserable person, too many cigarettes and too much whiskey; but he was loyal like an old dog, and Doyle needed loyalty.

Lamar moved rapidly through the forest. By all accounts, he was a better man in the woods than Luther on any given day, and he knew it. They were making good time on a direct route to the stranger's camp. Even though Lamar had never seen it, he knew exactly where it was based upon the description given to him by Luther. If Luther had been leading the way, even after having discovered it himself, they would most certainly have stumbled around in the woods for half a day before coming onto it again. For all of Lamar's deficiencies, he did have a good bearing in the forest, even without a compass, which he rarely bothered to carry. When dawn finally started to break, the two of them slowed down their pace considerably. "I figure his camp is just over this next swell by the stream you mentioned," said Lamar.

"How do you figure that without having ever been there before?" questioned Luther.

"Cuz I smell dog shit, and you said he's got a dog, and on account of the fact there's a stream runnin down this valley and it circles around this little hill. His camp is just ahead."

Luther shook his head more in irritation than anything else, but had learned to trust the smaller man's judgment long ago. They moved with extra caution. There was no way of telling whether the stranger had arrived back in camp yet or of knowing whether he was even involved or not, but things sort of pointed to the fact that he was. Plus, chances are, the dog may have been left in camp, otherwise T-Bone would have detected it at their camp and would have started barking. T-Bone was not a social dog.

"There it is," said Lamar. "Just where I said it would be." Luther nodded while giving the little guy an appraising stare. "There's no fire. It looks like no one's home, or else he's still in bed. We move up on it from here separately. Give me ten minutes to get around to the other side. When I move into camp, hold back and cover me in case someone is home. I'll check on the tent and see if he's inside. If he is, he's probably not involved and we should git. If it's empty, he's our man and we wait."

Ten minutes later, Lamar moved slowly into camp from the opposite side. As soon as he came into the clearing a yellow Labrador barked at him and approached in a protective manner with the hair raised on the back of her neck. Lamar dropped to one knee and held his hand out with some bear jerky in it. "Hello, girl," he said in a deceptively friendly voice. "How ya doin? I'm not here to hurt ya. I'm lost, and I was wondering if I could get some help. Is anybody home?" The dog approached the kneeling man in a trusting yet cautious manner and gratefully accepted the food held out to her. She let him scratch her head and pat her flank in a familiar gesture humans do when they befriend a dog. Lamar stood and walked over to the small dome tent.

"Hullo, is anyone home? I'm lost in the woods and I was wondering if I could get some help." He scratched gently on the tent wall. "Hullo?" After a moment of no response, he knelt in front of the doorway and unzipped the small tent and peered inside only to discover it was empty. "Hmm," he thought to himself. "I guess this clinches it." Next, he called out softly to Luther. "Looks like no one is home. Gee, he even left this fancy rifle here." Lamar started walking around camp with a more confident air as Luther joined him. "Campfire's cold," he said. Once again he approached the lab offering a friendly outstretched hand. "What do you know, old girl?" he said softly. "Did your master go and leave you all alone?" Lamar gently scratched the dog's head once again. When the unsuspecting animal was completely relaxed and at ease, Lamar removed the extra sharp skinning knife he wore on his belt and cut the poor dog's throat in one quick motion. The mortally wounded animal could only make one short yelp before falling to the ground and whimpering until the loss of blood slowly drained her life away.

"You fucking asshole," Luther said to him with a sneer.

"What did you expect me to do with the damn mutt, leave it and let it give us away?"

"You didn't have to enjoy it so much," he said.

"Wait until this dude brings back the babe," he said with a smile on his face. "If you got a weak stomach dealing with this mutt, you probably ought to head back to camp right now." Lamar continued walking around camp after wiping his hands on a shirt hanging from a branch. When he rifled through the personal possessions inside the tent he discovered a small radio that he smashed immediately. He also found and pocketed a 38 caliber Smith and Wesson revolver.

"This dude's got all kinds of paper notebooks and shit in here. It looks like he works for the conservation department or something," Lamar explained as he backed out of the tent with an armful of clothing he was stealing. "We best get back out of camp and prepare for company. I would imagine they should show up pretty quick now, wouldn't you think?" Before they moved back into the woods, Lamar tossed the dead dog into a pile of brush on the outskirts of camp in a half-hearted attempt at concealing her. Then he and Luther moved off a short distance into the trees where they could get a good view of the camp and surrounding area and waited. Luther kept the rifle.

Chapter Thirty-Three

A couple hours after dawn, Lonnie and his two companions approached his camp with caution. They stopped outside the perimeter and watched for a few minutes to see if it was occupied. It was evident there were still people following them as the barking of the dog could be heard occasionally in the distance. The space between them had remained somewhat constant for the past couple hours. Earlier, Lonnie had instructed Rachel and her son to move off the trail a short ways and wait for him while he made a dash for the airplane. It was a good quarter mile away, and he figured for what he needed to do there, they would not be necessary. Upon reaching the wreckage, he searched the cockpit for a pen and paper and quickly scrawled a message. "The pilot has been murdered. Passengers Rachel and son, Rusty, were abducted by four rouges bent on more foul play, including murder. They are camped to the northeast, about a three-hour hike. I have been able to rescue the two of them from these bandits, unharmed. We are now being pursued. My intent is to get to my own camp down the valley where I will attempt to radio in more details. These are armed and very dangerous men! They will, more likely, kill again if given the opportunity." He signed it, Ranger Lonnie Burch, and placed it on a passenger's seat where it would be easily discovered by rescuers. Before leaving, he grabbed a couple jackets and a sweater found strewn about the cabin. Ten minutes later, he returned to where he had left them, and they moved off at a right angle from the trail they were following. Lonnie made a deliberate attempt at disturbing the ground so their detour would not go unnoticed.

Lonnie made a whistling sound that could have easily been mistaken for a bird of some kind. After a moment he made it again. "What are you doing?" questioned Rachel softly.

"I'm calling my dog, Chewy. I left her in camp to keep an eye on things. It's strange she doesn't respond."

"Do you think she could have wondered off?"

"It's very unlikely. I'm going to walk into camp, but I want you and Rusty to remain here out of sight. I have a radio and gun in camp. If I can get to them, things will be a lot better. If anything goes wrong, get away. Keep moving down the valley and under no circumstances let yourself be caught." Rachel nodded in agreement, but secretly wished they could all just move down the valley right now without bothering to go into the camp. She watched with concern as Lonnie slowly circled the camp a ways before entering it from another direction. He didn't say a word as he moved out into the open but made a direct path to his tent where he hoped to find his side arm and rifle.

Lonnie hadn't moved fifteen paces into camp before he noticed things were not the way he had left them. For one, his shirt no longer hung from the peg on the tree where he had left it. He could also see from where he stood that his tent was not completely zipped up. This was no accident. He always made sure it remained tightly zipped when he left camp. While walking over to the tree where his shirt lay on the ground, he saw a bright red stain on it that he immediately recognized to be blood. A sturdy six-foot staff he used while hiking in the woods still leaned against the tree where he had left it. He picked it up and continued to move quickly to the tent. Once he unzipped it and crawled inside, it became clear. His things, what remained of them, were disheveled and tossed about. The rifle was missing and upon further searching, he realized the pistol was gone as well. By far, the most troubling thing was the smashed radio he found. Without another moment wasted, Lonnie backed out of the tent with the intent of vacating camp fast. There wasn't anything here any longer that could assist him in what lay ahead.

"Hold it right there, Buddy," a voice called out in a not so friendly tone.

Lonnie turned slowly with his staff in hand and was confronted by two dangerous looking men with rifles aimed directly at him. "What gives?" he asked feigning surprise. "What's the meaning of this? Are you robbing me? Where's my dog?"

"Hold up on the questions, fella," responded Lamar. "Where's the woman and kid? And don't tell me you don't know what I'm talking about."

"I don't know what you're talking about," he responded. Lonnie was looking around camp to see if there were any others. He called out for his dog, Chewy, knowing full well that his dog was now only a memory.

"The mutt's gone where it ain't gonna bother nobody no more," sneered Lamar as he and Luther cut the distance between them to just a few yards.

"Why are you doing this?"

"Let's just say because I don't like ya. Now cut the crap. I'm gonna ask just one more time, and if I don't like the answer, I'm gonna shoot ya in the stomach, and then I'm gonna skin ya alive."

Lonnie stared at the noticeably smaller Lamar incredulously while the sweat dripped down into the small of his back. Never before had he encountered such a personification of evil. His mind was racing while he tried to come up with a tactic to slow the pace. He needed time, and a bullet in the gut wouldn't give it to him. Lonnie had no illusions about what these men intended to do.

"I'm a conservation officer, you know. When I heard the plane come down yesterday, I called in on my radio and reported the location. This is a stupid thing you're doing here. One shot will bring in any deputies in the area." Lonnie didn't know where he was going with this. He only hoped he could stall long enough for Rachel and Rusty to get a head start before these thugs finished with him and started after them.

"Ok, dude, don't say I didn't warn ya." With that said, he raised the rifle as if to fire it.

Rachel watched the confrontation taking place from the cover of the woods feeling completely helpless to do anything. When she saw the two men walk into camp from the opposite direction while Lonnie searched inside the tent, she wanted to scream out. Fearing for her own safety and that of her son, she kept still, all the while searching for some way in which to help him. Things were moving so swiftly. Rachel knew Lonnie was trying to kill time so she and Rusty could get a head start, but couldn't bring herself to abandon him when he had already risked his own life to help her. Searching for something desperately, she ultimately focused on the only thing at hand. At her feet she picked up an egg-sized rock and threw it with all her might across camp. It sailed through the air behind them and struck a tree just as Lamar was leveling his rifle to shoot.

When he heard the sound, Lamar quickly spun around and fired his rifle in the direction of the tree. Lonnie reacted immediately. In a motion he hadn't used much since college, he hurled the heavy staff, as if it were a javelin, with all his strength at the best target he could find. It struck Luther full force in the chest, knocking him over. Lonnie wasted not a moment in making tracks for the nearest tree cover he could find. Lamar fumbled with the bolt on his rifle trying to chamber another round as Luther gasped on the ground trying to regain the wind that was severely knocked out of him by the blow. Lonnie entered the woods in the exact place where his assailants had recently been hiding. At the last moment, before a bullet went whistling by him, he spotted Chewy half concealed by a small bush lying in a pool of blood. Anger flushed in him as he ran deeper into the trees. There was no reason to kill the innocent dog other than pure meanness, plain and simple.

Lonnie spotted a pile of what turned out to be his own clothing, stolen earlier by Lamar, lying on the ground. Next to it, leaning against a tree, was his rifle. Years earlier, he had used this very same weapon to kill his first elk while hunting with his father. In a heartbeat, he picked it up and made sure there was still a round in the chamber before taking careful aim at his pursuers. He drew down on the first target that presented itself. Luther never knew what hit him. Hit cleanly in the heart, the one eyed bandit dropped like a rock, never to stir again. Lamar cursed as he suddenly realized his advantage had been compromised. He took off wildly through the trees in a desperate attempt to put as much distance between himself and the now armed Lonnie as he could. Rachel held Rusty down as Lamar went stampeding by not fifty feet from where they crouched. He never noticed them.

Lonnie chased after him only because he fled in the direction where Rachel was hiding. She called out to him as he came by. In the distance they could hear the crashing of timber and branches breaking as Lamar retreated into the forest. From another direction, the barking of a dog could still be heard, only this time it was much closer. The gunshots undoubtedly spurred them on to quicken their pace. Not wanting to hang around and confront them, Lonnie hastily put Rusty back on his shoulders and led Rachel off in the opposite direction towards the stream. When they reached it, he instructed her to follow him into the water. For the next half-mile they moved down the center of the stream in an attempt to conceal their scent from the trailing dog. Eventually, they came out of the water on the opposite shore and continued heading in a southerly direction down the valley.

"That was some mighty quick thinking back there on your part, Rachel. Thanks. You saved my life. I thought I was a goner for sure."

"It was all I could think of doing. He was going to murder you in cold blood. Was there any sign of your dog?" Lonnie explained to her how he had seen it dead in the bushes while he ran out of camp. "I'm sorry," she said.

"There was no reason to kill my dog. Chewy never hurt anybody. She's been my only companion since my---- well, for about six years now. I got her after finishing college when she was just a pup. I'll miss her." They continued walking for some time before speaking again. "Say Rusty, do you think you're up to doing a little walking on your own?"

"Sure. I can walk a hundred miles if someone would only let me." The two adults laughed. It was a welcome relief from the anxiety they had been feeling over the past day.

By the time Doyle entered Lonnie's camp with Grappa, Lamar had circled around and met them as they approached. He invented a story about how the ranger had beaten them back and laid in ambush for them until they arrived. According to Lamar's version of the story, Luther never had a chance, being shot cold blooded like, the moment they entered camp. It was only through his own quick reactions and skill that he managed to escape with his own life. "Lucky for you," Doyle said sarcastically. He would have much preferred if Lamar had been the one to get knocked off. Grappa inspected the body and commented on the nice shot the guy made. Lamar stashed the corpse at the edge of camp, on the opposite side from where the dog was located, to keep it out of the sun until such time as they were able to get back to bury it. Grappa took his rifle and ransacked his day pack for anything else of value.

It took almost forty minutes before T-Bone was able to pick up the trail again. When he did, and they were sure it was the right one, they pushed even harder than previously. Doyle had it in his head they were going to get these people no matter what, and make them pay for disrupting his operation. He wasn't that concerned over the death of Luther, although good employees were hard to find, especially in this business, but it was the principle of the thing. This ranger guy sneaked into his camp and made a fool out of him, and that was intolerable, not to mention the fact he could blow the whole lid off things. Doyle resigned himself to the reality of having to move his camp once this thing was behind them. "No big deal," he thought. "It's probably time anyway, perhaps to the eastern side of the Great Divide. Montana maybe."

For the rest of the day, Lonnie led his small party on a tireless escape through the heavy timber of the Bitterroot Mountain Range. He continuously used every tracking trick he could think of in order to shake their pursuers, but to no avail. They just kept coming on. Late in the day after moving over an open expanse of rock, climbing a small cliff face, and then traveling up the far side of a small stream for almost a mile, before doubling back on the opposite side a good way, Lonnie felt reasonably comfortable they had put a safe distance between them. Rusty carried out his part of the bargain too, by walking for long stretches at a time with no complaining, whatsoever. When the sun went down, each of them were dead tired. Lonnie hadn't slept in thirty-two hours and Rachel had precious little sleep herself the night before. Food up until this point hadn't been much of a consideration, but when Rusty asked if they had anything to eat, he realized it was going to become a problem if he didn't do something about it pretty soon.

"Rusty, how would you like to help me catch a fish so your mom has something to eat for dinner?" Lonnie asked.

"We don't have any fishing poles," he replied.

"Who said anything about fishing poles?

"How do you catch a fish without a pole?" he asked forlornly.

"Well, you just come with me and I'll show you."

Together, they walked a short distance to where the stream flowed slowly and undisturbed. Lonnie found a long pole like piece of dead wood. He used his knife to sharpen the end. With little Rusty sitting along the bank watching in amazement, Lonnie moved up and down the shoreline stalking the fish within the stream. After his third thrust, Lonnie pulled his spear out of the water with a smile on his face. A nice pound and a half salmon was skewered on it wiggling like a fish out of water wiggles. Rusty immediately became interested. "Let me try!" he pleaded.

Lonnie smiled nostalgically as if remembering something from long ago in his past. "Sure, Pal, but you have to find a stick first." Rusty set out without another thought and disappeared into the woods for a few minutes before returning with half of a downed tree limb.

"Will this work?" he asked.

Lonnie laughed again. "Sure it will." He went over and helped the excited boy to fashion himself a small spear. The two of them spent the next hour in a different world together, oblivious to their surroundings and the danger around them. When Rachel finally awoke from her catnap, she came looking for them and found a sight to behold. There, standing along the bank of the stream, was her son and Lonnie. They were not cognizant of her presence, and she did not give her position away but was content to watch silently as the two of them worked their spears in and out of the flowing water. On one occasion, she saw Lonnie pull a large fish from the stream and hand it to her son, who squealed with delight. He tossed it on shore next to at least two others. "Here, let me help you," the older man said. Together, they walked up the stream a ways until Lonnie spotted another fish. He stood behind Rusty and with a guiding hand helped the youngster to throw the spear with pinpoint accuracy into the stream below. The excitement the boy showed was proof enough of what was on the opposite end of the spear even before they lifted it from the water.

Rachel found herself to be just as thrilled as her son. She took a moment to examine this quiet man, who called himself Lonnie, with a renewed interest. He stood well over six feet tall and had thick, black wavy hair. His eyes were deep set and strikingly blue. He had high cheekbones and delicate features and it was obvious he was built like no other man she had ever been associated with. For the first time since she came into contact with him the day before, Rachel realized he was a very good-looking man. He obviously knew how to deal with young children. Perhaps he even had one or two of his own. This might explain why he took so readily to Rusty. For the boy's part, he had certainly taken a shine to Lonnie. Ever since the divorce, Rusty had been stand-offish towards men who came into contact with his mother. Strange how well they were getting along under the circumstances, she thought.

"Are we going to eat these fish tonight or merely catch them all evening?" Rachel inquired as she walked up and gave her position away.

"Aw, mom, we have to catch a bunch of them," answered her son.

"I'll bet we have enough for dinner and breakfast right now," Lonnie said. "Maybe your mom is right. How about I show you an old Indian way to cook up a bunch of salmon over the fire?"

Chapter Thirty-Four

Just after dark, Lonnie risked building a small fire only long enough to cook the fish they had caught. He instructed a very attentive Rusty on how to build a teepee fire. Once there was an accumulation of hot coals, he built a crude rotisserie over it using pieces of dry wood. The fish were rotated over the coals until they were quite done, and then the three of them ate ravenously. When everyone had eaten their fill, Lonnie took the remaining fish and scraps and wrapped them in leaves, depositing them further into the woods so the scent wouldn't give away their position to the trailing dog if it should eventually find his way to this spot. Afterwards, he insisted on extinguishing the fire, as the light from it would serve as a beacon exposing their location.

Sleep was hard to come by that night for Rachel and Lonnie, even though exhaustion nagged at them in a big way. The temperature dropped down into the high thirties and when the dampness infiltrated their clothing, it was hard not to shiver. Lonnie showed each of them how to stuff their outer clothing with dry grass in order to serve as insulation. He made small beds out of moss and leaves to ease the discomfort of the hard ground. A spot was chosen deeper into the forest, away from the stream, in order to keep their scent from crossing over and alerting the trailing hound. Rachel was confused about why they backtracked down the opposite side of the stream. "Wouldn't it be better to try to put as much distance between us as possible?" she asked.

"By coming back down the far side of the stream, we can keep watch on our trail. If we're followed, they'll be on our tracks and move right by us heading up the river. Then, after they go by, we can cross over again and get on their trail going back the way they came. It confuses the dog," he chuckled. "Tomorrow will be another long day. If there is no sight of them by morning, we can continue down the valley and make good our escape. It's still a good two days hike out from here, I figure."

"Lonnie, what brings you so far into these woods at this time of year with only your dog? You're a long way from civilization."

"I'm a conservation officer," he replied. In addition to keeping an eye out for illegal hunting and poachers, I monitor the health of the rivers and streams, and basically, the forest in general, including the animals and fish that live here. On this particular trip, I have been counting Sockeye salmon as they migrate up the streams. We like to keep tabs on their numbers as they move upstream to spawn. By counting them once they get this far inland, we have a better idea on the overall health and vitality of the entire population. It's a valuable food source, but because of this, there's a tendency to over fish them. Large commercial fishing boats sit at the entrance to the rivers where the salmon return each year to spawn. If we don't keep track of how many actually make it this far in to breed, the population may become so depleted it will threaten the entire ecosystem. More than just people depend on these fish to make a living."

"These fish come all the way from the ocean?"

"They're actually born in these streams. They spend their early lives here, then move downstream all the way to the ocean, sometimes a trip of two thousand miles or more, and move out to sea. When they reach maturity, they'll return to the exact stream where they were hatched and spawn themselves before they die. The cycle then repeats itself like it has for millions of years."

"How fascinating! You must really love it out here to spend so much time by yourself. Do you have any family, and how do they feel about you being gone for so long?"

Lonnie hesitated for a moment before answering her question. He didn't very often speak of his family or past with people, especially strangers, but this woman seemed to be a nice person and he liked her. She made him feel at ease with her soothing conversation. It had been a long time since he had spoken with a pretty female, and Rachel certainly was just that, even under these rustic conditions. "My mother died when I was nine years old from breast cancer. After that, my father raised me on a small ranch outside of Silvertown, Colorado. We had a great life together." He stopped speaking for a moment of reflection. Rachel could see that he was somewhere else.

"Do you still communicate with him?"

"Only in my prayers and dreams. He was a coal miner and died in a cave-in six years ago. After that, I finished college and moved out here."

"I'm sorry. Is that when you got your dog?"

"Yeah," he hesitated. "No more talking now. We need sleep if we're going to get through tomorrow. I'll keep an open ear in case our friends come by."

Rachel realized she must have touched on a subject still very sensitive to Lonnie and was sorry she had reminded him of it again. He was obviously a very intelligent and sensitive person. The death of his father must have been traumatic for him, so much so that he moved away from his home and friends and sought refuge out here in the wilderness. She eventually dropped off to sleep while thinking about what an interesting and complex person this man sitting next to her was.

Lonnie sat for a long time with his back up against a tree keeping an eye on the opposite side of the stream. Although it appeared he was being vigilant, in reality his thoughts were far away. The woman and her child had reawakened emotions within him he had tried to put out of his head. Little Rusty reminded him of himself when he was a small child. The boy's protective nature for his mother brought back memories of his own mom, long since stowed away in the back recesses of his mind. "How would his life be different today if she and Poppy were still alive?" he thought. The nagging question stayed with him for some time, and it led to other questions. "What if Poppy hadn't died in the mine?" Surely he would then have attended the Olympics and witnessed his greatest triumph. Lonnie felt the only thing in his life he was ever really good at was track and field, and he desperately wanted his father's approval and recognition for this. Lonnie mistakenly felt he had to work twice as hard in this endeavor to get his father's attention, to get his affection! School and studies held him back so much in trying to attain this. His lower grades embarrassed him, and he felt diminished in his father's eyes. To win a medal in the Olympics, well, how could he ignore that? Why did he have to die?

A lump started to form in his throat as his mind churned up these deep thoughts he had been running away from for so long. Without realizing it, Lonnie quietly sobbed. His breath caught in his chest and his body shuddered. When he felt a small patting sensation on his leg, he realized Rachel had discovered his grief. She slowly sat up next to him and put her arms around his shoulders and drew his head to her bosom. Lonnie tried to hold his emotions in check, but when she started to pat his head in a consoling manner, he sobbed.

Not even when Poppy was put into the ground on his ranch did Lonnie break down and cry. He held his tears in check and was a pillar of strength for Sara and the others. His brief moment of emotional release at the Olympics was certainly understandable---even good for him---but afterwards, he felt embarrassed and once again put on his stoic disguise and held his feelings inside. Lonnie had been running away from his past and isolating himself, avoiding any memories that might cause him to relive it. Over the years, this burden and lack of emotional release festered inside of him, until this very night when he was finally able to let go. Perhaps the catalyst was experiencing the close bond between Rachel and Rusty and the dangers they faced together; or maybe, after all this time, Lonnie was finally able to accept the fact that his father did love and respect him for who he was, regardless of his athletic accomplishments, and he was finally ready to get on with his life. Whatever the reason, this moment of release was to be a turning point for him.

Later, with almost no words at all, he apologized before drifting off into a deep sleep. Rachel continued to hold him and stroke his head gently, all the while wondering what it was that made this man who he was and what affected him so.

"Aw, shut up and quite yer bellyaching all the time!" Grappa scolded Lamar softly as the three of them slowly followed the lead of T-Bone. They had stopped for a few hours earlier in order to give the three-legged dog a rest, but were now once again hot on the trail. Doyle was now leading his men with a much more cautious approach. He was hoping they could come up on the small group while they were sleeping; therefore, he kept the hound from barking and insisted on silence in the ranks as they plodded along in the dark. Doyle was also painfully aware of the fact that the ranger had a rifle---and was willing to use it. He figured there were probably two or three rounds of ammunition in the weapon but doubted whether he had any more. Before leaving camp, Grappa had discovered a couple boxes of bullets in the tent while rummaging through it which would seem to confirm his suspicions.

The gibbous moon above illuminated the forest when it was able to penetrate the thick congestion of trees. The heavy ground cover of decaying wood and moss enabled them to move silently along. It was approaching 3:30 in the morning when T-Bone stopped to take a drink in the small stream. The poor dog had been worked hard over the past several hours and the strain and exhaustion were beginning to show on him. Doyle didn't really care about the well-being of his mutt. He had no affectionate feelings for it one way or another. The dog served a purpose, and that was to make his job easier by tracking his prey when it might be too difficult or too time consuming to do it himself. When the dog could no longer perform this function, Doyle wouldn't think twice about getting rid of it; out here that usually meant a bullet in the head. "C-mon dog, enough water already. Git a move on." Doyle snarled at the animal as he gave him a kick with the side of his foot in the flank. His mood had been getting darker and darker as the evening wore on. T-Bone turned on his master and growled viciously while taking a bite out of his leg. Doyle almost snapped at this blatant display of aggression. He unbuckled the thick belt holding up his pants and beat the helpless animal mercilessly. T-Bone whined loudly and cowered as he tried to avoid the brutal punishment directed upon him. "Damn dog. That'll teach you to bite me. The hell with him now; leave him lie for the coyotes," he said to his men. "Lamar, get up here and take over. The trail moves up the creek. I can see it from here."

"All right boss. Just don't kick me," he said.

"Well, don't try to bite me then!" They all had a good laugh at that one. The brief moment of anger and the subsequent laughter seemed to lighten the mood of everyone. They continued on the trail and never gave another thought to the exhausted and hurt animal left behind. Lamar used a small flashlight he carried in his pack to keep from losing the trail, although he felt he hardly needed it as even an idiot could follow the tracks running alongside the small waterway.

Lonnie watched the entire episode from behind a large tree on the far side of the stream. He had awakened when the bickering voices of Grappa and Lamar first reached him minutes earlier. He sneaked away from the still sleeping Rachel and Rusty to check it out. His heart went out to the poor dog, but there was little he could do to help. These were, without a doubt, the most bloodthirsty men he had ever encountered. While working for the forest service and conservation department over the past several years, he had a few run-ins with poachers and the like. Most of the time, once they realized they were busted, these people went along quietly preferring not to make their crime any worse than it already was.

The reputation of this particular group had preceded them. Two years earlier, a couple of officers had been murdered well to the north of here while investigating the indiscriminate killing of black bears. The department would collar certain bears in order to trace their movements and hibernating patterns. When these bears systematically turned up missing, an investigation was launched. It was later determined a poaching operation was working in the vicinity. After the murders of the officers, the ring picked up and disappeared. Lonnie was certain this particular group had a long history of violent crimes in the western states, and he was determined to do something about it. Unfortunately, he couldn't risk the safety and well being of Rachel and Rusty. It was imperative he got them out before attempting any police action. He was in no position at the moment to do anything, being outnumbered three to one. Protocol demanded he call for a back-up.

As he watched them move away following the stream, Lonnie reconfirmed to himself the best course of action was to elude these criminals at all costs. Once the woman and her child were in safe hands, he could lead the proper authorities back here and arrest them. Surely, a rescue operation must be combing the area at this very moment looking for the plane wreckage. He moved back to where Rachel slept and gently woke her. "Rachel, we have to move out. They're still on our trail. A few minutes ago they passed by on the other side moving upstream. Wake Rusty, and be very quiet," he whispered.

With extreme caution, Lonnie led the two of them across the stream. Rusty once again sat perched upon his shoulders. When they reached the opposite shore, he continued to follow the trail back in the direction from where they had come earlier. He doubted whether they could continue to elude the men for the amount of time it would take to hike out, so after some serious consideration, figured it would be best if they stayed in the area of the crash, rationalizing this is where help would come first. Once Doyle and his band of cut throats realized there were rescue parties in the area, they would undoubtedly disappear into the woods and start thinking about their own safety. It was imperative, however, they avoid detection until help arrived. Lonnie knew that eventually the lack of sleep and constant moving would take its toll on them. He also realized that when it was discovered what his plans were, Doyle would redouble his efforts to catch them. They were in a dangerous race, one in which they could ill afford to lose as the penalty for losing would be their very lives.

Chapter Thirty-Five

"They crossed here again," said Lamar. "They were sleeping right here and must have watched us go by last night. Those bastards! Look, this is where they had a fire. Shit, they was eatin fish for dinner. Now how do ya figure that?"

"I figure that ranger dude is a lot better than we gave him credit for," said Doyle. "He's heading back on our trail towards the crash sight. Pretty smart. He probably figures he can't outrun us, so he wants to stick in the area til help arrives. I think he's made his mistake though. The woman and kid will slow him for sure. Lamar, I want you and Grappa to double-time it after them. If he branches off the trail, leave a sign. When you catch 'em, you can do anything you want to em, just as long as you leave em dead. Watch for smoke, cuz I'm pretty sure he's gonna light a signal fire to let any surveillance planes know where he's at. I'm gonna follow behind ya, and then detour when I figure for sure where he's headed. I'm gonna try and stay high up and see if I can't spot any smoke. Stay on it until ya get him, Lamar, and I'll make ya real happy when it's done, understand?"

"I understand. Grappa, don't hold me back. We're gonna make tracks now. I got a hankerin for somethin only that lady can provide." The two of them moved out immediately in pursuit. Although Grappa was a large man, he had the ability to move quickly when necessary. Over the past couple of years, he had been on a lot of day hunts with Lamar and had learned to trust his tracking ability. He was content to follow behind and let his smaller companion utilize his considerable skills. He had no illusions about what they were going to do when they ultimately caught up with them. In fact, he was even looking forward to a little piece of the woman himself after leading them on this wild goose chase all night.

For the next three hours, Lamar and Grappa pursued their quarry without rest. On more than one occasion they thought they might have caught up with them, only to be disappointed by the sight of a frightened deer running off through the trees. At one point, the sound of a low flying airplane could be heard overhead. There wasn't any doubt in either of their minds what this meant. A rescue party was trying to locate wreckage from up above. Lamar raised his head and sniffed the air searching for any trace of smoke. He repeated this action every so often until eventually a smile came to his face. "Do you smell it," he said?

Grappa hadn't even considered smelling the air. When he answered with, "Smell what?" Lamar rolled his eyes in disgust.

"Smoke, you idiot! There's a fire burning somewhere. He's tryin to send a signal to the plane. We got him now. He must figure we lost his trail."

Throughout the early hours of the morning, Lonnie continued to move at the fastest pace they were capable of. They could hear no sounds of pursuit coming from behind, but on one occasion a frightened doe and fawn ran past them as they were stopping for a rest. The direction the deer came from concerned Lonnie, so without hesitation, he pushed on. When they heard the overhead sound of a small engine, he immediately stopped and built a fire. "I'm going to try and alert them with smoke, but we can't afford to hang around," he said. After igniting a small pile of tinder, he built it into a good size blaze before covering it completely with a pile of damp leaves and moss. It immediately sent up a column of white smoke. Lonnie then scraped an area around the fire all the way to the dirt before vacating the spot. "It's a foolhardy thing to do, but under the circumstances, we have no choice," he said. They moved quickly away from the fire and continued to travel back up the valley towards the wreck, with the hope that their signal would be picked up and help would soon be on the way.

Lamar followed his nose until it brought him to within eyesight of the fire. He and Grappa flattened to the ground and watched for awhile before coming to the conclusion the fire had been abandoned shortly after it had been set. Nevertheless, they split up before attempting to enter the area. When he approached the fire, Grappa immediately put it out by spreading the embers across the ground and stomping them with his boots. Lamar slowly moved around the perimeter until he picked up the trail again. "This way, he called out," and without another moment lost, they resumed the chase.

Doyle had veered off the trail earlier when he figured where Lonnie might be heading. In an attempt to keep to the high ground, he moved up a rugged slope running parallel to the valley below. He was sure Lonnie would be moving through this area. The higher he climbed, the better view he was able to get of the entire valley below. When Doyle heard the sound of a small search plane overhead, he sought cover under a rocky ledge. He sat there for some time before noticing a small, but very distinct, column of white smoke rising above the trees. "Just as I thought," said Doyle. "They're trying to signal the plane. Keep an eye on the valley away from the fire," he figured. "He would be stupid to send up a smoke signal and then wait underneath it to be caught. He's gonna light it and then move away." In a matter of minutes, three small figures could be seen moving along the edge of a clearing down below. "Right on schedule," he said with a smug tone of voice. "They're gonna follow the edge of that meadow around to the right, and then head into the thick timber once they get to the other side. If I can reach that point over there," he thought, indicating an outcropping of rock fifty yards around the ridge he was on, "I can pop them off one at a time while they're still in the open."

Lamar and Grappa moved quickly along the trail left in the soft ground. They knew they were getting closer by the minute. Lamar carried his rifle at port arms with the safety switch off, just waiting for an opportunity to get a clear shot. He was becoming more and more excited. His attention had switched from the ground immediately in front of him to the landscape fifty yards out that was visible through the trees. This was so much more stimulating than hunting bears or eagles, and the reward would be so much greater, he thought.

"I've got to stop and rest for a moment," called out Rachel. "Would it be okay to just take five minutes to catch my breath?" Lonnie had no reason to believe they were in imminent danger, but something, perhaps his sixth sense, told him they should not dwaddle.

"We can rest once we make it to the other side of this clearing," he answered as he paused for a moment to plead with her. "This is a bad spot to stop. We're too much in the open. Up ahead, the forest is thicker and it will give us better cover." Rachel agreed, and only hesitated for an instant longer in order to retie her sneaker before the three of them moved around the edge of the meadow.

When Doyle reached the rocky point that looked down upon the open meadow below, he hurriedly situated himself into a position where he might be able to make the three hundred yard shot to where Lonnie stood in the open talking to the woman. In the same instant, Lamar and Grappa came around a small group of trees not quite one hundred and fifty yards away, and immediately spotted little Rusty standing by his mother relieving himself against a rock. Grappa dropped to one knee and took careful aim at the tree where he expected Lonnie to walk out from behind and paused. Lamar, in a frenzied moment of bloodlust, raised his rifle and shot at the small boy. Luckily for Rusty, due to his small stature and Lamar's overexcitement, the shot went high, just barely missing taking his head off. Lonnie's reaction was immediate. He snatched Rusty up and quickly changed direction, heading off to his right and made for the trees adjacent to the meadow. Almost simultaneously, two shots rang out from above. The first bullet struck the earth in front of Rachel harmlessly, but the second proved to be more accurate. It grazed Lonnie on his left arm taking a long piece of meat with it. At first, Lonnie didn't even realize he was hit, but when they reached the cover of the trees and the blood was flowing freely down his arm, Rachel shrieked in alarm.

"You're hurt," she called out. Lonnie, feeling a sudden burning sensation in his bicep and a tingle running down his arm, was infuriated.

"Not now!" he shouted angrily, his voice taking on a tone she was not familiar with. "Get down." Lonnie moved back towards the meadow to where he might see where the attackers were coming from. He lay on the ground for almost a full minute before noticing Grappa sneaking up to his position from behind a tree eighty yards away. Obviously, he didn't realize Lonnie had doubled back and lay in wait for him. When the large man tried to move up to the next tree, Lonnie took the opportunity and shot, striking him in the thigh. He cursed when Grappa went down for he fully intended on killing the man. Earlier he had made every effort to avoid bloodshed, as he didn't want to traumatize the woman and her child, but now, it was a matter of life or death. These men were bent on killing them all, no matter what the consequences. Lonnie had never found himself in a position like this, and he had certainly never killed anyone before. When he shot Luther the day before, it was justified in his mind; nothing in his life had ever been more justified. He had hoped it would stop there, but obviously it hadn't. Lonnie realized if they were going to make it out alive, he was going to have to fight here and now.

Grappa dragged himself back behind the tree from where he had made his attack and sat there. He took the handkerchief tied around his neck and tied off his leg just above the wound in an attempt to stop the flow of blood. The pain was intense, as the bullet had struck his femur and shattered it. Lonnie crawled back the way he had come and went deeper into the woods so that he could change his position without it being discovered. He moved around to where he could get a line of sight on the guy up in the rocks. It was difficult to tell where the shots had come from, but after carefully scrutinizing the ridge, he recognized movement. The big guy was repositioning himself so he could get a better view of the valley below. Unlucky for him, thought Lonnie. The distance was almost three hundred yards, but certainly not impossible. He remembered what his father had told him years before. Get yourself a good rest, take a deep breath and then let half of it out, line the crosshairs up, and slowly squeeze the trigger. After going through the motions, his rifle kicked hard against his shoulder and caused him to blink. When he was able to refocus on the spot, he realized he must have missed for the man could be seen scampering for cover.

Once again, Lonnie backtracked his way deeper into the woods and returned to where Rachel and Rusty were hiding. Nobody said a word as Lonnie scoured the area. He recalled one shot being fired at them from down below and two more from up above. There was one more gun out there unaccounted for, and Lonnie had just one remaining bullet. It was better to retreat right now, he thought, and let them lick their wounds rather than risk firing off his last shot and missing. As long as they figured he had another round, Doyle would be extra cautious in approaching him again. But approach him they would, for that's what kind of men he was dealing with. "We've got to move away from here," Lonnie said. A trickle of blood continued to stream down his arm. He could feel the stickiness of the coagulating liquid in the palm of his hand, but tried to ignore it.

"We won't move another step until you let me take a look at your arm," Rachel answered stubbornly.

"When we've put a small distance between us, then you can doctor me, I promise. The bullet passed through my arm and didn't strike anything vital, just flesh. We can bandage it in a bit, but if we don't move now, there'll be no need for bandages when they finish with us." Lonnie hesitated while taking Rachel's hand. "Please?"

The three of them ran back into the woods they had been skirting earlier. Rachel held Rusty's hand and moved into the lead while Lonnie followed behind keeping an eye on their rear. They covered almost a mile before stopping and taking a breather in a section of the forest particularly congested with deadfall. Only after Lonnie was convinced they were not being followed, and he was satisfied that the terrain concealed their presence, did he allow Rachel to inspect his arm. It proved to be only a flesh wound, but it hurt like the dickens. She tore a piece of his shirt off and tied it around the wound after first packing it with a handkerchief he carried in his pocket. There was a depression in the rocks nearby that had collected rainwater from a downpour several days earlier.

This proved to be a Godsend, for they hadn't drunk anything in almost twenty-four hours. Afterwards, Lonnie used it to wash the dried blood off his arm.

"We can rest here for a bit," he said, while crouching down behind a large fallen tree and watching their back trail. "The odds are getting better. The big guy with the scar took one in the leg. I don't think he's going very far. That leaves two left, probably the worst two. I'm not sure what they'll do now, maybe call it quits and clear out, but I wouldn't bet on it. We still pose a threat to their operation. With us out of the way, they can continue on in another area with little pressure from the law. People disappear in these woods all the time. They just bury the bodies and no one is any the wiser."

Lonnie had been speaking without thinking and realized he had frightened Rachel even more than she already was. She sat there holding her son with tears in her eyes. Rusty, who was actually holding up quite well, patted his mom on the arm and said, "Don't worry, mom, Lonnie and me will take care of these guys. We won't let them get you."

"Nobody's going to get any of us as long as I can help it," Lonnie added. "Our chances are a lot better now than before. We're going to stay right here for the next few hours and get some rest. The longer we stay hidden, the harder it will be to find us. One way or another, help will soon be on the way and the bad guys will clear out at the first sign of it. Trust me, Rachel." Lonnie looked steadfast into her eyes. The tears made them even more attractive than they already were. Even though their lives were in considerable danger still, Lonnie was grateful for being given the opportunity to help this woman and her child. Last night, when he had broken down, she was there for him. Although he had awakened somewhat embarrassed, he didn't regret it happening. Rachel had shown compassion and understanding for him, and now it was his turn to reciprocate. Lonnie suddenly felt an urge to lean over and kiss her on the cheek, but instead patted her arm reassuringly. When Rusty looked up at him, he put his hand on the boy's small head and ruffled up his hair. "You two try to get some sleep now. We're not going anywhere for awhile." Rachel dried her tears and managed a smile before pulling Rusty next to her and closing her eyes.

Lamar moved up cautiously to Grappa's side after he was sure Lonnie had left the area. He was well aware of the fact his over excitement had ruined their opportunity to get a clean shot at the ranger, but he certainly wasn't going to take the blame for it. Once he realized his shot missed the intended target, he took cover behind a tree and waited for his next chance. He had called out to Grappa trying to encourage him on. "We've got them pinned down from above. I'll cover you. Try to get closer." When Grappa got hit in the leg, Lamar being the coward that he was, decided to stay put. His real expertise was shooting people in the back or when they were unaware of his presence. Confronting an armed man head on who knew how to use a gun wasn't his forte. "Bummer," he said to the big man. "Can you walk?"

"Not unless I have to, and I'm certainly not going to chase that guy anymore. You do it, ya stupid fuck! We had em, and you blew it."

Lamar nodded and said, "Yeah, I guess I got a little excited. I'm gonna move up the ridge to where Doyle is and see what he wants to do. Why don't you try and make it back to camp, it's only a couple miles from here. When we finish, we'll be regrouping back there before we clear out."

"I can't make it all the way back there by myself. I'm gonna need help."

"Ok, wait here then. I'll see what he wants to do."

Lamar checked one more time to make sure nobody had sneaked back up on him before moving out. He ran like a scared jackrabbit across the open meadow to the far side before climbing up to where Doyle was still hiding. When he reached him, the man had a cigarette in his mouth, and he was pulling on it deeply. "Now what, boss?"

"Doyle stared at him for a moment before speaking. "Where's Grappa?"

"He took one high up in the leg, says he can't walk much. It looks pretty bad. He's sittin down below under a tree waitin to hear from me."

"Can he make it back to camp?"

"Not unless we carry him, or he crawls."

"Then he'll never make the hike out either. Pretty soon this place is goin to be crawlin with rangers. We can't afford to waste time draggin his ass out of here, and we sure as hell can't leave him to rat us out."

"You want for me to fix him up? If it weren't for him getting excited and shootin so quick before I got myself situated, we would have gotten em for sure. I had em dead to rights out in the open."

"Yeah, fix him up good," Doyle said. "Then bury him. I'll meet ya in the meadow in an hour. We're still gonna get that guy and take care of business; then we're gonna have to clear out. Only one plane has flown over since yesterday, so they must not know where it went down. That should give us a bit longer. Afterwards, we're gonna have to get rid of his camp and bury Luther, too. I'm startin to feel like a fuckin undertaker!"

Lamar wasn't concerned about carrying out Doyle's instructions. He didn't really like Grappa anyway. The big guy was a pain in the butt, couldn't track worth a shit. The world would be a better place without him, he thought. When he approached the spot where he had left him, Grappa was still propped up next to the tree. "Heh, Grappa. How ya doin?" Lamar said with an exaggerated tone of sensitivity.

"How the hell do ya think I'm doin, ya shitty little fuck? I'm fuckin bleedin to death. This is all your fault," he accused.

"Well, don't you go frettin now, ol Lamar's gonna take care of you real good." Before Grappa had time to digest the true meaning or intent of Lamar's words, the crazed little lunatic pulled out the pistol he had stolen from Lonnie's tent and aimed it at him. "Is there anything you'd like me to say to your Mamma before I do ya in?"

"Why, you son of a bitch." Grappa attempted to raise the rifle he had resting by his side and defend himself, but all Lamar had to do was pull the trigger. Two shots thundered out from the 38 caliber Smith and Wesson, striking the injured man full in the chest before he could react. The heavy caliber bullet ripped into his flesh causing massive damage. Death was instantaneous.

Lamar showed no emotion as he went through Grappa's pockets, confiscating cigarettes and anything else of value. He dragged the still warm corpse off to an area where the soil did not appear to be so rocky and buried it quickly in a shallow grave. Within the hour, Doyle reappeared in the meadow toting his rifle. He had a fresh streak of blood across his neck that Lamar hadn't noticed earlier. Apparently, the ranger guy had hit him with his last shot. Lamar thought it was better not to mention it.

"Did he have any last words?" Doyle asked.

"Naw, he just called me an asshole."

Chapter Thirty-Six

The distant sound of gunshots alerted Lonnie as he sat behind a fallen tree keeping watch. He wasn't sure, but he thought the shots fired were those of a pistol rather than a rifle. This probably meant they were fired up close, as opposed to at a distance. He could only guess their purpose. Were they now starting to fight among themselves? The thought of deliberately murdering one of their own comrades had not even occurred to Lonnie, but he didn't put it past them. He fought the desire to sneak back and check things out, deciding it would be better if he stayed put for awhile longer and give everyone a bit more rest before moving again.

The day wore on and the sun moved across the sky. Unfortunately, there had been no further flyovers. This was disappointing to Lonnie as he figured it could only mean rescue attempts were concentrating on another spot. Certainly there would be more aerial surveillance of the area. His arm throbbed where it had been hit. He was lucky the bullet had struck him where it had and not a few inches closer to home, or he wouldn't be alive right now. When he figured they couldn't afford to rest any longer, he gently awakened Rachel. She opened her eyes with a start but didn't speak. "I think it's best if we move again," he said. "I would like to try and put a little more distance between us."

For the rest of the day, the three of them walked cautiously through the woods. Lonnie tried to keep them in the general vicinity of the crash sight but hesitated in bringing them too close. He considered stopping by his own camp and getting some badly needed food and water, but decided against it. When dusk came, Lonnie settled his small party about a mile from where the Cessna went down. "I'm going to leave you here for a bit while I sneak back to the plane and try to gather some food and warmer clothes. It should be all right. You'll be safe as long as you stay put. I'll be back in about an hour." Lonnie left her the rifle with strict instructions on how to use it only in an emergency. "Rusty, you stay here and keep an eye on your ma. Make sure she's safe and doesn't get into any trouble." He winked at Rachel who gave him the first smile he had seen from her since rescuing them the day before.

Rusty replied, "Maybe I should hold the gun."

Lonnie answered, "When you're eight years old young man, and not a day sooner."

Before he left, Rachel gave him a brief hug and said softly, "Hurry back." Lonnie walked away from them somehow feeling invigorated. Over the past couple of days, these two had come to mean a lot to him. He found himself moving with a new conviction and, for the first time in a long time, looked forward to getting back to someone's company.

Doyle and Lamar spent the remainder of the day trying to pick up the trail that had gone cold on them. Lamar tried to figure in which direction they were heading, then he made large sweeping circles in an attempt to pick up their sign. The longer it took, the more frustrated Doyle became. After awhile, his open criticism began to wear on Lamar, and soon the two were openly feuding with one another. The murder of Grappa had emboldened Lamar and gave him more courage. Usually Doyle could make him shudder in his boots when he looked at him crosswise, but as the day wore on, he realized his intimidation factor was waning. Pretty soon he would have to deal with Lamar, but for now he needed him. The southern misfit was still his best chance for picking up the trail. Once they found the hero and the woman and her kid, he would deal with them all. Then he could make his escape with all his contraband, making it look like Lamar was solely responsible for all the mayhem. "It was 'his' fingerprints on the flashlight in the cockpit after all," thought Doyle to himself.

Late in the day, the two of them decided to concentrate their efforts in the general vicinity of the crash sight and the ranger's camp. It made sense to them that they would try to stay in the area where the plane went down. After all, this would be the spot where the rescue would commence once the aircraft was discovered. Shortly before dark, Lamar discovered a fresh trail leading towards the wreck. By backtracking a ways, he realized they had been sitting for most of the day in one spot, thus leaving no trail. Doyle then decided the best course of action would be to back off and give them a false sense of security by not pushing too hard. Let them go to sleep feeling they had made their escape. Late in the evening, he and Lamar could follow the trail and catch them while they were sleeping.

The mountain air was exceptionally clear and brisk that night as Doyle and Lamar sat around the campfire eating bear jerky. Shooting stars were so much more visible when one moved away from the city lights. Doyle commented on how the good old days were a thing of the past, and how so many people were encroaching on their space. Lamar pulled from his pack a quart bottle of Beefeater gin and opened it. It was the remainder of the plane's stock. Over the next few hours, the two of them sat and drank. When the gin was gone, Doyle revealed a bottle of Canadian whiskey he had been carrying all day in his pack. He wasn't real keen on sharing it with Lamar and stirred up some bad feelings when he wouldn't share it at first. Ultimately he did let the smaller man have some. Eventually, the conversation turned to the plane crash and how Lamar had messed up by bringing the woman and her brat to camp. Lamar shot right back by saying it wasn't his fault and blamed it all on Grappa. He continued to wail on Doyle for always picking on him and humiliating him in front of other people. They argued and cut into each other more and more as the night wore on and as the alcohol took control of their senses. Lamar accidentally knocked over the whiskey bottle in one of his tirades.

"You stupid, inbred idiot!" yelled Doyle. "Why the fuck can't you ever get it right!" He screamed at Lamar unremittingly in a biting tone that finally pushed him over the edge. In the pretense of standing up to take a pee, Lamar walked over to an unsuspecting Doyle while pulling the 38 from his pocket and shot his drunken companion once in the head, ending his life immediately.

"Now, who's the stupid fuck?" he said as he kicked the dead man in the face. Let's hear you say it again," he scoffed. Lamar knelt beside Doyle's body and helped himself to his pair of pistols. "You won't be needin these anymore. I'd hate to see them go to waste. Well, good night. See ya in the morning," he said sarcastically as he moved to the other side of the fire and lay down to sleep for the remainder of the evening.

"There it is again," thought Lonnie to himself. This time he definitely recognized the shot as that of a 38 caliber pistol. The sound came from quite a distance away, perhaps as much as a mile. He was grateful for the obvious distance between them and it set his nerves at ease. Still, he wondered as to why there would be shooting this late at night. Could these men be killing one another, or perhaps they were merely shooting off into the night at shadows? Rachel and Rusty were sleeping soundly under the blanket he managed to retrieve from the wrecked airplane, and he saw little reason to disturb them. It was important they catch up on their sleep for tomorrow would certainly bring an end to their ordeal. Lonnie glanced over at Rusty and thought he detected a slight smile on the small boy's face. "Why not," he thought. "The child had just washed down three candy bars and a giant bag of potato chips with two root beers." Mom had thought the sugar rush would keep him from getting his rest, but from the looks of it now, there was little need to worry--for her either, as they were both sawing logs pretty well. Lonnie laid his head back down on his arm with Rusty curled up next to him and pretty soon he too, was sound asleep. The long night passed undisturbed for the three as they slept in relative comfort.

The following morning when Lamar woke up he had a fierce headache. There was a buzzing in his head that just wouldn't quit. He lay there for some time with his eyes closed before finally coming to his senses and realizing the buzzing wasn't in his head after all, but was in fact, an airplane flying overhead. Without hesitation, he jumped to his feet and almost tried to wake Doyle before remembering the events of the evening before. "Hmm," he said aloud. "It's about time someone took care of you." Without another moment wasted, he slung four rifles over his shoulders and started following the tracks that he knew would lead him to the people he was after. They would more than likely be concentrating on building a fire to signal the plane above, so he kept his eyes open for smoke. When he was able to see through the trees, Lamar noticed the plane was circling and at times would rock back and forth. Evidently, it had spotted someone on the ground and was signaling to them. This wasn't good news. So they now knew there were survivors. But it would still take time to get a rescue team in here and get them out, he figured. "I still have a little bit of time. Now, where is your signal fire?"

Lonnie woke up and started to move around at the crack of dawn. He let Rusty and Rachel continue to sleep for another hour before finally waking them. The night before when visiting the plane wreck, he was able to secure some warm clothing, a blanket, candy bars, soda pop, and most importantly, a small mirror that he intended on using to signal any flyovers. "Today we are going to do a bit of climbing. We're going to move to the top of that ridge over there and wait," he said. "Once we get to a clearing we can build a fire to light in a hurry when they come searching for us. This mirror will also help." He explained to Rusty how it could catch the sun light and be directed towards an airplane to signal it.

    It took almost two hours to make the climb, but eventually they were able to find a good spot that could be spotted from the air. Lonnie prepared a signal fire, to be lit on a moment's notice, with plenty of leaves and moss to pile on in order to create smoke. The three of them sat with their backs up against a large rock warming in the morning sun. They kept an eye on their back trail in the event someone should come up on them. For the first time in almost three days, they felt almost relaxed. Rachel talked about how she was on her way to her best friend's wedding to be the maid of honor. She also had to explain to Lonnie about what a cytotechnologist did. Being a male with no sisters, he had never really given it much thought. Rachel also touched on her personal life and talked about how she was divorced and what a difficult time she and Rusty had at first. Just as things were starting to come together for her this whole thing had to happen. After awhile, realizing she was doing all the talking, Rachel asked Lonnie to tell her about himself. "If you would rather not....." she started.

    "No, it's OK. I'm sorry about the other night. I've had this thing bottled up inside of me for a long time. Maybe it was good to finally let it out." Lonnie went on to explain about his past. He talked about losing his mother and the loneliness he felt after that, about trying so hard to always please his father, who was so set on his son becoming a college graduate. The harder he tried at school, the worse things seemed to get. Then he touched on how Sara had come into their lives, and how she had given him direction. She had encouraged his father to accept Lonnie's low average scholastic ability and to recognize him for his strengths, especially in athletics. Lonnie admitted that his lifelong goal had always been to please his father, to find a place in his heart next to his mother's. When the big day finally arrived, his father missed it and would never know.

    "Certainly he knew," said Rachel softly as she held his arm tenderly. "He must have been so very proud of you all your life.

Many times children don't always know how their parents feel about them because the parents aren't good at expressing themselves; that's why it helps to have two parents. What about Sara? She sounds like a wonderful person."

"Sara still lives on the ranch. After my father died, she gave birth to a baby girl, Megan. She's going to be six years old this fall. I try to get back there as often as I can, usually for Christmas and the holidays. Maynard, our neighbor and good friend, helps her out a lot. I think after all this is over, I may go back there for awhile. They could probably use some help around the ranch. Colorado is really a beautiful place. Have you ever been there?"

"No, I haven't, but I've always wanted to go there."

The distant sound of a small engine could be heard coming up the valley. Lonnie immediately hopped to his feet and ran to the woodpile with Rusty and together they lit it. Bright flames quickly rose up and consumed the dry wood piled in a vertical heap. Lonnie had Rusty fan it as he covered the crackling fire with dry leaves and moss. In an instant, a heavy white cloud of smoke rose up into the sky. Lonnie turned his attention to the small spotter plane far off to the southeast and used the mirror to signal it. Pretty soon they could see it change course and head directly towards them. All three waved in the air enthusiastically with their jackets and sweaters. Once it was overhead, it rocked its wings and circled a few times before heading back off to the south. "Now they know we're here," said Lonnie with a smile. "It shouldn't be too much longer. I would imagine they'll return with a rescue helicopter." He started to put out the fire.

"Why are you doing that?" questioned Rachel.

"I don't want to alert our friends as to where we are. The smart thing for them to do right now is to ski-daddle, but there's no telling what they might do. People like this are hardened criminals, and they don't always do the smart thing. It's best if we continue to be on the alert. It could be another few hours yet before help is on the ground."

Lamar moved rapidly through the trees. When he came to a clearing, he was able to detect smoke up on the ridge where he and Grappa had shot the eagle three days earlier. "So that's where you are," he thought. "Time is getting short, but don't count ol Lamar out just yet." He figured their trail ran right up the side of the ridge in a direct line from where he now stood to where the smoke was. In an attempt to keep his approach a secret, he circled around the ridge and started to climb it from another direction. Before doing so, he stashed his rifles and the pair of pistols he was carrying. They were so heavy around his waist that they were pulling his pants down. At the last minute, he also reached into his pocket and removed the 38 caliber "This will just slow me down," he thought. "After all, I do have a good sharp knife, and once I shoot the hero, that should be all I need." He nodded to himself in the affirmative as if to say he understood what must be done.

The three of them sat and watched the lower valley for another good hour. This time Rusty got into the conversation. "Where do all the animals go when the snow comes? What do they eat out here? There's no food. Are there Indians out here? How come there aren't any roads?" The questions came one right after another. It seemed that the thought of being rescued took a great load off the little guy's mind. Lonnie liked his line of questioning. They all had to do with the mountains and the forest, which was something he himself could relate to. While they talked, a large cow elk and calf ran by them coming from behind. "Something must have spooked them," Lonnie said. "I don't think there's anything to worry about from the direction they came from. The ridge continues to climb up into a rocky top."

"Those were elk?" Rusty asked. "How come we never saw any of those before?"

"Well," Lonnie responded, "An elk is a large animal and it covers a lot of ground. If someone is going to hunt an elk or find one, they just have to cover a lot of ground themselves." Lonnie remembered hearing Poppy say the same thing once to him when he was a small boy. In fact, Lonnie realized he was answering many of Rusty's questions with Poppy's old answers. This gave him a warm feeling. Somehow he had come full circle, sitting here passing on the knowledge to Rusty that his father had passed on to him when he was young and inquisitive. Rachel sat and took it all in, enjoying the interaction her son was having with Lonnie. When the sound of a falling rock was heard behind them, Lonnie said to Rusty, "Would you like to sneak with me and maybe see another elk?"

The old tom had been living in the area for almost twenty years. As mountain lions went, he was a true giant, weighing over two hundred pounds. Hunting for him had become more and more difficult over the past few months, and today marked the fourth day in a row that he had not eaten. It seemed that the deer and elk were moving out of the area. Much of the time he was reduced to eating rabbits and other small mammals, but today, he had larger prey on his mind. A cow elk and her small calf had been feeding in the meadow up in the higher ranges of the plateau. He had been stalking them for the better part of an hour when suddenly, the wind had shifted and they caught his scent. The mother elk immediately led her new offspring away down the side of the ridge, exposing herself and her calf to the humans sitting in the rocks. The big cat, feeling the frustration and the hunger pains gnawing at it, continued to search for something to eat, getting more desperate all the time.

Lonnie hadn't walked fifty yards with Rusty before they spotted the large cat perched on top of a nearby boulder watching them. It let out a terrifying cry that sounded like a woman screaming for her life as it rose from its crouched position. Lonnie reached out and slowly pulled Rusty back behind him. He shouted at the defiant animal and tried to intimidate it. When Rachel heard the shouts, she came up behind them and grabbed her son. "Don't move away," he said. "Stand next to me and shout at it. If you run, he'll chase you down." The three of them continued to gesture and scream at the hungry animal until eventually he realized this was not easy prey and took flight dropping over the side of the ridge and disappearing in the forest below. Rusty picked up a rock and threw it after him.

"That's enough to give someone heartburn this early in the morning," laughed Lonnie as they moved back to where they were sitting. He leaned his rifle against a rock.

"Will it come back?" asked a very tentative Rachel.

"No, I don't think so. There were too many of us for him. He must be plenty hungry to approach us like that. Usually mountain lions stay clear of humans. You were real brave back there, Rusty. I think you put a mighty big scare into that big old cat." They all laughed, releasing a bit of anxiety, and continued talking while standing there looking down into the valley below.

When Lamar heard the faint shouts, he didn't know what to think. Perhaps they were playing some kind of game or something, feeling relieved that help was on the way. He redoubled his climbing efforts, now directing his approach more towards where he had heard the voices. They obviously didn't figure he would still be coming for them. "Stupid people," he thought. "I'll throw you a little party."

Lamar belly crawled the last few feet until he reached an area where the trees gave way to an open space. It continued on up the side of the ridge to where he could see Lonnie and the woman. They were now talking in softer tones. He couldn't see the brat, but no matter, once he put a bullet through the hero's heart, he would throw the kid off the cliff. Lamar estimated the distance to be almost a hundred yards. He was sweating profusely from the climb, and as he took aim while resting his rifle on a rotten log, his scope fogged a bit. "Just relax," he thought. "It will all be over now real quick, just leave it to ol Lamar." BANG! The rifle reported as it kicked him in the shoulder. Lamar quickly opened his eyes feeling he had just made a pretty good shot. Sure enough, the ranger crashed backwards into the rock face and then collapsed to the ground. "Hmm, another great shot by yours truly," he said aloud to himself.

Rachel rushed to Lonnie's side as he lay there bleeding. She was hysterical. The bullet had struck him in the chest just below his left clavicle, barely missing his heart. Lonnie tried to speak, but was having trouble. They could hear Lamar calling to them from down below as he covered the last bit of ground between them. "Here I come, dawlin; ready or not." Lonnie tried to gesture, but was too weak. He managed to say "Gun!"

It was Rusty who brought his distraught mother back to reality. "Mom, the gun! Shoot him!" he called out.

Rachel realized this was their only chance. She quickly snatched up the rifle leaning against the rock and tried to recall everything Lonnie had taught her about firing it the night before. When she aimed it at Lamar, who was now only a matter of fifty feet away, he hesitated for a moment, suddenly feeling real fear. "Oops," he thought. Before he could react, she pulled the trigger and a loud click could be heard as the firing pin hit upon an empty chamber.

"Now that wasn't a very nice thing to do," Lamar laughed. "I guess, I'm a gonna have to spank ya for that one."

Rusty, who never missed a thing, hollered, "Put a bullet in it."

Rachel cursed herself for being so stupid. The first thing Lonnie had taught her was how to chamber a round, their only round. She hurriedly fumbled with the bolt on the weapon while Lamar continued to draw closer, laughing in the most sadistic way. When he was less than ten feet away, she aimed the weapon at him for the last time. He continued to smirk while saying, "Got no bullets left."

Rachel fired the rifle at Lamar from almost point blank range. She didn't even aim it, just pointed and pulled the trigger. The recoil from it knocked her back into Rusty, who was standing behind her, and they both fell to the ground. Lamar took the bullet right in the hip. He dropped his weapon, and the impact knocked him back down the hill. He tumbled and rolled all the way back to the trees, leaving a trail of blood in his wake. When he finally came to a stop, he crawled back into the cover of the forest. His wound was not mortal, but it hurt like hell. When he was out of sight from the people above, he propped himself up against a tree and sat there.

Rachel returned to Lonnie's side and immediately tried to stop the flow of blood by applying pressure to it. Rusty sat by his side holding his hand, tears streaming down both cheeks. Lonnie managed to speak the words, "Well done." The last thing he heard before slipping into unconsciousness was the sound of rotors in the distance chopping at the air and Rusty's voice calling out, "Mom, a helicopter!"

Lamar crawled further back into the forest and hid as the helicopter came and rescued the woman and her kid. As far as the ranger went, good riddance, Lamar thought. After it departed, he sat there for a long while gathering the strength to crawl back to his camp. He figured if he could make it to the horses, he could ride out and get medical attention somewhere and then start up business again somewhere else. After all, the operation was all his now.

At first, he wasn't sure what it was that he heard. It sounded like a woman shrieking hysterically. The noise came from behind the rocks directly in front of him. He held on to his bloody hip and tried to ease the pain and loss of blood by applying pressure to it. Lamar then focused his attention at the spot where he half expected to see the woman and her kid reappear. What he eventually saw frightened him beyond words. There, not twenty feet away, was the largest mountain lion he had ever seen in his life. Its huge yellow eyes were riveted to him as it slowly approached. Lamar cried piteously and wet himself as the great beast bared its fangs and prepared to pounce.

Epilogue

Lonnie spent three weeks in the hospital after he was airlifted to Boise. His wounds, though serious, struck neither bone nor artery and left no lasting ill effects. Rachel and her son Rusty accompanied him to the hospital and remained with him there for almost two weeks. When Lonnie needed a blood transfusion, it was she who provided the donor service. Upon release, Lonnie returned to his home in Silvertown for a few months where he convalesced in the company of Sara and her daughter, Megan. Shortly thereafter, he worked a deal with Maynard and purchased 120 acres from him so that he might use it to raise cattle. The Colorado DNR was more than happy to find a position for him working in the contiguous mountain ranges. The following autumn, Rachel came for a visit and fell in love with the state. After commuting back and forth for six months while Maynard and a number of Poppy's old friends helped Lonnie to build a small ranch home, she and Lonnie were married at the great waterfall in the Valley of the Monarch. Sara served as maid of honor, while Megan and Rusty were flower girl and ring bearer. Blue made a special trip out from Lincolnshire, Illinois, where he had been living with his lovely wife of three years and served as Lonnie's best man. Maynard took charge of the logistics and wore his father's tails and top hat. Father O'Brien performed the ceremony.

THE END

Printed in the United States
37151LVS00004B/196-261